OTHER BOOKS BY EOIN COLFER

Artemis Fowl

Artemis Fowl: The Arctic Incident

Artemis Fowl: The Eternity Code

Artemis Fowl: The Opal Deception

Artemis Fowl: The Lost Colony

Artemis Fowl: The Graphic Novel

Artemis Fowl: The Arctic Incident, The Graphic Novel

Airman

Half Moon Investigations

The Supernaturalist

The Wish List

Benny and Omar

Benny and Babe

Eoin Colfer's Legend of Spud Murphy

Eoin Colfer's Legend of Captain Crow's Teeth

Eoin Colfer's Legend of The Worst Boy in the World

ARTEMIS FOWL

THE TIME PARADOX

EOIN COLFER

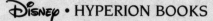

Disney • HYPERION BOOKS

New York

Can *you* crack the code? Decipher the code
that runs along the bottom of the pages of this
book to reveal a secret message.

Text copyright © 2008 by Eoin Colfer
All rights reserved. Published by Disney • Hyperion Books, an imprint of Disney Book Group.
No part of this book may be reproduced or transmitted in any form or by any means,
electronic or mechanical, including photocopying, recording, or by any information storage
and retrieval system, without written permission from the publisher. For information address
Disney • Hyperion Books, 114 Fifth Avenue, New York, New York 10011-5690.

New Disney • Hyperion paperback edition, 2009
1 3 5 7 9 10 8 6 4 2

Printed in the United States of America
This book is set in 13.5-point Perpetua.

ISBN 978-1-4231-0837-5

Library of Congress Cataloging-in-Publication Data on file.

Visit www.artemisfowl.com

For Grace: a new daughter,
granddaughter, niece, and cousin

PROLOGUE

Fowl Manor

Barely an hour north of Dublin's fair city lies the Fowl estate, where the boundaries have changed little in the past five hundred years.

The manor house is not visible from the main road, shrouded by a fan of oak trees and a parallelogram of high stone walls. The gates are reinforced steel with cameras perched upon their pillars. Were you allowed to pass through these discreetly electrified portals, you would find yourself on a pea-gravel avenue, meandering gently through what was once a manicured lawn, but has now been encouraged to evolve to a wild garden.

The trees grow dense as you approach the manor itself, soaring oak and horse chestnut intermingled with more delicate ash and willow. The only signs of cultivation are a driveway free of weeds and the glowing lamps that float overhead, seemingly without tether or cable.

Fowl Manor has been the site of many grand adventures over the centuries. In recent years the adventures have had more of a magical bent, though most of the Fowl family have been kept in the dark about this fact. They have no idea that the main lobby was completely destroyed when the fairy folk sent a troll to do battle with Artemis, the family's eldest son and a criminal mastermind. He was twelve years old at the time. Today, however, Fowl activity in the manor is entirely legal. There are no fairy special forces storming the battlements. No elfin police officers held captive in the cellar. Nor any signs of a centaur fine-tuning his listening devices or running thermal scans. Artemis has made peace with the Fairy People, and formed solid friendships among their ranks.

Though his criminal activities earned Artemis much, they cost him more. People he loved were distraught, injured, and even abducted because of his schemes. For the past three years his parents thought him dead while he fought demons in Limbo. And on his return, he was flabbergasted to find that the world had moved on without him, and he was now the older brother to two-year-old twin boys, Beckett and Myles.

〰〰〰〰〰〰〰〰〰〰〰 • 〰〰〰 • 〰〰〰〰〰〰 • 〰

CHAPTER 1

ESPRESSO AND TREACLE

ARTEMIS sat on an oxblood leather armchair, facing Beckett and Myles. His mother was in bed with a slight case of the flu, his father was with the doctor in her room, and so Artemis was lending a hand in entertaining the toddlers. And what better entertainment for youngsters than some lessons?

He had decided to dress casually in a sky blue silk shirt, light gray woolen pants, and Gucci loafers. His black hair was swept back from his forehead, and he was putting on a jolly expression, which he had heard appealed to children.

"Artemis need toilet?" wondered Beckett, who was squatting on the Tunisian rug, wearing only a grass-stained sweater, which he had pulled down over his knees.

"No, Beckett," said Artemis brightly. "I am trying to look jolly. And shouldn't you be wearing a diaper?"

"Diaper," snorted Myles, who had potty trained himself at the age of fourteen months, building a stepladder of encyclopedias to reach the toilet seat.

"No diaper," pouted Beckett, slapping at a still-buzzing fly trapped in his sticky blond curls. "Beckett hates diaper."

Artemis doubted that the nanny had neglected to put a diaper on Beckett, and he wondered briefly where that diaper was now.

"Very well, Beckett," continued Artemis. "Let's shelve the diaper issue for now, and move on to today's lesson."

"Chocolate on shelves," said Beckett, stretching his fingers high to reach imaginary chocolate.

"Yes, good. There is sometimes chocolate on the shelves."

"And espresso," added Beckett, who had a strange set of favorite tastes, which included espresso sachets and treacle—in the same cup, if he could manage it. Once Beckett had managed to down several spoons of this concoction before it was wrested away from him. The toddler hadn't slept for twenty-eight hours.

"Can we learn the new words, Artemis?" asked Myles, who wanted to get back to a mold jar in his bedroom. "I am doing 'speriments with Professor Primate."

Professor Primate was a stuffed monkey, and Myles's occasional lab partner. The cuddly toy spent most of its time stuffed into a borosilicate glass beaker on the 'speriment table. Artemis had reprogrammed the monkey's voice box to respond to Myles's voice with twelve phrases, including *It's alive! It's alive!* and *History will remember this day, Professor Myles.*

"You can go back to your laboratory soon," said Artemis approvingly. Myles was cut from the same cloth as himself, a natural-born scientist. "Now, boys, I thought today we might tackle some restaurant terms."

"Sneezes look like worms," said Beckett, who wasn't one for staying on topic.

Artemis was nearly thrown by this remark. *Worms* were most definitely not on the menu, though snails might well be. "Forget about worms."

"Forget worms?" said Beckett, horrified.

"Just for the moment," said Artemis reassuringly. "As soon as we have finished our word game, you may think on whatever pleases you. And if you are really good, then I might take you to see the horses."

Riding was the only form of exercise that Artemis had taken to. This was mainly because the horse did most of the work.

Beckett pointed to himself. "Beckett," he said proudly, worms already a distant memory.

Myles sighed. "Simple-toon."

Artemis was beginning to regret scheduling this lesson, but having begun he was determined to forge ahead.

"Myles, don't call your brother a simpleton."

"S'okay, Artemis. He likes it. You're a simple-toon, aren't you, Beckett?"

Θ • ΘＢＩＲＲ⊕ • ＢＤＩ⅍ᐰ • ⌷ • ⌷ＯＯ • Ο

"Beckett simple-toon," agreed the small boy happily.

Artemis rubbed his hands together. "Right, brothers. Onward. Imagine yourself seated at a café table in Montmartre."

"In Paris," said Myles, smugly straightening the cravat that he had borrowed from his father.

"Yes, Paris. And try as you will, you cannot attract the waiter's attention. What do you do?"

The infants stared at him blankly, and Artemis began to wonder if he wasn't pitching his lesson a little high. He was relieved, if a little surprised, to see a spark of comprehension in Beckett's eyes.

"Umm . . . tell Butler to jump-jump-jump on his head?"

Myles was impressed. "I agree with simple-toon."

"No!" Artemis said. "You simply raise one finger and say clearly '*Ici, garçon.*'"

"Itchy what?"

"What? No, Beckett, not *itchy*." Artemis sighed. This was impossible. *Impossible*. And he hadn't even introduced the flash cards yet or his new modified laser pointer, which could either highlight a word or burn through several steel plates, depending on the setting.

"Let's try it together. Raise one finger and say '*Ici, garçon.*' All together now . . ."

The little boys did as they were told, eager to please their deranged brother.

"Ici, garçon," they chorused, pudgy fingers raised. And then from the corner of his mouth, Myles whispered to his twin, "Artemis simple-toon."

Artemis raised his hands. "I surrender. You win, no more lessons. Why don't we paint some pictures?"

"Excellent," said Myles. "I shall paint my jar of mold."

Beckett was suspicious. "I won't learn anything?"

"No," said Artemis, fondly ruffling his brother's hair and immediately regretting it. "You won't learn a thing."

"Good. Beckett happy now. See?" The boy pointed to himself once more, specifically to the broad smile on his face.

The three brothers were stretched on the floor, up to their elbows in poster paint, when their father entered the room. He looked tired from his nursing duties, but otherwise fit and strong, moving like a lifelong athlete in spite of his bio-hybrid artificial leg. The leg used lengthened bone, titanium prosthetics, and implantable sensors to allow Artemis Senior's brain signals to move it. Occasionally, at the end of the day, he would use a microwavable gel pouch to ease his stiffness, but otherwise he behaved as if the new leg were his own.

Artemis climbed to his knees, smudged and dripping.

"I abandoned French vocabulary and have joined the twins in play." He grinned and wiped his hands. "It's quite liberating, actually. We are finger painting instead. I did try to sneak in a little lecture on cubism, but received a splattering for my troubles."

Artemis noticed then that his father was more than simply tired. He was anxious.

He stepped away from the twins and walked with Artemis Senior to the floor-to-ceiling bookcase.

"What is the matter? Is Mother's influenza worsening?"

Artemis's father rested one hand on the rolling ladder and lifted his weight from the artificial limb. His expression was strange, and one that Artemis could not recall ever seeing.

He realized his father was more than anxious. Artemis Fowl Senior was afraid.

"Father?"

Artemis Senior gripped the ladder's rung with such force that the wood creaked. He opened his mouth to speak, but then seemed to change his mind.

Now Artemis himself grew worried. "Father, you must tell me."

"Of course," said his father with a start, as if just remembering where he was. "I must tell you. . . ."

A tear fell from his eye, dropping onto his shirt, deepening the blue.

"I remember when I first saw your mother," he said. "I was in London, at a private party in The Ivy. A room full of scoundrels, and I was the biggest one in the bunch. She changed me, Arty. Broke my heart then put it together again. Angeline saved my life. Now . . ."

Artemis felt weak with nerves. His blood pounded in his ears like the Atlantic surf.

"Is Mother dying, Father? Is this what you are trying to tell me?"

The idea seemed ludicrous. Impossible.

His father blinked as if waking from a dream.

"Not if the Fowl men have something to say about it, eh, son? It's time for you to earn that reputation of yours." Artemis Senior's eyes were bright with desperation. "Whatever we have to do, son. Whatever it takes."

Artemis felt panic welling up inside him.

Whatever we have to do?

Be calm, he told himself. You have the power to fix this.

Artemis did not yet have all the facts, but nonetheless he was reasonably confident that whatever was wrong with his mother could be healed with a burst of fairy magic. And he was the only human on Earth with that magic running through his system.

"Father," he said gently. "Has the doctor left?"

For a moment the question seemed to puzzle Artemis Senior; then he remembered. "Left? No. He is in the lobby. I thought you might talk to him. Just in case there's a question I may have missed. . . ."

Artemis was only mildly surprised to find Dr. Hans Schalke, Europe's leading expert on rare diseases, in the

10

lobby, and not the usual family practitioner. Naturally his father would have sent for Schalke when Angeline Fowl's condition began to deteriorate. Schalke waited below the filigreed Fowl crest, a hard-skinned Gladstone bag standing sentry by his ankles like a giant beetle. He was belting a gray raincoat across his waist and speaking to his assistant in sharp tones.

Everything about the doctor was sharp, from the arrowhead of his widow's peak to the razor edges of his cheekbones and nose. Twin ovals of cut glass magnified Schalke's blue eyes, and his mouth slashed downward from left to right, barely moving as he talked.

"All of the symptoms," he said, his accent muted German, "on all of the databases, you understand?"

His assistant, a petite young lady in an expensively cut gray suit, nodded several times, tapping the instructions onto the screen of her smartphone.

"Universities too?" she asked.

"*All,*" said Schalke, accompanying the word with an impatient nod. "Did I not say all? Do you not understand my accent? Is it because I am from Germany coming?"

"Sorry, Doctor," the assistant said contritely. "All, of course."

Artemis approached Dr. Schalke, hand outstretched. The doctor did not return the gesture.

"Contamination, Master Fowl," he said without a trace of apology or sympathy. "We have not determined whether your mother's condition is contagious."

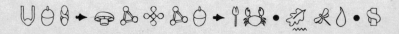

II

Artemis curled his fingers into his palm, sliding the hand behind his back. The doctor was right, of course.

"We have never met, Doctor. Would you be so good as to describe my mother's symptoms?"

The doctor huffed, irritated. "Very well, young man, but I am not accustomed to dealing with children, so there will be no sugarcoating."

Artemis swallowed, his throat suddenly dry.

Sugarcoating.

"Your mother's condition is possibly unique," said Schalke, banishing his assistant to her work with a shake of his fingers. "From what I can tell, her organs seem to be failing."

"Which organs?"

"*All* of them," said Schalke. "I need to bring equipment here from my laboratory at Trinity College. Obviously your mother cannot be moved. My assistant, Imogen, Miss Book, will monitor her until my return. Miss Book is not only my publicist but an excellent nurse. A useful combination, wouldn't you say?"

In his peripheral vision, Artemis saw Miss Book scurry around a corner, stammering into her smartphone. He hoped the publicist/nurse would display more confidence when caring for his mother.

"I suppose. All my mother's organs? *All* of them?"

Schalke was not inclined to repeat himself. "I am reminded of lupus, but more aggressive, combined with all three stages of Lyme disease. I did observe an

Amazonian tribe once with similar symptoms, but not so severe. At this rate of decline, your mother has days left to her. Frankly, I doubt we will have time to complete tests. We need a miracle cure, and in my considerable experience, miracle cures do not exist."

"Perhaps they do," said Artemis absently.

Schalke picked up his bag. "Put your faith in science, young man," advised the doctor. "Science will serve your mother better than some mysterious force."

Artemis held the door for Schalke, watching him walk the dozen steps to his vintage Mercedes-Benz. The car was gray, like the bruised clouds overhead.

There is no time for science, thought the Irish teenager. Magic is my only option.

When Artemis returned to his study, his father was sitting on the rug with Beckett crawling along his torso like a monkey.

"May I see Mother now?" Artemis asked him.

"Yes," said Artemis Senior. "Go now, see what you can find out. Study her symptoms for your search."

My search, thought Artemis. There are difficult times ahead.

Artemis's hulking bodyguard, Butler, waited for him at the foot of the stairs wearing full kendo armor, the helmet's face guard folded away from his weathered features.

"I was in the dojo, sparring with the holograph," he explained. "Your father called and told me I was needed immediately. What's going on?"

"It's Mother," said Artemis, passing him. "She's very ill. I'm going to see what I can do."

Butler hurried to keep pace, his chest plate clanking. "Be careful, Artemis. Magic is not science. You can't control it. You wouldn't want to accidentally make Mrs. Fowl's condition worse."

Artemis arrived at the top of the grand stairway, tentatively reaching his hand toward the bedroom door's brass knob as though it were electrified.

"I fear that her condition couldn't be worse. . . ."

Artemis went inside alone, leaving the bodyguard to strip off the kendo headgear and *hon-nuri* breastplate. Underneath he wore a tracksuit instead of his traditional wide-legged trousers. Sweat blossomed across his chest and back, but Butler ignored his desire to go and shower, standing sentry outside the door, knowing that he shouldn't strain too hard to listen, but wishing that he could.

Butler was the only other human who knew the full truth of Artemis's magical escapades. He had been at his young charge's shoulder throughout their various adventures, battling fairies and humans across the continents. But Artemis had made the journey through time to Limbo without him, and Artemis had come back changed. A part of Butler's young charge was magical now, and not just Captain Holly Short's hazel left eye that the time stream had given him in place of his own. On the journey from Earth to Limbo and back, Artemis had somehow managed to steal a few strands of magic from the fairies whose atoms were mixed with his in the time stream. When he had returned home from Limbo, Artemis had *suggested* to his parents in the compelling magical *mesmer* that they simply not think about where he had been for the past few years. It wasn't a very sophisticated plan, as his disappearance had made the news worldwide, and the subject was raised at every function the Fowls attended. But until Artemis could get hold of some LEP mind-wiping equipment, or indeed develop his own, it would have to suffice. He *suggested* to his parents that if anyone were to ask about him, they simply state it was a family matter and ask that their privacy be respected.

Artemis is a magical man, thought Butler. The only one.

And now Butler just knew Artemis was going to use his magic to attempt a healing on his mother. It was a dangerous game; magic was not a natural part of his makeup. Artemis could well remove one set of symptoms and replace them with another.

The boy entered his parents' bedroom slowly. The twins charged in here at all hours of the day and night, flinging

themselves on the four-poster bed to wrestle with his protesting mother and father, but Artemis had never experienced that. His childhood had been a time of order and discipline.

Always knock before entering, Artemis, his father had instructed him. *It shows respect.*

But his father had changed. A brush with death seven years earlier had shown him what was really important. Now he was always ready to hug and roll in the covers with his beloved sons.

It's too late for me, thought Artemis. I am too old for tussles with Father.

Mother was different. She was never cold, apart from during her bouts of depression when his father had been missing. But fairy magic and the return of her beloved husband had saved her from that, and now she was herself again. Or she had been until now.

Artemis crossed the room slowly, afraid of what lay before him. He walked across the carpet, careful to tread between the vine patterns in the weave.

Step on a vine, count to nine.

This was a habit from when he was little, an old superstition whispered lightly by his father. Artemis had never forgotten, and always counted to nine to ward off the bad luck should so much as a toe touch the carpet vines.

The four-poster bed stood at the rear of the room, swathed in hanging drapes and sunlight. A breeze slipped

16

into the room, rippling the silks like the sails of a pirate ship.

One of his mother's hands, pale and thin, dangled over the side of her bed.

Artemis was horrified. Just yesterday his mother had been fine. A slight sniffle, but still her laughing, warm self.

"Mother," he blurted upon seeing her face, feeling as though the word had been punched out of him.

This was not possible. In twenty-four hours his mother had deteriorated to little more than a skeleton. Her cheekbones were sharp as flint, her eyes lost in dark sockets.

Don't worry, Artemis told himself. In a few short seconds Mother will be well; then I can investigate what happened here.

Angeline Fowl's beautiful hair was frizzed and brittle, broken strands crisscrossing her pillow like a spiderweb. And there was an odd smell emanating from her pores.

Lilies, thought Artemis. Sweet, yet tinged with sickness.

Angeline's eyes opened abruptly, round with panic. Her back arched as she sucked a breath through a constricted windpipe, clutching at the air with clawed hands. Just as suddenly she collapsed, and Artemis thought for a terrible moment that she was gone.

But then her eyelids fluttered and she reached a hand for him.

"Arty," she said, her voice no more than a whisper. "I am

having the strangest dream." A short sentence, but it took an age to complete, with a rasped breath between each word.

Artemis took his mother's hand. How slender it was. A parcel of bones.

"Or perhaps I am awake and my other life is a dream."

Artemis was pained to hear his mother speak like this; it reminded him of the odd turns she used to suffer from.

"You're awake, Mother, and I am here. You have a light fever and are a little dehydrated, that's all. Nothing to be concerned about."

"How can I be awake, Arty?" said Angeline, her eyes calm in black circles. "When I feel myself dying. How can I be awake when I feel that?"

Artemis's feigned calm was knocked by this.

"It's the . . . fever," he stammered. "You're seeing things a little strangely. Everything will be fine soon. I promise."

Angeline closed her eyes. "And my son keeps his promises, I know. Where have you been these past years, Arty? We were so worried. Why are you not seventeen?"

In her delirium, Angeline Fowl saw through a haze of magic to the truth. She realized that he had been missing for three years and had come home the same age as he had gone away.

"I am fourteen, Mother. Almost fifteen now, still a boy for another while. Now close your eyes, and when you open them again, all will be well."

"What have you done to my thoughts, Artemis? Where has your power come from?"

Artemis was sweating now. The heat of the room, the sickly smell, his own anxiety.

She knows. Mother knows. If you heal her, will she remember everything?

It didn't matter. That could be dealt with in due time. His priority was to mend his parent.

Artemis squeezed the frail hand in his grip, feeling the bones grind against each other. He was about to use magic on his mother for the second time.

Magic did not belong in Artemis's soul and gave him lightning-bolt headaches whenever he used it. Though he was human, the fairy rules of magic held a certain sway over him. He was forced to chew motion sickness tablets before entering a dwelling uninvited, and when the moon was full, Artemis could often be found in the library listening to music at maximum volume to drown out the voices in his head—the great commune of magical creatures. The fairies had powerful race memories, and they surfaced like a tidal wave of raw emotion, bringing migraines with them.

Sometimes Artemis wondered if stealing the magic had been a mistake, but recently the symptoms had stopped. No more migraines or sickness. Perhaps his brain was adapting to the strain of being a magical creature.

Artemis held his mother's fingers gently, closed his eyes, and cleared his mind.

Magic. Only magic.

The magic was a wild force and needed to be controlled. If Artemis let his thoughts ramble, the magic would ramble too, and he could open his eyes to find his mother still sick but with different-color hair.

Heal, he thought. Be well, Mother.

The magic responded to his wish, spreading along his limbs, buzzing, tingling. Blue sparks circled his wrists, twitching like schools of tiny minnows. Almost as if they were alive.

Artemis thought of his mother in better times. He saw her skin radiant, her eyes shining with happiness. Heard her laugh, felt her touch on his neck. Remembered the strength of Angeline Fowl's love for her family.

That is what I want.

The sparks sensed his wishes and flowed into Angeline Fowl, sinking into the skin of her hand and wrist, twisting in ropes around her gaunt arms. Artemis pushed harder, and a river of magical flickers flowed from his fingers into his mother.

Heal, he thought. Drive out the sickness.

Artemis had used his magic before, but this time was different. There was resistance, as though his mother's body did not wish to be healed and was rejecting the power. Sparks fizzled on her skin, spasmed, and winked out.

More, thought Artemis. More.

He pushed harder, ignoring the sudden blinding headache and rumbling nausea.

Heal, Mother.

The magic wrapped his mother like an Egyptian mummy, snaking underneath her body, raising her six inches from the mattress. She shuddered and moaned, steam venting from her pores, sizzling as it touched the blue sparks.

She is in pain, thought Artemis, opening one eye a slit. In agony. But I cannot stop now.

Artemis dug down deep, searching his extremities for the last scraps of magic inside him.

Everything. Give her every last spark.

Magic was not an intrinsic part of Artemis; he had stolen it and now he threw it off again, stuffing all he had into the attempted healing. And yet it wasn't working. No, worse than that. Her sickness was growing stronger. Repelling each blue wave, robbing the sparks of their color and power, sending them skittering to the ceiling.

Something is wrong, thought Artemis, bile in his throat, a dagger of pain over his left eye. It shouldn't be like this.

The final drop of magic left his body with a jolt, and Artemis was thrown from his mother's bedside and sent skidding across the floor, then tumbling head over heels until he came to rest, sprawled against a chaise longue. Angeline Fowl spasmed a final time, then collapsed back onto her mattress. Her body was soaked with a strange, thick, clear gel. Magical sparks flickered and died in the coating, which steamed off almost as quickly as it had appeared.

Artemis lay with his head in his hands, waiting for the chaos in his brain to stop, unable to move or think. His own breathing seemed to rasp against his skull. Eventually the pain faded to echoes, and jumbled words formed themselves into sentences.

The magic is gone. Spent. I am entirely human.

Artemis registered the sound of the bedroom door creaking, and he opened his eyes to find Butler and his father staring down at him, concern large on their faces.

"We heard a crash; you must have fallen," said Artemis Senior, lifting his son by the elbow. "I should never have let you in here alone, but I thought that perhaps you could do something. You have certain talents, I know. I was hoping . . ." He straightened his son's shirt, patted his shoulders. "It was stupid of me."

Artemis shrugged his father's hands away, stumbling to his mother's sickbed. It took a mere glance to confirm what he already knew. He had not cured his mother. There was no bloom on her cheeks or ease in her breathing.

She is worse. What have I done?

"What is it?" asked his father. "What the devil is wrong with her? At this rate of decline, in less than a week my Angeline will be——"

Butler interrupted brusquely. "No giving up now,

gents. We all have contacts from our past that might be able to shed some light on Mrs. Fowl's condition. People we might prefer not to associate with otherwise. We find them and bring them back here as fast as we can. We ignore nuisances like passports or visas and get it done."

Artemis Senior nodded, slowly at first, then with more vigor.

"Yes. Yes, dammit. She is not finished yet. My Angeline is a fighter, are you not, darling?"

He took her hand gently, as though it were made of the finest crystal. She did not respond to his touch or voice. "We talked to every alternative practitioner in Europe about my phantom limb pains. Perhaps one of them can help us with this."

"I know a man in China," said Butler. "He worked with Madame Ko at the bodyguard academy. He was a miracle worker with herbs. Lived up in the mountains. He has never been outside the province, but he would come for me."

"Good," said Artemis Senior. "The more opinions we can call on the better." He turned to his son. "Listen, Arty, do you know someone who might be able to help? Anyone. Perhaps you have some underworld contacts?"

Artemis twisted a rather ostentatious ring on his middle finger so that the front rested against his palm. This *ring* was actually a camouflaged fairy communicator.

"Yes," he said. "I have a few underworld contacts."

CHAPTER 2

THE WORLD'S BIGGEST

Helsinki Harbor, the Baltic Sea

The giant sea monster that is the kraken sent its finned tentacles spiraling toward the ocean's surface, pulling its bloated body behind. Its single eye rolled manically in its socket, and its curved beak, the size of a schooner's prow, was open wide, filtering the rushing water through to its rippling gills.

The kraken was hungry, and there was room for only one thought in its tiny brain as it sped toward the holiday ferry above.

Kill . . . Kill . . . KILL . . .

"That is such dwarf manure," said Captain Holly Short of the Lower Elements Police, muting the sound file in her helmet. "For one thing, the kraken doesn't have tentacles, and as for 'kill, kill, kill' . . ."

"I know," said Foaly, the voice of mission control in her communicator. "I thought you might enjoy that passage. You know, have a laugh. Remember laughing?"

Holly was not amused. "It's so typical of humans, Foaly, to take something perfectly natural and demonize it. Krakens are gentle creatures, and the humans turn them into some kind of murderous giant squid. 'Kill, kill, kill.' Give me a break."

"Come on, Holly, it's just sensational fiction. You know those humans and their imaginations. Relax."

Foaly was right. If she got worked up every time the human media misrepresented a mythical creature, she would spend half her life in a rage. Over the centuries Mud Men had caught glimpses of the fairy folk, and had twisted the truth of these glimpses almost beyond recognition.

Let it go. There are decent humans. Remember Artemis and Butler.

"Did you see that human movie with the centaurs?" she asked the centaur on the other end of her helmet communicator. "They were noble and sporty. 'My sword for thee, Majesty, then off for a spot of hunting.' Fit centaurs, now that did make me laugh."

Thousands of miles away, somewhere in the earth's mantle below Ireland, Foaly, the Lower Elements Police's technical adviser, rubbed his paunch.

"Holly, that hurts. Caballine likes my belly."

Foaly had got married, or *hitched,* as centaurs called the ceremony, while Holly had been away with Artemis Fowl, rescuing demons in Limbo. A lot had changed in the three years she had been away, and sometimes Holly was finding it difficult to keep up. Foaly had a new bride to occupy his time. Her old friend Trouble Kelp had been promoted to LEP Commander, and she was back working at Recon with the Kraken Watch task force.

"Apologies, friend. That was mean," said Holly. "I like your belly too. I'm sorry that I wasn't there to see a hitching sash around it."

"Me too. Next time."

Holly smiled. "Sure. That's going to happen."

Traditionally, male centaurs were expected to take more than one bride, but Caballine was a modern fairy, and Holly doubted if she would stand for a new filly in the household.

"Don't worry, I'm joking."

"You'd better be, because I'm meeting Caballine at the spa this weekend."

"How's the new gear?" said Foaly, hurriedly changing the subject.

Holly spread her arms wide, feeling the wind ripple her fingers, seeing the Baltic Sea flash past below in shards of blue and white.

"It's wonderful," she said. "Absolutely wonderful."

* * *

Captain Holly Short of LEPrecon flew in wide lazy circles above Helsinki, enjoying the brisk Scandinavian air filtering through her helmet. It was just after five a.m. local time, and the rising sun set the Uspenski Cathedral's golden onion dome shimmering. Already the city's famed marketplace was strobed with headlights as vendors arrived to open up for the morning trade, or eager politicians' aides made their way toward the blue-gray facade of city hall.

Holly's target lay away from what would shortly be a bustling center of commerce. She adjusted her fingers, and the sensors in her armored gloves translated the movements to commands for the mechanical wings on her back, sending her spiraling down toward the small island of Uunisaari, half a mile from the port.

"The body sensors are nice," she said. "Very intuitive."

"It's as close as it gets to being a bird," said Foaly. "Unless you want to integrate?"

"No thank you," Holly said vehemently. She loved flying, but not enough to have a LEP surgeon stick a few implants in her cerebellum.

"Very well, Captain Short," said Foaly, switching to business mode. "Pre-op check. Three W's, please."

The three W's were every Reconnaissance officer's checklist before approaching an operation's zone: wings, weapon, and a way home.

Holly checked the transparent readouts on her helmet visor.

"Power cell, charged. Weapon on green. Wings and suit fully functional. No red lights."

"Excellent," said Foaly. "Check, check, and check. Our screens agree."

Holly heard keys clicking as Foaly recorded this information in the mission log. The centaur was known for his fondness for old-school keyboards, even though he himself had patented an extremely efficient virtual keyboard.

"Remember, Holly, this is just reconnaissance. Go down and check the sensor. Those things are two hundred years old, and the problem is more than likely a simple overheat. All you need to do is go where I tell you and fix what I tell you. No indiscriminate blasting involved. Understand?"

Holly snorted. "I can see why Caballine fell for you, Foaly. You're such a charmer."

Foaly snickered. "I don't rise to jibes anymore, Holly. Marriage has mellowed me."

"Mellowed? I'll believe that when you last ten minutes in a room with Mulch without throwing a hoof."

The dwarf Mulch Diggums had been at various times enemy, partner, and friend to Holly and Foaly. His greatest pleasure in life was stuffing his face, and not far behind that was irritating his various enemies, partners, and friends.

"Perhaps I need a few more years of marriage before I get *that* mellow. A few more centuries, in fact."

The island was large in Holly's visor now, surrounded by a monk's fringe of foam. Time to stop the chitchat and proceed with the mission, though Holly was tempted to circle in a holding pattern so she could talk some more with her friend. It seemed as though this was the first real conversation they'd had since her return from Limbo. Foaly had moved on with life in the past three years, but for Holly her absence had lasted only a few hours, and, though she had not aged, Holly felt cheated of those years. The LEP psychiatrist would have told her she was suffering from Post-time-travel-displacement Depression, and offered to prescribe a nice shot to cheer her up. Holly trusted happy-shots just about as much as she trusted brain implants.

"I'm going in," she said tersely. This was her first solo mission since debriefing, and she did not want anything less than a perfect report, even if it was only Kraken Watch.

"Copy," said Foaly. "You see the sensor?"

There were four bio-sensors on the island relaying information back to Police Plaza. Three pulsed a gentle green in Holly's visor display unit. The fourth sensor was red. Red could mean many things. In this case, *every* reading had risen above normal levels. Temperature, heartbeat, brain activity. All on the danger line.

It must be a malfunction, Foaly had explained. *If not, the other sensors would show something.*

"I have it. Strong signal."

"Okay. Shield and approach."

Holly twisted her chin sharply left until her neck bone clicked, which was her way of summoning the magic. It wasn't a necessary movement, since the magic was mostly a brain function, but fairies developed their own tics. She let a dribble of power into her limbs and vibrated out of the visible spectrum. Her Shimmer Suit picked up her frequency and amplified it so that a tiny spark of magic went a long way.

"I'm out of sight and going in," she confirmed.

"Understood," said the centaur. "Be careful, Holly. Commander Kelp will be reviewing this video, so stick to your orders."

"Are you suggesting that I occasionally stray from the rule book?" said Holly, apparently horrified by the very notion.

Foaly sniggered. "I am suggesting that you may not own a copy of the rule book, and if you do possess one, you certainly have never opened it."

Fair point, thought Holly, swooping down toward the surface of Uunisaari.

Whales are thought to be the world's largest creatures. They are not. The kraken can stretch to three miles in length and have been a staple of Scandinavian legend since the thirteenth century, when they appeared in the Orvar-Odd saga as the fearsome *lyngbakr*. Early descriptions of

⊖ẞ · Ⅰ○⊖ᒒ♉ẞ ➤ ♒∪∪Ⅰ⊗ · ⊖⊗ ➤

the kraken are the most accurate, describing the sea creature as an animal the size of a floating island whose real danger to ships was not the creature itself, but the whirlpool it created when it sank into the ocean. But by the Middle Ages the legend of the kraken had been confused with that of the giant squid, and each credited with the most fearsome attributes of the other. The squid was pictured as big as a mountain, while the peaceful kraken grew tentacles and developed a bloodlust to rival that of the deadliest shark.

Nothing could be further from the truth. The kraken is a docile creature whose main defenses are its sheer size and the bulk of shell, gas, and fat cells enclosing a melon-size brain, which provides it with just enough intelligence to feed itself and shed its shell. Underneath the crust of rock, weed, and coral, the kraken resembles nothing more than the common acorn barnacle, albeit a barnacle that could easily house an Olympic stadium or two.

Kraken enjoy a lifespan of several thousand years, thanks to an incredibly slow metabolism and a huge network of support systems surrounding their soft centers. They tend to settle in a food-rich or magical environment and remain there until the food or energy residue runs out. Nestling in the middle of an archipelago near a human port provides not only camouflage but an abundant source of edible material. And so this is where kraken are found, anchored to the seabed like gigantic limpets, vacuuming city waste through their gills and fermenting it into methane in their vast stomachs. But if human garbage is their salvation, it is also their damnation, for increasingly high toxin levels have rendered the kraken sterile, and now there are less than half a dozen of the ancient creatures left in the oceans.

This particular kraken was the oldest of the bunch. According to shell scrapings, old Shelly, as the small dedicated Kraken Watch referred to it, was more than ten thousand years old, and had been masquerading as an island in Helsinki Harbor since the sixteenth century, when the town was known as Helsingfors.

In all that time, Shelly had done little but feed and sleep, feeling no urge to migrate. Any need he may have felt to move on was dulled by the seepings of a paint factory built on his back more than a hundred years previous. For all intents and purposes, Shelly was catatonic, having emitted no more than a couple of methane flashes in over fifty years, so there was no reason to believe that this red light on his sensor was anything more than a crossed wire, and it was Holly's job to *uncross* it. It was a standard first-day-back-on-the-job kind of mission. No danger, no deadline, and little chance of discovery.

Holly turned her palms into the wind, descending till her boots scraped the roof of the island's small restaurant. Actually there were two islands, separated by a small bridge. One was a genuine island, and the other larger section was old Shelly nestled into the rock. Holly ran a quick thermal sweep, finding nothing but a few rodents and a blotch of heat from the sauna, which was probably on a timer.

Holly consulted her visor for the sensor's exact location. It was twelve feet underwater, tucked below a rocky ledge.

Underwater. Of course.

She stowed her wings, midair, then plunged feetfirst into the Baltic Sea, corkscrewing to minimize the splash. Not that there were any humans close enough to hear. The sauna and restaurant did not open until eight, and the nearest fishermen were on the mainland, their rods swaying gently like rows of bare flagpoles.

Holly vented the gas bags in her helmet to reduce buoyancy, and sank below the waves. Her visor informed her that the water temperature was a little over ten degrees, but the Shimmer Suit insulated her from cold shock and even flexed to compensate for the slight pressure increase.

"Use the Critters," said Foaly, his voice crystal clear through the vibration nodes over her ears.

"Get out of my head, centaur."

"Go on. Use the Critters."

"I don't need a tracer. It's right there."

Foaly sighed. "Then they shall die unfulfilled."

The Coded Radiation Tracers were microorganisms

bathed in radiation of the same frequency as the object being located. If you knew what you were looking for before leaving Foaly's workshop, then the Critters would bring you right to it; though they were a little redundant when the sensor was a few feet away and beeping on your screen.

"Okay," moaned Holly. "I wish you would stop using me as a guinea pig."

She pulled back a watertight flap on her glove, releasing a cloud of glowing orange mites into the water. They bunched for a moment, then sped off in a ragged arrow toward the sensor.

"They swim, they fly, they burrow," said Foaly, awed by his own achievement. "God bless their tiny hearts."

The Critters left a glowing orange wake for Holly to follow. She pulled herself below a sharp ledge, to find the Critters already excavating the growths covering the sensor.

"Now, come on. That is handy. Tell me that's not useful to a field officer."

It was very useful, especially since Holly only had ten minutes of air left; but Foaly's head was big enough as it was.

"A gill helmet would have been more useful, especially since you *knew* the sensor was underwater."

"You have more than enough air," argued Foaly. "Especially since the Critters are clearing the surrounding area."

The Critters ate away the rock and moss covering the sensor until it gleamed like the day it came off the assembly line. Once their mission was completed, the Critters flickered and died, dissolving in the water with a gentle fizz. Holly switched on her helmet lights and focused both beams on the alloy instrument. The sensor was the size and shape of a banana and covered with an electrolytic gel.

"The water is pretty clean, thanks to Shelly. I'm getting a decent picture."

Holly topped up her suit buoyancy a few notches until she was at neutral, and hung in the water as still as she could.

"Well, what do you see, Foaly?"

"The same as you," replied the centaur. "A sensor with a flashing red light. I need to take a few readings, if you wouldn't mind touching the screen."

Holly laid her palm on the gel so that the omnisensor on her glove could sync with the ancient instrument.

"Nine and a half minutes, Foaly, don't forget."

"Please," snickered the centaur, "I could recalibrate a fleet of satellites in nine and a half minutes."

It was probably true, thought Holly, as her helmet ran a systems check on the sensor.

"Hmm," sighed Foaly, thirty seconds later.

"Hmm?" repeated Holly nervously. "Don't hmm, Foaly. Dazzle me with science, but don't hmm."

"There doesn't seem to be anything wrong with this

sensor. It is remarkably functional. Which means . . ."

"That the other three sensors are malfunctioning," concluded Holly. "So much for your genius."

"I did not design these sensors," said Foaly, wounded. "They're old Koboi gear."

Holly shuddered, her body jerking in the water. Her old enemy Opal Koboi had been one of the People's leading innovators, until she decided that she would prefer to pursue all criminal avenues to crown herself queen of the world instead. Now she was housed in a specially constructed isolation prison cube suspended in Atlantis, and spent her time shooting off mail to politicians, pleading for early release.

"Apologies, old friend, for doubting your wonderfulness. I suppose I should check the other sensors. Above sea level, I do hope."

"Hmm," said Foaly again.

"Please stop that. Surely, now that I am here, I should check the remaining sensors?"

Silence for a moment as Foaly accessed a few files, then he spoke in hitched phrases while the information opened before him. "The other sensors . . . are not the pressing issue . . . right now. What we really need to know . . . is why would Shelly be redlining on *this* sensor. Let me just see . . . if we have ever had these kind of readings before."

Holly had no choice but to maintain contact with the

sensor, legs swaying underneath her, watching the air clock on her visor run down.

"Okay," said Foaly finally. "Two reasons for a kraken's readings to redline. One, Shelly is having a baby kraken, which is impossible since he's a sterile male."

"That leaves two," said Holly, who was certain that she would not like the second reason.

"And two. He's shedding."

Holly rolled her eyes in relief. "Shedding. That doesn't sound so bad."

"Weeeellll, it's a little worse than it sounds."

"What do you mean, a little?"

"Why don't I explain as you fly away as fast as you can."

Holly did not need to be told twice. When Foaly advised an officer to leave *before* he delivered one of his beloved lectures, then the situation was serious. She spread her arms wide, and the action was mimicked by the wings on her back.

"Engage," she said, pointing both arms to the surface; the engines ignited and blasted her clear of the Baltic, boiling the water wake as it hung in the air. Her suit was instantly dry as moisture slipped from its nonstick material and air resistance tugged at any remaining drops. In seconds she had climbed to a few hundred feet, the anxiety in Foaly's voice hurrying her along.

"A kraken sheds its shell once, and records show that Shelly dumped his three thousand years ago, so we presumed that was that."

"But now?"

"Now it seems as though Shelly has lived long enough to do it again."

"And why are we concerned about this?"

"We are concerned about this because kraken shed very explosively. The new shell has already grown, and Shelly will get rid of the old one by igniting a layer of methane cells and blasting it off."

Holly wanted to be sure she understood what was being said. "So you're saying that Shelly is going to light a fart?"

"No, Shelly is going to light *the* fart. He has stored enough methane to power Haven for a year. There hasn't been a fart like this since the last dwarf tribal gathering."

A computer representation of the explosion appeared in Holly's visor. To most fairies the image would be little more than a blur, but LEP officers were forced to develop the double focus necessary to read their screens and watch where they were going at the same time.

When the simulation put Holly clear of the projected blast radius, she dropped her boots, swinging in a loose ascending arc to face the kraken.

"Isn't there something we can do?"

"Besides take a couple of pictures? Nope. Too late for that. Only a few minutes to go. Shelly's inner shell is already at ignition temperature, so put your glare filter down and watch the show."

Holly lowered her shade. "This is going to make the

news all over the world. Islands don't just explode."

"Yes they do. Volcanic activity, gas leaks, chemical accidents. Believe me, if there's one thing the Mud Men *do* know, it's how to explain away an explosion. The Americans invented Area 51 just because a senator crashed a jet into a mountain."

"The mainland is safe?"

"Should be. A little shrapnel, maybe."

Holly relaxed, hanging from her wings. There was nothing she could do, nothing she *should* do. This was a natural process, and the kraken had every right to shed its shell.

Methane explosions. Mulch would love this.

Mulch Diggums was currently running a private investigations office in Haven with the pixie wheel-fairy Doodah Day. Mulch had, in his day, caused some methane disturbances himself.

Something pulsed gently in Holly's visor. A plasma splotch of red in the thermal sweep windows. There was life on the island, and not just insect or rodent. Multiple humans.

"Foaly. I have something."

Holly resized the window with a series of blink commands to track down the source. There were four hot bodies inside the sauna.

"*Inside* the sauna, Foaly. How did we miss them?"

"Their bodies were at the same temperature as the

brick walls," replied the centaur. "I'm guessing that one of the Mud Men opened the door."

Holly magnified her visor to plus four and saw that the sauna door was open a crack, a wedge of steam pushing through the gap. The building was cooling faster than the humans, and so now they showed up separately on her scanner.

"What are those Mud Men doing here? You said nothing opens until eight."

"I don't know, Holly. How would I know? They're humans. About as reliable as moon-mad demons."

It didn't matter *why* the humans were there, and wondering about it was a waste of time.

"I have to go back, Foaly."

Foaly put a camera on himself, broadcasting his live image to Holly's helmet.

"Look at my face, Holly. Do you see this expression? This is my *stern* face. Do not do it, Holly. Do not return to the island. Humans die every day, and we do not interfere. The LEP *never* interferes."

"I know the rules," said Holly, muting the growling centaur.

There goes my career again, she thought, angling her wings for a steep dive.

Four men sat in the sauna's outer room, feeling very smug that they had once again outwitted island authorities and managed to sneak a free sauna before work. It did help that one of the men was Uunisaari's security guard and had access to the keys, and a little five horsepower punt that accommodated the four friends, and a bucket of Karjala beer.

"Good temperature in the sauna today," said one.

A second wiped the steam from his glasses. "A little hot, I thought. In fact, even here it feels hot underfoot."

"Go jump in the Baltic, then," said the guard, miffed at this lack of appreciation for his efforts. "That will cool down your poor toesies."

"Don't pay any attention to him," said the fourth man, fastening his watch. "He has sensitive feet. Always some temperature problem."

The men, friends since childhood, laughed and swigged their beers. The laughing and swigging ceased abruptly when a section of the roof suddenly caught fire and disintegrated.

The guard coughed out a mouthful of beer. "Was someone smoking? I said no smoking!"

Even if one of his sauna buddies had answered, the guard would not have heard, as he had somehow managed to fly through the hole in the roof.

"My toes are *really* hot," said the bespectacled man as if hanging on to old topics of conversation could make new ones go away.

The others ignored him, busy doing what men

generally do in dangerous times: putting on their trousers.

There was no time for introductions or doors, so Holly drew her Neutrino sidearm and carved a six-foot hole in the roof. She was treated to the sight of four pale, semi-dressed Mud Men quivering in sudden fright.

I'm not surprised they're quivering, she thought. And that's only the beginning.

As she flew, she worked on her problem: how to get four humans out of the blast zone in as many minutes.

Until recently she would have had a second problem: the building itself. According to the fairy Book, fairies were forbidden to enter human buildings without an invitation. This was a ten-thousand-year-old hex that still had a little sting, causing nausea and loss of power to anyone who defied it. The law was an anachronism and a serious impediment to LEP operations, so after a series of public debates and a referendum, the hex had been lifted by demon warlock N°1. It had taken the little demon five minutes to unravel a hex that had stumped elfin warlocks for centuries.

Back to the original problem. Four large humans. Big explosion imminent.

The first human was easy enough and the obvious choice. He was blocking the others and wore nothing but a towel and a tiny security guard's cap, which perched on top of his skull like a nutshell on the head of a bear.

Holly grimaced. *I have to get him out of my sight as soon as possible, or I may never forget this image. That Mud Man has more muscles than a troll.*

Troll! Of course.

There had been several additions to the Recon kit while Holly had been in Limbo, most invented and patented by Foaly, naturally. One such addition was a new clip of darts for her Neutrino. The Centaur called them anti-gravity darts, but the officers called them floaters.

The darts were based on Foaly's own Moonbelt, which generated a field around whatever was attached to it, reducing the earth's gravitational pull to one fifth of normal. The Moonbelt was useful for transporting heavy equipment. Field officers quickly adapted the belt to their own specialized needs, attaching their prisoners to the pitons, which made them much easier to handle.

Foaly had then developed a dart that had the same effect as his Moonbelt. The dart used the fugitive's own flesh to conduct the charge that rendered him almost weightless. Even a troll seems less threatening when it is bobbing in the breeze like a balloon.

Holly slipped the clip from her belt, using the heel of one hand to ram it into the Neutrino.

Darts, she thought. Back to the Stone Age.

The big security guard was square in her sights, his lip wobbling petulantly.

⟩)⊕)◌ ⤳ • ⊗▢ • ⤳◌ ⚕ • ⚗ ⊙ •

No need for laser sights with this Mud Man, she thought. I could hardly miss.

And she didn't. The tiny dart pricked the man's shoulder, and he quivered for a moment until the anti-gravity field encircled him.

"Ooh," he said. "That's a little . . ."

Then Holly landed beside him, grasped his pale thigh, and hurled him into the sky. He went faster than a popped balloon, leaving a trail of surprised O's in his wake.

The remaining men hurriedly finished pulling on their pants; two tripped in their haste, banging heads before crashing to the ground. Plates of tomato-and-mozzarella rolls were batted aside; bottles of beer went spinning across the tiles.

"My sandwiches," said one man, even as he struggled with his purple jeans.

No time for panic, thought Holly, silent and invisible among them. She ducked low, avoiding pale swinging limbs, and quickly loosed off three more darts.

A strange calm descended on the sauna as three grown men found themselves floating toward a hole in the roof.

"My feet are—" began the bespectacled man.

"Shut up about your feet!" shouted sandwich man, swiping at him with a fist. The motion sent him spinning and bouncing like a pinball.

Foaly overrode Holly's MUTE.

"D'Arvit, Holly. You have seconds. *Seconds!* Get out of

there now! Even your suit armor will not stop an explosion of this magnitude."

Holly's face was red and sweating in spite of her helmet's climate control.

Seconds left. How many times have I heard that?

No time for subtleties. She lay flat on her back, tapping the readout on her Neutrino to select concussion beams, and fired a wide pattern blast straight up.

The beam bore the men aloft, as a fast-flowing river would bear bubbles, bouncing them off the walls and each other before finally popping them through the still-sparking circle in the roof.

The last man out looked down as he left, wondering absently why he was not gibbering in panic. Surely flying was grounds for hysteria?

That will probably come later, he decided. If there *is* a later for me.

In the steam of the sauna, it seemed to him that there was a small humanoid shape lying on the floor. A diminutive figure with wings, which leaped to its feet, then sped toward the flying men.

It's all true, thought the man. Just like Lord of the Rings. Fantasy creatures. All true.

Then the island exploded, and the man stopped worrying about fantasy creatures and began worrying about his trousers, which had just caught fire.

* * *

With all four men in the air, Holly decided that it was time to get herself as far from the supposed island as possible. She jumped from a squatting position, engaged her wings in the air, and shot into the morning sky.

"Very nice," said Foaly. "You know they're calling that move the Hollycopter, don't you?"

Holly drew her weapon, urging the weightless men farther away from the island with short bursts.

"Busy staying alive, Foaly. Talk later."

Foaly said. "Sorry, friend. I'm worried. I talk when I'm worried. Caballine thinks it's a defense mechanism. Anyway, the Hollycopter. You did the same takeoff during that rooftop shoot-out in Darmstadt. Major . . . I mean . . . *Commander* Kelp caught it on video. They're using the footage in the academy now. You wouldn't believe how many cadets have broken their ankles trying the same trick."

Holly was about to insist that he please shut up when Shelly ignited his methane cells, decimating his old shell and sending tons of debris hurtling skyward. The shock wave took Holly from below like a giant's punch, sending her pinwheeling. She felt her suit flex to avoid the impact, the tiny scales closing ranks like the shields of a demon battalion. There was a slight hiss as her helmet plumped the safety bags protecting her brain and spinal cord. The screens in her visor flickered, jumped, then settled.

The world spun by her visor in a series of blues and grays. The Artificial Horizon in her helmet did several revolutions, end over end, though Holly realized that in actuality she was the one revolving, and not the display.

Alive. Still alive. My odds must be getting short.

Foaly broke in on her thoughts. ". . . heart rate is up, though I don't know why. One would think you'd be used to these situations by now. The four humans made it, you will be delighted to know, since you risked your life and my technology to save them. What if one of my floaters had fallen into human hands?"

Holly used a combination of gestures and blinks to fire short bursts from several of her wings' twelve engines, wrestling back control of her rig.

She opened her visor to cough and spit, then answered his accusation.

"I'm fine, thanks for asking. And all LEP equipment is fitted with remote-destruct. Even me! So the only way your precious floaters were ever going to fall into human hands was if *your* technology failed."

"Which reminds me," said Foaly, "I need to get rid of those darts."

Below was pandemonium. It seemed as though half of Helsinki's inhabitants had already managed to launch themselves in various crafts, and a veritable flotilla was heading toward the explosion site, led by a coast guard vessel, two powerful outboards churning at its stern, nose up for speed. The kraken itself was obscured by smoke and dust, but charred fragments of its shell rained down like volcanic ash, coating the decks of the boats below and draping a dark blanket over the Baltic Sea.

Twenty yards to Holly's left, the floating men bobbed happily in the air, riding the last ripples of explosive shock, pants hanging in tattered ruins from their waists.

"I am surprised," said Holly, zooming in on the men. "No screaming or wetting themselves."

"A little drop of relaxant in the dart." Foaly chuckled. "Well, I say a little drop. Enough to have a troll missing his mommy."

"Trolls occasionally eat their mothers," commented Holly.

"Exactly."

Foaly waited until the men had dropped to within ten feet of the ocean's surface, then remote-detonated the tiny charge in each dart. Four small pops were followed by four loud splashes. The men were in the water no more than a few seconds before the coast guard reached them.

"Okay," said the centaur, obviously relieved. "Potential disaster averted, and our good deed done for the day. Kick up your boots and head back for the shuttle station. I have no doubt that Commander Kelp will want a detailed report."

"Just a second, I have mail."

"Mail! Mail! Do you really think this is the time? Your power levels are down, and the rear panels of your suit have taken a severe pasting. You need to get out of there before your shield fails altogether."

"I have to read this one, Foaly. It's important."

The mail icon flashing in Holly's visor was tagged with Artemis's signature. Artemis and Holly color-coded their mail icons. Green was social, blue was business, and red was urgent. The icon in Holly's visor pulsed a bright red. She blinked at the icon, opening the short message.

Mother dying, it read. *Please come at once. Bring N⁰1.*

Holly felt a cold dread in her stomach, and the world seemed to lurch before her eyes.

Mother dying. Bring N⁰1.

The situation must be desperate if Artemis was asking her to bring the powerful demon warlock.

She flashed back to the day, eighteen years ago, when her own mother had passed away. Almost two decades now, and the loss was still as painful as a raw wound. A thought struck her.

It's not eighteen years. It's twenty-one. I've been away for three.

Coral Short had been a doctor with LEPmarine, who patrolled the Atlantic, cleaning up after humans, protecting endangered species. She had been mortally injured when a particularly rancid-looking tanker they were shadowing accidentally doused their submarine with radioactive waste. Dirty radiation is poison to fairies, and it had taken her mother a week to die.

"I will make them pay," Holly had vowed, crying at her mother's bedside in Haven Clinic. "I will hunt down every last one of those Mud Men."

⊗ ⅄ • ↻ ⏦ ⚿ • ⌱ ⤳ ◗◖ ⚼ ⚲ ⏉ ⊙ ⌱ ⚟ ⚞ •

"No," her mother had said with surprising force. "I spent my career *saving* creatures. You must do the same. Destruction cannot be my legacy."

It was one of the last things she would ever say. Three days later, Holly stood stone-faced at her mother's recycling ceremony, her green dress uniform buttoned to the chin, the omnitool that her mother had given her as a graduation present in its holster on her belt.

Saving creatures. So Holly applied to Recon.

And now Artemis's mother was dying. Holly realized that she didn't think of Artemis as a human anymore, just as a friend.

"I need to go to Ireland," she said.

Foaly did not bother to argue, as he had sneaked a peek at this *urgent* mail on Holly's screen.

"Go. I can cover for you here for a few hours. I could say you're completing the Ritual. As it happens, there's a full moon tonight and we still have a few magical sites near Dublin. I'll send a message to Section Eight. Maybe Qwan will let N°1 out of the magi-lab for a few hours."

"Thanks, old friend."

"You're welcome. Now go. I'm going to get out of your head for a while and monitor the chatter here. Maybe I can plant a few ideas in the human media. I like the idea of an underground natural gas pocket. It's almost the truth."

Almost the truth.

Holly couldn't help applying the phrase to Artemis's

mail. So often the Irish boy manipulated people by telling them *almost the truth*.

She chided herself silently. Surely not. Even Artemis Fowl would not lie about something this serious.

Everyone had their limits.

Didn't they?

CHAPTER 3

ECHOES OF MAGIC

ARTEMIS SENIOR assembled his troops in Fowl Manor's conference room, which had originally been a banqueting hall. Until recently the soaring Gothic arches had been hidden by a false ceiling, but Angeline Fowl had ordered the ceiling to be removed and the hall restored to its original double-height glory.

Artemis, his father, and Butler sat in black leather Marcel Breuer chairs around a glass-topped table with space for ten more people.

Not so long ago there were smugglers seated at this table, thought Artemis. Not to mention crime lords, hackers, insider traders, counterfeiters, black marketers, and cat burglars. The old family businesses.

Artemis Senior closed his laptop. He was pale and

obviously exhausted, but the old determination shone brightly in his eyes.

"The plan is a simple one. We must seek out not just a second opinion, but as many opinions as possible. Butler will take the jet and go to China. No time for official channels, so perhaps you could find a strip where immigration is a little lax."

Butler nodded. "I know just the place. I can be there and back in two days, all going well."

Artemis Senior was satisfied. "Good. The jet is fueled and ready. I have already organized a full crew and an extra pilot."

"I just need to pack a few things, then I can be on my way."

Artemis could imagine what kinds of things Butler would pack, especially if there were no officials at the airstrip.

"What will you do, Father?" he asked.

"I am going to England," said Artemis Senior. "I can take the helicopter to London City Airport, and from there a limousine to Harley Street. There are several specialists I can talk to, and it will be far more efficient to send *me* there than to bring *them* all here. If any can shed even the most feeble ray of light on your mother's situation, then I will pay them whatever it takes to get them back here. Buy out their practices, if necessary."

Artemis nodded. Wise tactics. Still, he would expect no

less from the man who had successfully run a criminal empire for more than two decades, and a humanitarian one for the past few years.

Everything Artemis Senior did now was ethical, from his fair-trade clothes company to his shares in Earthpower, a consortium of like-minded businessmen who were building everything from renewable fuel cars to geothermal rods and solar panels. He had even had the Fowl cars, jet, and helicopter fitted with advanced emission filters to lighten the family's carbon footprint.

"I shall remain here," announced Artemis, without waiting to be told. "I can coordinate your efforts, set up a Webcam so that the Harley Street specialists can see Mother, supervise Dr. Schalke and Miss Book, and also conduct my own Internet search for possible cures."

Artemis Senior half smiled. "Exactly, son. I hadn't thought of the Webcam."

Butler was anxious to leave, but he had a point to make before going. "I am not comfortable with Artemis being left alone. A genius he may be, but he is still a habitual meddler and a magnet for trouble." The bodyguard winked at Artemis. "No offense, young sir, but you could turn a Sunday picnic into an international incident."

Artemis accepted the accusation graciously. "None taken."

"That thought has occurred to me," said Artemis Senior, scratching his chin. "But there is nothing for it. The nanny has agreed to take the twins to her cottage in Howth for a couple of days, but Arty is needed here, and so he will have to fend for himself."

"Which will not be a problem," said Artemis. "Have a little faith, please."

Artemis Senior reached across the table, covering his son's hand with his own. "Faith in each other is all we have now. We have to believe that saving your mother is possible. Do you believe it?"

Artemis noticed one of the upper windows swinging slowly ajar. A leaf curled into the room, riding a swirling breeze, then the window seemed to close itself.

"I absolutely believe it, Father. More with every minute."

Holly did not reveal herself until Artemis Senior's modified Sikorsky S-76C had lifted off from the rooftop heliport. Artemis was busy rigging a Webcam at the foot of his mother's bed when the elf shimmered into view with her hand on his shoulder.

"Artemis, I am so sorry," she said softly.

"Thanks for coming, Holly," said Artemis. "You got here quickly."

"I was aboveground, in Finland, chasing a kraken."

"Ah yes, Tennyson's beast," said Artemis, closing his eyes and remembering a few lines from the famous poem.

"Below the thunders of the upper deep;
Far, far beneath in the abysmal sea,
His ancient, dreamless, uninvaded sleep,
The Kraken sleepeth."

"Sleepeth? Not anymore. Watch the news headlines later. There was a natural gas explosion, apparently."

"I would guess that Foaly is up to his old spin-doctoring tricks?"

"Yes."

"Not many kraken left now," commented Artemis. "Seven, by my reckoning."

"Seven?" said Holly, surprised. "We're only tracking six."

"Ah, yes, six. I meant six. New suit?" he asked, changing the subject a little too quickly.

"Three years more advanced than the last one," replied Holly, filing the kraken tidbit for investigation at a later time. "It has autoarmor. If the sensors feel something big coming, the entire suit flexes to cushion the blow. It saved my life once today already."

A message icon beeped in Holly's helmet, and she took a moment to read the short text.

"N°1 is on the way. They're sending the Section Eight shuttle. No way to contain this now, so whatever we need to do has to be done fast."

"Good. I need all the help I can get."

Their conversation petered out as Angeline Fowl's

deathly illness completely occupied their thoughts. She radiated pallor, and the smell of lilies hung yellow in the air.

Artemis fumbled the Webcam and it rolled under the bed.

"Hellfire," he swore, kneeling to reach an arm into the dark space. "I can't . . . I just can't . . ."

And suddenly the enormity of the situation struck him hard.

"What kind of son am I?" he whispered. "A liar and a thief. All my mother has ever done was love me and try to protect me, and now she may die."

Holly helped Artemis to his feet. "You're not that person anymore, Artemis, and you love your mother, don't you?"

Artemis huffed, embarrassed. "Yes. Of course."

"Then you are a good son. And your mother will see that as soon as I cure her."

Holly clicked her neck, and magical sparks leaped from her fingertips, spinning in an inverted cone.

"No," blurted Artemis. "Wouldn't it be wise to check the symptoms first?"

Holly closed her fist, smothering the sparks. Suspicious.

She took off her helmet and stepped close to Artemis, closer than he liked people to be, staring hard into his mismatched eyes. It was strange to see her own eye looking back at her.

"Have you done something, Artemis?"

Artemis met her gaze steadily. It seemed that there was nothing in his eyes but sadness.

"No. I am more cautious with my mother than I would be with myself, that is all."

Holly's suspicion was born of years of experience with Artemis, and so she wondered why he would be reluctant to allow her to use magic now, when it had never bothered him before. Perhaps he had already tried this route himself. Perhaps the time stream had not stripped him of his stolen magic, as he had claimed.

She clamped her hands to the side of Artemis's head, then laid her forehead against his.

"Stop this, Holly," objected Artemis. "We have no time."

Holly did not answer, closing her eyes, concentrating. Artemis felt heat spread across his skull and the familiar buzz of magic. Holly was probing him. It lasted barely a second.

"Nothing," she said, releasing him. "Echoes of magic. But no power."

Artemis stumbled backward, dizzy.

"I understand your suspicion, Holly. I have earned it repeatedly. Now, would you please examine my mother."

Holly realized that up to this point she had avoided doing anything more than take a cursory glance at Angeline Fowl. This entire situation brought back too many painful memories.

"Of course, Artemis. I'm sorry about the probe. I had

to be sure that I could take all of this on face value."

"My feelings are not important," said Artemis, leading Holly by the elbow. "Now, my mother. Please."

Holly had to force herself to properly examine Angeline Fowl, and the moment she did, a deep-rooted dread sent pins and needles fluttering up and down her limbs.

"I know this," she whispered. "I know it."

"This condition is familiar to you?" asked Artemis.

His mother's face and arms were coated with a clear gel, which oozed from her pores and then steamed away. Angeline's eyes were wide, but only the whites were visible, and her fingers clutched the sheets as though hanging on to life.

Holly took a medi-kit from her belt, placed it on the bedside table, and used a swab to take a sample of the gel. "This gel. That smell. It can't be. It can't."

"It can't be what?" asked Artemis, his fingers tight on her forearm.

Holly ignored him, slipping her helmet on and opening a channel to Police Plaza.

"Foaly? Are you there?"

The centaur responded on the second buzz. "Right here, Holly. Chained to the desk. Commander Kelp has sent me a couple of mails asking where you are. I fobbed him off with the Ritual story. I reckon you have about—"

Holly interrupted his chatter. "Foaly, listen to me.

Artemis's mother. I think we have something . . . I think it's bad."

The centaur's mood changed instantly. Holly suspected that he had been waffling to hide his anxiety. After all, Artemis's message had been very grim.

"Okay. I'll sync with the manor systems. Ask Artemis for his password."

Holly lifted her visor to look Artemis in the eye. "Foaly wants your security password."

"Of course, of course." Artemis was drifting, and it took him a moment to remember his own secret word. "It's CENTAUR. All caps."

Below the earth's crust, Foaly stored the compliment in the corner of his brain that held treasured memories. He would take that one out later and gloat over a glass of sim-wine.

"Centaur. Right. I'm in."

A large plasma television on the wall flickered on, and Foaly's face appeared, first in blurred bubbles, then sharp focus. The Webcam in Artemis's hand whirred as the centaur remotely fiddled with its focus motor.

"The more points of view the better, eh?" he said, his voice pulsing from the television speakers in surround sound.

Artemis held the camera before his mother's face, his arm as still as possible.

"I take it, from Holly's reaction, that this condition *is* familiar to you?"

Holly pointed to the sheen covering Angeline's face. "See the gel, Foaly, from the pores. And the smell of lilies too—there can't be any doubt."

"It's impossible," muttered the centaur. "We eradicated this years ago."

Artemis was growing weary of these vague references. "*What* is impossible? Eradicated *what*?"

"No diagnosis just yet, Artemis; it would be premature. Holly, I need to run a scan."

Holly positioned the palm of her hand over Angeline Fowl's forehead, and the omnisensor in her glove bathed Artemis's mother with a matrix of lasers.

Foaly's finger swished like a metronome as the information was fed to his system. It was an unconscious movement that seemed too jolly for the situation.

"Okay," he said after half a minute. "I have what I need."

Holly closed her fist on the sensor, then stood with Artemis, clasping his hand in hers, silently awaiting the results. It did not take long, especially when Foaly had a good idea of his search parameters.

His face was grim as he read the results. "The computer has analyzed the gel. I am afraid it's Spelltropy."

Artemis noticed Holly's grip tightening. Whatever this *Spelltropy* was, it was bad.

He broke free from Holly, striding to the wall-mounted television. "I need an explanation, Foaly. Now, please."

Foaly sighed, then nodded. "Very well, Artemis.

Spelltropy was a plague among the Fairy People. Once contracted it was invariably fatal, and progressed to terminal stages in three months. From that point the patient has less than a week. This disease has everything: Neurotoxins, cell destruction, resistance to all conventional therapies, incredibly aggressive. It's amazing, really."

Artemis's teeth were clenched. "That's fabulous, Foaly. At last, something even you can admire."

Foaly wiped a bead of sweat from his nose, pausing before he spoke. "There is no cure, Artemis. Not anymore. I'm afraid your mother is dying. Judging by the concentration in the gel, I would say she has twenty-four hours, thirty-six if she fights. If it's any consolation, she won't suffer at the end."

Holly crossed the room, reaching up to grasp Artemis's shoulder, noticing how tall her human friend was becoming.

"Artemis, there are things we can do to make her comfortable."

Artemis shrugged her off, almost violently. "No. I can achieve wonders. I have talents. Information is my weapon." He returned his attention to the screen. "Foaly, forgive my outburst. I am myself now. You said that this Spelltropy was a plague—where did it begin?"

"Magic," said Foaly simply, then elaborated. "Magic is fueled by the earth, and when the earth could no longer

62

absorb the sheer bulk of pollutants, the magic became tainted also. Spelltropy first appeared about twenty years ago in Linfen, China."

Artemis nodded. It made sense. Linfen was infamous for its high pollution levels. As the center of China's coal industry, the city's air was laden with fly ash, carbon monoxide, nitrogen oxides, volatile organic compounds, arsenic, and lead. There was a joke among Chinese employers: If you hold a grudge against an employee, send him to work in Linfen.

"It is passed on through magic, and thus is completely impervious to magic. In ten years it had almost decimated the fairy population. We lost twenty-five percent of our numbers. Atlantis was worst hit."

"But you stopped it," Artemis insisted. "You must have found a cure."

"Not me," said Foaly. "Our old friend Opal Koboi found the antidote. It took her ten years, then she tried to charge through the nose for it. We had to get a court order to confiscate the supply of antidote."

Artemis was growing impatient. "I don't care about the politics, Foaly. I want to know what the cure was, and why we can't administer it to my mother."

"It's a long story."

"Abbreviate," snapped Artemis.

Foaly's eyes dipped, unable to meet Artemis's. "The cure occurred naturally. Many creatures contain important pharmacopoeia and act as natural magic enhancers. But because of human activities, more than twenty thousand of these potentially lifesaving species are made extinct every year. Opal developed a simple syringe gun to extract the cure for Spelltropy without killing the donor animal."

Artemis suddenly realized why Foaly couldn't look him in the eye. He cradled his head in his hands.

"Oh no. Don't say it."

"Opal Koboi found the antidote in the brain fluid of the silky sifaka lemur of Madagascar."

"I always knew," moaned Artemis, "that this would come back."

"Unfortunately, the silky sifaka is now extinct. The last one died almost eight years ago."

Artemis's eyes were haunted by guilt.

"I know," he whispered. "I killed it."

CHAPTER 4
MONKEY'S UNCLE

Fowl Manor, Almost Eight Years Ago

Ten-year-old Artemis Fowl closed the file he was working on, put his monitor to sleep, then rose from his study desk. His father would arrive momentarily for their meeting. Artemis Senior had confirmed the appointment that morning by internal mail, and he was never late. His time was precious, and he expected his son to be ready for their morning talk. Artemis's father arrived promptly at ten, leather greatcoat swishing around his knees.

"Minus fifteen in Murmansk," he explained, formally shaking his son's hand.

Artemis was standing on a specific flagstone before the fireplace. He was not actually required to stand in this spot, but he knew his father would sit in the Louis XV

chair by the hearth, and Artemis Senior did not like to crane his neck as he spoke.

His father lowered himself into the period chair, and Artemis enjoyed a quiet moment of satisfaction.

"The ship is ready, I take it?"

"Ready to sail," said his father, excitement flashing in his blue eyes. "This is a new market, Arty, my boy. Moscow is already one of the most commercial cities in the world. Northern Russia will inevitably follow."

"I gather Mother is not very pleased with your latest venture."

Recently, Artemis's parents had been arguing late into the night. The conflict in their otherwise happy marriage was over Artemis Senior's business interests. He controlled a criminal empire that had tentacles from the silver mines of Alaska to the shipyards of New Zealand. Angeline was a dedicated conservationist and humanitarian, and believed that Artemis Senior's criminal activities and ruthless exploitation of natural resources set a terrible example for her son.

"He will grow up just like his father," Artemis had heard her say one evening, through a little radio bug he'd planted in the aquarium.

"I thought you loved his father."

Artemis heard a rustling of material as his parents embraced. "I do. I love you more than life. But I love this planet too."

"My love," said Artemis Senior, so gently that it was difficult for the bug to pick up his voice. "The Fowl finances are in a delicate state right now. What capital we have is locked up in illegal ventures. I need one big deal so that I can begin the transition to completely legitimate businesses. Once we have some blue chip stock under our belts, then we can save the world."

Artemis heard his mother kiss his father. "Very well, my pirate prince. One big deal, then we save the world."

One big deal. A shipload of tax-free cola for the Russians. But more important, a pipeline of trade into the Arctic. Artemis suspected that his father would find it hard to abandon this pipeline after a single deal. There were billions to be made.

"The *Fowl Star* is fully loaded and ready for her voyage," Artemis's father informed his son later during their scheduled meeting in his study. "Remember, the world cannot be saved with good intentions alone. Leverage is needed, and gold is leverage."

Artemis Senior pointed to the Fowl crest and motto, carved into a wooden shield above the fireplace.

"*Aurum est potestas.* Gold is power; never forget that, Arty. Until the greens have wealth behind them, no one will listen."

Young Artemis was torn between his parents. His father embodied everything the family stood for. The Fowl dynasty had flourished for centuries because of their dedication to wealth, and Artemis had no doubt that his father would find a way first to increase their fortunes and then turn his attention to the environment. He loved his mother, but the Fowls' finances must be saved.

"Someday, control of the family business will fall to you," Artemis Senior told his son, standing to button his greatcoat. "And when that day comes, I will rest easy because I know you will put the Fowls first."

"Absolutely, father," said Artemis. "Fowls first. But that day will not come for decades."

Artemis Senior laughed. "Let's hope not, son. Now, I must be off; look after your mother while I am gone. And don't let her squander the family fortune, eh?"

The words were said in a lighthearted way, but a week later Artemis Fowl Senior was missing, presumed dead, and those words became the code his son would live by.

Look after your mother, but don't let her squander the family fortune.

Two months later, and Artemis was back at his desk, staring at the computer display in his study. On screen were the gloomy details of the family finances, which had dwindled rapidly since the disappearance of his father. He was the man of the house now, custodian of the Fowl empire, and must behave as such.

No sooner had Artemis Senior's ship been claimed by

the black Arctic waters than his debtors unanimously defaulted, and his cells of forgers, musclemen, thieves, and smugglers allied themselves to other organizations.

Honor among thieves? reflected Artemis bitterly. I think not.

Most of the Fowl money simply disappeared overnight, and Artemis was left with an estate to run and a mother who was heading rapidly toward a nervous breakdown.

It hadn't been long before the creditors were closing in, eager to claim their slice of the pie before only crumbs were left. Artemis had been forced to auction a Rembrandt sketch just to pay the mortgage on the manor and settle various other debts.

Mother was not making things any easier. She refused to believe that Artemis Senior was missing and forged ahead with her mission to save the world, hang the expense.

Artemis, meanwhile, was trying to mount expeditions to find his father. This is difficult when you are ten years old and not taken seriously by the adult world in general, in spite of various international art and music prizes, not to mention more than a dozen lucrative patents and copyrights filed worldwide. In time Artemis would build a fortune of his own, but *in time* was not soon enough. Money was needed now.

Artemis wanted to put together a proper situation room to monitor the Internet and world news channels.

That would take twenty computers at least. Also there was the team of Arctic explorers waiting in their Moscow hotel for him to wire the next portion of their payment. A payment that he didn't have.

Artemis tapped the screen with an elegant finger.

Something must be done, he thought.

Angeline Fowl was crying on her bed when Artemis entered the bedroom. His heart lurched at the sight, but he clenched his fist and told himself to be strong.

"Mother," he said, waving a bank account statement. "What is this?"

Angeline dried her eyes on a handkerchief, then rose to her elbows, slowly focusing on her son.

"Arty, little Arty. Come and sit with me."

Angeline's eyes were ringed with black mascara tears, and her complexion had faded to a white that was almost translucent.

Be strong.

"No, Mother. No sitting and talking. I want you to explain this fifty thousand euro check to a wildlife center in South Africa."

Angeline was bewildered. "South Africa, darling? Who's gone to South Africa?"

"You sent a check for fifty thousand euros to South Africa, Mother. I had that money put aside for the Arctic expedition."

"Fifty thousand. That figure is familiar. I'll ask your father when he gets in. He had better not be late for dinner again today, or I'll—"

Artemis lost his patience. "Mother, please. Try to think. We do not have spare funds for South African charities. All the staff have been let go except Butler, and he hasn't been paid in a month."

"Lemur!" shouted Angeline triumphantly. "I remember now. I bought a silky sifaka lemur."

"Impossible," snapped Artemis. "The *Propithecus candidus* is extinct."

His mother was suddenly passionate. "No. No, they found little silky in South Africa. They don't know how it managed to get there from Madagascar, probably on a poacher's boat. So I had to save it. It's the last one, Arty."

"In a year or two it will die," said Artemis coldly. "Then our money will have been wasted."

Angeline was horrified. "You sound just like . . ."

"Father? Good. Someone has to be rational."

Artemis's face was stern, but inside he quailed. How could he speak to his mother like this, when she was literally driven demented by grief?

Why have I not fallen to pieces? he wondered, and the answer came to him quickly. *I am a Fowl, and Fowls have always triumphed in the face of adversity.*

"But fifty thousand, Mother? For a lemur?"

"They may find a female," argued Angeline. "Then we will have saved a species."

There is no point in arguing, thought Artemis. Logic cannot prevail here.

"And where is lucky silky now?" he asked innocently, smiling as a ten-year-old should when discussing a small furry animal.

"He is safe in Rathdown Park. Living like a king. Tomorrow he is being flown to a special artificial habitat in Florida."

Artemis nodded. Rathdown Park was a privately funded nature reserve in Wicklow, specially constructed to protect endangered species. It had tighter security than the average Swiss bank.

"That's wonderful. Perhaps I will visit the fifty-thousand-euro monkey."

"Now, now, Artemis," his mother chided. "Silky is a lemur; they predate monkeys, as you well know."

I know but do not care! Artemis wanted to scream. *Father is missing, and you have spent the expedition money on a lemur!*

But he held his tongue. Mother was delicate at the moment, and he did not want to contribute to her instability.

"Rathdown doesn't usually accept visitors," continued Angeline. "But I am sure if I made a call they would make an exception for you; after all, the Fowls did pay for the primate village."

Artemis appeared delighted. "Thank you, Mother. That would be a real treat for me, and Butler too. You know how he likes small furry creatures. I would love to see the species we have saved."

Angeline smiled with a degree of madness that scared her son terribly.

"Well done, Artemis. This is one in the eye for the big-business men. Mother and son, united we shall save the world. I shall tease your father terribly when he gets home."

Artemis backed slowly toward the door, his heart in his shoes.

"Yes, Mother. United we shall save the world."

Once the door had closed behind him, Artemis stepped briskly downstairs, fingers conducting imaginary music as he plotted. He detoured to his bedroom and quickly dressed for a trip, then continued to the kitchen, where he found Butler slicing vegetables with a Japanese kodachi short sword. He was now chef and gardener as well as protector.

The huge bodyguard was making quick work of a cucumber.

"A summer salad," he explained. "Just greens, hard-boiled egg, and some chicken. I thought crème brûlée for dessert. It will give me a chance to try out my flamethrower." He glanced across at Artemis and was surprised to see him dressed in one of his two suits, the dark blue one he had worn recently to the opera in Covent Garden. Artemis had always been a neat dresser, but a suit and tie were unusual even for him.

"Are we going somewhere formal, Artemis?"

"Nowhere formal," said Artemis, with a coldness in his tone that the bodyguard had not heard before but would come to know well. "Just business. I am in charge of the family affairs now, and so I should dress accordingly."

"Ah . . . I detect a distinct echo of your father." Butler wiped the sword carefully, then pulled off his apron. "We have some typical Fowl family business to conduct, do we?"

"Yes," replied Artemis. "With a monkey's uncle."

Present Day

Holly was aghast.

"So in a fit of childish pique you murdered the lemur."

Artemis had composed himself and sat at a bedside chair, holding his mother's hand gently, as though it were a bird.

"No. I used to suffer from the occasional fit of pique, as you well know, but they generally did not last. An intellect such as mine cannot be overpowered by emotions for long."

"But you said that you killed the animal."

Artemis rubbed his temple. "Yes, I did. I didn't wield

the knife, but I killed it, make no mistake."

"How exactly?"

"I was young . . . younger," mumbled Artemis, uncomfortable with the topic. "A different person in many ways."

"We know what you were like, Artemis," said Foaly in a rueful tone. "You have no idea how much of my budget the Fowl Manor siege ate up."

Holly pressed for an answer. "How did you kill the lemur? How did you even get hold of it?"

"It was ridiculously easy," admitted Artemis. "Butler and I visited Rathdown Park and simply disabled the security while we were there. Later that evening we both popped back and picked up the lemur."

"So Butler killed it. I am surprised; it's not his style."

Artemis's eyes were downcast. "No, Butler didn't do it. I sold the lemur to a group called the Extinctionists."

Holly was horrified. "Extinctionists! Artemis, you didn't. That's horrible."

"It was my first big deal," said Artemis. "I delivered it to them in Morocco and they paid me a hundred thousand euros. It funded the entire Arctic expedition."

Holly and Foaly were speechless. Artemis had effectively put a price on life. Holly backed away from the human she had only moments ago considered a friend.

"I rationalized the whole thing. My father for a lemur. How could I not go through with it?"

Artemis had real regret in his eyes. "I know. It was a terrible thing to do. If I could turn back the clock . . ."

And suddenly he stopped. *He* couldn't turn back the clock, but he knew a demon warlock who could. It was a chance. *A chance.*

He laid his mother's hand gently on the bed, then stood to pace.

Plotting music, he thought. I need plotting music.

He selected Beethoven's Symphony No. 7 from his vast selection of mental music and listened to it as he thought.

Good choice. Somber yet uplifting. Inspiring stuff.

Artemis paced the carpet, almost unaware of his surroundings, lost in ideas and possibilities.

Holly recognized this mood.

"He has a plan," she said to Foaly.

The centaur pulled a long face, which wasn't difficult. "Why am I not surprised?"

Holly took advantage of Artemis's distraction to seal her helmet and speak privately to Foaly. She walked to the window and peered out at the estate through a gap in the curtains. The sinking sun wavered behind tree branches, and clumps of dahlias flashed red and white like fireworks.

Holly allowed herself time for a sigh, then focused on the situation.

"There's more at stake here than Artemis's mother," she said.

Foaly switched off the television so that Artemis could not hear him.

"I know. If there is an outbreak, it could be a disaster for fairies. We don't have any antidote left, remember?"

"We need to interview Opal Koboi. She must have kept records somewhere."

"Opal always kept her most valuable formulae in her head. I think she was caught off guard by the jungle fire; she lost all her donors in one fell swoop."

Koboi Industries had attracted the Madagascan lemurs by setting a sonix box in the Tsingy of Bemaraha. Virtually every lemur on the island had responded to the box's call, and they had all been wiped out by an unfortunate lightning fire. Luckily, the fairies had already treated most of their infected, but fifteen more fairies had died in quarantine wards.

Artemis stopped pacing and cleared his throat loudly. He was ready to share his plan, and he wanted the fairies' complete attention.

"There is a relatively simple solution to our problem," he said.

Foaly reactivated the television, his face filling the flat screen.

"*Our* problem?"

"Come, Foaly, don't pretend to be obtuse. This is a fairy plague that has mutated and spread to humans. You have no antidote and no time to synthesize one. Who knows how many cases of Spelltropy are incubating right now?"

Including my own, thought Artemis. I used magic on my mother, so therefore I probably have the disease.

"We will quarantine the manor," responded Foaly. "So long as no one uses magic on your mother, we can contain this."

"I seriously doubt that my mother is patient zero. That is simply too much of a coincidence. There are other cases out there, who knows how far along."

Foaly grunted, his version of conceding a point. "So tell me, Artemis, what is this *relatively simple solution?*"

"I go back in time and save the lemur," said Artemis, smiling brightly as though he had suggested a pleasant summer dip.

Silence. Complete silence for several moments, broken eventually by a strangled whinny from Foaly.

"Go back . . ."

". . . in time, " completed Holly incredulously.

Artemis sat in a comfortable armchair, steepled his fingers, and nodded once.

"Present your arguments, please. I am ready."

"How can you be so smug?" wondered Holly. "After all the tragedy we have seen, after all the havoc your plans have wreaked."

"I am determined, not smug," corrected Artemis. "There is no time for prudence here. My mother has hours left, and the Fairy People don't have much more."

Foaly was still gaping. "Do you have any idea how many constitution committee meetings we would have to sit through just to allow us to bring this issue to a Council meeting?"

Artemis wagged a finger dismissively. "Irrelevant. I have read the People's constitution. It does not govern humans or demons. If N°1 decides to help me, technically you have no legal power to stop him."

Holly joined the discussion. "Artemis, this is lunacy. Time travel was outlawed for a reason. The potential repercussions for the slightest interference could be catastrophic."

Artemis smiled mirthlessly. "Ah yes, the trusty *time paradox*. If I go back in time and kill my grandfather, then shall I cease to exist? I believe, as Gorben and Berndt did, that any repercussions are already being felt. We can only change the future, not the past or present. If I go back, then I have already been back."

Holly spoke kindly; she felt sorry for Artemis. Angeline's illness reminded her painfully of her own mother's final days.

"We cannot interfere, Artemis. Humans must be allowed to live their lives."

Artemis knew that to ram home his next argument he should stand and theatrically deliver the accusation, but he could not. He was about to play the cruelest trick of his life on one of his closest friends, and the guilt was almost unbearable.

"You have already interfered, Holly," he said, forcing himself to meet her eyes.

The words made Holly shiver; she buzzed up her visor. "What do you mean?"

"You healed my mother. Healed her and damned her."

Holly took a step back, raising her palms as though to ward off blows.

"Me? I . . . What are you saying?"

Artemis was committed to the lie now, and covered his guilt with a sudden burst of anger.

"You healed my mother after the siege. *You* must have given her Spelltropy."

Foaly came to his friend's defense. "Not possible, that healing was years ago. Spelltropy has a three-month incubation period, and it never varies by more than a few days."

"And it *never* affects humans," Artemis countered. "This is a new strain. You have no idea what you're dealing with."

Holly's face was slack with shock and guilt. She believed Artemis's words, though Artemis himself knew that he must have given his mother the disease when he adjusted her memory.

Father must have it too. Who gave it to me? And why am I not sick?

There were so many puzzles, but now was not the time

80

to unravel them. *Now* he needed to find the antidote, and to ensure fairy aid, he must play on their supposed guilt in this matter.

"But I'm clean," protested Holly. "I was tested."

"Then you must be a carrier," said Artemis flatly. He turned his gaze on the centaur's image. "That's possible, isn't it?"

Foaly was taken aback by Artemis's bluntness. "If this truly is a new strain, then yes, it's possible," he admitted. "But you can't draw any conclusions from supposition . . ."

"Normally I would agree. *Normally* I would have the luxuries of time and objectivity. But my mother is dying, and so I have neither. I must go back to save the lemur, and you are honorbound to help me, and if you won't help, then at least you must promise not to hinder my efforts."

The fairies were silent. Holly was lost in thought about what she might have done. Foaly was racking his considerable brain for responses to Artemis's arguments. He found none.

Holly removed her helmet and walked awkwardly to Angeline Fowl's bedside. Her legs felt strangely numb and the feeling was spreading.

"My mother died—poisoned by humans. It was an accident, but that didn't keep her alive." Tears dripped from her eyes. "I wanted to hunt those men down. I hated them." Holly wrung her hands. "I'm sorry, Artemis. I didn't know. How many others have I infected? You must hate me."

Take it back, thought Artemis. *Tell the truth now or your friendship can never be the same.* Then, *No. Be strong. Mother must live.*

"I don't hate you, Holly," said Artemis softly. *I hate myself, but the deception must continue.* "Of course none of this is your fault, but you *must* let me go back."

Holly nodded, then wiped her brimming eyes. "I will do more than let you go, I will escort you. A sharp pair of eyes and a quick gun hand will prove useful."

"No, no, no," shouted Foaly, increasing the screen's volume with each negative. "We can't simply alter the past whenever we feel like it. Perhaps Holly should save her mother, or bring Commander Julius Root back from the dead! This is totally unacceptable."

Artemis pointed a finger at him. "This is a unique situation," he said. "You have a plague about to erupt, and we can stop it here. Not only that, but you can reintroduce a species that was thought to be extinct. I may have caused one lemur to die, but Opal Koboi gathered the rest together for the lightning fire. The People are as guilty as I am. You harvested a living creature's brain fluid to save yourselves."

"We . . . we were desperate," argued Foaly, horrified that he would actually stutter.

"Exactly," said Artemis triumphantly. "You were willing to do anything. Remember how *that* felt, and ask yourself if you want to go through it again."

Foaly dropped his gaze, thinking back. That time had been a waking nightmare for the fairies. The use of magic had been suspended, and the lemurs were already extinct by the time a court order forced Opal to reveal the source of her antidote. He had worked sleeplessly to develop an alternative cure, but without success.

"We thought we were invincible. The only disease left was man." The centaur made up his mind. "The lemur must be alive," he stated. "The brain fluid can be stored for brief periods, but once it becomes inert, the fluid is useless. I was developing a charged container but . . ."

"This time you will succeed," Artemis assured him. "You will have a live subject and laboratory conditions. You can clone a female."

"Cloning is illegal, generally," mused Foaly. "But in extinction cases, exceptions have been made. . . ."

Holly's helmet beeped, drawing her attention to a craft landing in the driveway. She hurried to the window in time to see a slight shimmer cast a shadow on the moonlit driveway.

It must be a rookie pilot, thought Holly crossly. He hasn't activated his shadow lights.

"The shuttle's here," she informed Artemis.

"Tell the pilot to park around the back, in one of the stables. The doctor's assistant is making calls from my father's office. I don't want her going for a walk and bumping into a shielded fairy craft."

Holly relayed the instructions, and they waited tensely for the shuttle to maneuver to the back of the house. It seemed like a long wait, silent but for the rasp of Angeline's labored breathing.

"N°1 might not be able to do it," said Foaly almost to himself. "He is a young warlock, with barely any training. Time travel is the most difficult of magics."

Artemis did not offer a comment. There was no point. All his hopes rested on N°1.

He does it, or Mother dies.

He took Angeline's hand, stroking the rough parchment skin with his thumb.

"Hold on, Mother," he whispered. "I will only be a second."

CHAPTER 5

I NOW PRONOUNCE YOU

THE LITTLE DEMON known as N⁰1 cut a strange figure waddling down the LEP shuttle's gangplank. A small, stocky individual with gray armored plates and short limbs, he looked a little like a miniature upright rhino-ceros with fingers and toes, except for the head. The head was pure gargoyle.

I wish I had a tail, thought N⁰1.

In actual fact he did have a tail, but it was stubby and not good for much except making snow fans in Haven City's artificial weather park.

N⁰1 consoled himself with the observation that at least his tail didn't dangle down into the toilet. Some of the Hybras demons had trouble adjusting to the new-fangled seats on the recycling lounges in Haven. He had heard horror stories. Apparently there had been three emergency reattachments this month alone.

The transition from Limbo to normal time had been difficult for all demons, but there were many more positives than negatives. Restrictions imposed under the old tribal leader were now being lifted. Demons could eat cooked food if they felt like it. Family units were taking hold again. Even the most belligerent demons were a lot more relaxed with their mothers around. But it was difficult to shake off ten millennia of human-hating, and many of the buck demons were undergoing therapy or were on mood pills to stop them hopping a shuttle to the surface and chomping on the first human limb they saw.

Not Nº1, though, who had no limb-chomping ambitions whatsoever. He was something of an anomaly among demons. Nº1 loved everyone, even humans, especially Artemis Fowl, who had saved them all from the deathly dreariness of Limbo, not to mention Leon Abbot, the psychopathic ex–tribe leader.

So when the call came through to Section 8 that Artemis needed him, Nº1 had strapped himself into the division's shuttle and demanded to be taken aboveground. Commander Vinyáya had agreed because disagreeing could lead to all sorts of magical tantrums from the fledgling warlock. Once, in a fit of frustration, he had accidentally shattered the magnifying wall of the city's huge aquarium. Fairies were still finding minnows in their toilet ponds.

You can go, Vinyáya had told him. *But only if you take a squad of guards to hold your hand every step of the way.*

Which did not literally mean *hold his hand*, as Nº1 had found out when he tried to link with the captain of the guard.

"But, Commander Vinyáya said," he had objected.

"Stow the hand, demon," ordered the captain. "There'll be no hand-holding on my watch."

And so Nº1 appeared to approach Fowl Manor alone, though he was flanked by a dozen shielded fairies. Halfway up the avenue he remembered to shroud his real appearance with a shape-shifting spell. Any human who happened to be looking down the driveway would now see a small boy in flowing, flowered robes strolling toward the front door. This was an image Nº1 had seen in a human movie from the last century, and he thought it was appropriately nonthreatening.

Miss Book happened to appear at the doorway just as Nº1 reached it. The sight of him stopped the nurse-publicist in her tracks. She tugged off her glasses as though they were feeding false information to her eyes.

"Hello there, little boy," she said, smiling, though she probably would not have been so jolly had she been aware of the twelve plasma rifles pointed at her head.

"Hi," said Nº1 cheerily. "I love everyone, so no need to feel threatened."

Miss Book's smile faltered. "Threatened? Of course not. Are you looking for someone? Are you playing dress-up?"

Artemis appeared at the doorway, interrupting the conversation.

"Ah . . . Ferdinand, where have you been?" he said, quickly shepherding N°1 past the nurse. "This is the gardener's boy, Ferdinand," he explained. "A dramatic type. I'll summon his father to collect him."

"Good idea," said Miss Book doubtfully. "I know your mother's room is sealed, but don't let him upstairs all the same."

"Of course not," said Artemis. "I'll send him out the back way."

"Good," said the nurse. "I just need a breath of fresh air, then I will come to check on your mother."

"Take your time," said Artemis. "I can read the instruments."

I designed a few of them, he thought.

As soon as Miss Book disappeared around the corner, Artemis escorted his demon friend up the stairs.

"We're going upstairs," objected N°1 mildly. "Didn't that young lady tell you not to allow me upstairs?"

Artemis sighed. "How long have you known me, N°1?"

N°1 nodded craftily. "Ah, I see. Artemis Fowl *never* does what he is told to do."

Holly greeted N°1 on the landing, but refused to hug him until he dropped the shape-shifting spell.

"I hate the feel of those things," she said. "It's like hugging a wet sponge."

N°1 pouted. "But I enjoy being Ferdinand. Humans smile at me."

Artemis assured him that there was no surveillance in his study, and so the demon warlock waited until the door was closed behind them, then banished the spell with a click of his fingers. Ferdinand unraveled and fell from N°1's body in a flurry of sparks, leaving the small gray demon warlock wearing nothing but a wide grin.

Holly hugged him tightly. "I knew you would come. We need you desperately."

N°1 stopped smiling. "Ah, yes. Artemis's mother. Does she want a magical cure?"

"That's the last thing she wants," said Holly.

Once the situation was explained to N°1, he immediately agreed to help.

"You are in luck, Artemis," said the little demon, wiggling his eight fingers. "I did a module on time travel last week for the warlock diploma course I'm taking."

"Small class, I bet," commented Artemis dryly.

"Just me," admitted N°1. "And Qwan, of course, my teacher. Apparently I am the most powerful warlock Qwan has ever seen."

"Good," said Artemis. "Then transporting us all into the past shouldn't pose any problems for you."

Foaly had projected himself onto five of Artemis's various monitors. *"All?"* spluttered each image. "All! You can't take N°1 with you."

⦁ ⋃ ⚹ ⵛ ⵛ ⵣ ⋂ ⵄ ⵎ ⵄ ⵄ ⦁ ⵛ ⵣ ⵕ ⵄ ⦁ ⵦ ⦁

Artemis was not in the mood for argument. "I need him, Foaly. End of discussion."

Foaly looked as though his head would bulge through the screens. "It is most certainly not *end of discussion*. Holly is an adult, she can make her own decision, but N°1 is little more than a child. You cannot jeopardize him on one of your missions. A lot of hopes rest on that little demon. The future of the fairy families."

"None of us will have a future if N°1 doesn't bring us to the past."

"Please stop," said N°1. "All this arguing is making me dizzy. There is no time for it."

Artemis's face was red, but he held his tongue, unlike Foaly, who kept shouting, but at least he muted the screens.

"Foaly needs to vent," explained Holly. "Or he gets headaches."

The three waited until the centaur calmed himself, then N°1 spoke. "In any event, I cannot go with you, Artemis. That's not how it works."

"But you transported us from Limbo."

"Qwan did that. He is a master, I am but an apprentice. And anyway, we had no desire to go *back* to Limbo. If you wish to return *here*, I need to stay as a marker."

"Explain," said Artemis tersely.

N°1 spread his arms wide. "I am a beacon," he declared. "A shining supernova of power. Any magic I release into the ether will be attracted back to me. I send you into the past, and you will snap back to me like puppies on a leash." Nº1 frowned, not happy with his simile. "One of those retractable leashes."

"Yes, we get it," said Artemis. "How long will it take to weave the spell?"

Nº1 chewed his lip for a moment. "About as long as it takes you two to remove your clothing."

"Hurkk," said Artemis half-choking with surprise.

"D'Arvit," swore Holly.

"I think we all know what D'Arvit means," said Nº1. "But *hurkk* is not English. Unless you meant *hark*, which means *to remember something from the past*. Which I suppose could be relevant. Or perhaps you were speaking Dutch, and then *hurk* would translate as squat." Nº1 paused for a wink. "Which means *squat* to me."

Artemis leaned close to the demon's cornet-shaped ear. "Why do we need to take our clothes off?"

"That is a very good question," said Holly into the other ear.

"It's quite simple," said Nº1. "I am not so skilled as Qwan. And even *with* Qwan overseeing the last transfer, you two managed to switch an eye each, which was probably because someone was focusing on stealing magic. If you take clothes or guns in there, they could become a part of you." The demon raised a stiff finger. "Lesson number one of time transfers," he stated. "Keep it simple.

It's going to take all of your concentration just to reassemble your bodies. *And* you will be thinking for the lemur too."

N°1 noticed both Artemis's and Holly's awkward expressions and took pity on them.

"I suppose you could keep one thing, if you must. A small garment, but make sure it's your color, because you could be wearing it for a really long time."

Though they both knew that this was no time for modesty, neither Artemis nor Holly could suppress a blush. Holly covered her embarrassment by tearing off her Shimmer Suit as quickly as possible.

"I'm keeping the one-piece," she said belligerently, daring N°1 to argue. The *one-piece* looked similar to a swimsuit but was padded on the shoulders and back to support a wing rig. There were also heat and kinetic panels that could absorb energy from the wearer to power the suit.

"Okay," said N°1. "But I would advise you to remove the pads and any other electronics."

Holly nodded, tearing the pads from their Velcro strips.

Artemis gathered Holly's things. "I will put your helmet and suit in the safe, just to be certain they are secure. No need to take chances with the People's technology."

"Now you're thinking like a centaur," Foaly piped up.

It took only a minute to hide the fairy gear, and when he returned from the safe room, Artemis took off his shirt and trousers carefully, hanging them in his wardrobe. He placed his loafers on a shoe rack alongside several similar black pairs, and one brown, for casual days.

"Nice underwear," snickered Foaly from the screen, momentarily forgetting the gravity of the situation.

Artemis was wearing a pair of red Armani boxer shorts, which were pretty much the same color as his face.

"Can we get on with it?" he snapped. "Where do you need us to stand?"

"Wherever you need to be," replied N°1 simply. "It's far easier for me if you take off and land at the same point. It's hard enough shooting you down a wormhole faster than the speed of light without worrying about location too."

"We are in the right location," said Artemis. "This is where we need to be."

"You need to know *when* you want to arrive," added N°1. "The temporal coordinates are as important as the geographical ones."

"I know when."

"Very well," said N°1, rubbing his hands together. "Time to send you on your way."

Holly remembered something. "I haven't completed the Ritual," she said. "I'm low on magic, and without weapons, that could be a problem. We don't have an acorn."

"Not to mention a bend in the river," added Artemis.

N°1 smirked. "Those things *could* be problems. Unless . . ."

A spiral rune on the demon's forehead glowed red and spun like a Catherine wheel. It was hypnotizing.

"Wow," said Holly. "That's really . . ."

Then a pulsing beam of crimson magic blasted from the center of the rune, enveloping Holly in a cocoon of light.

"Now you're full to the brim," said Nº1, bowing low. "Thank you very much. I'm here all week. Don't forget to tip your goblins and bury those acorns."

"Wow," said Holly again when her fingertips stopped buzzing. "That's a neat trick."

"More than you know. That's my own signature magic. The Nº1 cocktail, if you like, which makes you a beacon in the time stream."

Artemis shuffled self-consciously. "How long do we have?"

Nº1 gazed at the ceiling while he ran some calculations. "Three hundred years . . . No, no, three days. Holly can bring you back at any point before that simply by making herself open to my power, but after three days the link grows weaker."

"Is there anything we can do about that?"

"Let's face facts: all-powerful I may be, but I'm a novice at this, so taking off from where you landed is vital. If you go beyond three days, then you are stuck in the past."

"If we do get separated, couldn't Holly come back and get me?" wondered Artemis.

"No, she could not," said Nº1. "It would be impossible

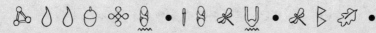

for you to meet at a point neither of you had experienced. This is a one-time deal only. It will take everything I have to hold you together for this trip. Any more and your atoms would lose their memory and simply forget where it is they are supposed to go. Both of you have already been in the time stream twice. I can transport objects forever and a day, but living beings break down without a warlock in the stream to shield them."

Holly asked a very pertinent question. "N°1, have you done this before?"

"Of course," said the demon. "Several times. On a simulator. And two of the holograms survived."

Artemis's determination barely flickered. "Two survived. The last two?"

"No," admitted N°1. "The last two were trapped in a time wormhole and consumed by quantum zombies."

Holly felt her pointy ears tingle, always a bad sign. Elfin ears could sense danger.

"Quantum zombies? You're not serious."

"That's what I said to Qwan. He wrote the program."

"This is irrelevant," said Artemis sharply. "We have no option but to go."

"Very well," said N°1, flexing his fingers. He bent his knees and rested his entire body weight on the tip of his tail.

"Power posture," he explained. "I do some of my best work in this position."

"So does Mulch Diggums," muttered Foaly. "Quantum zombies. I need to get a copy of *that* program."

A red haze blossomed around the demon warlock, tiny lightning bolts crackling across his horns.

"He's powering up," said Foaly from the screens. "You'll be off any second. Remember, try not to touch anything you don't have to. Don't talk to anyone. Don't contact me in the past. I have no desire not to exist."

Artemis nodded. "I know. Make as little impact as possible, in case the time paradox theory has some merit."

Holly was impatient to get going. "Enough science. Just blast us into the past. We'll bring the monkey back."

"Lemur," said Artemis and Foaly together.

Nº1 closed his eyes. When he opened them again they were pure crimson.

"Okay, ready to go," he said conversationally.

Artemis blinked. He was expecting Nº1's voice of power to be a bit less squeaky. "Are you sure?"

Nº1 groaned. "I know. It's the voice, isn't it. Not enough gravel. Qwan says I should go for less airy and more fairy. Trust me, I'm ready. Now hold hands."

Artemis and Holly stood there in their underwear, gingerly locking fingers. They had crossed space and time together, weathered rebellions, and tangled with demented despots. Coughed blood, lost digits, inhaled dwarf fumes, and swapped eyeballs, yet they found holding hands awkward.

N°1 knew he shouldn't, but he couldn't resist a parting crack.

"I now pronounce you . . ."

Neither hand-holder was amused, but before they had time to do more than scowl, twin bolts of red energy crackled from N°1's eyes, blasting his friends into the time stream.

"Man and elf," he said, finishing his joke, then chuckling delightedly.

On screen, Foaly snorted. "I'm guessing you're laughing to cover your anxiety?"

"Exactly right," said N°1.

Where Artemis and Holly had been standing, there were flickering copies of them both, mouths open to object to N°1's comment.

"That really freaks me out, the ghost images. It's like they're dead."

Foaly shuddered. "Don't say that. If they're dead, we all could be. How soon will they be back?"

"In about ten seconds."

"And if they're not back in ten seconds?"

"Then never."

Foaly started counting.

CHAPTER 6

I TO I

THERE IS A MOMENT of confusion when a land animal enters the water. Beast, human, or fairy, it doesn't matter. The surface is broken and every sense is suddenly shocked. The cold stings, motion slows, and the eyes are filled with smears of color and the snap of bursting bubbles. The time stream is like that moment sustained.

That's not to say that traveling through the time stream is a consistent experience. Never the same journey twice. The demon warlock Qwan, who was the planet's most experienced time-traveling fairy, wrote in his best-selling autobiography, *Qwan: My Time Is Now*, that *riding the time stream is like flying through a dwarf's intestine. There are very nice free-flowing stretches, but then you turn a corner to find the thing backed up and putrid. The problem being that the time stream is largely an emotional construct, and it absorbs ambient feelings from the real time it flows around. If you happen across a stretch of foul-smelling gunk, you can bet that the humans are killing something.*

Artemis and Holly were being dragged through a foul-smelling stretch that corresponded with an entire ecosystem being destroyed in South America. They could sense the animals' terror and even smell the charred wood.

Artemis felt too that Holly was losing herself in the maelstrom of emotions. Fairies were so much more sensitive to their environments than humans. If Holly lost concentration, her atoms would dissipate and be absorbed by the stream.

Focus, Holly, Artemis broadcast into the stream. *Remember who you are and why we are here.*

It was difficult for them both. Their particle memory had already been weakened by the Limbo journeys, and the temptation to meld with the stream was strong.

Artemis conjured a picture of his mother in his consciousness to bolster his determination.

I know when and where I want to be, he thought. Exactly when and where . . .

Fowl Manor, Almost Eight Years Ago

Artemis and Holly exited the time stream and entered ten-year-old Artemis's study. Physically this was a gentle enough experience, like jumping from a low wall onto thick carpet, but emotionally this particular trip was like a ten-minute blitz of the worst memories of their lives. The time stream: never the same ride twice.

Holly cried for her mother for a minute, but eventually the persistent chiming of a grandfather clock reminded her of where and when she was. She stood shakily and looked around her to find Artemis lurching toward the wardrobe. The sight of him cheered her a little.

"You have really let yourself go," she said.

Artemis was rummaging through the clothes on the rail.

"Of course nothing will fit," he muttered. "All too small."

Holly elbowed past him. "Not for me," she said, pulling a dark suit from its hanger.

"My first suit," said Artemis fondly. "For the family Christmas postcard. I had no idea really how to wear it. I remember fidgeting throughout the fitting. It's a Zegna, custom made."

Holly tore off a protective polyethylene wrap. "So long as it fits."

It was only then that Artemis's emotions settled enough for him to register Holly's comment.

"What do you mean, I have let myself go?"

Holly swung the wardrobe door so that its mirrored side faced Artemis.

"See for yourself," she said.

Artemis looked. In the mirror he saw a tall, slender boy, his face all but invisible under a wild mop of shoulder-length hair and even some bristles on his chin.

"Ah. I see."

"I'm surprised you do," said Holly. "Through all that hair."

"Accelerated aging. A side effect of the time stream," Artemis hypothesized, unconcerned. "When we return, the effects should be reversed." He paused, catching sight of Holly's reflection. "Perhaps you should check *yourself* in the mirror. I am not the only one to have changed."

Holly elbowed him aside, certain she was being kidded, but the half-smile died on her lips when she saw the fairy in the looking glass. It was her own face, but different, missing a few scars and a few decades' wear and tear.

"I am young," she gasped. "Younger."

"Don't be upset," said Artemis briskly. "It is temporary. All this is nothing more than dress-up. My physical maturity, your youth. In a moment or two we will be back in the stream."

But Holly *was* upset. She knew how this had happened.

I was thinking of Mother. Of our last hours together. Of how I was then.

And so that was how she had changed.

Look at me. Just out of the academy. In human terms, barely older than Artemis.

For some reason, this was a disturbing thought.

"Get some pants on," she snapped, buttoning a crisp white shirt up to her neck. "Then we can discuss your theories."

Artemis used his extra inches to reach up and tug a large box from the top of the wardrobe. In it were neatly folded layers of clothes, destined for one of Angeline Fowl's charity shops.

He tossed a silver wig to Holly.

"Seventies fancy dress party," he explained. "Mother went as a starship trooper, I seem to remember. Now cover those pointy ears."

"A hat would be easier," said Holly, pulling the wig over her auburn crew cut.

"No such luck, I'm afraid," sighed Artemis, selecting an old tracksuit from the box. "This is not exactly Harrods; we will have to make do."

Artemis's old loafers fit Holly well enough, and there were a pair of his father's sneakers in the box, which stayed on his feet when the toes were stuffed.

"Always good to be dressed when you're stealing monkeys," said Holly.

Artemis rolled up the tracksuit sleeves. "There's no need to dress at all, really. We simply wait for a few minutes, until my mother almost catches Butler sneaking upstairs with the lemur. I remember him sliding the cage through the doorway, then I brought her back upstairs. The moment that cage comes in here, we grab it, take off these ridiculous clothes, and wish our way back to N°1."

Holly checked herself in the mirror. She looked like a presidential bodyguard—from another planet. "That sounds so simple."

"It was simple. Will be. Butler never even entered the study. All we need to do is stand here and wait."

"And how did you find this particular moment?"

Artemis swept a sheaf of black hair back from his brow, revealing mismatched sorrowful eyes.

"Listen," he said, pointing toward the ceiling.

Holly tucked strands of silver hair behind one ear and cocked her head to one side to focus her considerable sense of hearing. She heard the grandfather clock, and the time travelers' beating hearts, but above them there was a strident, hysterical voice.

"Mother," said Artemis, eyes downcast. "It was the first time that she did not recognize me. She is at this moment threatening to call the police. In a moment she runs downstairs to the phone, and discovers Butler."

Holly understood. How could any son forget a moment like that one? Finding it again must have been easy and painful.

"I remember it clearly. We had just returned from Rathdown Park, the private zoo, and I thought I should check how she was feeling before flying to Morocco. In a month from now, she won't be able to look after herself anymore."

Holly squeezed his forearm. "It's fine, Artemis. This is all in the past. In a few minutes your mother will be back on her feet. She will love you as she always has."

Artemis nodded glumly. He knew it was probably true, but he also knew that he would never fully escape the specter of this bad memory.

Upstairs, Angeline Fowl's voice moved from her bedchamber to the upper landing, trailing shrill notes behind her.

Artemis pulled Holly back against the wall.

"Butler will be on the stairs now. We should keep to the shadows, just in case."

Holly couldn't help a flutter of nerves. "You're sure he stays outside? The last time I faced Butler as an enemy, I had the entire LEP on my side. I don't relish the thought of meeting him armed with nothing more than a silver wig."

"Calm yourself, Captain," said Artemis, unconsciously patronizing. "He stays outside. I saw it with my own eyes."

"Saw what with your own eyes?" asked Butler, who had appeared in the archway behind them, having let himself in through the adjoining bedroom door.

Artemis felt his pulse throb in his fingertips. How could this be? This was not the way it had happened. Artemis had never been on the receiving end of Butler's glare before, and understood for the first time just how terrifying his bodyguard could be.

"You two kids have been helping yourselves to the Fowl wardrobe, I see," continued Butler without waiting for an answer to his question. "Now, are you going to cause a fuss or are you going to come quietly? Let me give you a hint: the correct answer is *come quietly*."

Magic is the only way out, Holly realized.

She twisted her chin sharply to call on her fairy power. If she couldn't stun Butler, she would *mesmerize* him.

"Stand down, human," she intoned, voice loaded with hypnotic magic. But the *mesmer* is a two-pronged attack, audio and visual. Butler could hear the magical words, but eye contact was not consistent in the shadows.

"What?" he said, surprised. "How did you . . ." The hulking bodyguard had been drugged enough times to realize that his will was being sapped. Somehow these kids were putting him under. He staggered backward, his shoulder bashing against the arch.

"Sleep, Butler," said the little one in the starship trooper wig.

She knows me?

This was serious. These two had done some surveillance and decided to break in anyway.

I have to neutralize them before I pass out, thought Butler. If I go down, Master Artemis and Mrs. Fowl are defenseless.

He had two options: fall on the midget burglars or shoot them with the tranquilizer pistol he was carrying for the planned animal abduction at Rathdown Park.

He chose the second option. At least tranquilizer darts would not smother these two or crush their bones. Butler felt mildly guilty about his decision to "tranq" a couple of kids, but not overly so; after all, he worked for Artemis Fowl and knew exactly how dangerous children could be.

The starship trooper came out of the shadows, and Butler could see her eyes clearly. One blue, one tawny.

"Sleep, Butler," she said again in that melodious layered voice. "Aren't your eyelids heavy? Sleep."

She's hypnotizing me! Butler realized. He dragged out the pistol with fingers that felt as though they had been dipped in molten rubber then sprinkled with ball bearings.

"*You* sleep," he mumbled, then shot the girl in the hip.

Holly stared in disbelief at the hypodermic dart sticking out of her leg.

"Not again," she moaned, then collapsed to the floor.

Butler's head cleared immediately. The other intruder did not move an inch.

The little girl is the professional of the two, thought Butler, climbing to his feet. I wonder what this scruffy individual contributes to the partnership.

Artemis quickly saw that he had no choice but to reveal his identity and enlist Butler as an ally.

This will be difficult. I have nothing more than a passing resemblance to my younger self as proof.

Still, he had to try before his plan unraveled utterly.

"Listen, Butler," he began. "I have something to tell you—"

Butler didn't entertain another word. "No, no, no," he said briskly, shooting Artemis in the shoulder. "No more talking from either of you."

Artemis pulled out the dart, but it was too late. The tiny reservoir of sedative was empty.

"Butler!" he gasped, dropping to his knees. "You shot me."

"Everyone knows my name," sighed the bodyguard, bending to sling the intruders over his shoulders.

"I am intrigued," said ten-year-old Artemis Fowl, studying the two individuals in the Bentley trunk. "Something extraordinary has happened here."

"Hardly extraordinary," said Butler, checking the girl's pulse. "Two thieves somehow broke into the manor."

"They bypassed all the security. Not so much as a blip on the motion sensors?"

"Nothing. I just happened on them during a routine sweep. Hiding in the shadows, wearing cast-offs from the wardrobe."

Artemis tapped his chin. "Hmm. So you didn't find their clothes."

"Not a stitch."

"Which would mean that they broke in here and bypassed security in their underwear."

"That is extraordinary," admitted Butler.

Artemis took a penlight from his jacket pocket and shone it on Holly, setting the strands of her silver wig sparkling like a disco ball. "There's something about this one. Her bone structure is very unusual. The cheekbones are high, Slavic, perhaps, and the brow is wide and childlike. But the proportion of skull to torso is adult, not infant."

Butler chuckled low in his throat. "So they're aliens?"

"The young man is human, but she's something else," said Artemis thoughtfully. "Genetically enhanced, perhaps." He moved the beam of light along her cheekbone. "See here. The ears are pointed. Amazing."

Artemis felt an excitement buzzing on his forehead. Something was happening here. Something important. There were surely serious amounts of money to be earned from this situation.

He rubbed his palms briskly. "Very well. I cannot be distracted by this now. Long term, this strange creature could make our fortune, but right now we need to get that lemur."

Butler was crestfallen but covered it by slamming the trunk. "I had hoped we could forget the monkey. I was trained in several forms of martial arts; none of them had a monkey defense."

"It's a lemur, Butler. And I am aware that you believe this operation is beneath us, but my father's life is at stake."

108

"Of course, Artemis. Whatever you say."

"Exactly. So here is the plan. We will proceed to Rathdown Park as planned, and after we have done the deal with the Extinctionists, then I can decide what to do with our two guests. I presume they will be safe in the trunk?"

Butler snorted. "Are you kidding?"

Artemis did not smile. "Perhaps you have not noticed, Butler. I rarely *kid*."

"As you say, young master. You are not a kidder. Maybe someday, eh?"

"Perhaps when I find my father."

"Yes. Perhaps then. Anyway, to answer your question: this is your *father's* car, and there have been more prisoners in this trunk than you've had birthdays. Mafiya, Triad, Yakuza, Tijuana Cartel, Hells Angels. You name the gang, and a couple of them have spent a night in this trunk. In fact, your father had it specially modified. There's air-conditioning, a stay-cool light, soft suspension, and even drinking water."

"Is it secure? Remember, our captives already broke into the manor."

Butler closed the trunk. "Titanium lock, reinforced trunk door. No way out whatsoever. Those two are staying in there until we let them out."

"Excellent," said Artemis, sliding into the Bentley's rear seat. "Just give me a moment to do this one little thing,

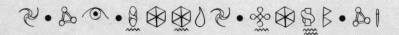

then let's forget about them and concentrate on the lemur."

"Excellent," echoed Butler, and then under his breath, "Monkey business. My favorite."

Rathdown Park

Even though Holly was ten pounds lighter than Artemis, she came to her senses before him. She was glad to be awake, as her dream had been terrible. While she was asleep, her knees and elbows struck the metal walls of the Bentley trunk, and she had imagined herself in an LEP submarine.

Holly lay huddled in the dark, swallowing and blinking to conquer the phobia. Her mother had been mortally injured in a metal box, and now she was inside one.

And it was thoughts of her mother that finally calmed Holly. She opened her eyes and explored the confined space with her vision and fingertips. It didn't take long to find the bubble light set into the steel wall. She snapped it on to find Artemis stretched beside her, and the sloping metal sheeting of a trunk door curling down past his arm. Her own borrowed shoes rested on the shining curve of a wheel arch. They were inside a vehicle.

Artemis groaned, twitched, and opened his eyes.

"Sell the Phonetix shares," he blurted, then remembered Butler and the darts. "Holly. Holly?"

Holly patted his leg. "It's okay, Artemis," she said in

Gnommish, in case the car was bugged. "I'm here. Where else could I be?"

Artemis shifted onto his side, flicking back the dense black hair obscuring his features, and spoke in the fairy tongue.

"We received the same dosage of tranquilizer, and yet you, the lighter person, are awake first. Magic?"

The side of Holly's face was thrown into deep shadow by the bubble light. "Yes. Nº1's signature magic is powerful stuff."

"Powerful enough to get us out of here?"

Holly spent a minute exploring the trunk's surface, running her fingertips along each weld in the metal. Finally she shook her head, silver wig sparkling. "Not a weak spot I can find. Even the air-conditioning vent is completely flush. No way out."

"Of course not," said Artemis. "We're inside the Bentley. The trunk is a steel box with a titanium lock." He breathed the cool air deeply. "How can this have happened? Everything is different. Butler was supposed to have deposited the cage in my study. Instead he creeps in through the bedroom and sedates us both. Now we don't know where we are, or indeed where the lemur is. Do they have it already?"

Holly pressed one ear to the trunk door. "I can tell you where we are."

Outside, the sounds of snuffling and snoring animals

drifted on the air. "We're close to animals. A park, I would guess, or a zoo."

"Rathdown Park," exclaimed Artemis. "And that fact tells us they do not, in fact, have the lemur. The schedule and situation have changed."

Holly was thoughtful. "We are not in control of this situation anymore, Artemis. Perhaps it's time to admit defeat and return home, when your younger self brings us back to the manor. *Perhaps* you can discover a cure in the future."

Artemis had been expecting this suggestion. "I considered that. The lemur is still our best option, and we are just a few feet away from it. Give me five minutes to get us out of here."

Holly was understandably dubious. "Five minutes? Even the great Artemis Fowl might have trouble breaking out of a steel box in five minutes."

Artemis closed his eyes and concentrated, trying to ignore his cramped surroundings and the sheaves of hair brushing his cheeks, and the itch of bristles on his chin.

"Face it, Artemis," said Holly impatiently. "We're stuck. Even Mulch Diggums would probably struggle with a lock like that if he happened to stroll by."

Artemis's brow flickered, irritated by this interruption, but then a smile spread across his face, made eerie by the stark lighting.

"Mulch Diggums strolling by," he whispered. "What are the chances of that?"

"Zero," said Holly. "Absolutely none. I would bet my pension on it."

At that moment something, or someone, tapped on the trunk door from the outside.

Holly rolled her eyes. "No. Not even you . . ."

Artemis's smile was smug beyond belief. "Just how large is your pension?"

"I do not believe it. I *refuse* to believe it. It is impossible."

More taps on the door now, followed by a delicate scraping and a muted swearword.

"What a guttural voice," said Artemis. "Very like a dwarf's."

"It could be Butler," argued Holly, irritated by Artemis's self-satisfied expression.

"Swearing in Gnommish. Hardly."

More metallic noises from the outside world.

Shhhnick. Chunk. Clackack.

And the trunk's lid swung upward, revealing a slice of starry night with the glinting silhouette of a gigantic pylon behind it. A bedraggled head popped into the space, features smeared with mud and worse. This was a face that only a mother could love, and then perhaps only if her sight were failing. The dark close-set eyes peered out from above a dense beard that shivered slightly, like seaweed in a current. The creature's teeth were large, square, and not made any more appealing by the large insect wriggling between two molars.

⚭ ✳ ⬡ ⬡ ⊙ ⚭ ☙ • ⚭ ⬢ ⚭ • ⬡ ⚭ ⬡ ⬡ • ⋃

It was, of course, Mulch Diggums.

The dwarf snagged the unfortunate insect with his tongue, then chewed it delicately.

"Ground beetle," he said with relish. "*Leistus montanus.* Nice bouquet, solid earthy shell; then once the carapace cracks, a veritable explosion of flavors on the palate."

He swallowed the unfortunate creature, then funneled a mighty burp though his flapping lips.

"Never burp when you're tunneling," he advised Artemis and Holly as casually as though they were sitting around a café table. "Dirt coming down, air coming up. Not a good idea."

Holly knew Mulch well. This chitchat was simply for distraction while he took a peek around.

"And now to business," said the dwarf finally, discarding the dead beard hair he had used to pick the lock. "I seem to have a human and an elf trapped in a car. So I ask myself, should I let 'em out?"

"And what do you answer yourself?" asked Artemis with barely contained impatience.

Mulch's black pebble eyes danced in the moonlight. "So, the Mud Boy understands Gnommish. Interesting. Well, understand *this*, human. I let you out as soon as I get my money."

Ah, thought Holly. There is money involved. Somehow these two have set up a deal.

Holly had endured her prison for long enough. Mulch

is not yet my friend, she thought. So there's no need to be polite.

She drew a knee to her chin, tugging on it with both hands for an extra pound of elastic force.

Mulch realized what she was about to do. "Hey, elf. No—"

Which was as far as he got before his face was batted with the trunk door. The dwarf tumbled backward into the hole he had climbed out of, sending up an *oof* of wind and dirt.

Holly clambered over Artemis to the fresh air. She gulped down great gasps, chest out, face to the sky.

"Sorry," she said between breaths. "That space is tiny. I don't like tiny."

"Claustrophobic?" asked Artemis, rolling from the trunk.

Holly nodded. "I used to be. I thought I had overcome it. Lately, though . . ."

There was a commotion in the dwarf hole. A blue riot of swearing, and a scuffling in the earth.

Holly quickly recovered herself and leaped into the pit, tackling Mulch before he could unhinge his jaw and disappear.

"He could be useful," she grunted, bundling the protesting dwarf up the incline. "And he has already seen us, so the damage has been done."

"That's a pincer hold," exclaimed Mulch. "You're LEP."

He twisted around, snagging Holly's wig with his beard hair. "I *know* you. Holly Short. *Captain* Holly Short. One of Julius Root's pet rottweilers." Suddenly the dwarf's already creased brow wrinkled further in confusion. "But this is impossible."

Before Artemis could instruct Holly not to ask, she went ahead and did it.

"Why is it impossible, Mulch?"

Mulch did not reply, but his eyes betrayed him, glancing guiltily over his shoulder at a scuffed Tekfab backpack. Holly deftly spun the dwarf around and opened the bag's main compartment.

"Quite a treasure trove we have here," she said, rummaging in the backpack. "Medi-kit, rations, adhesive com-pads. And look, an old omnitool." Then she recognized the inscription laser etched into the base. "It's *my* old omnitool."

In spite of their years of friendship, Holly turned the full force of her anger on Mulch.

"Where did you get this?" she shouted. "How did you get it?"

"A present," offered Mulch lamely. "From my . . . eh . . ." He squinted to read the writing on the base. "From my mother. She always called me Holly because of my, erm, prickly personality."

Holly was angrier than Artemis had ever seen her. "Tell me, Diggums. The truth!"

Mulch thought about fighting. It was in the curve of his fingers and the baring of his teeth, but the moment passed quickly, and the dwarf's natural passive nature surfaced.

"I stole all this stuff from Tara," he admitted. "I'm a thief, aren't I? But in my defense, I had a difficult childhood, which led to low self-esteem, which I projected onto others and punished them by stealing their possessions. So in a very real way, I am the victim here. And I forgive me."

Mulch's trademark waffle reminded Holly of the friend he would become, and her anger evaporated as quickly as it had appeared. She traced the laser inscription with a fingertip.

"My mother gave me this," she said quietly. "Most reliable omnitool I ever had. Then, one night in Hamburg, my fugitive locked himself in a car. So I reached for my omnitool and it was gone. The target was apprehended by humans; I lost my first fugitive; and Commander Root had to send in an entire team of techies to clean up. It was a disaster. And all this time it was you."

Mulch was puzzled. "All this time? I stole this from a belt in a locker in Tara *an hour ago*. I *saw* you there. What's going on here . . . ?" Then Mulch blinked and clapped his hairy palms. "Oh, bless my bum-flap. You're time travelers."

Holly realized that she had said too much. "That's ridiculous."

The dwarf was actually doing a little jig now. "No. No,

it all adds up. You're talking about *future* events in the *past* tense. You sent back a note so that I would come and rescue you here and now." Mulch clapped his hands to his cheeks in mock horror. "What you're doing is so much more illegal than anything I could ever do. Imagine the reward I would get for turning you over to Julius Root."

"Sent back a note?" scoffed Holly. "That's absurd, isn't it, Artemis?"

"Most certainly," said Artemis. "But if someone were to send back a note from the future, when and where would they send it to?"

Mulch jerked a thumb toward Holly. "There's a junction box beside her locker. Looked like it hadn't been touched for years. I was checking it out because sometimes they have valuable tech in 'em. Not this one, though, just an envelope addressed to me. And inside a note asking me to come to this place and set you free."

Artemis smiled. Satisfied. "I imagine there was an incentive offered for our rescue?"

Mulch's beard hair crackled. "A large incentive. No . . . a *stupendous* incentive."

"Stupendous, eh? Very well, you shall have it."

"When?" asked Mulch hungrily.

"Soon. I just need you to do me one more favor."

"I knew it," said the dwarf, through grinding teeth. "Never do the job until you see the cash. Why should I trust you?"

Artemis took a step forward, eyes narrow behind a curtain of dark hair. "You don't need to trust me, Mulch. You need to be afraid of me. I am a Mud Boy from your future, and I could be in your past too, if you choose not to cooperate. I found you once, I could certainly do it again. The next time you break into a car trunk, there could be a gun and a badge waiting for you."

Mulch felt apprehension tingling in his beard hair, and his beard hair was rarely wrong. As his grandmother used to say: *Trust the hair, Mulch. Trust the hair.* This human was dangerous, and he had enough trouble in his life already.

"Okay, Mud Boy," he said grudgingly. "One more favor. And then you'd better have a stupendous amount of gold for me."

"I will. Fear not, my pungent friend."

The dwarf was deeply offended. "Don't call me *friend*. Just tell me. What. You. Want. Done."

"Simply follow your nature and dig us a tunnel. I need to steal a lemur."

Mulch nodded as though lemur-napping was the most natural thing in the world.

"And from whom are we stealing it?"

"From me."

Mulch frowned, then the penny dropped. "Ah . . . time travel throws up all sorts of twists, doesn't it?"

Holly slipped the omnitool into her pocket. "Tell me about it," she said.

CHAPTER 7

TALK TO THE ANIMALS

Rathdown Park, County Wicklow, Ireland

The Fowl Bentley was protected by a fingerprint scanner, and a keypad that required an eight-digit code. The code was changed every month, and so it took Artemis a few seconds to mentally rewind almost eight years and remember the right set of numbers.

He slid across the front seat's tan leather upholstery and pressed his thumb to a second scanner tucked behind the steering wheel. A spring-loaded compartment slid smoothly from the dash. It was not a large compartment, but big enough to hold a clip of cash, platinum credit cards, and a spare cell phone in its cradle.

"No gun?" said Holly, when Artemis emerged from the car, though one of Butler's guns would be clunky in her fingers.

"No gun," confirmed Artemis.

"I wouldn't be able to hit an elephant with one of Butler's pistols even if I had one."

"Elephants are not the quarry this evening," said Artemis, speaking in English now that they were out of the trunk. "Lemurs are. At any rate, as we could hardly shoot at our opponent on this particular adventure, perhaps it's better that we are unarmed."

"Not really," said Holly. "I may not be able to shoot you or the lemur, but I bet that more *opponents* will turn up. You have a knack for making enemies."

Artemis shrugged. "Genius inspires resentment. A sad fact of life."

"Genius *and* robbing stuff," Mulch chimed in from his perch on the lip of the car trunk. "Take it from one who knows, nobody likes a smart thief."

Artemis drummed his fingers on the fender.

"We have certain advantages. Elfin magic. Digging talents. I have almost eight more years of experience in the art of mischief-making that the other Artemis does not have."

"Mischief-making?" Holly scoffed. "I think you're being a little gentle on yourself. Grand larceny is closer to the mark."

Artemis stopped drumming. "One of your fairy powers is speaking in tongues, correct?"

"I'm talking to you, aren't I?" responded Holly.

"Just how many tongues can you speak in?"

Holly smiled. She knew Artemis's devious mind well

enough to realize exactly where he was going with this.

"As many as you want."

"Good," said Artemis. "We need to split up. You take the aboveground route into Rathdown Park, Mulch and I travel underground. If we need a distraction, use your gift."

"It would be a pleasure," said Holly, and immediately turned translucent, as though she were a creature of purest water. The last thing to go was her smile.

Just like the Cheshire cat.

Artemis remembered a few lines from *Alice's Adventures in Wonderland*:

> *"But I don't want to go among mad people,"*
> said Alice.
> *"Oh, you can't help that," said the cat.*
> *"We're all mad here."*

Artemis glanced at the pungent dwarf searching his living beard for stored insects.

We're all mad here too, he thought.

Holly approached the main door of Rathdown institute with care even though she was shielded. The People had thought themselves invisible to Butler once before and had paid with trauma and bruises. She would not underestimate the bodyguard, and the fact that he was once again her

enemy set her stomach churning with nervous acid.

The human clothes jumped and scratched along her frame. They were not built for shielding, and in a matter of minutes they would shake to pieces.

I miss my Neutrino, she thought, looking at the reinforced steel door with the dark unknown beyond it. And I miss Foaly and his satellite linkups.

But at heart Holly was an adventurer, and so the idea of quitting never even occurred to her.

It was difficult to operate mechanisms while shielded, so Holly powered down for the few seconds necessary to jimmy the door with her omnitool. It was an old model, but Holly's mother had paid an extra few ingots for upgrades. The standard omnitool would open any door operating on a simple mechanical lock and key system. This one could short electronic locks too, and even deactivate simple alarms.

But that shouldn't be necessary, she thought. As far as Artemis remembers, he turned off all the alarms.

The thought didn't give much comfort. Artemis had been wrong about this trip already.

In less than five seconds the omnitool did its job and vibrated gently, like a cat purring at its own cleverness. The heavy door swung open silently under the lightest touch, and Holly buzzed up her shield.

Stepping into the Rathdown institute, Holly felt more mission anxiety than she had in years.

⊕ · ◊β⊕◊℞ ⊗℞ · ⊗♑ · ◊β ℞℞ ·

I'm a rookie again. Some kid straight out of the academy, she realized. My mind is experienced, but my body is overruling it.

And then: *I better get this monkey quick, before adolescence kicks in.*

Young Artemis had turned off the security on his way into the institute. It had been an easy thing to bypass all the alarms with the director's pass card. Earlier in the day, when he had been given the guided tour, he had posed several complicated questions on the validity of the theory of evolution. The director, a committed evolutionist, had allowed Artemis's arguments to distract him long enough to have his pocket picked by Butler. Once the pass card was in the bodyguard's possession, he simply slotted it into a battery-powered card cloner in his breast pocket, and whistled a few bars of Mozart to cover the whirr of the machine.

Two minutes later all the information they needed was stored in the cloner's memory, the director's card was back in the man's pocket, and Artemis suddenly decided that maybe evolution wasn't a bad theory after all.

Though there are more holes in it than a Dutch dam made of Swiss cheese, he had confided to Butler on the way home from Rathdown Park. Butler had been encouraged by this statement. It was almost a straightforward joke.

Later that evening young Artemis had popped a button

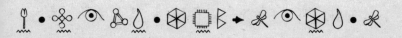

camera into the air-conditioning duct at the rear of the Bentley.

All the better to keep an eye on our guests.

The female was interesting. *Fascinating*, in fact. The darts would wear off soon, and it would be intriguing to watch her reaction, much more so than that of the hirsute teenager, even though his broad forehead suggested intelligence and his general features had a lot in common with the Fowl family's own. In fact, he reminded Artemis of an old photo he had once seen of his father as a boy, working on an archaeological dig in South America. Perhaps the male captive was a distant cousin hoping to claim some kind of birthright now that Father was missing. There was much to be investigated here.

The button camera was broadcasting to his cell phone and ten-year-old Artemis checked the screen occasionally as Butler guided him through Rathdown Park toward the lemur's cage.

"Focus, Artemis," chided the bodyguard. "One dastardly crime at a time."

Artemis glanced up from his phone. "Dastardly, Butler? *Dastardly?* Honestly, we are not cartoon characters. I do not have a villainous laugh or an eye patch."

"Not yet. Though you'll have an eye patch soon enough if you don't concentrate on the job at hand."

They were passing underneath Rathdown Park's aquarium through a Plexiglas tunnel that allowed scientists

and the occasional visitor to observe the species housed in the million-gallon tank. The tank mimicked as far as possible the inhabitants' natural environment. Different compartments had different temperatures and different vegetation. Some were salt water, others were fresh, but all housed endangered or rare creatures.

Tiny bulbs dotted the ceiling above, simulating stars, and the only other light came from the bioluminescence of an albino lantern shark, which shadowed Artemis and Butler along the tunnel until its snout bumped Plexiglas.

Artemis was more interested in his cell phone than the shark's eerily glowing photophores.

Events were unfolding on his screen that were close to incredible. Artemis stopped in his tracks to fully absorb what he was seeing.

The Fowl Manor intruders had escaped the Bentley trunk with the help of an accomplice. Another nonhuman.

I am entering a new world here. These creatures are potentially more lucrative than a lemur. Should I abandon this venture and concentrate on the nonhumans?

Artemis maximized the volume on his handset, but the tiny microphone attached to the button camera could only pick up snatches of the conversation.

It was mostly in some alien tongue, but some of the talk was in English, and he heard the word *lemur* more than once.

Perhaps this lemur is more valuable than I realized. The animal is the bait that lures these creatures in.

A minute passed with only the small revolting dwarf-like thing in the screen, perching its disproportionately large backside on the rim of the trunk; then the female appeared, only to promptly disappear, Rathdown Park's famous pylons filling the screen where she had been.

Artemis tightened his grip on the phone.

Invisibility? The energy involved in creating a reflective field or needed to generate high-speed vibration must be incredible.

He quickly navigated the phone's menu and activated the digital thermal imager, a decidedly nonstandard option, and was relieved to see the female creature's form blossom on screen in warm tones.

Good. Not gone, just hard to see.

Keeping one eye on his phone, Artemis called to his bodyguard. "Butler, old friend. Slight change of plan."

The bodyguard knew better than to hope the lemur hunt was off. "We're still on the trail of a little creature, though, I'll bet."

"Creatures," said ten-year-old Artemis. "Plural."

Fourteen-year-old Artemis was not enjoying the view. To distract himself he composed a haiku describing the sight before him.

> *Pale, shuddering globes*
> *Churn their poisonous cargo*
> *Bald heads in a bag*

Mulch Diggums was not feeling quite so poetic. He stopped digging and rehinged his jaw.

"Could you please stop shining that flashlight on my backside? I blister easily. We dwarfs are extremely photosensitive, even to artificial light."

Artemis had taken the flashlight from the Bentley's breakdown kit and was following Mulch through a fresh tunnel to the lemur's cage. The dwarf had assured him that the tunnel was sufficiently short for him to hold in the dirt and air until they reached the other end, making it safe for Artemis to be directly behind him.

Artemis averted the light for a few seconds, thinking that a bum blister was the last thing he wanted to see; but after a while the beam strayed back onto the pale, wobbling flesh once more.

"Just a quick question. If you can hold in all the diggings, then why does your bum-flap need to be open?"

Mulch was spitting large wads of dwarf phlegm onto the wall to shore up the tunnel.

"In case of emergency," he explained, "I could swallow a buried lug of metal, or a strip of old tire. Now, those I would have to evacuate on the spot, annoying Mud Boy to the rear or not. No sense in ruining my trousers too, is there, dopey?"

"I suppose not," said Artemis, thinking that with such a wide-bore loaded weapon pointed at him, he could bear being called *dopey*.

"Anyway," continued the dwarf, hawking another wad at the wall, "you should consider yourself privileged. Not many humans have seen a dwarf working with spit. This is what you might call an ancient art. First you—"

"I know, I know," interrupted Artemis impatiently. "First you excavate, then you strengthen the walls with your spittle, which hardens on contact with the air, providing it's out of your mouth, obviously. And it's luminous too, amazing material."

Mulch's behind wobbled in surprise. "How do you know these secrets?"

"You told me, or rather, you will tell me. Time travel, remember?"

The dwarf peered over his shoulders, eyes red in the glow of his spittle. "Just how close do we become?"

"Very close. We get an apartment together, and after a whirlwind courtship you marry my sister and honeymoon in Vegas."

"I love Vegas," said Mulch wistfully. Then, "Such snide wit. I can see how we might be friends. All the same, keep your comments to yourself, or we might have to see how funny you are covered in tunnel waste."

Artemis swallowed hard, then moved the flashlight away from Mulch's behind.

The plan was a simple one. They would tunnel underneath the compound and wait below the lemur's cage for Holly to contact them on the short-range LEP

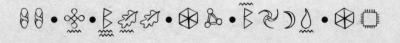

adhesive communicator stuck to Artemis's cheek, part of Mulch's stash. From that point forward, the plan became fluid. Either they would pop up and grab the lemur while Holly caused consternation among the animals, or if young Artemis had already secured the lemur, Mulch would dig a hole under Butler and make it easier for Holly to relieve the boy of his prize.

All very straightforward, thought Artemis. Which is unusual for me.

"Okay, Mud Boy," said Mulch, scooping a bulb-shaped hollow with his flat fingers. "We are here. X marks the monkey."

"Lemur," corrected Artemis automatically. "Are you certain you can distinguish this particular animal's scent from all the others?"

Mulch held a hand to his heart in mock affront. "I? Certain? I am a dwarf, human. A dwarf nose can tell the difference between grass and clover. Between black hair and brown. Between dog poo and wolf poo."

Artemis groaned. "I shall take that as a yes."

"And so you should. Keep this up and I may choose not to marry your sister."

"If I had a sister, I'm sure she would be inconsolable."

They crouched in the hollow for several minutes, the park's nighttime growls and snores drifting down through the clay. By some curious anomaly, once the sounds penetrated the tunnel's coating of dwarf spittle, they were

130

trapped inside and bounced off the walls in conflicting waves. Artemis felt as though he were literally in the lion's den.

As if this wasn't disturbing enough, he noticed that Mulch's cheeks were glowing bright pink. All of them.

"Problems?" he asked, unable to mask a nervous tremor.

"I've been holding in this gas for a long time," replied the dwarf through clenched teeth. "It's coming out soon. You got any sinus problems?"

Artemis shook his head.

"Pity," said Mulch. "This would have cleared them right up."

If it hadn't been for Artemis's determination to save his mother, he would have bolted right then.

Luckily for Artemis's nasal passages, Holly beeped him on the ad-com. The communicator was a basic vibration model that sent signals directly to Artemis's ear without any external noise. Artemis heard Holly's words but not her voice. The ad-com was only sophisticated enough to produce robotic tones.

"In position. Over."

Artemis placed a finger on the communicator, completing the circuit that allowed him to speak.

"Received. We are directly below the target's cage. Can you see the opposition?"

"Negative. No visual. But I do see the lemur. He seems to be asleep on a low branch. I can easily reach him."

"Negative, Holly. Hold your position. We will secure the target. You watch for my younger self."

"Understood. Don't hang around, Arty. Get up, get down, and back to the car."

Arty?

Artemis was surprised that Holly would call him that. It was his mother's pet name for him.

"Got it. Up, down, and back."

Arty?

Mulch tapped him urgently on the shoulder. "Whenever you're ready, Mud Boy. Now would be great."

"Very well. Proceed. Try to be quiet."

Mulch changed position and pointed the crown of his head at the tunnel roof, squatting low on his haunches.

"Too late for quiet," he grunted. "Pull your jacket over your face."

Artemis barely had time to do what he'd been asked, when Mulch released a thundering cylinder of gas and earth, spraying the boy with undigested clods. The shell of dwarf spittle cracked in a thousand places, and Mulch was borne aloft by a churning pillar of force, easily punching through to the surface.

Once the dust had settled somewhat, Artemis scrambled after him into the cage. Mulch had pinballed off a low cage ceiling and was unconscious, blood matting his already tangled hair, his bum-flap fluttering like a wind sock while the remainder of the tunnel waste escaped.

Low cage ceiling?

The lemur in the next cage seemed highly amused by all the commotion, and hopped up and down on a truncated branch wedged between the bars.

The next cage, realized Artemis. We are not in the lemur's cage. What cage are we in?

Before he had time to investigate, his cheek beeped, and an emotionless robotic voice droned into his ear.

"Get Mulch out of there, Arty. Get back down now."

What is it? wondered Artemis. What's in this cage?

Then a four-hundred-pound Ugandan mountain gorilla crashed into him, leaving the thought behind like a speech bubble.

Young Artemis and Butler were watching all of this through the slot windows of a camouflaged hide that sat in front of the cages. The hide had been built inside a rockery and water feature and allowed close study of the various animals without disturbing the natural rhythms of their day. The director had been kind enough to let Artemis sit in the observer's chair earlier that day.

"Someday we'll be able to run the hide's thermal imaging camera and all this equipment from that chair," he had said.

"Perhaps sooner than that," Artemis had replied.

"Oh dear," said Butler, the phrase sounding over-delicate in his gravelly voice. "That must really have hurt."

He reached into his pocket for the dart gun. "I'd better lend a hand, or at least a dart."

Butler had been busy with his darts. Two night workers lay unconscious on cots at the rear of the hide.

Through the slot window they had a clear view of the male intruder being shaken like a rag doll by an enormous gorilla. The cage's third occupant had collapsed and appeared to be racked by an energetic bout of flatulence.

Incredible, thought Artemis. This day is full of surprises.

He tapped a few keys on the computer keyboard before him, redirecting the compound's thermal imaging camera.

"I don't think a dart will be necessary," he said. "Help is already on the way."

Sure enough, a red-hearted glow bounced across the cobbled walkway, hovering before the gorilla cage.

"Now, this should be interesting," mused ten-year-old Artemis.

Holly was forced into action. She had been discreetly tucked away behind the broad trunk of an imported baobab tree, shield off, conserving magic, keeping an eye out for young Artemis, when Mulch blew a hole in the earth into the wrong cage. He exploded from the ground in a minicyclone of debris and bounced off a few surfaces like a cartoon pinball, before collapsing onto the cage floor.

The cage's resident, a black-and-gray bull gorilla, shot

straight up, woken from deep sleep. His eyes were wide but blurred, his teeth yellow and bared.

Stay down, Artemis, she thought. Stay in the hole.

No such luck. Artemis clambered to the surface, carefully navigating the simple climb. The time stream had not granted him any agility. As Artemis often said, the physical was not his area.

Holly thumbed her ad-com. "Get Mulch out of there, Arty," she shouted. "Get back down now."

It was too late. The gorilla had decided these new-comers were a threat to be dealt with. It rolled from its nest of leaves and bark, landing on eight knuckles, the impact sending a jarring wave along its arm hair.

Holly buzzed up her shield as she ran, silver strands floating behind her as the wig fell apart, marking her trail.

The gorilla attacked, grabbing a surprised Artemis Fowl by the shoulders, roaring in his face, head back, teeth like a bear trap.

Holly was at the gate, powering down, pulling the omnitool from her pocket, jabbing the business end into the lock. She surveyed the scene inside the cage while she waited for the tool to work.

Mulch was up and on his elbows now, shaking a groggy head. It would be a moment or two before he was in any shape to help, if he deigned to help a human stranger.

Anyway, it was immaterial; a moment or two would be too late for Artemis.

The omnitool beeped and the cage door swung open, a narrow walkway extended from the footpath crossing a moat and slotting into grooves on the habitat floor.

Holly charged across without hesitation, waving her arms, shouting, making herself a target.

The gorilla huffed and snorted, gathering Artemis close to its chest, warning Holly to stay back. Artemis's head flopped on his shoulders, and his eyes were half closed.

Holly stopped ten feet from the animal and lowered her arms and gaze. A nonthreatening stance.

The gorilla made a few fake attacks, thundering to within a foot of Holly then contemptuously turning his back, all the while grunting and barking, pressing Artemis to his chest. Artemis's hair was slicked back with blood, and a crimson trickle leaked from the corner of his left eye. One arm was broken, and blood pouched the sleeve of his tracksuit.

Holly was shocked. Appalled. She felt like crying and running away. Her friend was injured, possibly dead.

Get a grip! she told herself. *You are older than you look.*

One of the fairy magical powers was the gift of tongues, and this encompassed a rudimentary grasp of some of the more sophisticated animal tongues. She would never be discussing global warming with a dolphin, but she knew enough for basic communication.

With gorillas it was as much about body language as what was actually said. Holly squatted low, elbows crooked, knuckles on the earth, spine curved forward—the posture of a friend—then she funneled her lips and hooted several times. *Danger!* the hoots said. *Danger is near!*

The gorilla did a comical double take, amazed to hear gorilla-speak coming from this creature. It sensed a trick but was not sure what that trick might be. And when in doubt, beat your chest.

The gorilla dropped Artemis, stood tall on two feet, thrusting forward chin and pectorals, and began beating its chest with open palms.

I am king here. Do not trifle with me, was the clear message.

A wise sentiment indeed, but Holly had no choice.

She darted forward, hooting all the time, throwing in the odd terrified screech, and then, against the advice of every wildlife expert who had ever held a steadi-cam, she looked directly into the animal's eyes.

Leopard, she hooted, layering her voice with the fairy *mesmer*. *Leopard!*

The gorilla's fury was replaced by dull confusion, which was in turn pushed aside by terror.

Leopard! Holly hooted. *Climb!*

Moving with less than its customary grace, the gorilla stumbled toward the rear of the cage, moving as though underwater, senses dulled by the *mesmer*. Trees and foliage were batted aside, leaving a wake of sap-crowned trunks and flattened grass. In moments the animal had disappeared deep into the dark recesses of its artificial habitat.

Fearful gibberings floated from the upper canopy.

Holly would feel bad later for putting the beast under a spell, but now there was not a heartbeat to waste on guilt. Artemis was grievously injured, perhaps mortally so.

The gorilla had dropped Artemis like a carcass that had been picked clean. He lay there, still as the dead.

No. Don't think that.

Holly raced to her friend's side, skidding the final yard on her knees.

Too far gone. He's too far gone.

Artemis's face was pale as bone. His long black hair was matted with blood, and the whites of his eyes were twin crescents through hooded lids.

"Mother," he said, the word riding on a breath.

Holly reached out her hands, magic already dancing on her fingertips, shooting off in arcs like tiny sun flares.

She froze before the magic could make the jump to Artemis's body.

If I heal Artemis will I also damn him? Is my magic tainted with Spelltropy?

Artemis thrashed weakly, and Holly could actually hear bones grating in his sleeve. There was blood on his lips too.

He will die if I don't help. At least if I heal him, there is a chance.

Holly's hands were shaking, and her eyes were blurred with tears.

138

Pull yourself together. You are a professional.

She didn't feel very professional. She felt like a girl out of her depth.

Your body is playing tricks on your mind. Ignore it.

Holly cupped Artemis's face gently in both hands.

"Heal," she whispered, almost sobbing.

The magical sparks leaped like dogs unleashed, sinking into Artemis's pores, knitting bones, healing skin, staunching internal bleeding.

The sudden transition from death's door to hale and hearty was rough on Artemis. He shuddered and bucked, teeth chattering, hair frizzing in an electric halo.

"Come on, Artemis," said Holly, bending over him like a mourner. "Wake up."

There was no reaction for several seconds. Artemis looked like a healthy corpse, but then that was how he usually looked. Then his mismatched eyes opened, lids flickering like hummingbird wings as his system rebooted. He coughed and shuddered, flexing fingers and toes.

"Holly," he said when his vision had cleared. His smile was sincere and grateful. "You saved me again."

Holly was laughing and crying at the same time, tears spilling onto Artemis's chest.

"Of course I saved you," she said. "I couldn't do without you." And because she was happy and flushed with magic, Holly leaned down and kissed Artemis, magic sparking around the contact like tiny fireworks.

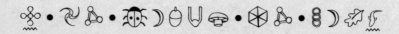

* * *

Ten-year-old Artemis Fowl was keeping one eye on the drama unfolding in the gorilla cage.

"Troglodytes gorilla," he commented to Butler. "Given the name by Dr. Thomas S. Savage, an American missionary to western Africa, who first scientifically described the gorilla in 1847."

"You don't say," murmured the bodyguard, who was more interested in the brute's bite radius than its proper name.

They had used the commotion as cover to slip out from the artificial hide and across the small courtyard to the lemur's cage, which was beside the gorilla's.

The strange newcomers were far too busy to notice them swipe the cage's key-card lock and open the gate door.

"Look at those two. Wasting time. You wouldn't catch me doing that."

Butler snorted, as he usually did immediately before delivering a deadpan line. "Most people never catch you doing anything, Artemis."

Artemis allowed himself a chuckle. This was an interesting day, and he was enjoying the challenges that it presented.

"And there we are," said Artemis quietly. "The last silky sifaka lemur in the world. The hundred-thousand-euro primate."

The lemur was perched high in a Madagascar palm, clinging to the branches with its long grasping toes and opposable thumb digits. Its coat was snow white with a brown patch on the chest.

Artemis pointed at the animal. "That coloring results from chest scent-marking with the sternal-gular gland."

"Uh-huh," said Butler, who cared slightly less about this than he did about the gorilla's scientific name. "Let's just grab the animal and get out of here before our friends next door regroup."

"I think we have a moment or two," said Artemis.

Butler studied the strangers in the adjacent cage. It was surprising that the male was not in pieces by now, but somehow the female had appeared from nowhere and chased the gorilla off. Impressive. That one had a few tricks up her sleeve. There was serious technology behind her. Perhaps some kind of camouflage software in the clothing, which would explain the sparks. The Americans, he knew, were developing an all-terrain camouflage suit. One of his military contacts had sent him a link to a leaked video on the Internet.

There was another creature in the cage, the hairy individual who had released the first two from the Bentley, picking what was supposed to be an unpickable lock in the process. The creature was neither man nor beast, a rough stumpy character who had been propelled through the earth by some force, and was now suffering from a debilitating attack of gas. Somehow, this *thing* had managed to dig a thirty-yard tunnel in a matter of minutes. If it hadn't been for the fact that the cages were modular with overlapping walls, then the creature would have been in the same cage as the lemur. As it was, while it emerged directly below the lemur, it was one cage over.

Butler knew that Artemis would be just itching to study these strange creatures, but now was not the time. They were in a position of total ignorance, and people in that position often died without being enlightened.

The bodyguard drew his dart pistol, but Artemis recognized the sound of a gun sliding from a holster and waved his index finger.

"That's our last option. I don't want our little friend breaking his neck on the way down. First we try gentle persuasion."

From his pocket, Artemis tugged a small ziplock bag containing an amber gel flecked with black and green.

"My own concoction," he explained. "The sifakas are from the Indriidae family of primates, which, as you know, is a strictly vegetarian family."

"Who wouldn't know that?" wondered Butler, who had not exactly put away his pistol.

Artemis unzipped the bag, releasing a sweet thick aroma that wound its way upward, toward the lemur.

"Sap concentrate, with a potpourri of African vegetation. No lemur could resist this. But if this particular primate's brain is stronger than his stomach, fire away. One shot, if you please, and avoid the head. The needle alone would probably be enough to crack that tiny skull."

Butler would have snorted, but the lemur was moving. It crawled along the branch, dipping its pointed nose to catch the odor, touching the smell with a darting pink tongue.

"Hmm," said the bodyguard. "That concoction won't work on humans, I suppose."

"Ask me again in six months," said Artemis. "I am doing some pheromone experiments."

The lemur scampered forward now, hypnotized by the glorious aroma. When the branch ran out, it dropped to the ground and hopped forward on two legs, fingers outstretched toward the bag.

Artemis grinned. "This game is over."

"Maybe not," said Butler. In the cage beside them, the long-haired boy was on his feet, and the female was making a very strange noise.

The corona of magic around fourteen-year-old Artemis and Holly faded, and along with it went the dreamlike trance insulating Artemis's mind.

He was instantly alert. Holly had kissed him. Artemis backpedaled, jumping to his feet and spreading his arms wide to counteract the sudden dizziness.

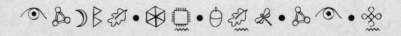

"Eh, thanks," he said awkwardly. "That was unexpected."

Holly smiled, feeling a little embarrassed "Artemis. You're okay. Any more healings and you'll be nothing but scar tissue held together by magic thread."

Artemis thought that it would be nice to stay here and talk like this, but one cage over his future was escaping with his past.

He understood immediately what had happened. Mulch's nose had led them to the right place, but the cages were built like interlocking blocks, and so the lemur had been above them, but also in the next cage. He should have remembered that, if he had been here before. But Artemis had no memory of visiting the central compound. As far as he was aware, the park director had brought the lemur into a special viewing room. This was confusing.

"Very well," he said. "I see where we are . . ."

He was thinking aloud, steadying his mind, trying to forget the kiss for now. Think about it later.

Artemis rubbed the red sparks from his eyes, then turned as quickly as the post-healing vertigo would allow. There he was, his younger self, enticing the silky sifaka lemur with a bag of amber paste.

Sap, I bet. Perhaps with a few twigs and leaves. Wasn't I a clever boy.

An immediate solution was needed. A fluid quick-fire plan. Artemis rubbed his eye sockets as if that could sharpen his mind.

"Mulch, can you tunnel?"

The dwarf opened his mouth to answer, but threw up instead.

"I dunno," he said finally. "My head's a bit flippy floppy. Stomach too. That bash really shook me." His belly made a sound like an outboard motor. "'Scuse me. I think I gotta . . ."

He did indeed *gotta*. Mulch crawled into a fern patch and let fly with the remainder of his stomach contents. Several leaves wilted on the spot.

No use, thought Artemis. I need a miracle, or that lemur is gone and dead.

He grabbed Holly's shoulders. "Do you have any magic left?"

"A little, Artemis. A few sparks, maybe."

"Can you talk to the animals?"

Holly twisted her chin to the left until her neck bone clicked, checking the tank.

"I could do that, anything except trolls. They don't fall for that trick."

Artemis nodded, muttering to himself. Thinking.

"Okay. Okay. I want you to scare that lemur away from me. The younger me. And I need confusion. Can you do that?"

"I can try."

Holly closed her eyes, breathed deeply through her nose, filling her lungs, then threw her head back, and howled. It was a fantastic noise. Lions, apes, wolves, and eagles. They

145

were all in there. The howl was punctuated by the staccato chatter of monkeys and the hiss of a thousand snakes.

Artemis the elder stepped back, instinctively terrified. Some primal part of his brain interpreted this message as fear and pain. His skin crawled and he had to fight his every instinct not to run and hide.

Artemis the younger reached down to the lemur, dangling the ziplock bag in front of its twitching nose. The lemur laid the pads of its fingers on Artemis's wrist.

I have him, thought the Irish boy. The money for the expedition is mine.

Then a wall of unholy sound blasted him like a force-ten wind. Young Artemis staggered back, dropping the bag of paste, suddenly irrationally terrified.

Something wants to kill me. But what? Every animal in the world, it sounds like.

The park's residents were thoroughly spooked too. They screeched and chattered, rattling their cages, hurling themselves against the bars. Monkeys tried repeatedly to leap across the moats surrounding their islands. A thousand-pound Sumatran rhino charged the heavy doors of its cage, rattling the hinges with each attack. A red wolf snarled and snapped, an Iberian lynx hissed, slashing the air, and a snow leopard chased its tail, flicking its head and mewling anxiously.

Butler could not help but shift his focus.

"It's the female creature," he stated. "Making some kind of sound. It's riling these animals up. I'm a bit disturbed myself."

Artemis did not take his gaze from the lemur. "You know what to do," he said to his bodyguard.

Butler knew. If there is an obstacle preventing the completion of a mission, remove the obstacle. He strode quickly to the bars, poked the pistol's muzzle through the mesh, and put a dart into the female's shoulder.

She stumbled backward, her fantastic orchestra of animal sounds squawking to a halt.

Butler felt a shudder of guilt, which almost caused him to misstep on his way to Artemis's side. Twice now he had tranq'ed this girl, or whatever she was, without having any idea what the chemicals were doing to her nonhuman system. His only consolation was that he had loaded small dosage darts as soon as he had secured the night watchman. She shouldn't be out too long. A few minutes tops.

The lemur was spooked now, tiny hands tickling the space before him. The sap cocktail was tempting, but there was danger here of the worst kind, and the urge to live was overriding the desire for a tasty treat.

"No," said Artemis, seeing fear cloud the creature's eyes. "It's not real. There is no danger."

The little simian was not convinced, as if it could read the boy's intention in the sharp angles of his face.

The silky sifaka squeaked once as though pinpricked, then scampered along Artemis's arm, over his shoulder, and out the cage door.

Butler lunged for the tail but missed by a hair. He closed his fingers into a fist.

"Perhaps it's time to admit defeat on this one. We are dangerously unprepared, and our adversaries have . . . abilities we know nothing about."

His charge's reply was to hurry after the lemur.

"Artemis, wait," sighed Butler. "If we must proceed, then I will take the lead."

"They want the lemur," Artemis panted as he ran. "And so it becomes more valuable than it was. When we catch the animal, then we are in a position of power."

Catching the animal was easier said than done. The lemur was incredibly agile and found purchase on the smoothest of surfaces. It darted without a wobble along a metal railing, leaping fully ten feet to the lower branches of a potted palm, and from there jumped to the compound wall.

"Shoot!" hissed Artemis.

It occurred to Butler briefly that he did not care for Artemis's expression. Almost cruel, his brow creased where a ten-year-old's brow should not have creases. But he would worry about that later, for now he had an animal to sedate.

Butler was quick, but the silky sifaka was quicker. In a

flash of fur it scaled the wall and dropped outside into the night, leaving a blurred white jet stream in its wake.

"Wow," said Butler, almost in admiration. "That was fast."

Artemis was not impressed by his bodyguard's choice of words. "*Wow*? I think this merits more than a *wow*. Our quarry has escaped, and with it the funds for my Arctic expedition."

At this point Butler was fast losing interest in the lemur. There were other less ignoble ways to raise funds. He shuddered to think of the ribbing he would have to endure if an account of this night somehow made it to Farmer's Bar in LA, which was owned by one ex-blue-diamond bodyguard and frequented by many more.

But in spite of his distaste for the mission, Butler's sense of loyalty forced him to share a fact that the park director had mentioned earlier, when Artemis was busy studying the alarm system.

"There is something that I know, which you may not know," he said archly.

Artemis was not in the mood for games. "Oh, really. And what would that be?"

"Lemurs are tree creatures," replied Butler. "That little guy is spooked, and he's going to climb the biggest tree he can find, even if it isn't actually a tree. If you see what I mean."

Artemis saw immediately, which wasn't difficult, as the

huge structures cast a lattice of moonshadows over the entire compound. "Of course, old friend," he said, his frown-crease disappearing. "The pylons."

Things were going disastrously wrong for Artemis the elder. Mulch was injured, Holly was unconscious *again*, feet sticking out of the dwarf's hole, and he himself was fast running out of ideas. The deafening clamor of a hundred endangered species going berserk was not helping his concentration.

The animals are going ape, he thought. Then: *What a time to develop a sense of humor.*

All he could do was prioritize.

I need to get Holly out of here, he realized. *That is the most important thing.*

Mulch moaned, rolling onto his back, and Artemis saw that there was a bleeding gash on his forehead.

He stumbled to the dwarf's side. "I imagine you're in great pain," he said. "It's to be expected with such a laceration." Bedside manner was not one of Artemis's strong suits. "You will have a rather large scar, but then looks are not really important to you."

Mulch squinted at Artemis through a narrowed eye. "Are you trying to be funny? Oh my God, you're not. That was actually the nicest thing you could think of to say."

He dabbed at his bloody forehead with a finger. "Ow. That hurts."

"Of course."

"I will have to seal it. You know all about *this* dwarf talent, I suppose."

"Naturally," said Artemis, keeping a straight face. "I've seen it a dozen times."

"I doubt it," grunted Mulch, plucking a wiggling beard hair from his chin. "But I don't have much choice now, do I? With the LEP elf in dreamland, I won't be getting any magical help from that quarter."

Artemis heard a rustling in the undergrowth at the rear of the cage. "You'd better hurry it up. I think the gorilla is overcoming his fear of fairies."

Wincing, Mulch introduced the beard hair to his gash. It took off like a tadpole, poking through the skin, stitching the flaps together. Though he groaned and shuddered, Mulch managed to stay conscious.

When the hair had finished its work and the wound was tied up tighter than a fly in a ball of spiderweb, Mulch spat on his hand and rubbed the gooey mess onto the wound.

"All sealed," he proclaimed; then, upon seeing the glint in Artemis's eye, "Don't get any ideas, Mud Boy. This only works on dwarfs, and what's more, my beard hair only works on me. You poke one of my lovelies into your skin, and all you'll get is an infection."

The rustling in the undergrowth grew louder, and Artemis Fowl decided to forego further information,

which for him was almost unheard of.

"Time we were off. Can you seal the tunnel behind us?"

"I can bring the whole lot down easy as pie. You'd better take the lead, though; there are better ways to go than being buried alive in . . . shall we say, recyclings. Need I say more?"

There was no need to say another syllable. Artemis jumped into the hole, grabbed Holly's shoulders, and began dragging her down the tunnel, past the blobs of luminous spittle, toward the proverbial light at the end. It was like traveling through space toward the Milky Way.

The sounds of his own body were amplified. Gulping breath, drumming heartbeat, the bend and creak of muscle and sinew.

Holly rolled along easily, her suit hissing on the rough surface like a nest of vipers. Or maybe there were snakes down here, the way Artemis's luck was going.

I am trying to do something good for a change, he reminded himself. And this is how the fates reward me. A life of crime was infinitely easier.

Surface noise was amplified by the tunnel's acoustics. The gorilla sounded furious now. Artemis could hear the slap of fists on chest and an enraged huffing.

He realizes he has been tricked.

His theorizing was cut short by Mulch's appearance in the tunnel, the spittle bandage on his forehead casting a zombie glow on his face.

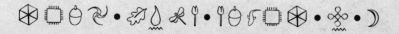

"Gorilla coming," he said as he gulped down lungfuls of air. "Gotta go."

Artemis heard twin thumps as the gorilla landed on the tunnel floor. The huge simian roared a challenge down the hole, and the noise grew in ferocity with every foot it traveled.

Holly moaned, and Artemis pulled harder on her shoulders.

Mulch sucked down air as fast as he could, bundling Artemis and Holly deeper into the tunnel. Twenty yards to go. They would never make it. The gorilla was advancing, pulverizing each spittle lantern as he passed it, roaring with bloodlust. Artemis swore he saw a flash of teeth.

The tunnel seemed to shudder with each blow. Large sections collapsed. Mud and rock clattered down on Artemis's head and shoulders. Dirt pooled in Holly's eye sockets.

Mulch's cheeks ballooned, and he opened his lips the merest fraction to speak.

"Okay," he said in a helium voice. "The tank is full."

The dwarf gathered Artemis and Holly in his burly Popeye arms and vented every bubble of air in his body. The resulting jet stream propelled the group down the length of the tunnel. The trip was short, jarring, and confusing. The breath was driven from Artemis's lungs, and his fingers were stretched to cracking, but he would not let go of Holly.

He could not let her die.

The unfortunate gorilla was blown head-over-rump by the windstorm and yanked back up the tunnel as though tethered to an elastic cable. It whooped as it went, digging its fingers into the tunnel wall.

Artemis, Holly, and Mulch popped from the tunnel mouth, bouncing and skittering along the ditch in a tangle of limbs and torsos. The stars above them were speed-streaked, and the moon was a smear of yellow light.

An old famine wall halted their progress, crumbling under the impact of three bodies.

"For more than a hundred and fifty years this wall stood," coughed Artemis. "Then *we* come along."

He lay on his back, feeling thoroughly defeated. His mother would die, and Holly would soon hate him when she worked out the truth.

All is lost. I have no idea what to do.

Then one of the notorious Rathdown pylons sharpened in his vision—more specifically, the figures clambering along its service ladder.

The lemur has escaped, Artemis realized. And is climbing as high as it can.

A reprieve. There was still a chance.

What I need to save this situation is a full LEP surveillance and assault kit. Perhaps I will have Nº1 send one back for me.

Artemis disentangled himself from the others and decided that underneath the pillar's cornerstone would be

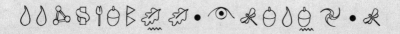

154

a secure spot. He tugged off the remaining stones stacked on top, then wiggled his fingers under the final boulder, and heaved. It came away easily, revealing nothing but worms and damp earth. No package from the future; for whatever reason that particular trick would only work once.

So. No help. I must make do with what is available.

Artemis returned to where Holly and Mulch lay. Both were moaning.

"I think I split a gut getting rid of that wind," said Mulch. "There was a bit too much fear in the mix."

Artemis's nose wrinkled.

"Will you be okay?"

"Give me a minute and I'll be plenty strong enough to carry that huge amount of gold you promised me."

Holly was groggy. Her eyes fluttered as she tried to pull herself together, and her arms flopped like fish out of water. Artemis did a quick pulse and temperature check. Slight fever but steady heartbeat. Holly was recovering, but it would be several minutes before she could control her mind or body.

I must do this on my own, Artemis realized. No Holly, no Butler.

Just Artemis versus Artemis.

And perhaps an omnitool, he thought, reaching into Holly's pocket.

* * *

The Rathdown electricity pylons had been featured in Irish news headlines several times since their erection. Environmentalists protested vehemently that the appearance of the gigantic pylons blighted an otherwise beautiful valley, not to mention the possible detrimental effect the uninsulated power lines could have on the health of anyone or anything living below their arcs. The national electricity board had countered these arguments by pleading that the lines were too high to harm anything, and that to construct smaller pylons around the valley would blight ten times more land.

And so a half dozen of these metal giants bridged Rathdown Valley, reaching a height of three hundred feet at their zenith. The pylon bases were often ringed by protesters, so much so that the power company had taken to servicing the lines by helicopter.

On this night, as Artemis raced across the moonlit meadow, kicking up diamond dewdrops, there were no protesters ringing the pylons, but they had planted their signs like moon flags. Artemis slalomed through this obstacle course while simultaneously craning his neck to track the figures above.

The lemur was on the wire now, silhouetted by the moon, scampering easily along the metal cable, while Artemis the younger and Butler were stranded on the small platform at the pylon's base, unable to venture any farther.

Finally, thought Artemis. A stroke or two of luck.

Stroke one was that the lemur was suddenly up for grabs. Stroke the second was that while his young nemesis had chosen to follow the silky sifaka directly up the pylon the animal was scaling, he himself could go up the adjacent pole, which just happened to be the service pylon.

Artemis reached the pylon's base, which was secured by a cage. The heavy padlock submitted instantly to a quick jab from the omnitool, as did the steel equipment locker. Inside were various tools, walkie-talkies, and a Faraday suit. Artemis tugged on the heavy overalls, wiggling his fingers into the attached gloves, tucking his long hair inside the hood. The flame-retardant and steel-thread suit had to completely enclose him to act as a protective Faraday cage. Otherwise he could not venture out on the wires without being burned to a criminal-mastermind cinder.

More luck. An elevator platform ran along the side of the pylon. It was locked and key-coded. But locks quailed when faced with an omnitool, and a key code was of little value when it was a simple matter to unscrew the control panel and activate the pulley manually.

Artemis held tight to the safety rail as the tiny elevator shuddered and whined its way into the night sky. The valley spread out below him as he rose, and a westerly wind crept over the hills, tugging a strand of hair from his hood. Artemis gazed north, and for a fanciful moment imagined he could see the lights of Fowl Manor.

Mother is there, he thought. Unwell now and unwell in the future. Perhaps I can just talk to my younger self. Explain the situation.

This thought was even more fanciful than the last. Artemis had no illusions about what he had been like at the age of ten. He had trusted no one completely but himself. Not his parents, not even Butler. At the first mention of time travel, his younger self would have his bodyguard shoot a dart first and ask questions later. A *lot* of questions and at great length. There was no time for explanations and debate. This battle would have to be won by wits and guile.

The elevator grated into its brackets at the top of the pylon. A skull and crossbones sign was riveted to the tall safety gate. Even if Artemis had not been a genius, the sign would have been difficult to misinterpret, and just in case a total idiot did manage to scale the pylon, there was a second sign depicting a cartoon man being zapped by electricity from a cartoon pylon. The man's skeleton was clearly visible, X-ray style.

Apparently electricity is dangerous, Artemis might have commented had Butler been by his side.

There was yet another lock on the safety gate, which delayed Artemis about as long as the first two. Outside the safety gate was a small platform covered with wire mesh, with twin power lines humming directly beneath.

There are half a million volts running through those lines, thought Artemis. I do hope there are no rips in this suit.

Artemis squatted low, peering along the line. The lemur had paused halfway between the two pylons and was chattering to himself as if weighing up his options. Luckily for the small creature, it was only touching one line and so no current flowed through its body. If it put so much as a toe on the second line the shock would spin it a hundred feet into the air, and it would be stone dead before it stopped revolving.

On the far pylon, Artemis the younger scowled at the animal while simultaneously trying to tempt it back with his bag of paste.

There is nothing to do but go out on the wires and bring the lemur back yourself.

The hotsuit was equipped for moving across the wires. There was a safety cord wrapped around his waist and a lightning rod in a long pocket on his thigh. Below the platform was a small sled on insulated runners that the engineers used to hand-crank themselves between pylons.

Brains count for little now, he realized. What I need is balance.

Artemis groaned. Balance was not his forte.

Taking a deep breath, he crouched low and drew the lightning rod from his pocket. Almost as soon as it cleared the material, jets of white-hot sparks jumped from the power lines connecting with the tip of the rod. The stream buzzed and hissed like a neon snake.

You are equalizing voltage, that's all. The electricity cannot hurt you.

Perhaps not, but Artemis could already feel the hair standing on his neck. Was that anxiety, or were a couple of volts sneaking in somewhere?

Don't be absurd. If there is a hole, all the volts will worm inside, not just a couple.

Artemis was vaguely familiar with the technique for wire-walking, as the national broadcasting service had done a news special on the high-wire daredevils who risked their lives to keep the lights of Dublin burning. It wasn't so much wire-walking as wire-crawling. The cables were extremely taut, and the maintenance engineers clipped on their safety lines, lay on the sled, then turned the winch until they reached the maintenance site.

Simple. In theory. For a professional on a calm morning.

Not so easy for an amateur in the dead of night with only the stars and the ambient light of nearby Dublin to guide him.

Artemis sheathed his lightning rod and gingerly clipped his safety line to one of the cables.

He held his breath, as though that could possibly make a difference, and laid his gloved hands on the metal sled.

Still alive. A good start.

Artemis inched forward, the metal warm under his clumsy gloved hands, until he was lying flat on the sled with the double-handled winch in front of his face. It was a delicate maneuver and would have been impossible had the cables not been tethered together at regular intervals. He began to twist, and almost immediately the strain on his arms was tremendous as he moved his own bodyweight.

The gym. Butler, you were right. I'll do weights, anything, just get me off these cables with that lemur under my arm.

Artemis slid forward, feeling the runners scrape the rough metal of the cables, their intense hum setting his teeth on edge and sending constant shivers coursing along his arched spine. The wind was low, but still threatened to topple him from his lofty perch, and the ground seemed like another planet. Distant and uninviting.

Twenty feet later his arms ached, and he was noticed by the opposition.

A voice floated across from the other pylon. "I advise you to stay where you are, young man. If that suit has the tiniest rip, then one slip and those cables will liquefy your skin and melt your bones."

Artemis scowled. *Young man?* Had he really been so obnoxious? So patronizing?

"It would take less than a second for you to die," continued ten-year-old Artemis. "But that's quite long enough to be in mortal agony, don't you think? And all for nothing, as the lemur will obviously return for this treat."

Yes, he had been smug as well as obnoxious and patronizing.

Artemis chose not to reply, concentrating his energy on staying alive and enticing the silky sifaka toward him. From his considerable reservoir of knowledge on just about everything, Artemis plucked the fact that smaller simians were comforted by a purring noise. Thank you, Jane Goodall.

So he began to purr, much to the amusement of his younger self.

"Listen, Butler. There's a cat on the wire. A big tom, I would say. Perhaps you should throw him a fish."

But the mocking tone was undercut with tension. Young Artemis knew exactly what was going on.

More purring and it seemed to be working. The ghostly sifaka took a few cautious steps toward the elder Artemis, his beady black eyes glittering with starlight and perhaps curiosity.

Holly would be proud. I am talking to an animal.

Even as he purred, Artemis winced at how ludicrous the situation had become. It was a typical Fowlesque melodrama. Two parties hunting for a lemur on the highest power lines in Ireland.

Artemis looked along the dip of the lines across to the other pylon, where Butler stood, jacket tail flapping around his thighs. The bodyguard leaned into the wind, and the intensity of his stare seemed to pierce the darkness, homing in on Artemis the elder like a laser.

I miss my bodyguard, thought Artemis.

The lemur scampered closer, encouraged by the purring and perhaps fooled by the steel-gray hotsuit.

That's right. I am another lemur.

Artemis's arms were shaking from the strain of turning the handles at such an awkward angle. Every muscle in his body was stretched to its limit, including several he had never used before. His head was dizzy from keeping his balance.

All this and animal impersonations too.

One yard now. That was the distance between Artemis and the lemur. There were no more taunts from the other side now. Artemis glanced across and found that his nemesis had his eyes closed and was breathing deeply. Trying to come up with a plan.

The lemur jumped onto the sled and touched Artemis's gloved hand tentatively. Contact. Artemis stayed stock still, apart from his lips, which burbled out a comforting purr.

That's it, little fellow. Climb onto my arm.

Artemis looked into the lemur's eyes, and for perhaps the first time realized that it had emotions. There was fear in those eyes, but also a mischievous confidence.

How could I have sold you to those madmen? he wondered.

⊗ ◐ ⧊ ⧫ ⟲ ◉ ◊ • ⟲ ▢) ⊗ ⊗ ⧈ • ◐ ◐ ℱ

The lemur suddenly committed itself and scampered onto Artemis's shoulder. It seemed content to sit there while Artemis ferried it back to the service pylon.

As Artemis retreated, he kept his eye fixed on his younger self. He would never simply accept defeat like this. Neither of them would. Young Artemis's eyes suddenly snapped open and met his nemesis's stare.

"Shoot the animal," he said coldly.

Butler was surprised. "Shoot the monkey?"

"It's a . . . never mind. Just shoot it. The man is protected by his suit, but the lemur is an easy target."

"But the fall . . ."

"If it dies, it dies. I will not be thwarted here, Butler. If I cannot have that lemur, then no one will have it."

Butler frowned. Killing animals was not in his job description, but he knew from experience that there was no point in arguing with the young master. At any rate, it was a bit late to protest now, perched atop a pylon. He should have spoken up more forcefully earlier.

"Whenever you're ready, Butler. The target is not getting any closer."

Out on the cables, Artemis the elder could scarcely believe what he was hearing. Butler had drawn his pistol and was climbing over the rails to get a better shot.

Artemis had not intended to speak, as interaction with his younger self could have serious repercussions for the future, but the words were out before he could stop them.

"Stay back. You don't know what you're dealing with."

Oh, the irony.

"Ah, he speaks," called young Artemis across the abyss. "How fortunate that we can understand each other. Well, understand this, stranger, I will have that silky sifaka or it will die. Make no mistake."

"You must not do this. There's too much at stake."

"I must do it. I have no choice. Now send the animal over, or Butler will shoot."

Through all of this, the lemur sat perched on fourteen-year-old Artemis's head, scratching the stitching of his hood.

So the two boys who were one boy locked eyes for a long tense moment.

I would have done it, thought Artemis the elder, shocked by the cruel determination in his own blue eyes.

And so he gingerly reached up one hand and plucked the silky sifaka from his head.

"You have to go back," he said softly. "Go back for the nice treat. And if I were you, I'd stick close to the big human. The little one isn't very nice."

The lemur reached out and tweaked Artemis's nose, much as Beckett might have done, then turned and trotted along the cable toward Butler, nose sniffing the air, nostrils flaring as they located the sweet scent of Artemis's goody bag.

In a matter of seconds it sat curled in the crook of

young Artemis's elbow, contentedly dipping its long fingers into the sap. The young boy's face glowed with victory.

"Now," he said, "I think it best that you stay exactly where you are until we leave. I think fifteen minutes should be fine. After that, I advise you to be on your way and count yourself fortunate that I did not have Butler sedate you. Remember the pain that you are feeling now. The ache of utter defeat and hopelessness. And if you ever consider crossing swords with me again, review your memory of this pain, and perhaps you will think twice."

Artemis the elder was forced to watch as Butler stuffed the lemur into a duffel bag, and boy and bodyguard commenced their climb down the service ladder. Several minutes later the Bentley's headlights scythed the darkness as the car pulled away from Rathdown Park and onto the motorway. Straight to the airport, no doubt.

Artemis reached up and gripped the winch handles. He was not beaten yet—far from it. He intended to cross swords with his ten-year-old self again just as soon as he possibly could. If anything, the boy's mocking speech had fueled his determination.

Remember the pain? thought Artemis. I hate myself. I really do.

CHAPTER 8

A BLOB OF PHLEGM

BY THE TIME Artemis had made his way down from the pylon, Holly had disappeared. He'd left her by the tunnel mouth, but there was nothing in the spot now except mud and footprints.

Footprints, he thought. Now I suppose I need to track Holly. I really must read *The Last of the Mohicans*.

"Don't bother following those," said a voice from the ditch. "False trail. I laid it in case the big human took our LEP friend along for a snack."

"That was good thinking," said Artemis, squinting through the foliage. A shaggy shadow detached itself from a hillock and became Mulch Diggums. "But why did you bother? I thought the LEP were your enemy."

Mulch pointed a stubby mud-crusted finger. "You are my enemy, human. You are the planet's enemy."

· ⏣ 🝔 ⬡ 🝔 ⬡ ⏣ ⚓ 🝔 · 🝔 ⊙ · 🜋 🝔 🜛 ⬡ 🝔 🝕

"And yet you are willing to help me for gold."

"A *stupendous* amount of gold," said Mulch. "And possibly some fried chicken. With barbecue sauce. And a large Pepsi. And maybe more chicken."

"Hungry?"

"Always. A dwarf can eat only so much dirt."

Artemis didn't know whether to giggle or groan. Mulch would always have trouble grasping the gravity of situations, or perhaps he liked to give that impression.

"Where's Holly?"

Mulch nodded toward a grave-shaped mound of earth.

"I buried the captain. She was moaning quite loudly. *Arty* this and *Arty* that, with a few *Mothers* thrown in."

Buried? Holly is claustrophobic.

Artemis dropped to his knees and scooped the earth from the mound with his bare hands. Mulch let him at it for a minute, then sighed dramatically.

"Let me do it, Mud Boy. You'll be there all night."

He strolled over and casually thrust his hand into the mound, chewing his lip as he searched for a specific spot.

"Here we go," grunted the dwarf, yanking out a short branch. The mound vibrated then collapsed into small heaps of pebbles and clay. Holly was underneath, unhurt.

"It's a complex structure called a na-na," said Mulch, brandishing the twig.

"As in . . . ?"

"As in 'Na-na-ne-na-na, you can't see me,'" said the

dwarf, then slapped himself on the knee, exploding in a fit of giggles.

Artemis scowled, shaking Holly's shoulders gently.

"Holly, can you hear me?"

Holly Short opened bleary eyes, rolled them around for a while, then focused.

"Artemis, I . . . Oh gods."

"It's okay. I don't have the lemur . . . Well, actually, I do. The other me, but don't worry, I know where I'm going."

Holly dragged at her cheeks with delicate fingers. "I mean, *Oh gods, I think I kissed you*."

Artemis's head pounded, and Holly's mismatched eyes seemed to hypnotize him. She still had a blue eye, even though her body had rejuvenated itself in the tunnel. Another paradox. But though Artemis felt hypnotized, even slightly dazed, he knew he was not *mesmerized*. There was no fairy magic here.

Artemis looked into those elfin eyes, and he knew that this younger, somehow more vulnerable Holly felt the same way, at this particular tangle of time and space, as he did.

After all we have been through. Or maybe because of it.

A memory smashed the delicate moment like a rock thrown through a spiderweb.

I lied to her.

Artemis rocked backward with the strength of the thought.

Holly believes that she infected Mother. I blackmailed her.

He knew at that instant that there was no recovering from such a brutal fact. If he confessed, she would hate him. If he did not, he would hate himself.

There must be something I can do.

Nothing came to mind.

I need to think.

Artemis took Holly's hand and elbow, helping her to stand and step from the shallow gravelike hole.

"Reborn," she quipped, then punched Mulch on the shoulder.

"Oww. 'Why-for, miss, dost thou torment me?'"

"Don't quote Gerd Flambough at me, Mulch Diggums. There was no need to bury me. A simple broadleaf across my mouth would have done."

Mulch rubbed his shoulder. "A broadleaf desn't have the same artistry. Anyway, do I look like a fern type of guy? I am a dwarf and we deal in mud."

Artemis was glad of the banter. It gave him a minute to compose himself.

Forget your adolescent confusion about Holly. Remember Mother wasting away in her bed. There are less than three days left.

"Very well, troops," he said with forced joviality. "Let's move it out, as an old friend of mine would say. We have a lemur to catch."

"What about my gold?" asked Mulch.

"I shall put this as simply as possible. No lemur, no gold."

Mulch tapped his lips with eight fingers, and his beard hairs vibrated like the tendrils of a sea anemone. Thinking.

"How much is *stupendous*, exactly, in bucket terms?"

"How many buckets do you have?"

Mulch took this as a serious question. "I have a lot of buckets. Most of them are full of stuff, though. I could empty them, I suppose."

Artemis almost gnashed his teeth. "It was a rhetorical question. A lot of buckets. As many as you like."

"If you want me to go any farther down this monkey road, I need some kind of down payment. A good-faith deposit."

Artemis slapped his empty pockets. He had nothing.

Holly straightened her silver wig. "I have something for you, Mulch Diggums. Something better than a stupendous amount of gold. Six numbers, which I will reveal when we get there."

"Get where?" asked Mulch, who suspected that Holly was being melodramatic.

"The LEP equipment lockup at Tara."

Mulch's eyes glowed with dreams of sky-skis and dive bubbles, laser cubes and fat vacuums. The motherload. He'd been trying to crack an LEP lockup for years.

"I can have anything I want?"

"Whatever you can get onto a hovertrolley. One trolley."

Mulch spat a marbled blob of phlegm into his palm.

"Shake on it," he said.

Artemis and Holly looked at each other.

"It's your lockup," said Artemis, stuffing his hands into his pockets.

"It's your mission," countered Holly.

"I don't know the combination."

And then the trump. "We're here for your mother."

Artemis smiled ruefully. "You, Captain Short, are getting as bad as me," he said, and sealed the deal with a sopping handshake.

CHAPTER 9

THE FROG PRINCE

The Fowl Lear Jet, Over Belgium

Young Artemis made a video call from his PowerBook to the ancient town of Fez in Morocco. Even as he waited for the connection, Artemis silently fumed that it was necessary to make this intercontinental trip at all. Even Casablanca would have been more convenient. Morocco was hot enough without having to drive cross-country to Fez.

On screen a window popped open, barely containing the huge head of Dr. Damon Kronski, one of the most hated men in the world, but revered, too, in certain circles. Damon Kronski was the current president of the Extinctionists organization. Or as Kronski said in his most notorious interview: *The Extinctionists are not just an organization. We are a religion.* Not a statement that endeared him to the peace-loving churches of the world.

The interview had run for months on Internet news sites and was sampled every time the Extinctionists made the headlines. Artemis had viewed it himself that very morning and was repulsed by the man he was about to do business with.

I am swimming with sharks, he realized. And I am prepared to become one of them.

Damon Kronski was an enormous man, whose head began its slope into his shoulders just below the ears. Kronski's skin was translucent, redhead white with a scattershot of penny freckles, and he wore violet sunglasses that were clamped in place by the folds of his brow and cheeks. His smile was broad, shining, and insincere.

"Little Ah-temis Fowl," he said with a pronounced New Orleans drawl. "You find your daddy yet?"

Artemis gripped the armrest of his chair, squeezing dents in the leather, but his smile was as shiny and fake as Kronski's. "No. Not yet."

"Well now, that's a pity. Anything I can do to help, you be sure to let your uncle Damon know."

Artemis wondered if Kronski's amiable uncle act would fool a drunken half-wit. Perhaps it was not supposed to.

"Thank you for the offer. In a few hours we may be able to help each other."

Kronski clapped his hands delightedly. "You have located my silky sifaka."

"I have. Quite a specimen. Male. Three years old. Four feet in length from head to tail. Easily worth a hundred thousand."

Kronski feigned surprise. "A hundred? Did we really say a hundred thousand euros?"

There was steel in Artemis's eyes. "You know we did, Doctor. Plus expenses. Jet fuel is not cheap, as you are aware. I would like to hear you confirm it, or I will turn this plane around."

Kronski leaned close to the camera, his face ballooning in the screen.

"I'm generally a good judge of character, Ah-temis," he said. "I know what people are capable of. But you, I have no idea what you might do. I think it's because you haven't reached your limit yet." Kronski leaned back in his chair, the leather creaking under his weight. "So, very well. One hundred thousand euros, as we agreed. But a word of warning . . ."

"Ye-es?" said Artemis, stretching the word to two syllables, in the New Orleans fashion, to demonstrate his lack of awe.

"You lose my lemur, my little silky, then you'd better be ready to cover *my* expenses. The trial is all set up, and my people don't like to be disappointed."

The word *expenses* sounded a lot more sinister when Kronski used it.

"Don't worry," snapped Artemis. "You will get

your lemur. Just have my money ready."

Kronski spread his arms wide. "I've got rivers of gold here, Ah-temis. I've got mountains of diamonds. The only thing I don't have is a silky sifaka lemur. So hurry down here, boy, and make my life complete."

And he hung up a second before Artemis could click the terminate-call button.

Psychologically, that puts Kronski in the power seat, thought Artemis. I must learn to be quicker on the mouse.

He closed the PowerBook lid and reclined his chair. Outside, sunlight was burning through the lower layers of mist, and jet trails drew tic-tac-toe patterns in the sky.

Still in busy airspace. Not for long. Once we hit Africa, the jet streams will thin out considerably. I need a few hours' sleep; tomorrow will be a long and distasteful day.

He frowned. *Distasteful, yes, but necessary.*

Artemis hit the recline button and closed his eyes. Most boys his age were swapping football cards or wearing out their thumbs on game consoles. *He* was in a jet, twenty thousand feet over Europe, planning the destruction of a species with a deranged Extinctionist.

Perhaps I am too young for all this.

Age was immaterial. Without his efforts, Artemis Fowl Senior would be lost forever in Russia, and that was simply not going to happen.

Butler's voice came over the jet's intercom. "All quiet up front, Artemis. Once we get out over the

Mediterranean, I'm going to put her on autopilot for an hour and try to wind down. . . ."

Artemis stared at the speaker. He could sense that Butler had more to say. Nothing but static and the beep of instruments for a moment, then . . . "Today, Artemis, when you told me to shoot the lemur, you were bluffing. You *were* bluffing, weren't you?"

"It was no bluff," said Artemis, his voice unwavering. "I will do whatever it takes."

Tara

Access to the Tara shuttleport was hindered by several steel doors, various scans and codes, tamper-proof bio-locks, and a 360^0 surveillance network at the entrance, which is not as easy to set up as it is to say. Of course, all of this could be bypassed if one knew a secret way in.

"How did you know I had a secret way in?" pouted Mulch.

In response, Artemis and Holly simply looked at him as though he were an idiot, waiting for the penny to drop.

"Stupid time travel," muttered the dwarf. "Told you all about it myself, I suppose."

"You will," confirmed Holly. "And I don't see what you're so upset about. It's not as if I can report you to anyone."

"True," admitted Mulch. "And there is all that lovely loot."

The three sat in a stolen Mini Cooper outside the

boundary fence of the McGraney farm, underneath which was concealed the Tara shuttleport. Thirty thousand cubic feet of terminal hidden by a dairy farm. The first light of dawn was diluting the darkness, and the lumpy silhouettes of grazing cows ambled across the meadow. In a year or two, Tara would become a bustling tourist hub for the fairies, but for the moment, all tourism had been suspended since the Spelltropy outbreak.

Mulch squinted at the nearest beast through the back window. "You know something, I'm a tad peckish. I couldn't eat a whole cow, but I'd put a fair dent in one."

"Mulch Diggums hungry. Stop the presses," commented Artemis drily. He opened the driver's door and stepped onto the grassy verge. A light mist clung to his face, and the clean smell of country air ran through his system like a stimulant.

"We need to get going. I have no doubt that the lemur is already twenty thousand feet in the air."

"That's a nimble lemur," sniggered the dwarf. He climbed over the front seat, tumbling onto the verge.

"Nice clay," he said, giving the ground a lick. "Tastes like profit."

Holly stepped from the passenger seat and sideswiped Mulch's behind with her loafer.

"There will be no profit for you if we can't get into the terminal unseen."

The dwarf picked himself up. "I thought we were

supposed to be friends. Easy with the kicking and the punching. Are you always this aggressive?"

"Can you do it or not?"

"Of course I can. I said so, didn't I? I've been running around this terminal for years. Ever since my cousin——"

Artemis butted in on the conversation. "Ever since your cousin Nord, if I'm not mistaken. Ever since Nord was arrested on pollution charges, and you broke him out. We know. We know everything about you. Now, let's move on with the plan."

Mulch turned his back to Artemis, casually unbuttoning his bum-flap. This action was among the worst insults in a dwarf's arsenal. Second only to what was known as the Tuba, which involves a cleaning of the pipes in someone's direction. Wars have been fought over the Tuba.

"Moving on, chief. Stay here for fifteen minutes, then make your way to the main entrance. I would take you with me, but this tunnel is too long to hold things in, if you catch my drift." He paused for a wink. "And if you stand too close, that's exactly what you'll be catching."

Artemis smiled through gritted teeth. "Very well. Most amusing. Fifteen minutes it is, Mr. Diggums, the clock is ticking."

"Ticking?" said Mulch. "Fairy clocks haven't ticked for centuries."

Then he unhinged his jaw and leaped with astonishing grace, diving into the earth like a dolphin slicing through a wave, but without the sunny disposition or cute grin.

Though Artemis had seen this a dozen times, he could not help being impressed.

"What a species," he commented. "If they could take their minds off their stomachs for a few minutes, they could rule the world."

Holly climbed onto the hood of the car, rested her back against the windshield, feeling the sun on her cheeks.

"Maybe they don't want to rule the world. Maybe that's just you, Arty."

Arty.

Guilt gnawed at Artemis's stomach. He gazed at Holly's fine familiar features and realized that he couldn't keep lying to her any longer.

"It's a pity we had to steal this car," continued Holly, eyes closed. "But the note we left was clear enough. The owner should find it without a problem."

Artemis didn't feel so bad about the car. He had bigger nails in his coffin.

"Yes, the car," he said absently.

I need to tell her. I have to tell her.

Artemis put a toe on the Mini's front tire and climbed onto the hood beside Holly. He sat there for a few minutes, concentrating on the experience. Storing it away.

Holly glanced at him sitting next to her. "Sorry about earlier. You know, the thing."

"The kiss?"

Holly closed her eyes. "Yes. I don't know what's happening to me. We're not even the same species. And when we go back, we will be ourselves again." Holly covered her face with her free hand. "Listen to me. Babbling. The LEP's first female captain. That time stream has turned me into what you would call a teenager again."

It was true. Holly was different: the time stream had brought them closer together.

"What if I'm stuck like this? That wouldn't be so bad, would it?"

The question hung in the air between them. A question heavy with insecurity and hope.

If you answer this question, it will be the worst thing you have ever done.

"It wasn't you, Holly," Artemis blurted, his forehead hot, his calm cracked.

Holly's smile froze, still there but puzzled. "What wasn't me?"

"You didn't infect my mother. I did it. It was me. I had a few sparks left over from the tunnel, and I made my parents forget I'd been missing for three years."

Holly's smile was gone now. "I didn't . . . but you told me . . ." She stopped in midsentence, the truth washing across her face like a disease.

Artemis pressed on, determined to explain himself. "I had to do it, Holly. Mother is dying . . . will be dying. I needed to be certain of your help. . . . Please understand . . ."

He trailed off, realizing that there was no explaining away his actions. Artemis allowed Holly several minutes to fume, then spoke again. "If there had been another way, Holly, believe me."

No reaction. Holly's face was carved in stone.

"Please, Holly. Say something."

Holly slid from the hood, her feet connecting solidly with the earth.

"Fifteen minutes are up," she said. "Time to move out."

She strode across the McGraney boundary without a backward glance, legs cutting twin swathes in the green-black grass. Dawn sunlight shimmered on the tip of each blade, and Holly's passage set a surging ripple of light flashing across the meadow.

Extraordinary, thought Artemis. *What have I lost?*

There was nothing to do but trudge after her.

Mulch Diggums was waiting for them inside the holographic bush at the shuttleport's concealed entrance. In spite of a thick coating of mud, his smug expression was easy to read.

"You won't be needing an omnitool, Captain," he said. "I got the door open all on my lonesome."

Holly was more than surprised. The shuttleport's main door needed a twenty-digit code, plus a palm-print scan, and she knew that Mulch was about as technologically minded as a stink worm. Not that Holly wasn't relieved, as she had anticipated a thirty-minute slog resetting the log once she opened the door herself.

"So . . . tell me."

Mulch pointed down the corridor toward the subterranean escalator. A small figure was spread-eagled on the ramp, his head covered in a blob of shining goo.

"Commander Root and his heavy mob have cleared out. Only one security guard left."

Holly nodded. She knew where Julius Root had gone. Back to Haven to wait for her report from Hamburg.

"The guard was on his rounds up here when I tunneled in, so I swallowed him briefly and gave him a lick of dwarf spit. Everyone reacts differently to the phlegm helmet. This little pixie tried to escape. Slapped the sensor, spouted the code, then staggered around a bit before the sedative got him."

Artemis pressed past into the access tunnel. "Perhaps our luck is finally turning," he said, certain he could feel Holly staring daggers into the back of his head.

"A pity he didn't open the lockup," sighed Mulch. "Then I could have double-crossed you two and made off with the shuttle."

Artemis froze. "Shuttle?" he braved Holly's hostile gaze to ask. "A shuttle, Holly. Do you think we could still beat my younger self to Morocco?"

Holly's eyes were flat, and her tone was neutral. "It's possible; it depends on how long it takes me to cover our tracks."

The shuttle was what LEP pilots would call a

snowgood, as in *Snowgood for anything but the recycling smelter*. Butler, Artemis knew, would have been more straightforward in his assessment of the vehicle.

He could hear the big bodyguard's voice in his head. *I have driven some heaps in my time, Artemis. But this pig is . . .*

". . . is barely out of the Stone Age," murmured Artemis, then chuckled ruefully.

"Another joke, Mud Boy? You're really in fine form today. What is it this time? Did you tell some poor trusting fool that they caused a plague?"

Artemis hung his head wearily. This could go on for years.

Mulch had stumbled across the shuttle when he'd tunneled to the port wall and wind-blasted a sheet of metal cladding from a service tunnel wall. He knew the panel would be loose because he had utilized this point of entry on previous visits. The shuttle had been up on blocks and under a lube tent, and so Mulch could not resist a little peek. Lo and behold, a tunnel scraper in for refitting. Just the thing for hopping around the People's network of subterranean access tunnels.

It had been a simple matter for Holly to reverse the clunky shuttle back down the monorail to the tunnel access hatch.

Meanwhile, Artemis had been covering their tracks, removing all traces of their visit to the shuttleport. Wiping video crystals and replacing the lost time with loops. There wasn't much he could do about the unconscious sprite or the loader-worth of LEP hardware they had helped themselves to from the lockup, but Mulch had no problem taking credit for those.

"Hey, I'm already public enemy number one," he had said. "It's not as if I can go any higher on the list."

So now they were seated inside the tunnel scraper, which was slotted into a launching bracket, drawing a few minutes' charge from the coupling dock before they dropped into the abyss. Holly spent the time falsifying a report for the tunnel authorities.

"I'm telling them that the shuttle paddle has been upgraded as per the service order, and the ship has been requested by the North African shuttleport to do a supply artery de-clogging. It's a drone flight, so they won't be looking for any personnel on board."

Artemis was determined to give the mission every chance of success, in spite of the bridges he had burned. So if a question had to be asked, he would ask it.

"Will that work?"

Holly shrugged. "I doubt it. There's probably a smart missile waiting for us on the other side of that door."

"Really?"

"No. I'm lying. Not nice, is it?"

Artemis shook his head miserably. He would have to

think of some way to make it up to Holly. At least partially.

"Of course it will work. For now, at least. By the time Police Plaza puts all of this together, we should have returned to the future."

"And we can fly without a paddle?"

Holly and Mulch shared a guffaw and a few words in Gnommish that were too fast for Artemis to catch. He did think he heard the word *cowpóg* which translated as *moron*.

"Yes, Mud Boy. We can fly without a paddle, unless you're planning to scrape some residue from the tunnel walls. Usually we leave that to the robots."

Artemis had forgotten how cutting Holly could be with people she wasn't fond of.

Mulch sang a few bars of the old human song "You've Lost That Loving Feeling." He crooned at Holly, clutching an imaginary microphone in his fist.

Holly was not smiling now. "You're about to lose all feeling in your legs, Diggums, if you don't shut it."

Mulch noticed Holly's expression and realized that now was not the best time to be needling her.

Holly decided that it *was* time to terminate the conversation. She remote-opened the access hatch and withdrew the docking clamps.

"Buckle up, boys," she said, and dropped the small craft into a steep dive, down an enormous hole, like dropping a peanut into the mouth of a hungry hippo.

CHAPTER 10
A FOWL MOOD

Fez, Morocco

Ten-year-old Artemis was about as miserable as Butler could remember seeing him, except for perhaps the time he had lost a science prize to an Australian postgraduate. The bodyguard glanced in the mirror of the rented Land Rover and saw that his young charge was sitting in a puddle of perspiration, his expensive suit virtually dissolving on his spare frame.

He's in a Fowl mood, thought Butler, in a rare moment of wit.

A perforated box sat belted on the seat beside Artemis. Three black fingers poked from one of the holes, as the captured lemur explored his prison.

Artemis has barely looked at the creature. He is trying to objectify it. It is no small thing to cause the extinction of a species, even to save one's father.

Artemis, meanwhile, was cataloging the causes of his misery. A missing father and a mother teetering on the brink of nervous collapse were numbers one and two. Followed by a team of Arctic explorers running up expenses in a Moscow hotel room, doubtless living on room service—caviar with everything. Damon Kronski figured high on the list too. A repulsive man with repellant ideals.

The local airport, Fez Saïss, had been closed, and so Butler had been forced to detour the Lear to Mohammed V International in Casablanca and rent a Land Rover there. And not a modern Land Rover either. This one belonged in the last millennium and had more holes than a block of Gruyère cheese. The air-conditioning had spluttered its last more than a hundred miles ago, and the seat padding had worn so thin that Artemis felt like he was sitting on a jackhammer. If the heat didn't bake him, the vibration would shake him to death.

Still, in spite of all these things, a thought struck Artemis, causing the corner of his mouth to twitch into a half smile.

That strange creature and her human companion were utterly fascinating.

They were desperate to have this lemur, and they would not give up. He was certain of it.

Artemis turned his attention to the city suburbs bouncing past his window. The desert highway was suddenly thick with traffic as they neared the city center. Giant trucks thundered past, tires taller than a grown man, their flatbeds stuffed with sullen human cargo. Harried donkey hooves clicked on the broken asphalt, their backs piled high with sticks, laundry, or even furniture. Thousands of dusty mopeds slalomed through the lanes, often bearing entire families on their rusting frames. The roadside buildings shimmered in the late-afternoon sun like mirages. Ghost houses with tea-drinking specters seated out at the front.

Closer to the town center the buildings were denser with no tracts of desert in between. Dwellings were interspersed with garages and video stores, tea shops and pizza parlors. All were the same sandblasted orange color, with patches of original paint poking through below the lintels.

Artemis felt, as he always did when visiting developing nations, mild surprise at the coexistence of ancient and modern. Goat herders toted iPods on spangled chains and wore Manchester United shirts. Shacks had satellite dishes bolted to their corrugated roofs.

Until recent times, Fez had been a place of real importance, being the depot for the caravan trade from the south and east. It was known as a center of Arab wisdom, a holy city, and a place of pilgrimage when the route to Mecca was closed by weather conditions or overrun with bandits.

Now it had become a place where outlawed Extinct-ionists did deals with desperate Irish criminals.

The world is changing more rapidly now than it ever has before, thought Artemis. *And I am helping to change it for the worse.*

Not a comforting thought, but comfort was not a luxury he expected to enjoy in the near future.

Artemis's cell phone buzzed as an incoming text message arrived, having made its way from Fez to Ireland and back to Morocco.

He checked the screen, and a mirthless smile exposed his incisors.

The leather souk. Two hours, read the message.

Kronski wished to make the exchange in a public place.

Apparently the doctor trusts me about as much as I trust him. Smart man.

Holly piloted the shuttle as though she were angry with it, slamming the mining craft around bends until its air brakes screamed and its readout needles shot into the red. She wore a flight helmet hardwired directly into the shuttle's cameras, so a wraparound view of the shuttle was available to her at all times; she could even choose a remote view beamed to the shuttle from the tunnel's various cameras. This particular stretch of tunnel saw little traffic, and so the motion-sensitive lights would pop on barely ten yards before the shuttle entered a stretch.

Holly tried hard to enjoy the experience of flying and forget everything else. Being a pilot for the LEP was what she had dreamed of since childhood. As she cut yet another corner with inches to spare, and she felt the shuttle strain to its limits in her hands, the tension drained from her body as though absorbed by the craft.

Artemis lied to me and blackmailed me, but he did it for his mother. A good reason. Who's to say that I would not have done the same thing myself? If I could have saved my mother, I would have done whatever I needed to do, including manipulate my friends.

She could understand what Artemis had done—even though she felt it was unnecessary—but that did not mean she could forgive him just yet.

And how could she forget it? It felt as though she had completely misjudged their friendship.

That won't happen again.

One thing that Holly was certain of—the most she and Artemis could ever have now was what they had always had: grudging respect.

Holly patched into the passenger-seat bubble-cam on the shuttle ceiling and was gratified to see Artemis clutching the armrests on his seat. Perhaps it was the camera feed, perhaps his face was actually green.

You blew it, Mud Boy, thought Holly, and then: *I hope it's your face and not the feed.*

There was a natural vent in the Moroccan desert south of Agadir, where tunnel gas filtered up through a foot of sand. The only evidence of this was a slight coloration of the sand above the vent, which was quickly dispersed by the winds as soon as the sand reached the surface. Nevertheless, a thousand years of the process had left the dunes with curious red streaks, which the local villagers swore was blood from the victims of Raïsuli, a famous twentieth-century bandit. It was highly unlikely that anyone swallowed these claims, least of all the villagers themselves, but it made good reading in the guidebooks and drew visitors to the otherwise unremarkable area.

Holly drilled the craft through the vent, sealing the shuttle's own air filters against the tiny sand particles. She was flying virtually blind with only a three-dimensional model of the vent to navigate by. Luckily it was a short leg of the trip and it took mere seconds for the shuttle to punch through to the African sky. In spite of the craft's insulated skin, its passengers soon began to feel the heat. Especially Mulch Diggums. Unlike the other fairy families, dwarfs were not surface creatures and did not dream of golden sun on their upturned faces. Anything higher than sea level gave them vertigo.

Mulch burped wetly. "This is too high. I don't like this. Hot, too darned hot. I need to go to the bathroom. For what, I'm not sure exactly. Just don't follow me in there. Whatever you hear, don't come in."

When a dwarf gave this sort of advice, it was wise not to ignore it.

Holly sent a charge through the windshield to clear it, then pointed the shuttle's nose northeast toward Fez. With a bit of luck, they could still beat little Artemis to the rendezvous point.

She set the autopilot and swiveled her seat to face Artemis, whose face was just returning to its normal pallor.

"You're sure about the rendezvous point?" she asked.

Artemis wasn't sure about anything, and this uncertainty fogged his brain.

"Not sure, Holly. But I clearly remember making the exchange at the souk in Fez. At the very least it is a place to start. If Kronski and my younger self do not show up, then we proceed to the Extinctionists' compound."

Holly frowned. "Hmm. This scheme is not up to your usual standards, and our time is running out. We don't have a couple of days to play around with. Time is the enemy."

"Yes," agreed Artemis. "Time is the crux of this entire misadventure."

Holly took a nutri-bar from the tiny refrigerator and returned to her controls.

Artemis studied his friend's back, trying to read her body language. Hunched, rounded shoulders, and arms crossed in front of her body. She was cutting herself off, hostile to communication. He needed to produce some masterstroke to get himself back into her good books.

Artemis pressed his nose to the porthole, watching the

Moroccan desert flash past in streaks of ocher and gold. There must be something that Holly wanted. Something she regretted not doing, that in some way he could facilitate.

After a moment's concentrated thought, it came to him. Hadn't he seen a field holograph pack on one of the storage rails? And wasn't there someone to whom Holly had never said good-bye?

Police Plaza, Haven City, The Lower Elements

Commander Julius Root was up to the quivering tip of his fungus cigar in paperwork. Not that it was actual paperwork. There hadn't been any LEP files written on real paper in a centaur's age. It was all saved on a crystal and kept in a central core somewhere in info-space, and apparently now Foaly's people were trying to grow memory plants, which meant that someday information could be stored in plants or dung heaps, or even the cigar sticking out of Root's mouth. The commander did not understand any of this, nor did he want to. Let Foaly have the worlds of nano and cyber technologies. He would take the world of everyday LEP problems. And there were plenty of those.

First, his old enemy Mulch Diggums was running riot aboveground. It was almost as if the dwarf were taunting him. His latest crime spree involved breaking into shuttleports, then selling his booty to exiled fairies living among the humans. At each site he would leave a nice pyramid of recycled earth in the middle of the floor, like a calling card.

Then there were those blasted swear toads. A couple of college graduate warlocks had granted the power of speech to the common bloated tunnel toad. Naturally, being college graduates, they had only granted the toads the power of bad language. Now, thanks to an unforeseen side effect, namely fertility, there was a virtual epidemic of these toads running around Haven, offending every citizen they hopped into.

The goblin gangs were growing in strength and audacity. Only last week they had fireballed a patrol car on its route through a goblin town.

Julius Root leaned back in his swivel chair, allowing the smoke from his cigar to form a cloud around his head. There were days when he felt like hanging up his holster for good. Days when it felt as though there was nothing to keep him in the job.

The hologram ring buzzed on the ceiling like a disco ball. Incoming call. Root checked the caller ID.

Captain Holly Short.

Root allowed himself a rare grin.

Then there were days when he knew exactly what he had to do.

I have to groom the best people to take over when I am gone.

People like Captain Kelp, Foaly—gods help me—and Captain Holly Short.

Root had handpicked Holly from the ranks. Promoted her to captain, the first woman in the LEP's history. And she had done him proud. Every recon so far had been successful, without a single mind-wipe or time stop.

She's the one, Julius, said Root's inner voice. *Smart, fearless, compassionate. Holly Short will make a splendid captain. Who knows, maybe a great commander.*

Root wiped the smile from his face. Captain Short did not need to see him smiling proudly like a doting grandfather. She needed discipline, order, and a healthy dollop of respect/fear for her commanding officer.

He tapped the accept pad on his desktop screen, and the hologram ring blasted a Milky Way of stars from its projectors, which swirled and solidified into the flickering form of Captain Holly Short wearing a human suit. Undercover, obviously. He could see her exactly as she was, but she could not see him until he stepped into the footprint of the holographic ring, which he did.

"Captain Short, all is well in Hamburg, I trust?"

Holly seemed speechless for a moment; her mouth hung open and her hands reached out as if to touch the commander. In her time he was dead, murdered by Opal Koboi, but here and now Julius Root was as vital as she remembered.

Root cleared his throat. "All *is* well, Captain?"

196

"Yes. Of course, Commander. All is well, for the moment. Though it might be an idea to have Retrieval on standby."

Root dismissed this idea with a wave of his cigar. "Nonsense. Your record so far speaks for itself. You have never needed backup before."

Holly smiled. "Always a first time."

Root blinked. Something on the hologram ring's floating gaseous readout had caught his eye.

"Are you calling me from Africa? What are you doing in Africa?"

Holly slapped her palm against the instrument panel on her end. "No, I'm in Hamburg, in the observation hide. Stupid machine. The projectors are all wrong too. I look about ten years old on the monitor. I'm going to strangle Foaly when I get back."

Root couldn't help but smile at that, but he tucked it away quickly.

"Why the hologram, Short? What's wrong with a plain old communicator? Do you know how expensive it is to beam sound and vision through the earth's crust?"

Holly's image flickered and stared at its feet, then up again.

"I . . . I just wanted to thank you, Jul . . . Commander."

Root was surprised. *Thank him.* For months of impossible tasks and double shifts.

"Thank me, Captain? This is most irregular. I'm not

sure I'm doing my job right if fairies are thanking me."

"Yes, yes you are," blurted Holly's image. "You do a fine job, more than fine. No one appreciated . . . appreciates you enough. But I do now. I know what you were . . . are trying to do for me. So thank you, and I won't let you down."

Root was surprised to find that he was actually touched. It wasn't every day he was faced with such genuine emotion.

Look at me, he thought. Blubbering at a hologram. Wouldn't Foaly love this.

"I . . . 'hem . . . I accept your thanks, and I believe them to be heartfelt. Although I don't expect an expensive hologram call during every mission; just the once will be fine."

"Understood, Commander."

"And be careful in Hamburg. Make sure to check your equipment."

"I will, Commander," said Holly, and Root could have sworn she rolled her eyes, but it could have been another glitch in the program.

"Anything else, Captain?"

Holly reached out her hand; it shimmered and wavered slightly with the motion. Root was not sure what he was supposed to do. Hologram etiquette was very clear: hugging and shaking were not encouraged. After all, who wants to embrace a pixellated image?

But still the hand was there.

"Wish me luck, Commander. One officer to another."

Root grunted. With any other subordinate he would have suspected toadying, but Captain Short had always impressed him with her candor.

He reached out his hand and felt a slight tingle as it touched Holly's virtual digits.

"Good luck, Captain," he said gruffly. "And try to tone down that maverick streak. Someday I won't be around to help you."

"Will do, Commander. Good-bye," said Holly, and then she was gone. But in the seconds before her holographic image fizzled out, Julius Root could have sworn he saw rough holographic tears glint on her cheeks.

Stupid machine, he thought. I will demand that Foaly recalibrate the lot of them.

Holly stepped out of the holo-booth, which resembled an ancient shower unit with a rubber curtain. With the touch of a button it collapsed and self-sealed into the portable briefcase.

There were tears in her eyes as she strapped herself into the pilot's chair and flicked off the autopilot.

Artemis squirmed slightly in the copilot's chair.

"So, are we even?"

Holly nodded. "Yes. We're even. But your elf-kissing days are over."

"I see," said Artemis.

"It's not a challenge, Artemis. Over is over."

"I know," said Artemis neutrally.

The sat in silence for a while, watching low mountains speed across the desert toward them, then Holly leaned across and punched Artemis gently on the shoulder.

"Thanks, Arty."

"You are most welcome. All I did was have an idea."

Mulch emerged noisily from the bathroom, scratching and grunting.

"*Wooo-oh*, that's better. Thank the gods for sound-proofing, eh?"

Holly winced. "Close the door and let the extractor fan do its work."

Mulch slammed the door with a flick of his heel. "I was thinking in there, you know, rooo-minating."

"I don't think I want to hear this."

Mulch plowed on, regardless. "That little lemur. The silky whatever. You know who he reminds me of with that buzz-cut hairdo?"

They had all been thinking it.

"Commander Root," said Holly, smiling.

"Yep. A miniature Commander Root."

"Julius Junior," said Artemis.

They crested the Atlas mountain foothills, and Fez was revealed like the heart of the land, its arteries clogged with vehicles.

200

"Jayjay," said Holly. "That's his name. Now, let's go get him."

She switched on the shuttle's shield and initiated their descent into Fez.

CHAPTER 11
PIGEON DROPPINGS

The Leather Souk, Fez Medina

Holly inflated a cham-pod and suckered it to the shadowy underside of the stone balcony overlooking Fez's leather souk. When the coast was clear, she and Artemis climbed through the tiny access port, wiggling into the blow-up seats. Artemis's knees knocked against his chin, clicking his teeth.

"Like I said, you're getting tall," said Holly.

Artemis blew a raven lock from his eye. "And hairy."

"Your hair was the only thing that stopped little Arty from recognizing himself, so be glad of it."

Holly had liberated the cham-pod duffel bag from the Tara lockup along with a single Neutrino handgun and suitable disguises. Artemis wore a knee-length brown shirt and thong sandals, while Holly's fairy characteristics were hidden by an abaya and head scarf.

The cham-pod was an old portable model and was basically a ball with a transparent outer layer that was inflated by a tank of chromo-variable gas, which could change color to imitate the background. That was about as high-tech as it got. No directional equipment, no on-board weaponry, just a one-way touch screen and two cramped seats.

"No air filters?" wondered Artemis.

"Unfortunately not," said Holly, pulling her scarf across her nose. "What is that smell?"

"Diluted pigeon droppings," replied Artemis. "It's highly acidic and, of course, plentiful. The tannery workers use it to soften the hides before dyeing them."

The leather souk spread out below them was a spectacular sight. Huge stone vats were arranged across the courtyard in honeycomb patterns, each filled with either vegetable dyes such as saffron or henna, or acidic softeners. The leather workers stood in the dye vats, thoroughly soaking each skin, including their own, and when the hide had attained the desired hue, it was stretched on a nearby rooftop to dry.

"People say that Henry Ford invented the production line," said Artemis. "This place has been going for six hundred years."

The souk was enclosed by high walls painted white

but mottled by dye and dust. Ocher stains spread across the ancient brick like the faded map of some exotic archipelago.

"Why did Kronski choose the souk?" wondered Holly. "The stink is almost unbearable, and I say that as a friend of Mulch Diggums."

"Since birth Kronski has suffered from anosmia," Artemis explained. "He has no sense of smell. It amuses him to conduct his business here, as whoever he happens to be meeting will be virtually assaulted by the smell from the acid vats. Their concentration is shattered and his is unaffected."

"Clever."

"Fiendishly. The area is a tourist attraction, so many people will pass through, but none hang around for too long."

"So plenty of spectators but not many witnesses."

"Apart from the locals, and Kronski doubtless has a dozen of those on his payroll who will see what he wants them to see." Artemis leaned forward, his nose brushing the plastic portal. "And here is our fiendish Extinctionist now. Right on cue."

The souk below was thronged with leather workers and merchants, long since inured to the sharp odor of the vats. Groups of die-hard tourists flitted through, determined to capture the scene on their cameras but unwilling to suffer the heat and smells for longer than a few shutter clicks.

And among them all, serene and smiling, strode Dr. Damon Kronski, dressed in a preposterous tailored camouflage suit, complete with a general's peaked hat.

Holly was sickened by the man and how obviously he relished his surroundings.

"Look at him. He loves this."

Artemis did not comment. He had sold the lemur and judged that to be a crime worse than Kronski's. Instead he searched the souk for a smaller version of himself.

"There I am. West corner."

Holly switched her gaze to locate young Artemis. He stood almost hidden by a huge tiled urn brimming with mint-green dye. The sinking sun was a chopped silver disk on its surface.

Artemis smiled. *I remember standing in that exact spot so the glare would distract Kronski. It is the only vat touched by the sun at this time. A little payback for the smell. Childish, perhaps, but then, I was a child.*

"It looks like your memory is accurate on this occasion," said Holly.

Artemis couldn't help but be relieved. His recollection had been hit-and-miss up to now.

He straightened suddenly. *Hit-and-miss. How could I not have seen it? These memory malfunctions could only mean one thing.*

No time to pursue that thought now. The exchange was afoot.

Artemis tapped the touch screen with his index finger, expanding a section and closing in on a plinth at the center of the souk. The low table stone was grooved and curved from centuries of being piled high with hides. Wet henna glistened on its surface and dribbled down its sides like blood from a head injury.

"There," said Artemis. "That's where we agreed to make the exchange. Kronski lays the suitcase on the rock. I hand it over."

"*Him*. The lemur is a male, and his name is Jayjay," said Holly, making it real.

"I hand over Jayjay. Then we go our separate ways, simple as that. There were no complications."

"Perhaps we should wait until after the handoff?"

"No. What happens afterward is an unknown quantity. At least now we have some foreknowledge."

Holly studied the scene with a veteran's eye. "Where's Butler?"

Artemis touched another point on the screen. It rippled slightly, flexed, and enlarged his selection.

"In that window. Watching over everything."

The window was a high rectangle in the flaking white wall, painted black by shade and depth.

"You think you're invisible, don't you, my friend," Holly whispered, then highlighted the window with a thumb and activated a night-vision filter. In the sudden glow of body heat, a hulking figure appeared in the

206

window, still as stone except for a beating heart.

"I remember that Butler wanted to make the exchange, but I talked him out of it. He's up there right now, fuming."

"Butler fuming is not something I want to see up close."

Artemis laid a hand on her shoulder. "Then don't get too close. A distraction is all we need. I wish there had been an LEP jumpsuit in that lockup. If you were invisible to man *and* machine, I would be more comfortable with this."

Holly twisted her chin, calling her magic, and blobs of her disappeared until there was nothing left in the seat but haze.

"Don't worry, Artemis," she said, her voice sounding almost robotic because of the vibration. "I have been on missions before. You are not the only smart one in the souk."

Artemis was not in the least cheered by this. "All the more reason to be careful. I wish there'd been a set of wings in the terminal. What sort of lockup doesn't have wings?"

"Potluck," said Holly, her voice floating through the expandable seal that operated as a doorway. "We got what we got."

"We got what we got," repeated Artemis, following Holly's progress down the steps and across the courtyard with the infrared filter. "Terrible grammar."

* * *

Ten-year-old Artemis felt as though he had been dipped in a jar of honey and left to bake on the surface of the sun. His garments had molded themselves to his skin, and a tornado of flies revolved around his head. Artemis's throat was sandpaper dry, and he could hear his breath and pulse as though he were wearing a helmet.

And the stench. The stench was a hot wind gusting in his nose and eyes.

I must persevere, he thought with a focused determination beyond his years. Father needs me. Also, I refuse to be cowed by this odious man.

The souk was a confusing kaleidoscope of pumping limbs, splashing dye, and evening shadows. And from Artemis's point of view, things were even more confusing. Elbows flashed past, urns rang like bells, and the air was shattered by sharp bolts of French and Arabic above his head.

Artemis allowed himself a moment to meditate. He closed his eyes and took shallow breaths through his mouth.

Very well, he thought. To business, Dr. Kronski.

Luckily the doctor was enormous, and as Artemis made his way through the souk, he quickly spotted Kronski on the opposite diagonal.

Look at that poser. A camouflage suit! Does he honestly believe himself a general in some war against the animal kingdom?

Artemis himself drew surprised stares from the locals. Tourists were not unusual in the souk, but lone ten-year-old boys in formal suits, carrying monkey cages, were rare in any part of the world.

It is a simple matter. Walk to the center and set down the cage.

But even walking through the souk was not simple. Workers bustled through the lanes between vats, laden with dozens of sopping hides. Strings of dye flew through the air, striping the clothes of tourists and other workers. Artemis was forced to tread carefully and give way several times before he eventually reached the small clearing at the center.

Kronski was there before him, perched on the tiny stool that folded out from the top of his hunting cane, puffing on a thin cigar.

"Apparently I'm missing out on half the experience," he said, as though they were simply continuing a conversation. "The best part of a cigar is the aroma, and I can't smell a thing."

Artemis was silently infuriated. The man looked completely comfortable, with barely a drop of sweat on his brow. He forced himself to smile.

"Do you have the money, Damon?" At least he could annoy the good doctor by neglecting his title.

Kronski did not seem annoyed. "Got it right here, Ahtemis," he said, patting his breast pocket. "A hundred thousand is such a trifling amount, I managed to stuff every last note into my suit pocket."

Artemis could not resist a jibe. "And what a lovely suit it is."

Kronski's violet-colored glasses flashed in the last rays of the sun. "Unlike your own, my boy, which appears to be losing its *character* in this heat."

It was true, Artemis felt that the only thing holding him upright was the dried sweat on his spine. He was hungry, tired, and irritable.

Focus. The end justifies the sacrifices.

"Well, obviously I have the lemur, so can we please proceed."

Kronski's fingers twitched, and Artemis could guess what he was thinking: *Take the lemur from the boy. Just grab it. No need to part with the hundred thousand.*

Artemis decided to nip this kind of thinking in the bud. "In case you're entertaining any rash notions of reneging on our agreement, let me just say one word to you: *Butler*."

One word was enough. Kronski knew Butler's reputation but not his whereabouts. His fingers twitched once more, and then were still.

"Very well, Ah-temis. Let's get this business over with. I'm sure you appreciate that I need to inspect the merchandise."

"Of course. And I'm sure that *you* appreciate that I will need to see a sample of your currency."

"Why, of course." Kronski wiggled his hand into a

pocket and withdrew a fat envelope brimming with purple five hundred euro notes. He carelessly selected one and passed it across to Artemis.

"Gonna smell it, are you, Ah-temis?"

"Not exactly." Artemis flipped open his cell phone and selected a UV and magnetic currency scanner from its augmented menu. He passed the note in front on the purple light, checking for the watermark and metal strip.

Kronski pressed a hand to his heart. "I am wounded, boy, injured, that you think I would cheat you. Why, it would cost more than a hundred thousand to forge a hundred thousand. A good set of plates cost twice that."

Artemis closed the phone. "I am not a trusting person, Damon. You'll learn that about me." He placed the cage on the stone plinth. "Now, your turn."

In that moment, Kronski's entire attitude changed. His offhand nature vanished, to be replaced with a giddiness. He smiled and tittered, tiptoeing to the cage like a child to a Christmas tree.

Perhaps a normal child, thought Artemis sourly. Christmas morning held no surprises for me, thanks to the X-ray scanner on my cell phone.

Obviously the prospect of extinguishing the life's spark of another species excited Kronski hugely. He leaned over the cage daintily, squinting through the airholes.

"Yes, yes. All *appears* to be in order. But I will need to take a closer look."

"A hundred thousand euros buys you all the closer looks you need."

Kronski tossed the envelope to Artemis. "Oh, take it, you tiresome boy. You really distress me, Ah-temis. A boy like you can't have many friends."

"I've got one friend," retorted Artemis, pocketing the money. "And he's bigger than you."

Kronski opened the box just enough to grab the lemur by the scruff of the neck. He hoisted the animal aloft like a trophy, checking him from all angles.

Artemis took a step back, casting suspicious glances around the souk.

Perhaps nothing is going to happen, he thought. Perhaps those creatures were not as resourceful as I believed. I may have to be content with the hundred thousand for now.

And then the resourceful creatures arrived.

Holly did not have wings to fly, but that did not mean she couldn't cause havoc. There had been no weapons in the LEP lockup beyond the single Neutrino, but there had been some mining equipment, including a few dozen blaster buttons, which Holly was now sprinkling into the unattended dye vats around the souk, with a double helping underneath Butler's window.

Though she was invisible, Holly took extra care with her movements, as shielding without a suit was wild magic

indeed. Any sudden gestures or collisions could cause her body to vent magical fireworks, which would look strange igniting out of thin air.

So—softly, softly was the way to move.

Holly dropped the last of the buttons, feeling totally vulnerable in spite of her invisibility.

I miss Foaly's guidance, she thought. It's nice to have an all-seeing eye.

As if he could read her mind, Artemis's voice came from the mike-bud in her ear. Another gift from the lockup.

"Kronski is opening the cage. Get ready to blow the buttons."

"All set. I'm at the northwest corner if Jayjay tries to run."

"I see you on the filter. Detonate at will."

Holly climbed into an empty vat and fixed her gaze on Kronski. He had the lemur out now, holding it away from his body. Perfect.

She ran a finger along the small strip in her hand until all the tiny lights had turned green. A one word message scrolled across the strip: *Detonate?*

Absolutely, thought Holly, and pressed the YES box.

A vat blew, sending a column of red dye shooting twenty feet into the air. Several more vats quickly followed suit, thumping like mortars, hurling their contents into the Moroccan sky.

A symphony of color, thought Artemis from his perch. Butler's view is totally obscured.

Below in the souk, pandemonium was instantaneous. The leather workers roared and shouted, oohing like spectators at a fireworks show as each new colored fountain erupted. Some realized that their precious leathers were being coated with the wrong hues and began to feverishly gather their wares and tools. Within seconds it was raining gouts of dye, and the spaces between the vats were thronged with frantic workers and spooked tourists.

Young Artemis stood stock still, ignoring the flying dye, his gaze fixed on Damon Kronski and the lemur in his fist.

Watch the animal. They want the animal.

Kronski squealed with each explosion, balancing on a single leg like a scared ballet dancer.

Priceless, thought Artemis, and shot a few seconds of video on his phone. Something else was about to happen, he felt sure of it.

And he was right. Artemis had a vague impression that the earth exploded in front of Kronski's feet. Mud mushroomed upward, something moved in the curtain of earth, and then the lemur was gone.

Dr. Kronski was left holding a blob of slime, which glowed slightly in the evening shadows.

The last drops of dye fell, and slowly the chaos retreated. The leatherworkers shook their heads in wonder, then began to curse their luck. A day's profit gone.

Kronski squealed for several seconds after the dust had cleared, holding the note like an opera singer.

Artemis grinned nastily. "It isn't over until the fat lady sings, so I suppose it's over."

The doctor was snapped out of it by Artemis's tone. He composed himself, standing on two feet and breathing deeply as the red spots retreated from his cheeks. It was not until he tried to wipe the gunk from his hand that he realized the lemur was no longer in his grasp. As he stared in disbelief at his fingers, Kronski felt the stuff coating his fingers harden into a glowing gauntlet.

"What have you done, Artemis?"

Ah, thought Artemis. Suddenly you can pronounce my name.

"I have done nothing, Damon. I delivered the lemur, you lost him. The problems here are all yours."

Kronski was livid; he tore off his glasses to reveal red-rimmed eyes. "You have tricked me, Fowl. Somehow you are a participant in this. I cannot host an Extinctionist conference without a strong opening. The execution of that lemur was my big 'Hello, everyone.' "

Artemis's phone beeped, and he glanced at the screen. A brief text from Butler.

Mission accomplished.

He pocketed the cell phone and smiled broadly at Kronski.

"A strong opening. I may be able to help you with that. For a price, naturally."

Artemis the elder sat in the cham-pod watching events unfurling below. Everything had gone exactly to plan, with the exception of the dye vats, which actually exceeded Artemis's expectations.

Butler's view is completely blocked, he thought. And then he froze suddenly. Of course! I wouldn't have placed Butler in that window at all. I would have put a decoy there, as it is one of the five logical places for a sniper to set up. In fact, I would have put a decoy in all five spots and then had Butler hide himself somewhere on the souk floor, ready to step in if those pesky lemur-nappers showed up again, which they very well could, as they seem to know my every move. I, Artemis Fowl, have been bamboozled by myself.

Suddenly, a horrifying thought struck him.

"Holly!" he shouted into the microphone pad adhered to his thumb. "Abort! Abort!"

"What . . ." came the crackly response. "The noise . . . I think . . . damaged."

Then a few seconds of white noise, sharp snaps, and silence.

It was too late. Artemis could only press his face against the screen and watch helplessly as one of the leatherworkers shrugged off his shoulder blanket and straightened, revealing himself to be far taller than he had previously appeared. It was, of course, Butler, with a handheld infrared scanner extended before him.

Butler. Don't do it, old friend. I know you were never comfortable with my schemes.

In three quick strides the bodyguard moved to Holly's vat and netted the elf in his blanket. She struggled and fought, but never had a chance against Butler's formidable strength. In ten seconds Holly was hog-tied and hoisted over the bodyguard's shoulder. In five more seconds Butler was out of the gate and lost in the gathering crowds of the medina.

It all happened so quickly that Artemis's jaw did not have time to drop. One moment he was in control, enjoying the smugness that comes with being the smartest person in the metaphorical room. The next he was crashing back to earth, having sacrificed his queen for a rook, realizing he was up against somebody just as smart as he was, only twice as ruthless.

He felt the pallor of desperation creep across his forehead, leaving pins and needles in its wake.

They have Holly. The Extinctionists will put her on trial on charges of breathing human air.

A thought occurred to him: Every defendant is entitled to a good lawyer.

CHAPTER 12

GONE FOREVER

La Domaine des Hommes, Extinctionists' Compound, Fez

Artemis the younger agreed to accompany Dr. Kronski to his gated compound near the medina. Kronski's Land Rover was considerably more luxurious than Artemis's rented model, complete with powerful air-conditioning, water cooler, and white tiger upholstery.

Artemis ran a finger through the fur and was not surprised to find that it was real.

"Nice seats," he commented drily.

Kronski did not answer. He hadn't spoken much since losing the lemur, except to mutter to himself, cursing the unfairness of it all. It didn't seem to bother him that his suit was covered in dye, which was transferring itself to his expensive upholstery.

• ⋃ ⚭ ⁋⁋ ⚙ ᛒ 🐿 ◗ • ∞ 🌰 ᛒ 🦞 🦀 🦀 🦀 •

Though it took barely five minutes to reach the compound, Artemis was glad of the thinking space. By the time the Land Rover was cleared through the reinforced gates, he had any wrinkles in his strategy straightened out, and he'd used the spare two minutes to plot one of the romance novels he occasionally wrote under the pseudonym Violet Tsirblou.

A guard with bulk to match Butler's waved them through, underneath a walkway arch in the twelve-foot wall. Artemis kept his eyes open on the way in, noting the armed guards patrolling the ten-acre compound, and the position of the generator hut, and the staff quarters.

Information is power.

The residential chalets were built in the style of Californian beach houses, flat roofs, and plenty of glass, clustered around a man-made beach, complete with a wave machine and lifeguard. There was a large conference center in the middle of the compound, with a scaffold-clad spire jutting from its roof. Two men were perched on the scaffolding, putting the finishing touches to a brass icon on the spire's tip. And even though most of the icon was wrapped in canvas, Artemis could see enough to know what it was. A human arm with the world in its fist. The symbol of the Extinctionists.

Kronski's driver parked in front of the compound's grandest chalet, and the doctor led the way inside wordlessly. He flapped a hand toward a hide-covered sofa, and disappeared into his bedroom.

Artemis was hoping for a shower and a change of clothes, but apparently Kronski was too upset for courtesy, so Artemis was forced to tug at the collar of his itchy shirt and wait for his host's return.

Kronski's reception lounge was a macabre space. One wall was covered with certificates of extinction, complete with photographs of the unfortunate animals and the dates on which the Extinctionists managed to murder the last one of the particular species.

Artemis browsed the photo wall. Here was a Japanese sea lion and a Yangtze river dolphin. A Guam flying fox and a Bali tiger.

All gone forever.

The only way to see these creatures would be to somehow build up enough momentum to travel faster than the speed of light and go back in time.

There were further horrors in the room, all labeled for educational purposes. The sofa was upholstered with the pelts of Falkland Island wolves. The base of a standing lamp was fashioned from the skull of a western black rhinoceros.

Artemis struggled to maintain his composure.

I need to get out of here as quickly as possible.

But the faint voice of his conscience reminded him that leaving this place would not mean that it no longer existed, and selling the strange creature to Kronski would only draw more people to it.

Artemis conjured a picture of his father in his mind.

Whatever it takes. Whatever I have to do.

Kronski entered the room, showered and wearing a flowing kaftan, his eyes red rimmed as though he'd been crying.

"Sit down, Ah-temis," he said, gesturing toward the sofa with a hide-bound fly swatter.

Artemis eyed the seat. "No. I think I'll stand."

Kronski sank into an office chair. "Oh, I get it. Grown-up sofa. It's difficult to be taken seriously when your feet don't touch the ground."

The doctor rubbed his eyes with stubby thumbs, then donned his trademark glasses.

"You have no idea what it's been like for me, Ah-temis. Hounded from country to country because of my beliefs, like some common criminal. And now that I have *finally* found somewhere to call home—now that I have persuaded the committee to meet here—I lose my trial animal. That lemur was the centerpiece of the entire conference."

Kronski's voice was steady and he seemed to have recovered himself since his breakdown at the leather souk.

"The Extinctionists' committee are very powerful men, Ah-temis. They are accustomed to comfort and convenience. Morocco is hardly convenient. I had to build this compound to entice them down here, and promise a big opening to the conference. And now all I have to show is a shining hand."

Kronski brandished his hand, which was largely slime-free, but it did seem to glow faintly.

"All is not lost, Doctor," said Artemis soothingly. "I can provide you with something that will rejuvenate your society and make it globally relevant."

Kronski's frown was skeptical, but he leaned forward, arms slightly outstretched.

His face says no, thought Artemis. But his body language says yes.

"What are you selling, Ah-temis?"

Artemis opened the gallery on his phone and selected a photograph.

"This," he said, passing the phone to Kronski.

The doctor studied the photograph, and the skepticism in his eyes grew more pronounced.

"What is this? Photo manipulation?"

"No. Genuine. This creature is real."

"Come on, Ah-temis. What we've got here is latex and bone implants. Nothing more."

Artemis nodded. "That's a fair reaction. So you don't pay until you're satisfied."

"I already paid."

"You paid for a lemur," Artemis countered. "This is an undiscovered species. Possibly a threat to mankind. This is what the Extinctionists are all about. Imagine how many members will clamor to donate to your church when you uncover this threat."

Kronski nodded. "You put together a good argument for a ten-year-old. How much do I pay?"

"You pay five million euros. Nonnegotiable."

"Cash?"

"Diamonds."

Kronski pouted. "I won't pay a single stone until I verify the authenticity of your product."

"That's fair."

"That's mighty accommodating of you, Fowl. How do you know I won't double-cross you? After all, I'm pretty sure that you had a hand in whatever happened back at the souk. Payback is fair play where I come from."

"You might double-cross me, Damon. But you won't double-cross Butler. You are not a stupid man."

Kronski grunted, impressed. "I got to hand it to you, boy. You've got all the angles figured. You present 'em well too." He stared absently at his glowing hand. "You ever think it strange, Ah-temis, how a kid like you winds up going eyeball to eyeball with an old crook like me?"

"I don't understand the question," said Artemis truthfully.

Kronski clapped his hands and laughed. "It delights me, Ah-temis," he said, "that a boy such as you exists. It makes my day." The laughter stopped suddenly, as though cut off by a guillotine. "Now, how soon can I inspect the creature?"

"Immediately," replied Artemis.

"Good. Well, text your man to come hither. Let's say it takes him thirty minutes to get here, another ten to clear security. We can meet him in the grand lodge in one hour."

"I said immediately," said Artemis, clicking his fingers. Butler stepped out from behind a curtain, a Kevlar duffel bag under one arm.

Kronski squealed briefly, then rolled his eyes in frustration. "I can't control that. . . . Ever since the koala in Cleveland. It's so embarassing. . . ."

File and save, thought Artemis. Koala in Cleveland.

"Anyway," continued the doctor, "how did he get in here?"

Butler shrugged. "I came in the same way you did, Doctor."

"You were in the Land Rover," breathed Kronski. "Very clever."

"Not really. More lax on your part than clever on ours."

"I will remember that. Do you have the merchandise with you?"

Butler's mouth tightened, and Artemis knew that he was being pushed to the limits of his loyalty by this transaction. The lemur had been bad enough, but this female in the bag was some kind of person.

Wordlessly, the bodyguard placed the duffel on the desktop. Artemis tugged on the zipper, but Butler stopped him.

"She has some kind of hypnotizing skills. I once met a guy in Laos who could put the whammy on you, but

nothing like this. She tried it outside the souk and I nearly ran into a camel, so I taped her mouth. Also, as we know, she can turn invisible. When I opened the bag first, she wasn't there. I think her juice is running out, though. There could be more stunts; who knows what tricks she has hidden in those pointed ears. Are you prepared to take that risk?"

"Yes," said Kronski, almost foaming at the mouth. "Absolutely yes. Open the bag."

Butler removed his hand, and Artemis unzipped the duffel, exposing the figure inside.

Kronski stared into the mismatched eyes, ran a hand across the inhumanly wide brow, tugged one of the ears, then staggered to the office bar and poured himself a glass of water with shaky hands.

"Five million at today's market price," he said. "You said five and we agreed. No upping the price now."

Artemis smiled. The doctor was hooked.

"Five million," he said. "Plus expenses."

Artemis the elder rode back to the landing site on a collapsible LEP scooter designed to resemble a 1950s human Lambretta. The resemblance was only bumper deep, as there were not many Lambrettas that came equipped with clean nuclear batteries, Gnommish satellite navigation, and self-destruct buttons.

The Ifrane road outside the imperial city was part of the

fertile Fez river basin and was lined with olive groves and golf courses.

Ancient and modern. Coexisting.

Overhead the stars seemed closer and fiercer than at home in Ireland, shining down like stadium lights, as though Africa were somehow closer to the rest of the universe.

I lost her. I lost Holly.

But he did have a plan. A half-decent plan. All it needed was a bit of fairy technology to open a few doors, and then there was still a chance. Because without Holly, all was lost. There would be no future for any of them.

It took almost an hour to find the particular golf course where Holly had parked the LEP shuttle. Not that there was much evidence of a craft in that spot, besides a slightly flat plane of sand in the bunker. Holly had nosed the shuttle deep into the dry sand and left the shield powered on. Artemis only found it himself with the help of the bike's navigation systems.

He collapsed the scooter into a Frisbee-size disk and climbed down through the roof hatch.

Mulch Diggums was idly swiveling himself in the pilot's chair.

"That's my scooter, Mud Boy," he said. "That came off the trolley, so I take it with me."

Artemis shut the hatch behind him. "Where's the lemur? Where's Jayjay?"

Mulch answered these questions with some of his own. "Where's Holly? Have you lost her?"

"Yes," Artemis admitted miserably. "The boy outwitted me. He knew we would come for the lemur. He sacrificed it to get Holly."

"Smart," said Mulch. "Anyway, I'm off, see you . . ."

"See you? *See you*? One of your fairy comrades is in danger and you're just going to desert her?"

Mulch raised his palms. "Hey, calm down, Mud Boy. The LEP are not my comrades. We had a deal: I get you the little furry fellow and you get me a trolley of LEP tech goodies. Job done, both parties happy."

At that moment Jayjay poked his head around the bathroom door.

"What's he doing in there?"

Mulch grinned. "Take two guesses."

"Lemurs cannot use advanced plumbing."

"See for yourself. Whatever's in there, I'm blaming Jayjay."

He clicked his furry fingers, and the lemur ran along his arm, onto his head.

"See? He accepts responsibility." Mulch frowned. "You're not going to trade this fellow for Captain Short, are you?"

"No point," said Artemis, accessing the LEP central database. "It would be like trying to trade a hairpin for Excalibur."

Mulch chewed his lip. "I'm familiar with the Excalibur story, so I know what you're trying to say there. A hairpin is useless, Excalibur is wonderful, and so on. But in some instances a hairpin is extremely useful. Now, if you had said a *rubber* hairpin . . . Do you see what I'm getting at?"

Artemis ignored him, tapping furiously at the V-board that had appeared in front of him. He needed to know everything he could about the Extinctionists, and Foaly had an extensive file on them.

Mulch tickled Jayjay under the chin. "I was getting pretty fond of Captain Short, against my better judgment. I suppose I could dig in and rescue her."

This was a genuine offer and a fair point, so Artemis spared a moment to address it.

"Not possible. Kronski has seen the tunnel rescue before and he won't fall for it again. At any rate, you wouldn't survive the temperature during the day. Even underground you wouldn't be safe. The earth is so dry that cracks can penetrate up to fifty feet in open ground. One pinprick of midday sun and you would crisp like an old book in a furnace."

Mulch winced. "Now you see *that* image works really well. So what are you going to do?"

Artemis used the advanced fairy technology to print a leopard print card with an Extinctionists' hologram flashing silver and purple in the center.

"I'm going to the Extinctionists' banquet tonight," he

said, flicking the card with his forefinger. "After all, I have been invited. All I need is a disguise and some medical supplies."

Mulch was impressed. "That's very good. You're almost as devious as I am."

Artemis turned back to the V-board. It would take time to firm up his cover.

"You have no idea," he said.

The night of the Extinctionists' banquet was upon him, and Kronski's nerves were frazzled. He danced around his chalet wearing nothing but a bath towel, anxiously humming his way through the tunes from *Joseph and the Amazing Technicolor Dreamcoat*. Kronski often dreamed that *he* was wearing the technicolor coat, and it was fashioned from the pelts of all the animals he had hunted to extinction. He always awoke smiling.

Everything has to be perfect. This is the biggest night of my life. Thank you, little Ah-temis.

There was a lot riding on this conference, and the banquet generally set the tone for the entire weekend. Pull off something big at the banquet trial and the members would be buzzing about it for days. The Internet would be alive with chatter.

And it doesn't get any bigger than a brand-new sentient species. The Extinctionists are about to go global.

And just in time. Truth be told, the Extinctionists were

old news. Subscriptions were dropping off, and for the first time since its inception, the conference was not a total sellout. In the beginning it had been wonderful, so many exciting species to hunt and nail to the wall. But now countries were protecting their rare animals, especially the big ones. There was no flying to India for a tiger shoot anymore. And the sub-Saharan nations took it extremely badly if a group of well-armed Extinctionists showed up in one of their reserves and began taking potshots at elephants. It was getting to the point where government officials were refusing bribes. *Refusing bribes.*

There was another problem with the Extinctionists, though Kronski would never admit it aloud. The group had become a touchstone for the lunatic fringe. His heartfelt hatred for the animal kingdom was attracting bloodthirsty crazies who could not see past putting a bullet in a dumb beast. They could not grasp the philosophy of the organization. Man is king, and animals survive only so long as they contribute to the comfort of their masters. An animal without use is wasting precious air and should be wiped out.

But this new creature changed everything. Everyone would want to see her. They would film the entire trial and execution, leak the tape, and then the world would come to Damon Kronski.

One year of donations, thought Kronski. Then I retire to enjoy my wealth. Five million. This fairy, or whatever it is, is worth ten times that. A hundred times.

Kronski jiggled in front of the air conditioner for a minute then selected a suit from his wardrobe.

Purple, he thought. Tonight I shall be emperor.

As an afterthought he plucked a matching tasseled Caspian tiger-skin hat from an upper shelf.

When in Fez, he thought brightly.

The Fowl Lear Jet, 30,000 Feet Over Gibraltar

Ten-year-old Artemis Fowl tried his best to relax in one of the Lear jet's plush leather chairs, but there was a tension knot at the base of his skull.

I need a massage, he thought. Or some herbal tea.

Artemis was perfectly aware what was causing the tension.

I have sold a creature . . . a person . . . to the Extinctionists.

Being as smart as he was, Artemis was perfectly capable of constructing an argument to justify his actions.

Her friends will free her. They almost outsmarted me, they can certainly outsmart Kronski. That fairy creature is probably on her way back to wherever she came from right now, with the lemur under her arm.

Artemis distracted himself from this shaky reasoning by concentrating on Kronski.

Something really should be done about that man.

A titanium PowerBook hummed gently on Artemis's

fold-out tray. He woke the screen and opened his personal Internet browser program that he had written as a school project. Thanks to a powerful and illegal antenna in the jet's cargo bay, he was able to pick up radio, television, and Internet signals almost anywhere in the world.

Organizations like the Extinctionists live and die on their reputations, he thought. It would be an amusing exercise to destroy Kronski's reputation using the power of the Web.

All it would take was some research and the placement of a little video on a few of the Net's more popular networking sites.

Twenty minutes later Artemis junior was putting the finishing touches to his project when Butler ducked through the cockpit door.

"Hungry?" asked the bodyguard. "There's some hummus in the fridge, and I made yogurt-and-honey smoothies."

Artemis embedded his video project onto the final Web site.

"No, thank you," mumbled Artemis. "I'm not hungry."

"That will be the guilt gnawing at your soul," said Butler candidly, helping himself from the fridge. "Like a rat on an old bone."

"Thank you for the simile, Butler, but what's done is done."

"Did we have to leave Kronski the weapon?"

"Please, I put remote-destruct charges in my hardware,

do you really think such an advanced race will leave their technology unprotected? I wouldn't be surprised if that gun is melting in Kronski's hands. I had to leave it as a sweetener."

"I doubt the creature is melting."

"Stop this, Butler. I made a deal and that's the end of it."

Butler sat opposite him. "Hmm. So you are governed by some sort of code now. Honor among criminals. Interesting. So what's that you're cooking up on your computer?"

Artemis rubbed the tense spot on his neck. "Please, Butler. All of this is for my father. You know it must be done."

"One question," said Butler, ripping the plastic from a cutlery set. "Would your father want it to be done this way?"

Artemis did not answer, just sat and rubbed his neck.

Five minutes later Butler took pity on the ten-year-old. "I thought we might turn the plane around and give those strange creatures a little help. Fez Saïss airport has reopened, so we could be back there in a couple of hours."

Artemis frowned. It was the right thing to do, but it was not on his agenda. Returning to Fez would not save his father.

Butler folded his paper plate in half, trapping the debris from his meal inside.

"Artemis, I would like to swing the jet around, and I

intend to do that unless you instruct me not to. All you need to do is say the word."

Artemis watched his bodyguard return to the cockpit, but said nothing.

Morocco

The Domaine des Hommes was buzzing with limo-loads of Extinctionists coming in from the airport, each one wearing their hatred for animals on their sleeve, or on their heads or feet. Kronski spotted a lady sporting thigh-high Ibex boots. Pyrenean, if he wasn't mistaken. And there was old Jeffrey Coontz-Meyers with his quagga-backed tweed jacket. And Contessa Irina Kostovich, her pale neck protected from the evening chill by a Honshu wolf stole.

Kronski smiled and greeted each one warmly and most by name. Every year there were fewer newcomers to the ranks, but that would all change after the trial tonight. He skipped along toward the banquet hall.

The hall itself had been designed by Schiller-Haus in Munich, and was essentially a huge prefabricated kit, which arrived in containers and was erected by German specialists in less than four weeks. Incredible, really. It was an impressive structure, more formal in appearance than the chalets, which was only proper, as serious business was conducted inside. Fair trials and then executions.

Fair trials, thought Kronski, and giggled.

The main doors were guarded by two burly Moroccan gentlemen in evening wear. Kronski had considered crested jumpsuits for the guards, but dismissed the idea as too Bond.

I am not Dr. No. I am Dr. No-Animals.

Kronski breezed past the guards, down a corridor carpeted with sumptuous local rugs, and into a double-height banquet hall with a triple-glazed glass roof. The stars seemed close enough to reach out and capture.

The decor was a tasteful blend of classic and modern. Tasteful except for the gorilla-paw ashtrays on each table and the row of elephant-foot champagne coolers on stands outside the kitchen doors. Kronski squeezed through the double doors, past a brushed-steel kitchen, to the walk-in freezer at the rear.

The creature sat flanked by three more guards. She was cuffed to a plastic baby chair borrowed from the compound's creche. Her features were alert and sullen. Her weapon lay out of reach on a steel trolley.

If looks were bullets, thought Kronski, picking up the tiny weapon and weighing it on his palm, I would be riddled.

He pointed the weapon at a frozen ham hock hanging on a chain and pulled the tiny trigger. There was no kickback and no obvious flash of light, but the ham was now steaming and ready to serve.

Kronski raised the violet-colored sunglasses that he wore day and night, to make sure his vision was accurate.

"My goodness," he said in wonderment. "This is quite a toy."

He stamped on the steel floor, sending a bong reverberating through the chamber.

"No tunneling out this time," he announced. "Not like at the souk. Do you speak English, creature? Do you know what I am saying to you?"

The creature rolled her eyes.

I would answer you, her expression said, *but there is tape across my mouth*.

"And for good reason," said Kronski, as though the sentence had been spoken aloud. "We know all about your hypnotism tricks. And the invisibility." He pinched her cheek as one would a cute infant. "Your skin feels almost human. What are you? A fairy, is that it?"

Another eye roll.

If eye-rolling were a sport, this creature would be a gold-medal winner, thought the doctor. Well, perhaps silver medal. Gold would surely go to my ex-wife, who's no slacker in the eye-rolling department herself.

Kronski addressed the guards. "*Est-ce qu'elle a bougé?*" he asked. "Has she moved?"

The men shook their heads. It was a stupid question. How could she move?

"Very well. Good. All proceeds according to my plan."

Now Kronski rolled his own eyes. "Listen to me. *All proceeds according to my plan.* That is *so* Doctor No. I should go and get myself some metal hands. What do you think, gentlemen?"

"Metal hands?" said the newest guard, unaccustomed to Kronski's rants. The other two were well aware that many of the doctor's questions were rhetorical, especially the ones about Andrew Lloyd Webber or James Bond.

Kronski ignored the new guy. He placed a finger on pursed lips for a moment, to communicate the importance of what he was about to say, then took a deep whistling breath through his nose.

"Okay, gentlemen. Everyone listening? This evening couldn't be more important. The future of the entire organization depends on it. Everything must be totally perfect. Do not take your eyes off the prisoner and do not remove her restraints or gag. No one is to see her until the trial begins. I paid five million in diamonds for the privilege of a grand reveal, so no one gets in here but me. Understood?"

This was not a rhetorical question, though it took the new guy a moment to realize it.

"Yes, sir. Understood," he blurted, a fraction after the other two.

"If something does go wrong, then your final job of the evening will be burial duty." Kronski winked at the new guard. "And you know what they say: last in first out."

* * *

The atmosphere at the banquet was a little jaded until the food arrived. The thing about Extinctionists was that they were picky eaters. Some hated animals so much that they were vegetarians, which limited the menu somewhat. But this year Kronski had managed to poach a chef from a vegetarian restaurant in Edinburgh who could do things with a zucchini that would make the most hardened carnivore weep.

They started with a subtle tomato-and-pepper soup in baby turtle shells. Then a light parcel of roast vegetables in pastry with a dollop of Greek yogurt, served in a monkey-skull saucer. All very tasty, and by now the wine was relaxing the guests.

Kronski's stomach was so churned with nerves that he could not eat a single bite, which was most unusual for him. He hadn't felt this giddy since his very first banquet in Austin all those years ago.

I am on the verge of greatness. Soon my name will be mentioned in the same sentence as Bobby Jo Haggard or Jo Bobby Saggart. The great evangelist Extinctionists. Damon Kronski, the man who saved the world.

Two things would make this banquet the greatest ever held.

The entrée and the trial.

The entrée would delight everyone, meat-eaters and vegetarians alike. The vegetarians could not eat it, but at least they could marvel at the artistry it took to prepare the dish.

Kronski tapped a small gong beside his place setting and stood to introduce the dish, as was the custom.

"Ladies and gentlemen," he began. "Let me tell you a story of extinction. In July 1889, Professor D. S. Jordan visited Twin Lakes in Colorado and published his discoveries in the 1891 Bulletin of the United States Fish Commission. He found what he proclaimed to be a new species, the yellowfin cutthroat. In his report Jordan described the fish as silvery olive with a broad lemon-yellow shade along the sides, lower fins bright golden yellow, and a deep red dash on each side of the throat, hence the "cutthroat." Until about 1903, yellowfin cutthroats survived in Twin Lakes. The end for the yellowfin came soon after the introduction of the rainbow trout to Twin Lakes. Other trout interbred with the rainbows, but the yellowfins quickly disappeared and are now completely extinct."

Nobody shed a tear. In fact, there was a smattering of applause for the *E* word.

Kronski raised a hand. "No, no. This is not a cause for joy. It is said that the yellowfin was a very tasty fish, with a particularly sweet flavor. What a pity we shall never taste it." He paused dramatically. "Or shall we . . . ?"

At the rear of the room a large false wall slid aside to reveal a red velvet curtain. With great ceremony, Kronski drew a remote control from his jacket and zapped the curtain, which pulled back with a smooth swish. Behind it was an enormous trolley bearing what appeared to be a miniature glacier. Silver and steaming.

The guests sat forward, intrigued.

"What if there had been a flash freeze more than a hundred years ago in Twin Lakes?"

A twittering began among the diners.

No.

Surely not.

Impossible.

"What if a frozen chunk of lake had been trapped by a landslide deep in an uncharted crevasse and was kept solid by near zero currents."

Then that would mean . . .

Inside that chunk . . .

"What if that chunk surfaced a mere six weeks ago on the land of my good friend Tommy Kirkenhazard. One of our own faithful members."

Tommy stood to take a bow, waving his Texas gray wolf Stetson. Though his teeth were smiling, his eyes were shooting daggers at Kronski. It was obvious to the entire room that there was bad blood between the two.

"Then it would be possible, outrageously expensive, and difficult, but possible to transport that chunk of ice here. A chunk that contains a sizeable shoal of yellowfin cutthroat trout." Kronski drew breath to allow this

240

information to sink in. "Then we, dear friends, could be the first people to eat yellowfin in a hundred years."

This prospect even had a few of the vegetarians salivating.

"Watch, Extinctionists. Watch and be amazed."

Kronski clicked his fingers, and a dozen kitchen staff wheeled the ponderous trolley into the center of the banqueting area, where it rested on a steel grille. The workers then stripped off their uniforms to reveal monkey costumes underneath.

Have I gone over the top with the monkey rigs? Kronski wondered. Is it just too Broadway?

But a quick survey of his guests assured him that they remained enthralled.

The kitchen staff were actually trained circus acrobats from one of the Cirque du Soleil knockoffs touring north Africa. They were only too glad to take a few days out of their schedule to put on this private show for the Extinctionists.

They swarmed up the huge ice block, anchoring themselves on with ropes, crampons, or grappling hooks, and began demolishing it with chainsaws, flaming swords, and flamethrowers, all produced seemingly from nowhere.

It was a spectacular indulgence. Ice flew, showering the guests, and the buzz of machinery was deafening.

Quickly the shoal of yellowfin poked through the blue murk of ice. They hung, wide-eyed and frozen in midturn, their bodies caught by the flash freeze.

What a way to go, thought Kronski. With absolutely no inkling. Wonderful.

The performers began carving the fish in blocks from the ice, and each one was passed down to one of a dozen line cooks, who had appeared from the side doors wheeling gas burners. Each individual block was slid into a heated colander to steam off excess ice, then the fish were expertly filleted and fried in olive oil with a selection of chunky cut vegetables and a crushed clove of garlic.

For the vegetarians there was a champagne mushroom risotto, though Kronski did not anticipate many takers. The nonmeat eaters would accept the fish just to stab it.

The meal was a huge success, and the level of delighted chatter rose to fill the hall.

Kronski managed to eat half a fillet, in spite of his nerves.

Delicious. Exquisite.

They think that was the highlight, he thought. They ain't seen nothing yet.

After coffee, when the Extinctionists were loosening their cummerbunds or turning fat cigars for an even burn, Kronski instructed his staff to set up the courtroom.

They responded with the speed and expertise of a Formula One pit team, as well they should after three months of being whipped into shape. Literally. The team of workers swarmed across the grid where the melted ice sloshed below like a disturbed swimming pool, a few stray yellowfins floating on the surface. They covered this section of floor and exposed a second pit, this one lined with steel and covered with scorch marks.

Two podiums and a dock were wheeled into the center of the hall, taking the place of the ice trolley. The podiums had computers on their swivel tops, and the wooden dock was occupied by a cage. The cage's resident was masked by a curtain of leopard skin.

The diners' chatter ceased as everybody held their breath for the big reveal. This was the moment everyone had waited for, these millionaires and billionaires paying through the nose for a few moments of ultimate power: holding the fate of an entire species in their hands, showing the rest of the planet who was boss. The guests did not notice the dozen or so sharpshooters placed discreetly on the upper terrace in case the creature on trial displayed any new magical powers. There was little chance of a subterranean rescue, as the entire hall was built on a foundation of steel rods and concrete.

Kronski milked the moment, rising slowly from his seat and sauntering across to the prosecutor's podium.

He steepled his fingers, allowing the moment to build, then began his presentation.

"Every year we put a rare animal on trial."

There were a few hoots from the audience, which Kronski waved away good-naturedly.

"A *real* trial, where the host prosecutes, and one of you lucky people gets to defend. The idea is simplicity. If you can convince a jury of your unprejudiced peers . . ."

More hooting.

". . . that the creature in this cage contributes positively to human existence on this planet, then we will free the creature, which, believe it or not, did happen once in 1983. A little before my time, but I am assured that it actually happened. If the defense counsel's peers are not convinced of the animal's usefulness, then I press this button." And here, Kronski's bulbous fingers twiddled playfully with an oversize red button on his remote control. And the animal drops from its cage into the pit, passing the laser eye beam, which activates the gas-powered flame jets. Voilà, instant cremation.

"Allow me to demonstrate. Indulge me; it's a new pit. I've been testing it all week."

He nodded at one of the staff, who yanked up a section of the grid with a steel hook. Kronski then picked a melon from a fruit platter and tossed it into the pit. There was a beep followed by an eruption of blue-white flame gouts from nozzles ranged around the pit walls. The melon was burned to black floating crisps.

The display drew an impressed round of applause, but not everyone appreciated Kronski's grandstanding.

Jeffrey Coontz-Meyers cupped both hands around his mouth. "Come on, Damon. What have we got tonight?

Not another monkey. Every year it's monkeys."

Generally interruptions would irritate Kronski, but not tonight. On this night all hectoring, however witty, would be swept from people's memories the second that curtain was drawn aside.

"No, Jeffrey, not another monkey. What if—"

Jeffrey Coontz-Meyers groaned vocally. "Please, no more *what if's*. We had half a dozen with the fish. Show us the blasted creature."

Kronski bowed. "As you wish."

He thumbed a button on his remote control, and a large view screen descended from the rafters, covering the back wall. Another button pushed, and the curtain concealing the caged creature swished smoothly to one side.

Holly was revealed, cuffed to the baby chair, her eyes darting and furious.

At first the main reaction was puzzlement.

Is it a little girl?

It's just a child.

Has Kronski gone mad? I knew he sang to himself, but this?

Then the Extinctionists' eyes were drawn to the screen, which was displaying a feed from a camera clamped to the cage.

Oh my lord. Her ears. Look at her ears.

She's not human.

What is that? What is it?

Tommy Kirkenhazard stood. "This'd better not be a

hoax, Damon. Or we'll string you up."

"Two points," said Kronski softly. "First, this is no hoax. I have unearthed an undiscovered species; as a matter of fact, I believe it to be a fairy. Second, if this was a hoax, you would not be stringing anyone up, Kirkenhazard. My men would cut you down before you could wave that ridiculous hat of yours and shout 'Yee-haw.'"

Sometimes it was good to send a shiver down people's spines. Remind them where the power was.

"Of course, your skepticism is to be expected, welcomed, in fact. To put your minds at rest, I will need a volunteer from the audience. How about you, Tommy? How's that backbone of yours?"

Tommy Kirkenhazard gulped down half a glass of whiskey to bolster his nerves, then made his way to the cage.

Good performance, Tommy, thought Kronski. It's almost as if we hadn't arranged this little confrontation to give me a bit more credibility.

Kirkenhazard stood as close to Holly as he dared, then reached in slowly to tweak her ear.

"My saints, it's no fake. This is the real deal." He stood back, and the truth of what was happening filled his face with joy. "We got ourselves a fairy."

Kirkenhazard rushed across to Kronski's podium and pumped his hand, clapping his back.

And so my biggest critic is converted. The rest will follow like sheep. Useful animals, sheep.

Kronski silently congratulated himself.

"I will prosecute the fairy, as is the tradition," Kronski told the crowd. "But who will defend? What unlucky member will draw the black ball. Who will it be?"

Kronski nodded at the maître d'.

"Bring the bag."

Like many ancient organizations, the Extinctionists were bound by tradition, and one of these traditions was that the creature on trial could be defended by any member of the assembly, and if no member was willing, one would be chosen by lottery. A bag of white balls, with one black. The spherical equivalent of the short straw.

"No need for the bag," said a voice. "I will defend the creature."

Heads turned to locate the speaker. It was a slender young man with a goatee and piercing blue eyes. He was wearing tinted glasses and a lightweight linen suit.

Kronski had noticed him earlier, but could not put a name to the face, which disturbed him.

"And you are?" he asked, while swiveling his laptop so that the built-in camera was aimed at this stranger.

The young man smiled. "Why don't we give your identification software a moment to whisper the answer to you."

Kronski thumbed ENTER, the computer captured an image, and five seconds later it plucked membership details from the Extinctionists' file.

Malachy Pasteur. Young French-Irish heir to an abattoir empire. Made a sizeable donation to the Extinctionists' coffers. His first conference. As with all attendees, Pasteur was thoroughly vetted before his invitation was issued. A valuable addition to the ranks.

Kronski was all charm.

"Mr. Pasteur. We are delighted to welcome you to Morocco. But tell me, why would you wish to defend this creature? Her fate is almost certainly sealed."

The young man walked briskly to the podium. "I enjoy a challenge. It is a mental exercise."

"Defending *vermin* is an exercise?"

"*Especially* vermin," retorted Pasteur, lifting the lid on his laptop. "It is easy to defend a servile, useful animal like the common cow. But this? This will be a hard-fought battle."

"A pity to be crushed in battle so young," said Kronski, his lower lip hanging with mock sympathy.

Pasteur drummed his fingers on the podium. "I have always liked your style, Dr. Kronski. Your commitment to the ideals of Extinctionism. For years I have followed your career, since I was a boy in Dublin, in fact. Lately, however, I feel that the organization has lost its way, and I am not the only one with this feeling."

Kronski ground his teeth. So that was it. A naked challenge to his leadership.

"Be careful what you say, Pasteur. You tread on dangerous ground."

Pasteur glanced at the floor below him where ice water still sloshed in the pit beneath. "You mean I could sleep with the fishes? You would kill me, Doctor? A mere boy? I don't think that would bolster your credibility much."

He's right, fumed Kronski. I can't kill him. I must win this trial.

The doctor forced his mouth to smile. "I don't kill *humans*," he said. "Just animals. Like the animal in this cage."

Kronski's many supporters applauded, but that still left many silent.

I was wrong to come here, Kronski realized. It is too remote. Nowhere for private jets to land. Next year I will find somewhere in Europe. I will announce the move as soon as I crush this whelp.

"Allow me to explain the rules," continued Kronski, thinking, *Explaining the rules puts me in charge and gives me the upper hand, psychologically speaking.*

"No need," said Pasteur brusquely. "I have read several transcripts. The prosecutor puts his case, the defender puts his case. A few minutes of lively debate, then each table votes. Simple. Can we please proceed, Doctor. No one here appreciates their time being wasted."

Clever, young man. Putting yourself on the same side as the jury. No matter. I know these people, and they will never acquit a beast, no matter how pretty she is.

"Very well. We shall proceed." He selected a document on

his desktop. His opening statement. Kronski knew it by heart, but it was comforting to have the words easily accessible.

"People say that we Extinctionists hate animals," began Kronski. "But this is not the case. We do not hate poor dumb animals; rather, we love humans. We love humans and will do whatever it takes to ensure that we, as a race, survive for as long as possible. This planet has limited resources, and I, for one, say we should hoard them for ourselves. Why should humans starve when dumb animals grow fat? Why should humans freeze when beasts lie toasty warm in their coats of fur?"

Malachy Pasteur made a noise somewhere between a cough and a chuckle. "Really, Dr. Kronski, I have read several variations on this speech. Every year, it seems, you trot out the same simplistic arguments. Can we please focus on the creature before us tonight?"

A tittering ripple spread among the banquet guests, and Kronski had to struggle to contain his temper. It seemed he had a battle on his hands. Very well, then.

"Most amusing, boy. I was going to take it easy on you, but now the gloves are off."

"We are delighted to hear it."

We? We?

Pasteur was swinging the Extinctionists his way without their even knowing it.

Kronski summoned every last drop of charisma from inside himself, flashing back to his youth, to those long summer days spent watching his evangelist daddy whip up the crowds inside a canvas tent.

He raised his arms high, each finger bent back until the tendons strained.

"This is not what we are about, people," he thundered. "We did not travel all this way for some petty verbal sparring. *This* is what the Extinctionists are about." Kronski pointed a rigid finger at Holly. "Ridding our planet of creatures like this."

Kronski shot a sideways glance at Pasteur, who was leaning chin on hands, a bemused look on his face. Standard opposition behavior.

"We have a new species here, friends. A *dangerous* species. It can make itself invisible, it can hypnotize through speech. It was *armed*."

And to much oohing from the crowd, Kronski drew forth Holly's Neutrino handgun from his pocket.

"Do any of us wish to face a future where this could be pointed in our faces? Do we? The answer, I think, is clearly no. Now, I'm not going to pretend that this is the last one of its kind. I feel certain that there are thousands of these fairies, or aliens, or whatever, all around us. But does that mean we should grovel and release this little creature? I say no. I say we send a message. Execute one, and the rest will know we mean business. The governments of the world despise us now, but tomorrow they will come banging down our door for guidance."

Time for the big finish. "We are Extinctionists, and our time is now!"

It was a good speech and drew wave after wave of applause, which Pasteur rode out with the same bemused expression.

Kronski accepted the applause with a boxer's rolling of the shoulders, then nodded toward the opposite podium.

"The floor is yours, boy."

Pasteur straightened and cleared his throat . . .

. . . Artemis straightened and cleared his throat. The fake beard glued to his chin itched like crazy, but he resisted the impulse to scratch it. In a fair arena he would destroy Kronski's arguments in about five seconds, but this was not a fair arena, or even a sane one. These people were bloodthirsty, jaded billionaires, using their money to buy illicit excitement. Murder was just another service that could be purchased. He needed to handle this crowd carefully. Push the right buttons. First of all he had to establish himself as one of them.

"When I was young, and the family wintered in South Africa, my grandfather would tell me stories of a time when people had the right attitude toward animals. 'We kill 'em when it suits us,' he said to me. 'When it serves our purposes.' This is what the Extinctionists used to be about. A species was not *protected* unless we humans benefited from its survival. We kill when it *benefits* us. If an animal is using the planet's resources and not directly contributing to our health, safety, and comfort, we wipe it out. Simple as that. This was an ideal worth fighting for. Worth killing for. But this . . ." Artemis pointed at the pit below him and Holly in her cage. "This is a circus. This is an insult to the memory of our ancestors who gave their time and gold to the Extinctionists' cause."

Artemis worked hard on his eye contact, connecting with as many people as possible in the audience, lingering for a moment with each one.

"We have an opportunity to learn from this creature. We owe it to our predecessors to find out if she can contribute to our coffers. If this is, in reality, a fairy, then who knows what magic it possesses? Magic that could be yours. If we kill this *fairy*, we will never know what unimaginable wealth dies with it."

Artemis bowed. He had made his point. It would not be enough to sway the bloodthirsty Extinctionists, he knew, but it might be enough to make Kronski feel a little less cocky.

The doctor was waving his hands before the echo of Artemis's voice had faded.

"How many times must we listen to this argument?" he wondered. "Master Pasteur accuses me of repeating myself, while he repeats the tired argument of every defense counsel we have ever listened to." Kronski tapped his lips in horror. "Ooh, let us not kill the creature, for it is potentially the source of all our power and wealth. I remember spending a fortune on a sea slug that was supposed to cure arthritis. All we got was very expensive goo. This is all supposition."

"But this creature is magical," objected Artemis, banging the podium with his fist. "We have all heard how she can turn invisible. Even now her mouth is taped so she cannot hypnotize us. Imagine the power we could wield if we were to unlock the secrets of these gifts. If nothing else, they would better prepare us to deal with the rest of her kind."

Kronski's main problem was that he agreed with much of his opposition's argument. It made perfect sense to save the creature and tease her secrets from her, but he could not afford to lose this argument. If he did, he might as well hand over the leadership.

"We have tried to interrogate her. Our best men tried, and she told us nothing."

"It is difficult to talk with a taped mouth," Artemis noted drily.

Kronski drew himself to his full height, lowering the timbre of his voice for effect. "The human race faces its most deadly enemy, and you want to cozy up to it. That is not how we Extinctionists do things. If there is a threat, we wipe it out. That is how it has always been."

This brought a roar of approval from the crowd; bloodlust trumps logic every time. Several members were

254

on their feet, hollering. They'd had enough of the argument and wanted some action.

Kronski's face was flushed with victory.

He thinks it's over, thought Artemis. Poor man. And then: *This beard really itches.*

He waited calmly until the furor had trailed away, then came out from behind the podium. "I was hoping to spare you this, Doctor," he said. "Because I respect you so much."

Kronski flapped his lips. "Spare me what, Master Pasteur?"

"You know what. I think you have pulled the wool over everyone's eyes long enough."

Kronski was not in the least worried. The boy was beaten and everything else was was just irritating chatter. Still, why not let Pasteur dig a hole for himself?

"And what wool would that be?"

"Are you certain you want me to continue?"

Kronski's teeth glittered when he smiled. "Oh, absolutely certain."

"As you wish," said Artemis, approaching the dock. "This creature was not our original defendant. Up until yesterday we had a lemur. Not quite a monkey, Mr. Coontz-Meyers, but close enough. I say we had a lemur, but in truth we *almost* had a lemur. It went missing at the pickup. Then, and this is important, then we were sold this creature by the *same* boy who sold us the lemur, undoubtedly paid for from Extinctionists' funds. Does anyone else think this is a little off? I do. This boy keeps his lemur and sells us a supposed fairy."

Kronski was not so cocky now. This Pasteur fellow had a lot of information.

"*Supposed* fairy?"

"That's right. Supposed. We have only your word for it, and of course that of Mr. Kirkenhazard, who apparently is your worst enemy. Nobody is falling for that ruse, I assure you."

"Examine the thing yourself," blurted Kronski, glossing over the Kirkenhazard accusation. "This is an easy argument to win."

"Thank you, Doctor," said Artemis. "I believe I shall."

Artemis approached the cage. This was the tricky part, as it required sleight of hand and coordination, which were the elements in every plan that he usually left to Butler.

His pocket bulged slightly with a couple of adhesive nu-skin bandages taken from Mulch's medi-kit. He had told the security guard that they were nicotine patches and so had been allowed to bring them through to the banquet. The bandage adhesive was activated by skin contact, and it molded itself to the contours it was applied to, assuming the color and texture of the surrounding skin.

Artemis's fingers hovered over his pocket, but it was not yet time to touch a bandage. It would simply stick to his own hand. Instead he reached into his other pocket for the phone he had stolen from the Bentley, back at Rathdown Park.

"This phone is invaluable to me," he told the Extinctionists. "It's a little bulkier than other phones, but that is because I have been installing add-ons for years. This phone is an amazing thing, really. I can stream television, watch movies, check my stocks, all the standard stuff. But I also have an X-ray camera and display. Just give me a second." Artemis pressed a few buttons, linking the phone by Bluetooth to the laptops, and from there to the large view screen.

"Ah, here we are," Artemis said, passing the phone in front of his hand. On screen an arrangement of phalanges, metacarpals, and carpals stood out darkly inside a pale foam of flesh. "You see the bones of my hand quite clearly. This is a very good projection system you have, Dr. Kronski. I congratulate you."

Kronski's smile was as fake as the congratulations had been.

"Do you have a point, Pasteur, or are you just showing us how clever you are?"

"Oh, I have a point, Doctor. And that point is, that were it not for the width of the brow and the pointed ears, this creature seems remarkably like a little girl."

Kronski snorted. "A pity about the ears and brow. But for them you would have an argument."

"Precisely," said Artemis, and passed the phone before

Holly's face. On screen, he played a short movie file he had constructed back in the shuttle. It showed Holly's skull with dark, dense shapes on her temples and ears.

"Implants," crowed Artemis. "Clearly the result of surgery. This *fairy* is a clever fake. You have tried to dupe us, Kronski."

Kronski's denials were lost in the roar of the crowd. The Extinctionists surged to their feet, decrying this despicable con job.

"You lied to me, Damon!" shouted Tommy Kirkenhazard, with something like anguish. "To *me*."

"Put *him* in the pit," called Contessa Irina Kostovich, her face as feral as that of the Honshu wolf on her shoulder. "Make *Kronski* extinct. He deserves it for dragging us here."

Kronski upped the volume on his podium mike. "This is ridiculous. If you have been tricked, then so have I. No! I will not believe it. This boy, this Pasteur, is lying. My fairy is real. Just give me a chance to prove it."

"I have not finished, Doctor," cried Artemis, stepping boldly to the dock. In both hands he held a Nu-skin patch, slipped into his palms during the confusion. He could feel pinpricks of heat on his flesh as the adhesive was activated. He had to act quickly or his plans would be reduced to two flesh-colored pads on his own hands.

"These ears do not seem right to me. And your friend Mr. Kirkenhazard was most gentle with them."

Artemis scrunched one Nu-skin patch into a rough cone, sealing the adhesive on itself. He thrust the other hand through the bars and made a great show of tugging on the tip, while in reality spreading the second bandage over Holly's ear, covering the entire tip and most of the auricle.

"It's coming away," he grunted, making sure to mask the cage's camera with his forearm. "I have it."

Seconds later the bandage was dry, and one of Holly's ears was totally obscured. Artemis looked her in the eye and winked.

Play along, the wink said. *I will get you out of this.*

At least Artemis hoped this was what his wink communicated and not something like *Any chance of another kiss later?*

Back to business.

"It's a fake," called Artemis, holding high the crumpled flesh-colored bandage. "It came off in my hand."

Holly obligingly presented her profile to the Webcam. No more pointed ear.

Outrage was the dominant reaction from the Extinctionists.

Kronski had tricked them all, or worse, he had been bamboozled by a boy.

Artemis held the supposed fake ear aloft, squeezing it as though he were strangling a poisonous snake.

"Is this the man we want to lead us? Has Dr. Kronski displayed sound judgment in this case?"

Artemis threw the "ear" into the watery pit. "And *supposedly* this creature can hypnotize us all. I rather think her mouth is covered so she cannot speak."

With one sharp movement he ripped the tape from Holly's mouth. She winced and shot Artemis a dour glare, but then quickly dissolved into tears, playing the part of human victim to perfection.

"I didn't want to do it," she sobbed.

"Do what?" Artemis prompted.

"Dr. Kronski took me from the orphanage."

Artemis raised an eyebrow. *The orphanage?* Holly was ad-libbing.

"He told me if I had the implants, then I could live in America. After the operation I changed my mind, but the doctor wouldn't let me go."

"An orphanage," said Artemis. "Why, that's bordering on the unbelievable."

Holly's chin dropped. "He said he'd kill me if I told."

Artemis was outraged. "He said he'd kill you. And this is the man steering our organization. A man who hunts humans as well as animals." He pointed an accusing finger at a bewildered Kronski. "You, sir, are worse than the creatures we all despise, and I demand you release this poor girl."

Kronski was finished, and he knew it. But something could still be salvaged from this mess. He still had the group's account numbers, and he was the only one with the combination to the compound safe. He could be out of this place in two hours with enough riches to last a few years. All he had to do was somehow stop this Pasteur boy hamming it up.

And then he remembered. *Ham!*

"And what about this?" he shouted, brandishing Holly's gun. "I suppose this is fake too."

The Extinctionists drew back, cowering behind their seats.

"Absolutely," sneered Artemis. "A child's toy. Nothing more."

"Would you stake your life on it?"

Artemis appeared to hesitate. "N . . . no need for dramatics, Doctor. Your cause is lost. Accept it."

"No," snapped Kronski. "If the gun is real, then the creature is real. And if she is not real, as you insist, then you have nothing to fear."

Artemis summoned his courage. "Very well, do your worst." He stood squarely before the tiny needle barrel, offering his chest.

"You are about to die, Pasteur," said Kronski, without much sympathy.

"Perhaps I would be, if you could squeeze your chubby finger into the trigger guard," said Artemis, almost as if he were goading the doctor into action.

"To hell with you then!" barked Kronski, and pulled the trigger.

Nothing much happened. A spark and a slight hum from the inner workings.

"It's broken," gasped the doctor.

"You don't say," said Artemis, who had remote-destructed the Neutrino's charge pack from the shuttle.

Kronski raised his palms. "Okay, boy. Okay. Give me a moment to think."

"Just let the girl go, Doctor. Save a shred of dignity. We don't execute humans."

"I am in charge here. I just need a second to gather myself. This wasn't supposed to happen. This is not how she said it would go. . . ."

The doctor rested his elbows on the lectern, rubbing his eyes beneath the round, tinted spectacles.

How *she* said it would go? thought Artemis. Were there unseen forces at work here?

While Artemis was puzzling and Kronski's world collapsed around his ample shoulders, cell phones began to ring in the banquet hall. A lot of people were receiving messages all of a sudden. In moments the room rang with a discordant symphony of beeps, *brrr's*, and polyphonic tunes.

Kronski ignored this strange development, but Artemis was anxious. He had things under control now and did not need anything to redress the scales, or for that matter, tip Kronski over the edge.

The reactions to the incoming messages were a mixture of shock and glee.

Oh my God. Is this true? Is it real?

Play it again. Turn up the volume.

I don't believe this. Kronski, you fool.

That's the last straw. We are a joke. The Extinctionists are finished.

Artemis realized that all these messages were in fact the same message. Someone had an Extinctionists database and was sending them all a video.

Artemis's own phone trilled gently. Of course it would; he had put his fake identity on every Extinctionist database he could find. And as his phone was still linked to the giant screen, the video mail began to play automatically.

Artemis recognized the scene immediately. The leather souk. And the main player was Kronski, standing on one leg, squealing with a high-pitched ruptured-balloon intensity. Comical was not the word for it. Ridiculous, farcical, and pathetic were words that came close. One thing was certain, having seen this video, no one in their right mind could respect this man ever again, much less follow his lead.

While the video played, a short message scrolled below the picture.

Here we see Dr. Damon Kronski, president of

• ⧊ ⧉ ⬡ • ⚿ ⬡ ⧗ ⚏ ⧉ • ⬡ ⧊ • ⬡ ⚿ ⌇ •

the Extinctionists, displaying surprising balance for a man his size. This reporter has learned that Kronski turned against animals when he was mauled by an escaped koala at one of his politician father's rallies in Cleveland. Witnesses to the mauling say that young Damon "squealed so sharp he coulda cut glass." A talent the good doctor does not seem to have lost. Squeal, baby, squeal!

Artemis sighed. I did this, he realized. It's just the kind of thing I would do.

At another time he would have appreciated this touch, but not now. Not when he was so close to freeing Holly.

Speaking of Holly . . .

"Artemis, get me out of here," she hissed.

"Yes, of course. Time to go."

Artemis rifled through his pockets for a handy wipe. Inside the wipe were three long coarse hairs donated by Mulch Diggums. Dwarf hairs are actually antennae that dwarfs use to navigate in dark tunnels, and have been adapted by the resourceful race to serve as skeleton keys. No doubt Holly's omnitool would have been handier, but Artemis could not risk losing that to security. The wipe had kept the hairs moist and pliable until they were needed.

Artemis removed the first hair, blew a speck of

moisture from its tip, and inserted it into the cage lock, working it through the cogs. As soon as he felt the hair harden in his fingers, he turned the makeshift key and the door sprang open.

"Thank you, Mulch," he whispered, then went to work on Holly's centrally locked cuffs. The third hair would not even be needed. In seconds, Holly was free and rubbing her wrists.

"Orphanage?" said Artemis. "You don't think that was overdoing it?"

"Boo-hoo," said Holly briskly. "Let's just get back to the shuttle."

It was not to be that straightforward.

Kronski was being herded into a corner by a group of Extinctionists. They harangued and even slapped and poked the doctor, ignoring his arguments, while overhead the video message played again and again.

Oops, thought Artemis, closing his phone.

Inevitably perhaps, Kronski cracked. He batted his tormentors aside like bowling pins, clearing a circle of breathing space for himself, then, panting, he pulled a walkie-talkie from a clip on his belt. "Secure the area," he wheezed into the device. "Use all necessary force."

Even though the Domaine des Hommes security were technically working for the Extinctionists, their loyalties lay with the man who paid their salaries. That man was Damon Kronski. He might dress like a demented peacock and have the manners of a desert dog, but he knew the combination to the safe and paid the wages on time.

The sharpshooters on the upper terrace sent a few warning shots over the heads of the crowd, which caused utter pandemonium.

"Lock the building down," said Kronski into the walkie-talkie. "I need time to gather my funds. Ten thousand dollars in cash for every man who stands by me."

There was no need for further incentive. Ten thousand dollars was two years' wages to these men.

Doors and shutters were slammed down and manned by burly guards, each one brandishing a rifle or a custom-made Moroccan nimcha sword with rhino grips, which Kronski had made for the security team.

The spooked Extinctionists bolted toward bathrooms or alcoves, anywhere that might have a window. They frantically punched numbers into their phones, screaming for help from anyone, anywhere.

A few were more resourceful. Tommy Kirkenhazard pulled out a ceramic handgun he had smuggled in under his hat and took a few potshots at the upper terrace from behind a heavy teak bar. He was answered by a volley from above with shattered bottles, mirrors, and glasses sending slivers flying like arrowheads.

With a straight-fingered jab to the solar plexus, a tall Asian man quickly disarmed a door guard.

"This way!" he called, flinging the fire door wide. The portal was quickly jammed with Extinctionist torsos.

Artemis and Holly sheltered behind the cage, watching for a way out.

"Can you shield?"

Holly twisted her chin, and one arm rippled out of sight. "I'm low on juice. I have just about enough for a minute or two. I've been saving it."

Artemis scowled. "You are always low on juice. Didn't N°1 fill you up with his signature magic?"

"Maybe if your bodyguard hadn't plugged me with a dart—twice. Maybe if I hadn't had to heal you at Rathdown Park. And maybe if I hadn't been shielding in the souk, trying to find your monkey."

"Lemur," said Artemis. "At least we saved Jayjay."

Holly ducked as a hail of glass shot over her head. "My goodness, Artemis. You sound like you actually care about an animal. Nice beard, by the way."

"Thank you. Now, do you think you could shield for long enough to disarm those two guards on the kitchen door behind us?"

Holly sized the two men up. Both had shotguns and were radiating enough malevolence to ripple the air. "Shouldn't be a problem."

"Good. Do it quietly. We don't want another bottleneck. If we do get separated, let's meet somewhere close. At the souk."

"Okay," said Holly, vibrating into invisibility.

A second later Artemis felt a hand on his shoulder and heard a disembodied voice in his ear.

"You came for me," whispered Holly. "Thank you."

Then the hand was gone.

All magic has a price. When fairies shield, they sacrifice fine motor skills and clear thought. It is infinitely more difficult to do a jigsaw when your body is vibrating faster than a hummingbird's wings, even if your brain could stop rattling for long enough to focus on the puzzle.

In the LEP Academy, Holly had picked up a tip from an Atlantean gym coach. It really helped to beat the shield-shakes if you sucked your lower abdominals in and up, strengthening your core. It gave you something to focus on and held your torso a little tighter.

Holly practiced the exercise as she crossed the banquet floor toward the kitchen. As a frantic butter-knife-wielding Extinctionist missed her by a shade, she thought that sometimes being invisible was more dangerous than being in plain sight.

The two guards at the door were actually growling at anyone who ventured too close. They were big, even for humans, and Holly was glad that no fine motor skill would be called for. Two quick jabs into the nerve cluster above the knee should be plenty to bring these guys down.

Simple, thought Holly, then: *I shouldn't have thought*

that. Whenever you think that, something goes wrong.

Of course she was dead right.

Someone started firing on Kronski's guards. Silver darts streaked through the air, then punctured skin with a sickening thunk.

Holly knew instinctively who the shooter was, and her suspicions were confirmed when she spotted a familiar silhouette anchored in the roof beams.

Butler!

The bodyguard was draped in a desert blanket, but Holly identified him from the shape of his head and also from his unmistakable shooting position: left elbow cocked out a little more than most marksmen preferred.

Young Artemis sent him back to clear a path for us, she realized. *Or maybe Butler made the decision himself.*

Whichever it was, Butler was not helping as much as he'd hoped. With the guards dropping, the Extinctionists were piling over their fallen captors, desperate to be free of this building.

Caged Extinctionists, thought Holly. *I'm sure Artemis appreciates that irony.*

Just as Holly drew back her fists, the two guards at the kitchen door clutched their necks and pitched forward, unconscious before they hit the floor.

Nice shooting. Two shots in under a second from eighty yards out. With darts too, which are about as accurate as wet sponges.

She was not the only one to notice the unguarded door. A dozen hysterical Extinctionists rushed the portal, screaming like rock-band fans.

We need to exit this building. Now.

Holly turned toward Artemis, but he was lost in a clump of advancing Extinctionists.

He must be somewhere in there, she thought; then she was pinned by the mob, borne aloft and into the kitchen.

"Artemis," she called, completely forgetting that she was still invisible. "Artemis!"

But he was nowhere to be seen. The world was a melee of elbows and torsos, sweat and screams. Voices were in her ears and ragged breath on her face, and by the time she had disentangled herself from the pack, the banquet hall was virtually deserted. A few stragglers, but no Artemis.

The souk, she thought. I will find him in the souk.

Artemis tensed himself to run. As soon as Holly took the guards out of commission, he would sprint as fast as he could and pray that he didn't trip and fall.

Imagine, to endure all of this, only to be defeated by a lack of coordination. Butler would be sure to say *I told you so* when they met in the afterlife.

Suddenly the pandemonium level jumped a few notches, and the screaming of the Extinctionists reminded Artemis of Rathdown Park's panicked animals.

Caged Extinctionists, he thought. Oh, the irony.

The kitchen door guards fell, clutching their throats.

Nice work, Captain.

Artemis bent low, like a sprinter waiting for the gun, then catapulted himself from his hiding place behind the dock.

Kronski hit him broadside with his full weight, tumbling them both through the railings into the dock. Artemis landed heavily on the baby chair, and it collapsed underneath him, one of its arms raking along his side.

"This is all your fault," squealed Kronski. "This was supposed to be the best night of my life."

Artemis felt himself being smothered. His mouth and nose were jammed by sweat-soaked purple material.

He intends to kill me, thought Artemis. I have pushed him too far.

There was no time for planning, and even if there were, this was not one of those situations where a handy mathematical theorem could be found to get Artemis out of his predicament. There was only one thing to do: lash out.

So Artemis kicked, punched, and gouged. He buried his knee in Kronski's ample stomach and blinded him with his fists.

All very superficial blows that had little lasting effect—except one. Artemis's right heel brushed against Kronski's chest. Kronski didn't even feel it. But the heel connected briefly with the oversize button on the remote control in the doctor's pocket, releasing the dock trapdoor.

The second his brain registered the loss of back support, Artemis knew what had happened.

I am dead, he realized. Sorry, Mother.

Artemis fell bodily into the pit, breaking the laser beam with his elbow. There was a beep, and half a second later the pit was filled with blue-white flame, which blasted black scorch marks in the walls.

Nothing could have survived.

Kronski braced himself against the dock rails, perspiration dripping from the tip of his nose into the pit, evaporating on the way down.

Do I feel bad about what just happened? he asked himself, aware that psychologists recommended facing trauma head-on in order to avoid stress later in life.

No, he found. I don't. In fact, I feel as though a weight has been lifted from my shoulders.

Kronski raised himself up with a great creaking and cracking of knees.

Now, where's the other one? he wondered. I still have some weight to lose.

Artemis saw the flames blossom around him. He saw his skin glow blue with their light and heard their raw roar, then he was through, unscathed.

Impossible.

Obviously not. *Obviously* these flames had more bark about them than bite.

Holograms?

The pit floor yielded beneath his weight with a hiss of pneumatics, and Artemis found himself in a sub-chamber, looking up at heavy steel doors swinging closed above him.

The view from inside a swing-top bin.

A very high-tech swing-top bin, with expanding gel hinges. Fairy design, without a doubt.

Artemis remembered something Kronski had said earlier.

This is not how she said it would go. . . .

She . . . She . . .

Fairy design. Endangered species. What fairy had been harvesting lemur brain fluid even before the Spelltropy epidemic?

Artemis paled. Not her. Please, not her.

What do I have to do? he thought. How many times must I save the world from this lunatic?

He scrambled to his knees and saw he had been funneled onto a padded pallet. Before he could roll off, octobonds sprang from recessed apertures along the pallet's steel rim, trussing him tighter than a tumbled rodeo cow. Purple gas hissed from a dozen overhead nozzles, shrouding the pallet.

Hold your breath, Artemis told himself. Animals don't know to hold their breath.

He held on until it felt as though his sternum would split, and then just as he was about to exhale and suck in a huge breath, a second gas was pumped into the chamber, crystallizing the first. It fell onto Artemis's face like purple snowflakes.

You are asleep now. Play possum.

A small door sank smoothly into the floor, with a sound like air being blown through a straw.

Artemis peeked through one half-closed eye.

Magnetic field, he thought dully, a band of steel creasing his forehead.

I know what I will see, but I have no wish to see it.

A pixie stood framed by the doorway, her tiny, beautiful features twisted with their customary pouting cruelty.

"This," squealed Opal Koboi, pointing a vibrating finger, "is not a lemur."

CHAPTER 13

THE HAIRY ONE IS DEAD

The Leather Souk

Butler jogged from the Extinctionists' compound to the leather souk. Artemis was waiting in the building where they had planned the previous day's exchange. Police presence in Fez amounted to no more than a couple of two-man patrols, and so it was easy for someone of Butler's experience to sneak around without being detected. Though it was hardly illegal to visit a medina, it was certainly frowned on to stroll around a tourist area with a large rifle strapped to one's back.

Butler ducked into a dark corner and quickly broke down his dart rifle into almost a dozen parts, slotting them into various garbage bins. It was possible that he could slip the Fez Saïss Airport customs men some *baksheesh* and simply stow the weapon under his seat, but these days it was better to be safe than sorry.

Ten-year-old Artemis was sitting at a prearranged spot in one of the sniper windows, picking nonexistent lint from his jacket sleeve, which was his version of nervous pacing.

"Well?" he asked, steeling himself for the answer.

"The female got out," said Butler. He thought it better not to mention that the long-haired male had everything under control until Artemis's video arrived.

Artemis caught the implication. "The female? The other one was there too?"

Butler nodded. "The hairy one is dead. He attempted a rescue, and it didn't work out."

Artemis gasped.

"Dead?" he said. "Dead?"

"Repeating the word won't change its meaning," said Butler sharply. "He tried to rescue his friend, and Kronski killed him for it. But what's done is done, eh? And at least we have our diamonds."

Butler checked his temper. "We should move out for the airport. I need to run the preflight checks."

Artemis was left stunned and silent, unable to take his eyes from the bag of diamonds, which winked accusingly from their slouched perch on his lap.

Holly was not having any luck. Her shield was so weak that she switched it off to save her last spark for a small healing if it was needed; and no sooner had her image solidified than one of Kronski's goons spotted her and walkie-talkied his entire squad. Now she was running for her life through the medina, praying that Artemis was at the meeting point and that he had thought to bring the scooter.

No one was taking potshots at her, which was encouraging, unless Kronski wanted to do the potshotting himself.

No time to think about that now. Survival was the priority.

The medina was quiet this late in the evening, with only a few straggling tourists and die-hard merchants still walking the streets. Holly dodged between them, pulling down whatever she could reach to get in the way of the stampede of security men behind her. She tugged over towers of baskets, upended a kebab stand, and shouldered a table of spices, dashing a white wall with multicolored arcs.

The thunder of footsteps behind her did not recede in the least. Her tactics were not working. The security guards were simply too large and were bustling past the obstacles.

Dodge and weave, then. Lose them in the alleyways.

This tactic was no more succesful than the last. Her pursuers were familiar with the medina's layout and coordinated their pursuit on handheld radios, herding Holly toward the leather souk.

Where I'll be in the open. An easy target.

Holly raced on, Artemis's loafers cutting into her heels. A series of cries and curses arose behind her as she barged without apology through bands of tourists and shoulder-slammed tea boys, sending trays flying.

I am corralled, she thought desperately. You'd better be waiting, Artemis.

It occurred to Holly that she was leading the posse directly to Artemis, but there was no other option. If he was waiting, then he could help; if not, she was on her own anyway.

She jinked left, but four huffing guards blocked the alleyway, all hefting vicious long-bladed knives.

The other way, I think.

Right, then. Holly skidded into the leather souk, heels throwing up dust fans.

Where are you, Artemis?

She cast her gaze upward toward their observation point, but there was nothing there. Not even the telltale shimmer of a hide.

He's not here.

She felt panic scratch at her heart. Holly Short was an excellent field officer, but she was way out of her jurisdiction, her league, and her time.

The leather souk was quiet now, with only a few workers scraping skins on the surrounding rooftops. Lanterns crackled below the roofline, and the giant urns

lurked like alien pods. The smell was just as bad as it had been the previous day, possibly worse, as the vats had had longer to cook. The stench of droppings hit Holly like a soft, feverish glove, further addling her mind.

Keep running. Find a nook.

Holly spent half a moment considering which body part she would trade for a weapon, then sprinted for a doorway in the adjacent wall.

A guard appeared, dragging his knife from its sheath. The blade was red. Maybe blood, maybe rust. Holly switched direction, losing a shoe in the turn. There was a window one floor up, but the wall was cracked: she could make the climb.

Two more guards. Grinning. One held a net, like a gladiator.

Holly skidded to a halt.

We're in the desert! Why does he have a fishing net?

She tried again. An alleyway barely broad enough for an adult human. She was almost there when a fat guard with a ponytail to his waist and a mouthful of yellowed teeth wedged himself into the avenue, blocking it.

Trapped. Trapped. No escape and not enough magic to shield. Not even enough to mesmerize.

It was difficult to stay calm, in spite of all her training and experience. Holly could feel her animal instincts bubbling in the pit of her stomach.

Survive. Do what you have to do.

But what could she do? One unarmed child-size fairy against a squadron of armed muscle.

They formed a ragged circle around her, weaving between the urns in a slow-motion slalom. Each set of greedy glittering eyes focused on her face. Closer and closer they came, spreading their arms wide in case their prey made a dart for freedom.

Holly could see their scars and pockmarks, see the desert in their nails and on their cuffs. Smell their breath and count their fillings.

She cast her eyes toward the heavens.

"Help," she cried.

And it began to rain diamonds.

Below the Extinctionists' Compound

"That is not a lemur," repeated Opal Koboi, drumming a tiny toe on the floor. "I know it is not a lemur because it has no tail and it seems to be wearing clothes. This is a human, Mervall. A Mud Boy."

A second pixie appeared in the doorway. Mervall Brill. One of the infamous Brill brothers who would break Opal out of her padded psych cell some years later. His expression was a mixture of puzzlement and terror. Not pretty on any face.

"I don't understand it, Miss Koboi," he said, twiddling the top button on his crimson lab coat. "It was all set up for the lemur. You *mesmerized* Kronski yourself."

Opal's nostrils flared. "Are you suggesting this is somehow my fault?" She clutched her throat as if the very idea caused her breath to fail.

"No, no, no," said Mervall hurriedly. "It could not be Miss Koboi's fault. Miss Koboi is, after all, perfection itself. Perfection does not make mistakes."

This outrageous statement would be recognized as blatant toadying by right-minded people, but Opal Koboi found it fair and rational.

"Exactly. Well said, Mervall. A pity your brother does not have a tenth of your wisdom."

Mervall smiled and shuddered. The smile was in acceptance of the compliment; the wince was because the mention of his twin had reminded him that his brother was at this moment locked in a cage with a red river hog, as punishment for not complimenting Opal's new boots.

Miss Koboi was having a bad day. Currently, two out of seven were bad. If things got any worse, even though the wages were astronomical, the Brill brothers would be forced to seek alternative employment.

Mervall decided to distract his boss. "They're going crazy up there. Firing weapons. Dueling with cutlery. Those Extinctionists are an unstable lot."

Opal leaned over Artemis and sniffed gently, wiggling her fingers to see if the human was awake.

"The lemur was the last one. I was *this* close to being all-powerful."

"How close?" asked Mervall.

Opal squinted at him. "Are you being funny?"

"No. I sincerely wondered. . . ."

"It's an expression," snapped the pixie, striding back toward the main chamber.

Mervall nodded slowly. "An expression. I see. What should I do with the human?"

Opal did not break her stride. "Oh, you might as well harvest him. Human brain fluid is a good moisturizer. Then we pack up and find that lemur ourselves."

"Should I dump his drained corpse in the animal pit?"

Opal threw up her arms. "Oh, for heaven's sake. Must I tell you how to do everything? Can't you show a little initiative?"

Mervall wheeled the pallet after his boss.

The animal pit it is, then, he thought.

The Leather Souk

Diamonds rained down in glittering showers. Falling stars twinkling in the lamplight.

Young Artemis's fee, Holly realized. He is throwing me a lifeline.

For a moment the guards were transfixed. Their faces wore the dazed expression of children who have woken and are surprised to find themselves in a good mood. They stretched out their fingers, watching the diamonds bounce and tumble.

Then one broke the spell. *"Des diamants!"* he cried.

Hearing the word spoken aloud galvanized his companions. They dropped to their knees, patting the dusky ground for the precious stones. More dived into the pungent vats as they registered tiny plops made by stones impacting on liquid.

Mayhem, thought Holly. Perfect.

She glanced upward just in time to see a small hand withdraw into the black rectangle of a window.

What made him do it? she wondered. That was a most un-Artemislike gesture.

A guard diving past her leg reminded her that things were still pretty dire.

In their greed, they have forgotten me, but perhaps they will remember their duty when the stones are pocketed.

Holly spared a moment to salute up at young Artemis's window, then raced out of his view toward the nearest alley, only to be flattened by a puffing Damon Kronski.

"Two for two," he huffed. "I got both of you. This must be my lucky day."

When will this end? thought Holly incredulously. How can these things continue to happen?

Kronski pressed down on her like an enraged elephant,

frown lines framing his tinted glasses, sweat flowing in sheets down his face, dripping from his pouting lip.

"Except, this is *not* my lucky day, is it," he shouted, a keen note of hysteria on the edge of his tone. "You saw to that. You and your accomplice. Well, my gas chamber took care of him. Now I will take care of you!"

Holly was stunned.

Artemis dead?

She would not believe it. Never. How many people had written Artemis Fowl off and lived to regret it? Plenty. She was one of them.

Holly, on the other hand, was proving easier to kill. Her vision was blurring, her limbs were treading water, and the weight of the world was on her chest. The only sense firing on all cylinders was her sense of smell.

What a way to go. Inhaling motes of pigeon droppings with your last breath.

She heard her ribs groan.

I wish Kronski could smell this.

An idea sparked in her brain, the last ember in a dying grate.

Why shouldn't he smell it? It's the least I can do.

Holly reached deep into her core of magic, searching for that last spell. There was a flicker deep inside. Not enough to shield, or even *mesmerize*, but perhaps a minor healing.

Usually healing spells were used on recent wounds, but

Kronski's anosmia was a lifelong ailment. Fixing it now could be dangerous and would almost certainly be painful.

Oh well, thought Holly. If it hurts him, it hurts him.

She reached up a hand past the forearm on her throat, inching it along Kronski's face, willing the magic into her fingertips.

Kronski did not feel threatened. "What's this? Are you playing 'got your nose'?"

Holly did not answer. Instead she closed her eyes, jammed two fingers up Kronski's nostrils, and sent her last sparks of magic down those channels.

"Heal," she said. A wish and a prayer.

Kronski was surprised but not initially upset.

"Hey, what the . . ." he said, then sneezed. The sneeze was powerful enough to pop his ears and roll him off his captive. "What are you, five years old? Sticking fingers up my nose." Another sneeze. Bigger this time. Blowing a trumpet of steam from each nostril.

"This is pathetic. You people are really—"

A third sneeze, this one traumatizing the entire body. Tears streamed down Kronski's face. His legs jittered and his glasses shattered in their frames.

"Oh my," said Kronski, when he had his limbs under control. "Something's different. Something has changed."

Then the smell hit him.

"Aarrgh," said Kronski, then began to squeal. His

tendons tightened, his toes pointed, and his fingers ripped holes in the air.

"Wow," said Holly, massaging her throat. This was a stronger reaction than expected.

The smell was bad, but Kronski acted like he was dying. But what Holly did not fully grasp was the power of the doctor's awakened sense of smell. Imagine the joy of seeing for the first time, or the euphoria of a first step. Then square that feeling and make it negative. Take a ball of poison, dip it in thorns and manure, wrap it in a poultice of festering bandages, boil the whole lot in a cauldron of unspeakably vile excretions, and shove it up your nose.

This is what Kronski could smell, and it was driving him out of his mind.

He lay flat on his back, flinching and pawing the sky.

"Foul," he said, repeating the word over and over. "Foul, foul. Fowl, Fowl."

Holly crawled to her knees, coughing and spitting onto the dry sand. Her entire being felt battered and bruised from back to spirit. She looked at Kronski's expression and realized that there was no point in asking him questions. The president of the Extinctionists was beyond logical conversation for the time being.

Possibly for good, she thought. I don't see him leading any international organizations for a while.

Holly noticed something. One of Kronski's lenses had

completely shattered, revealing the eyeball underneath. The iris was a strange violet, almost the same shade as the spectacles had been, but this was not what caught Holly's attention. The edge of the retina was ragged, as though it had been nibbled on by tiny sclera fish.

This man has been *mesmerized*, Holly realized. A fairy is controlling him.

She climbed to her feet and hobbled one-shoed down the nearest alley, the voices of squabbling greed fading behind her.

If a fairy is involved, then nothing is as it seems. And if nothing is as it seems, then perhaps Artemis Fowl still lives.

Below the Extinctionists' Compound

Mervall Brill winked at himself in the chrome door of a body freezer.

I am a handsome chap, he thought. And this lab coat covers the paunch rather well.

"Brill!" called Opal from her office. "How is that brain fluid coming?"

Merv jumped. "Just sucking him dry now, mistress."

The pixie put his weight behind the trolley with its human cargo, trundling it down a short corridor to the lab itself. Being stuck in this tiny facility with Opal Koboi was no picnic. Just the three of them for weeks on end, draining the fluids from endangered species. Opal could afford to hire a thousand lab assistants to work for her, but she was uberparanoid about secrecy. Opal's level of paranoia was such that she had begun to suspect plants and inanimate objects of spying on her.

"I can grow cameras!" she had shrieked at the Brill brothers during one briefing. "Who's to say that despicable centaur Foaly hasn't succeeded in splicing surveillance equipment to plants? So get rid of all the flowers. Rocks, too. I don't trust them. Sullen little *blëbers*."

So the Brill twins had spent an afternoon scouring the facility for anything that might contain a bug. Even the recycling toilet scent blocks had to go, as Opal was convinced they were photographing her when she used the facilities.

Still, though, Mistress Koboi is right to be paranoid, Merv admitted as he barged through the lab double doors. If the LEP ever found out what she was doing here, they would lock her up forever and a day.

The double doors led to a long triple-height laboratory. It was a place of misery. Cages were stacked to the ceiling, each one filled with a trapped animal. They moaned and keened, rattling their bars, butting the doors. A robot food-pellet dispensing machine whirred along the network, spitting gray pellets into the appropriate cages.

The center island was a series of operating pallets. Scores of animals lay sedated on the tables, secured, like Artemis, with rigid octobonds. Artemis caught sight of a

Siberian tiger, paws in the air and bald patches shaved into its skull. On each patch there sat what looked like a tiny slice of liver. As they passed, one of the slices made a squelching sound, and a tiny light emitting diode on its ridge flashed red.

Merv stopped to peel it off, and Artemis saw to his horror that the thing's underside was spiked with a dozen dripping spines.

"Full to the brim, Mr. Super Genetically Modified Leech Mosquito thing. You are a disgusting abomination, yes you are. But you sure know how to siphon brain fluid. I'd say you're due for a squeezing."

Merv pumped a foot pedal to open a nearby fridge and finger-tinkled the beakers inside until he found the right one.

"Here we go. SibTig BF."

He placed the beaker on a chrome work surface, then squeezed the leech like a sponge until it surrendered its bounty of brain fliud. Afterward the leech was casually tossed into the trash.

"Love you lots," said Mervall, returning to Artemis's pallet. "Miss you loads."

Artemis saw everything though the slit of an open eye. This was a depraved, horrible place, and he had to get out of here.

Holly will come for me, he thought, and then: *No, she won't. She'll think I'm dead.*

This realization chilled his blood.

I went into the flames.

He would have to save himself, then. It would not be the first time. Stay alert; a chance will come and you must be ready to take it.

Mervall found room on the operating section and parked Artemis neatly in it.

"And he squeezes it into an impossible space. They said it couldn't be done. They were wrong. Mervall Brill is the king of trolley parking." The pixie belched. "Which is not the future I had in mind for myself as a younger pixie."

Then, somewhat moodily, he trawled a low-level aquarium with a perforated jug, until it was full of convulsing superleeches.

Oh no, thought Artemis. Oh, please.

And then he was forced to close his eyes as Mervall turned to face him.

Surely he will see my chest heaving. He will sedate me, and it will all be over.

But Mervall apparently did not notice. "Ooh, I hate you guys. Disgusting. I tell you something, human, if your subconscious can hear me, be glad you're asleep, because you do *not* want to go through this awake."

Artemis almost cracked then. But he thought of his mother, with less than a day left to her, and he kept silent.

He felt his left hand being tugged, and heard Mervall grunt.

"Stuck tight. Just a tick."

The grip loosened, and Artemis tracked Mervall's movement with his ears and nose. A brush of soft belly on his elbow. Breath blowing past his ear. Mervall was at his left shoulder, reaching across.

Artemis opened his right eye just enough to roll his pupil into the slit. There was an operating light directly overhead, craned in above the operating table on a thick flat chrome arm.

Chrome. Reflective.

Artemis watched Mervall's actions in the surface. The pixie tapped the octobond's touch-sensitive control pad, revealing a Gnommish keyboard. Then, singing a popular pixie pop song, he tapped in his password. One number with each beat of the chorus.

"'Pixies rock hard!'" he sang. "'Extreme pixie hard rock, baby.'"

Which seemed unlikely to Artemis, but he was glad of the song, as it gave him time to file Mervall's pass code.

Mervall released one of the bonds, allowing him to extend Artemis's forearm. Even if the human did happen to wake up, all he could do was flail.

"Now, my little leech, do your nasty work for Aunt Opal, and I will reward you by squeezing your innards into a bucket." He sighed. "Why are all my best lines wasted on annelids?"

He plucked a leech from the jug, pinched it to make the

spines stick out, then slapped it onto Artemis's exposed wrist.

Artemis felt nothing but an immediate sense of well-being.

I'm being sedated, he realized. An old troll trick. Cheer you up before you die. It's a good trick, and anyway, how bad can dying be? My life has been one trial after another.

Mervall was checking his chronometer. His brother had been in that recycling cage behind the galley for an awfully long time. That red river hog might decide to have himself a bite of pixie meat.

"I'll just check," he decided. "Be back before the leech is full. First blood, then brain. You should have complimented Mistress Opal's boots, brother."

And off he toddled down the center aisle, plucking the mesh of each cage as he passed, driving the animals wild.

"'Pixies rock hard!'" he sang. "'Extreme pixie hard rock, baby.'"

Artemis was finding it hard to motivate himself. It felt so easy lying on the pallet, just letting all his troubles run out of his arm.

When you decide to die, Artemis thought sluggishly, it doesn't matter how many people want to kill you.

He did wish the animals would calm down. Their chattering and chirping were interfering with his mood.

There was even a parrot somewhere, squawking a phrase. "Who's your mama?" it asked over and over again. "Who's your mama?"

My mama is Angeline. She's dying.

Artemis's eyes opened.

Mama. Mother.

He lifted his free arm and bashed the unwelcome leech against one of the octobonds. It exploded in a spatter of mucus and blood, leaving half a dozen spines jutting from Artemis's arms like the spears of tiny soldiers.

That's going to hurt eventually.

Artemis's throat was dry, his neck was twisted, and his vision was impaired, but even so, it took him barely a minute to activate the keypad with Mervall's code and retract the bonds.

If these are alarmed, I'm in trouble.

But there was no siren. No pixies came running.

I have time. But not much.

He picked the spines from his skin, wincing not from pain, but from the the sight of the red-rimmed holes in his wrist. A rivulet of blood ran from each wound, but it was slow and watery. He would not bleed to death.

Coagulant in the spines. Of course.

Artemis zombie-walked across the lab, gradually straightening out the kinks. There were hundreds of eyes on him. The animals were silent now, noses, beaks, and snouts pressed against the wire mesh, waiting to see what would develop. The only sound came from the food-pellet robot zipping through its routine.

All I need to do is escape. No need for confrontation or saving the world. Leave Opal be, and run away.

But of course in the world of Artemis Fowl, things are rarely straightforward. Artemis donned network goggles he found hanging from a low peg, activated the V-board, and used Mervall's password to log on to the network. He needed to know where he was and how to get out.

There were design plans to the entire facility stored on a desktop file. No security, no encryption. Why would there be? It wasn't as if any of the humans above would wander down, and even if they did, humans could not read Gnommish.

Artemis studied the plans with care and growing anxiety. The facility consisted of a series of interconnected modules housed in ancient tunnels beneath the Extinctionists' compound, but there were only two ways out. He could go out the way he had come in, which was not ideal, as it led straight back up to Kronski. Or he could choose the shuttleport on the lower level, which would mean stealing and piloting a shuttle. His chances of overriding complicated theft-prevention safeties before Opal had him vaporized were minimal. He would have to go up.

"Do you like my little laboratory?" said a voice.

Artemis stared past the goggle display. Opal stood before him, hands on hips.

"Quite a place, isn't it?" she continued in English. "All these tunnels were just here, waiting for us. Perfect. As soon as I found them, I knew I had to have them, which is why I persuaded Dr. Kronski to move here."

Information is power, thought Artemis. Don't give her any.

"Who are you?" he asked.

"I am the future queen of this world, at the very least. You may refer to me as Mistress Koboi for the next five minutes. After that you may refer to me as *Aaaaarrrrgh*, hold your throat, die screaming, and so on."

As pompous as I remember.

"I seem to be bigger than you, Mistress Koboi. And as far as I can see, you have no weapons."

Opal laughed. "No weapons?" she cried, spreading her arms. "These creatures have given me all the weapons I need." She stroked the sleeping tiger. "This big kitty augments my mind control. Those sea slugs focus my energy beams. A shot of liquidized dolphin fin mixed with just the right amount of cobra venom turns the clock back a hundred years."

"This is a weapons factory," breathed Artemis.

"Exactly," said Opal, gratified that *someone* finally understood. "Thanks to these animals and their fluids, I have become the most powerful magician since the demon warlocks. The Extinctionists have been rounding up the creatures I need. Fools. Tricked by a cheap blast of holographic flames. As if I would kill these wonderful creatures before I drained their juices. You humans are such idiots. Your governments spend their fortunes looking for power, when all the time it is cavorting around your jungles."

"That's quite a speech," said Artemis, wiggling his fingers, tapping the V-board that only he could see.

"Soon I will be—"

"Don't tell me, soon you will be invincible."

"No, actually," said Opal, with admirable patience. "Soon I will be able to manipulate time itself. All I need is the . . ."

And suddenly everything fell into place for Artemis. Everything about this whole affair. And he knew he would be able to escape.

"The lemur. All you need is the lemur."

Opal clapped. "Exactly, you bright Mud Boy. That wonderful lemur brain fluid is the last ingredient I need for my magic boosting formula."

Artemis sighed. "Magic boosting formula? Listen to yourself."

Opal missed the mocking tone, possibly because she didn't hear it a lot. "I had a whole bunch of lemurs before, but the LEP appropriated them to cure some plague, and I lost the rest in a fire. All my test subjects gone, and their fluids are quite impossible to replicate. There is *one* left, and I need him. He is my cloning model. With that lemur

I will control time itself." Opal stopped speaking for a moment, tapping her bow lips with a finger. "Wait a moment, human. What do you know of my lemur?" She took the finger away from her mouth and ignited a pulsing sphere of flame at its tip, melting her nail varnish. "I asked you, what do you know of my lemur?"

"Nice boots," said Artemis, then selected an option on the goggle screen with a flick of his finger.

Are you sure you wish to open all the cages? asked the computer.

The Extinctionists were sneaking back into the compound, led by the intrepid Tommy Kirkenhazard, who brandished his empty pistol with decidedly more bravado than he felt.

"I got stuff in that compound," he repeatedly told the mass huddled behind him. "Expensive stuff. And I ain't leaving it behind."

Most of the rest had *expensive stuff* too, and now that Kronski was catatonic in the souk, and his guards seemed to have fled with their sparkling booty, this seemed the best time to reclaim their belongings and head for the airport.

Much to Kirkenhazard's relief, the compound appeared to be utterly deserted, though the gelatinous group was spooked several times by night shadows jumping in the Moroccan wind.

I ain't never shot nothing with an empty gun, he

thought. But I don't imagine it's too effective.

They reached the door to the main hall, which hung from its frame on a single hinge.

"Okay, folks," said Kirkenhazard. "There ain't no porters around to carry our stuff, so you got to hump it yourselves."

"Oh, my lord," said Contessa Irina Kostovich, and swooned into the arms of a Scottish oil baron.

"Gather whatever you can, and we meet back here in fifteen minutes."

The contessa was muttering something.

"What was that?" asked Kirkenhazard.

"She said she has a pedicure booked for the morning."

Kirkenhazard held up a hand, listening. "No. Not that. Does anyone else hear rumbling?"

The animals charged through the open cage doors with savage glee, hopping, jumping, flying, and sliming. Lions, leopards, various monkeys, parrots, gazelles, hundreds of creatures all with one idea in mind: *Escape*.

Opal was not amused.

"I cannot believe you did that, Mud Person. I will wring your brain out like a sponge."

Artemis ducked his head low, not caring at all for the brain/sponge imagery. If he avoided Opal's regal stare, then she could not *mesmerize* him. Unless her augmented powers allowed her access to the brain without the conduit of the optic nerve.

Even if he had not ducked, he would have been shielded by the tide of creatures that engulfed him, snapping, buffeting, and kicking.

This is ridiculous, he thought as a monkey's elbow drove the air from his lungs. If Opal does not get me, the animals will. I need to direct this stampede.

Artemis squatted behind one of the operating tables, pulling out the tiger's anaesthetic drip as he passed, and squinted through the spokes of passing legs for an appropriate animal.

Opal roared at the creatures in an amalgamation of their tongues. It was a piercing sound and split the animal phalanx down the center so that it flowed around her. As the herd passed, Opal took potshots with pulsing blasts of energy that erupted from her fingers, and scythed through entire rows of creatures, knocking then senseless to the ground. Cages tumbled like building blocks, refrigerators spewed their contents across the tiles.

My distraction is being chopped down, thought Artemis. Time for an exit.

He spied a set of hooves stomping toward him, and steadied himself for a jump.

It's a quagga, he realized. Half horse, half zebra, and there hasn't been one in captivity for a hundred years. Not exactly a thoroughbred stallion, but it will have to do.

The ride was a little rougher than Artemis was accustomed to on the Fowl Arabians. No steadying stirrups, no creaking saddle, no snapping reins. Not to mention the fact that the quagga was unbroken and scared out of its wits.

Artemis patted its neck.

Ludicrous, he thought. This entire affair. A dead boy escaping on an extinct animal.

Artemis grabbed tufts of the quagga's mane and tried to direct it toward the open doorway. It bucked and kicked, whipping its striped head around to nip at Artemis with strong, square teeth. He dug in his heels and held on.

Opal was busy protecting herself from a wave of animal vengeance. Some of the larger predators were not as cowed as their cousins, and decided that the best way to remove the threat posed by Opal Koboi was to eat her.

The tiny pixie twirled like a demonic ballerina, shooting blasts of magical energy that ballooned at her shoulders, gathered force in roiling spheres at her elbows, and shot forth with liquid pulsations.

Artemis had never seen anything like it. Stricken animals simply froze in midair, their momentum utterly drained, dropping to the ground like statues, immobile but for their terrified rolling eyes.

She is powerful indeed. I have never seen a force like this. Opal must never be allowed to capture Jayjay.

Opal was running out of magic. Her bolts fizzled out or spiraled off target like errant squibs. She abandoned them and drew two pistols from her belt. One was immediately batted from her hand by the tiger that had lumbered to join the fray, but Opal did not submit to hysteria and quickly thumbed that other gun to a broad-spread setting and slashed the barrel from side to side as she fired, releasing a fan of silver energy.

The tiger was the first to drop, with a look on its face that said *Not again*. Several more followed, cut off in midscreech, howl, or hiss.

Artemis hauled back on the quagga's spiked mane, jumping it onto an operating table. The beast snorted and complained but did as it was bid, skittering the length of one table and leaping across to the next.

Opal loosed a shot in their direction, but it was absorbed by a brace of condors.

The door was directly before them, and Artemis feared the quagga would falter. But no, it butted through to the corridor connecting the lab to the holographic flame chamber.

Artemis quickly opened the control panel in his stolen network goggles and chose the ramp setting.

It took maddening moments for the platform to extend itself, and for those seconds Artemis rode the quagga around in circles to take its mind off dislodging the unwelcome rider on its back and to make them both a more difficult target if Opal followed them through the corridor.

An eagle swooped by, its feathers raking Artemis's

cheek. A muskrat clambered along his torso, hopping to the rising platform.

There was light above. The sickly wavering beams of a faulty strip light. But light nevertheless.

"Come on, girl," said Artemis, feeling very much the cowboy. "Yee-haw."

The Extinctionists gathered aroun Tommy Kirkenhazard's raised finger, listening intently as if the noise emanated from inside the finger.

"Ah, I don't hear nothing," admitted Tommy. "I must have been dreaming. After all, it's been a stressful night for human-lovers."

Then the lodge burst open, and the Extinctionists were utterly engulfed in a sea of beasts.

Kirkenhazard went down under a couple of Chacma baboons, vainly pulling the trigger on his empty gun and shouting over and over: "But we killed you, darn it. We killed you."

Though there would be no fatalities in the compound that night, eighteen people were hospitalized with bites, skin burns, broken bones, and various infestations. Kirkenhazard fared the worst. The baboons ate his gun and the hand holding it, and then turned the unfortunate man over to a groggy tiger, who found himself waking in a very bad mood.

Not one of the Extinctionists noticed a small, dark craft

rising silently from behind one of the chalets. It flew across the central park and scooped up a long-haired youth from the back of what looked like a small striped donkey. The craft spun in a tight arc like a stone in a sling, then hurtled into the night sky as though it had to be somewhere in a real hurry.

Pedicures, and indeed all spa treatments, were canceled for the next day.

Opal was desolate to find that, on top of everything else, her boots were ruined.

"What is that stain?" she demanded of Mervall and his recently liberated twin, Descant.

"Dunno," muttered Descant, who was still a bit moody from his time in the cage.

"It's a dropping of some kind," volunteered Mervall quickly. "Judging from the size and texture, I would say one of the big cats got a little nervous."

Opal sat on a bench and extended the boot. "Pull it off, Mervall."

She placed her sole on Mervall's forehead and pushed until he tumbled backward, clutching the dropping-laden footwear.

"That Mud Boy. He knows about my lemur. We must follow him. He is tagged, I take it."

"Oh yes," confirmed Mervall. "All the newcomers are sprayed on landing. There's a radioactive tracer in his every pore right now. Harmless, but there's nowhere on this planet that he can hide from us."

"Good. Excellent, in fact. I think of everything, do I not?"

"You do, mistress," droned Descant. "Brilliant, you are. Astounding is your fabulosity."

"Why, thank you, Descant," said Opal, as ever oblivious to sarcasm. "And I thought you'd be upset after the pigpen. Fabulosity isn't a word, by the way. In case you're thinking of writing how wonderful I am in your diary."

"Point taken," Descant said seriously.

Opal offered her other foot to Mervall. "Good. Now set the self-destructs on this place and let's get the shuttle prepped. I want to find this human and kill him immediately. We were too nice last time, with the leeches. This time, immediate death."

Mervall winced. He was holding two boots covered in tiger droppings, and he'd prefer to wear those than be in that human's shoes.

Artemis lay flat on his back in the cargo hold, wondering it he could possibly have dreamed the past few minutes. Superleeches, sleeping tigers, and a grumpy quagga.

He felt the floor vibrate beneath him and knew that they were moving at several times the speed of sound. Suddenly the vibration disappeared, to be replaced by a far more sedate hum. They were slowing down!

Artemis hurried to the cockpit, where Holly was glaring at a readout as if she could change the information displayed there. Jayjay was in the copilot's seat and seemed to be in charge of steering.

Artemis pointed at the lemur. "This may seem like a silly question, but is Jayjay . . ."

"No. Autopilot. And nice to see you alive, by the way. You're welcome for the rescue."

Artemis touched her shoulder. "Once again, I owe you my life. Now, I hate to move directly from gratitude to petulance, but why have we slowed down? Time is running out. We had three days, remember? There are only hours left."

Holly tapped the readout. "We were pinged by something at the compound. Someone's computers have downloaded our schematics. Can you tell me any more about that?"

"Opal Koboi," said Artemis. "Opal is behind everything. She's harvesting animal fluids to increase her own magic. If she gets her hands on Jayjay, she'll be invincible."

Holly did not have time to be incredulous. "That's wonderful. Opal Koboi. I knew this little trip was missing a psychotic element. If Opal pinged us, then she'll be on our tail in something a little more war-worthy than this clunker."

"Shields?"

"Nothing much. We might fool human radar but not fairy scanners."

"What can we do?"

"I need to keep us up here in the air lanes with all the human traffic. We stay subsonic and don't draw attention to ourselves. Then at the last moment we make a break for Fowl Manor. It won't matter if Opal sees us then, because by the time she catches us, we'll be back in the time stream."

Mulch Diggums poked his head through from the mail box. "Nothing much in here. A few gold coins. What say I keep them? And did I hear someone mention Opal Koboi?"

"Don't worry about it. Everything is under control."

Mulch guffawed. "Under control? Like Rathdown Park was under control. Like the leather souk was under control."

"You're not seeing us at our best," Artemis admitted. "But in time you will come to respect Captain Short and me."

Mulch's expression doubted it. "I'd better go and look up *respect* in the dictionary, because it mustn't mean what I think it means, eh, Jayjay?"

The lemur clapped his delicate hands and chattered with what sounded like laughter.

"It looks like you've found an intellectual equal, Mulch," said Holly, returning to her instruments. "It's a pity he isn't a girl; then you could marry him."

Mulch imitated shock. "Romance outside your species. Now *that's* disgusting. What kind of weirdo would kiss

someone when they weren't even part of the same
species?"

Artemis massaged his suddenly pounding temples.

It's a long way to Tipperary, he thought. And then a few
more miles to Dublin.

"A shuttle?" said Opal. "A fairy shuttle?"

The Koboi craft was hovering at an altitude of thirty
miles, tipping the border of space. Starlight winked on the
hull of their matte-black shuttle, and the earth hung below
them wearing a stole of clouds.

"That's what the sensors show," said Mervall. "An old
mining model. Not much under the hood, and zero
firepower. We should be able to catch it."

"Should?" said Opal, stretching an ankle to admire her
new red boots. "Why should?"

"Well, we had her for a while. Then she went subsonic.
I would guess their pilot is riding the human flight lanes
until they feel safe."

Opal smiled devilishly. She liked a challenge.

"Okay, let's give ourselves every advantage. We have the
speed and we have the weapons. All we need is to point
ourselves in the right direction."

"What an incrediferous idea." Descant smirked.

Opal was pained. "Please, Descant. Use short words.
Don't force me to vaporize you."

This was a hollow threat, as Opal had not been able to

produce so much as a spark since the compound. She still had the basics—mind control, levitation, that kind of thing—but she would need some serious bed rest before she could muster a lightning bolt. The Brills did not need to know that, though.

"Here's my idea. I ran the lab tapes through voice recognition and got a regional match. Whoever that Mud Boy is, he lives in central Ireland. Probably Dublin. I want you to get us down there as fast as you can, Descant, and when that mining shuttle drops out of the air lanes"— Opal closed her tiny fingers around an imaginary ant, squeezing the blood from its body—"We will be waiting."

"Fabulicious," said Descant.

Fowl Manor, Dublin, Ireland

The sun had risen and was sinking again by the time Holly had dragged the spluttering shuttle over the Fowl Estate wall.

"We're close to the deadline, and this piece of junk is close to dead," she said to Artemis. Holly placed a hand on her heart. "I can feel N°1's spark dying inside, but there's still time."

Artemis nodded. The sight of the manor somehow made his mother's plight seem even more urgent.

I have to go home.

"Well done, Holly. You did it. Set us down in the rear

courtyard. We can access the house by the kitchen door."

Holly pressed a few buttons. "Around the back it is. Scanning for alarms. Found two and a sneaky third. Motion sensors, if I'm not mistaken. Only one alarm is being remotely monitored, and the other two are self-contained. Should I disable the remote alarm?"

"Yes, Holly, please disable the alarm. Anybody home?"

Holly checked the thermal imaging. "One warm body. Top floor."

Artemis sighed, relieved. "Good. Just Mother. She will have taken her sleeping tablets by now. *Little me* can't be back yet."

Holly set the shuttle down as gently as she could, but the gears were stripped and the suspension bags were drained. There were dents in the stabilizers, and the gyroscope was spinning like a weather vane. The landing gear stripped a channel of cobblestones from the courtyard surface, tumbling them like bricks of turf before the plow.

Artemis gathered Jayjay in his arms.

"Are you ready for more adventures, little man?"

The lemur's round eyes were filled with anxiety, and he looked to Mulch for reassurance.

"Always remember," said Mulch, tickling the creature's chin, "that *you* are the smart one."

The dwarf found an old duffel bag and began stuffing the remaining contents of the fridge inside.

"No need for that," said Holly. "The ship is yours. Take

it, dig up your booty, and fly far away. Dump this heap in the sea and live off your earnings for a few years. Just promise me that you won't sell to humans."

"Only the junk," said Mulch. "And did you say that I could keep the shuttle?"

"Actually, I'm asking you to scrap it. You'll be doing me a favor."

Mulch grinned. "I'm a generous person. I could do you a favor."

Holly smiled back. "Good. And remember, when we meet again, none of this ever happened, or it probably won't."

"My lips are sealed."

Artemis squeezed past him. "Now, there's something I would pay to see. Mulch Diggums with his mouth closed."

"Yes, nice meeting you too, Mud Boy. I look forward to robbing you in the future."

Artemis shook his hand. "I look forward to it myself, believe it or not. We will have some fine times."

Jayjay reached out for a handshake. "You look after the human, Jayjay," said Mulch seriously. "He's a bit dim, but he means well."

"Good-bye, Mr. Diggums."

"Later, Master Fowl."

Opal was on her third round of the Gola Schweem meditative circle chant when Mervall burst into her private chamber.

"We found the shuttle, mistress," he panted, clutching a flexi-screen to his chest. "They went supersonic for barely a minute over the Mediterranean. But it was enough."

"Humm humm haaa. Rahmumm humm haaaa," intoned Opal, finishing her chant. "Peace be inside me, tolerance all around me, forgiveness in my path. Now, Mervall, show me where the filthy human is so that I may feed him his organs."

Mervall proferred the flexi-screen. "Red dot. East coast."

"Military?"

"No, surprisingly. It's a residence. No defenses whatsoever."

Opal climbed out of her snuggle-me chair. "Good. Run a few scans. Warm up the cannons and get me down there."

"Yes, mistress."

"And Mervall?"

"Mistress?"

"I think little Descant has a crush on me. He told me earlier that I was very phototractive. Poor little simpleton. Could you tell him that I am unavailable? If you don't, I shall have to have him killed."

Merv sighed. "I shall tell him, mistress. I feel sure he will be disconnipted."

Artemis found himself scratching Jayjay's head as they moved through the manor.

"Be calm, little chap. No one can hurt you now. We're safe."

Holly was behind him on the stairs, guarding the rear, two fingers rigidly extended. The fingers were not a loaded weapon, but they could break bones with enough momentum behind them.

"Come on, Artemis. Nº1 is weaker now, so we have to jump soon."

Artemis stepped around a weight-sensitive pad on the twelfth step. "Nearly there. Seconds away."

His study was exactly as he had left it, the wardrobe still open, a scarf drooping from the top shelf like an escaping snake.

"Good," said Artemis, his confidence growing. "This is the spot. The exact spot."

Holly was panting. "About time. I'm having trouble holding on to the signal. It's like running after a smell."

Artemis put an arm around her shoulder. A group of three; tired, hungry, but excited.

Holly's shoulders shook with an exhaustion and tension she had kept hidden until now.

"I thought you were dead," she said.

"Me too," admitted Artemis. "Then I realized that I couldn't die, not in this time."

"I presume you're going to explain that to me."

"Later. Over supper. Now can we open the time stream, friend?"

There was a sudden swish as the bay window curtain slid back. Young Artemis and Butler were there, both wearing foil suits. Butler unzipped his suit to reveal a large gun strapped across his chest.

"What was that about a time stream?" asked ten-year-old Artemis.

Mulch Diggums was burying a gold coin as a sacrifice to Shammy, the dwarf god of good fortune, when the earth exploded underneath him, and he found himself straddling the blade of a shuttle icebreaker prow.

I never even heard that coming, he thought. And then: *So much for Shammy.*

Before he could gather himself sufficiently to figure up from down, Mulch found himself tumbled to the base of a silver ash tree, with the barrel of a Neutrino restricting the movement of his Adam's apple. His beard hairs instinctively realized that the gun was not friendly, and twined themselves around the barrel.

"Nice shuttle," said Mulch, playing for time until the stars in his vision flickered out. "Whisper engine, I'm guessing."

Three pixies stood before him. Two males and a female. Generally, pixies were not very threatening creatures, but the males were armed and the female had a look in her eyes.

"I bet," said Mulch, "that you would set the world on fire just to watch it burn."

Opal tapped the suggestion into a small electronic notepad on her pocket computer.

"Thanks for that. Now, tell me everything."

I'll resist for a minute, then feed her some misinformation, thought Mulch.

"I'll tell you nothing, pixie she-devil," he said, Adam's apple knocking nervously against the gun barrel.

"Oooh," said Opal, stamping with frustration. "Isn't anyone afraid of me?"

She stripped off a glove and placed a thumb on Mulch's temple. "Now, show me everything."

And with a few remaining sparks of ill-gotten magic, she sucked every memory of the past few days from Mulch's brain. It was an extremely unpleasant sensation, even for someone used to expelling large amount of material from his person. Mulch gibbered and bucked as the last few days were vacuumed from his head. When Opal had what she wanted, the dwarf was left unconscious in the mud.

He would wake up an hour later with the starter chip for an LEP shuttle in his pocket and no idea how he'd gotten there.

Opal closed her eyes and flicked through her new memories.

"Ah," she said, smiling. "A time stream."

"There isn't time for this," insisted Artemis.

"I think there is," argued ten-year-old Artemis. "You

have broken into my house again; the least you can do is explain that time stream comment. Not to mention the fact that you are alive."

Artemis the elder flicked his hair away from his face.

"You must recognize me now. Surely."

"This is not a shampoo commercial. Please stop flicking your hair."

Holly was bent almost double, her hand on her heart.

"Hurry," she groaned, "or I'll have to go without you."

"Please," Artemis pleaded. "We need to go. It's a matter of life and death."

Young Artemis was unmoved. "I had a feeling you would be back. This is where it all began, right on this spot. I reviewed the security tapes, and you simply appeared in this room. Then you followed me to Africa, so I thought if I saved the creature's life you might end up back here with my lemur. We simply blocked our heat signatures and waited. And here you are."

"That's pretty flimsy reasoning," said Artemis the elder. "We were obviously after the lemur. Once we had the lemur, why would we return here?"

"I realize the logic was flawed, but I had nothing to lose. And, as we can see, a lot to gain."

Holly did not have the patience for a Fowl gloating session. "Artemis, I know you have a heart. You're a good person even if you don't know it yet. You sacrificed your diamonds to save my life. What will it take for you to let us go?"

Young Artemis considered this for an infuriating minute and a half.

"The truth," he said eventually. "I need to know the absolute truth about all of this. What kind of creature are *you*? Why does *he* look so familiar? What makes the lemur so special? Everything."

Artemis the elder clutched Jayjay to his chest. "Get me a pair of scissors," he said.

Opal ran into the manor, casually squashing the magical nausea that flared upon entering a human dwelling without permission.

A time stream, she thought, almost giggling with excitement. Finally I can test my theories.

The manipulation of time had long been Opal's ultimate goal. To be able to control one's passage through time was the greatest power. But her magic was not strong enough without the lemur. It took teams of LEP warlocks to slow time down for a few hours; the magic required to open a door to the tunnel was stupendous. It would be easier to shoot down the moon.

Opal tapped this into her notepad.

Reminder. Shoot down the moon? Viable?

But if she could gain entrance to the tunnel, Opal felt sure that she would quickly master the science involved.

It's more than likely an intuitive organism; and after all, I am a genius.

She scaled the stairs, mindless of the scuff marks the high human steps inflicted on her new boots. Mervall and Descant trailed behind, surprised at this lack of footwear prudence.

"I got thrown into the pigpen for boots," muttered Descant. "Now she's scratching those ones on the stairs. Typical Koboi inconsistency. I think I'm getting an ulcer."

Opal reached the upper landing and raced immediately through an open doorway.

"How does she know that's the right room?" wondered Descant.

"Oh, I don't know," said Mervall, resting his hands on his knees. Scaling human steps is not easy for pixies. Big heads, short legs, tiny lungs. "Maybe it's the magical red glow coming from the doorway, or perhaps it's the deafening howl of the temporal winds."

Descant nodded. "You could be right, brother. And don't think I don't know sarcasm when I hear it."

Opal traipsed from the room, her expression sour.

"They have gone," she announced. "And the tunnel is about to close. Also my boots are ruined. So, boys, I am looking for someone to blame."

The Brill brothers took one look at each other, then turned and ran as fast as their tiny legs would carry them.

Not fast enough.

⊖ → ⚸ • ⏂ ◊ ⏂ • ⚴ ⊙ • ⚵ ✧ ✦ ◊ ⏂ •

CHAPTER 14

THE HOLE IN THE ACE

HOLLY felt herself relax as soon as they entered the stream.

Safe for the moment.

Jayjay was safe. Soon Artemis's mother would be well, and when that was accomplished, Holly decided that she would punch her erstwhile friend in his smug face.

I did what I had to do, Artemis had said. *And I would do it again.*

And she had kissed him. Kissed him!

Holly understood Artemis's motives, but it wounded her deeply that he had felt the need to blackmail her.

I would have helped anyway. Definitely.

Would you? Would you have disobeyed orders? Was Artemis right to do it his way?

These were questions that Holly knew would haunt her for years. If she had years left to her.

The journey was more arduous than before. The time stream was eroding her sense of self, and there was a syrupy temptation to relax her concentration. Her world seemed less important wrapped in its sparkling waves. Being part of an eternal river would be a pleasant way to exist. And if the fairy races were wiped out by plague, what of it?

N°1's presence pricked her consciousness and bolstered her resolve. The little demon's power was evident in the stream, a shimmering thread of crimson pulling them on through the miasma. Things moved in the shadows. Darting, sharp things. Holly sensed teeth and hooked fingers.

Had N°1 mentioned something about quantum zombies? That was probably a joke. Please let that be a joke.

Concentrate! Holly told herself. Or you will be absorbed.

She could feel other presences traveling with her. Jayjay was surprisingly calm, considering his surroundings. Somewhere in the periphery was Artemis, his sense of purpose keen as a blade.

N°1 is going to get a shock, thought Holly, when he sees us pop through.

N°1 didn't seem very shocked when the group tumbled from the stream, solidifying on the floor of Artemis's study.

"See any zombies?" he asked with a spooky wiggling of his fingers.

"Thank the gods," proclaimed Foaly from the television screens, then exhaled loudly through his broad nostrils. "That was the longest ten seconds of my life. Did you get the lemur?"

There was no need for an answer, as Jayjay decided he liked the sound of Foaly's voice and gave the nearest screen a lick. The little primate's tongue crackled, and he scampered back, shooting Foaly a glare.

"One lemur," said the centaur. "No female?"

Holly shook the stars from her eyes, the fog from her brain. The stream lingered in her head like the last moments of sleep.

"No. No female. You'll have to clone him."

Foaly peered past Holly to the shuddering form on the ground behind her.

The centaur raised an eyebrow.

"I see we have an——"

"Let's talk about that later," said Holly sharply, interrupting the centaur. "For now we have work to do."

Foaly nodded thoughtfully. "I'm guessing, from the look of things, that Artemis has a plan of some sort. Is that going to be a problem for us?"

"Only if we try to stop it," said Holly.

Artemis took Jayjay into his arms, stroking the little

lemur's Mohawk and calming him with a rhythmic clicking of his tongue.

Holly felt that she too would be calmed—not by Artemis's clicking, but by the sight of her own face in the mirror. She was herself again; her one-piece fit snugly. A grown woman. No more teenage confusion. She would feel even better once she retrieved her gear. There was nothing like a Neutrino on the hip for a self-confidence boost.

"Time to see Mother," said Artemis grimly, selecting a suit from the wardrobe. "How much fluid should I administer?"

"It's powerful stuff," said Foaly, entering some calculations on his keyboard. "Two cc's. No more. There is a syringe gun in Holly's medi-kit on the bedside table. Be very careful with the brain drain. There's an anaesthetic tab in there too. Give Jayjay a swab, and he won't feel a thing."

"Very well," Artemis said, pocketing the kit. "I shall go in alone. I do hope Mother recognizes me."

"So do I," agreed Holly. "Or she may object to lemur brain juice being injected into her by a total stranger."

Artemis's hand hovered over the crystal doorknob on his parents' bedroom door. In its facets he could see a dozen reflections of his own face. Each one was drawn and worried.

Last chance. My last chance to save her.

I am forever trying to save people, he thought. I'm supposed to be a criminal. Where did it all go wrong?

No time for drifting. There was more at stake here than gold or notoriety. His mother was dying, and her salvation was perched on Artemis's shoulder, searching his scalp for ticks.

Artemis closed his fingers over the knob. Not another moment to waste on thoughts; time now for action.

The room seemed colder than he remembered, but this was doubtless his imagination.

All minds play tricks. Even mine. The perceived cold is a projection of my mood, nothing more.

His parents' bedroom was rectangular in shape, stretching along the west wing from front to rear. It was actually more of an apartment than a room, with a lounge area and office corner. The large four-poster bed was angled so that tinted light from a medieval stained-glass porthole would fall across the studded headboard in summer.

Artemis placed his feet carefully on the rug, like a ballet dancer, avoiding the vine pattern in the weave.

Step on a vine, count to nine.

Bad luck was the last thing he needed.

Angeline Fowl was splayed on the bed, as though thrown there. Her head was angled back so sharply that the line from her neck to her chin was almost straight, and her skin was pale enough to seem translucent.

She's not breathing, thought Artemis, panic fluttering in his chest like a caged bird. I was wrong. I am too late.

Then his mother's entire frame convulsed as she dragged down a painful breath.

Artemis's resolve almost left him. His legs were boneless rubber and his forehead burned.

This is my mother. How can I do what needs to be done?

But he would do it. There wasn't anyone else who could.

Artemis reached his mother's side and gently pushed strands of hair back from her face.

"I am here, Mother. Everything will be fine. I found a cure."

Somehow, Angeline Fowl heard her son's words, and her eyes flickered open. Even her irises had lost their color, fading to the ice blue of a winter lake.

"Cure," she sighed. "My little Arty found the cure."

"That's right," said Artemis. "Little Arty found the cure. It was the lemur. Remember, the Madagascan lemur from Rathdown Park?"

Angeline raised a bone-thin finger, tickling the air before Jayjay's nose. "Little lemur. Cure."

Jayjay, unsettled by the bedridden woman's skeletal appearance, ducked behind Artemis's head.

"Nice lemur," said Angeline, a weak smile twitching her lips.

I am the parent now, thought Artemis. She is the child.

"Can I hold him?"

Artemis took a half-step back. "No, Mother. Not yet. Jayjay is a very important creature. This little fellow could save the world."

Angeline spoke through her teeth. "Let me hold him. Just for a moment."

Jayjay crawled down the back of Artemis's jacket, as though he understood the request and did not want to be held.

"Please, Arty. It would comfort me to hold him."

Artemis nearly handed the lemur over. Nearly.

"Holding him will not cure you, Mother. I need to inject some fluid into one of your veins."

Angeline seemed to be regaining her strength. She inched backward, sliding her head up the headboard. "Don't you want to make me happy, Arty?"

"I prefer *healthy* to happy for the moment," said Artemis, making no move to hand over the lemur.

"Don't you love me, son?" crooned Angeline. "Don't you love your mommy?"

Artemis moved briskly, tearing open the medi-kit and closing his fingers around the transfusion gun, a single tear rolling down his pale cheek.

"I love you, Mother. I love you more than life. If you could only know what I have been through to find little

Jayjay. Just be still for five seconds, then this nightmare will be over."

Angeline's eyes were crafty slits. "I don't want you to inject me, Artemis. You're not a trained nurse. Wasn't there a doctor here, or was I dreaming that?"

Artemis primed the gun, waiting for the charge light to flash green. "I *have* administered shots before, Mother. I gave you your medicine more than once the last time you were . . . ill."

"Artemis!" snapped Angeline, the flat of her hand slapping the sheet. "I demand that you give the lemur to me now! This instant! And summon the doctor."

Artemis plucked a vial from the medi-kit. "You are hysterical, Mother. Not yourself. I think I should give you a sedative before I administer the antidote." He slid the vial into the gun and reached for his mother's arm.

"No," Angeline virtually screeched, slapping him away with surprising strength. "Don't touch me with your LEP sedatives, you stupid boy."

Artemis froze. "LEP, Mother? What do you know of the LEP?"

Angeline tugged her lip, a guilty child. "What? Did I say LEP? Three letters, no more. They mean nothing to me."

Artemis took another step away from the bed, gathering Jayjay protectively in his arms.

"Tell me the truth, Mother. What is happening here?"

Angeline abandoned her innocent act, pounding the

mattress with delicate fists and squealing in frustration.

"I despise you, Artemis Fowl. You bothersome human. How I loathe you."

Not words one expects to hear from one's mother.

Angeline lay flat on the bed, steaming with rage. Literally steaming. Her eyeballs rolled in their sockets, and tendons stood out like steel cables on her arms and neck. All the time she ranted.

"When I have the lemur I will crush you all. The LEP, Foaly, Julius Root, all of you. I will send laser dogs down every tunnel in the earth's crust until I flush out that odious dwarf. And as for that female captain, I will brainwash her and make her my slave." She cast a hateful look at Artemis. "Fitting revenge, don't you agree, *my son*." The last two words dripped from her lips like poison from a viper's fangs.

Artemis held Jayjay close; he could feel the small creature shivering against his chest. Or perhaps the shivering was his own.

"Opal," he said. "You followed us home."

"Finally!" shouted Artemis's mother, in Opal's voice. "The great boy genius sees the truth." Angeline's limbs stiffened, and she levitated from the bed, surrounded by a roiling mist of steam. Her pale blue eyes cut through the fog, spearing Artemis with their mad glare.

"Did you think you could win? Did you believe that the battle *was* won? How charmingly deluded. You do not even possess magic. I, on the other hand, have more magic than any other fairy since the demon warlocks. And once I have the lemur, I will be immortal."

Artemis rolled his eyes. "Don't forget invincible."

"I haaate you!" squealed Opal/Angeline. "When I have the lemur, I will . . . I will . . ."

"Kill me in some horrible fashion," suggested Artemis.

"Precisely. Thank you."

Angeline's body pivoted stiffly until she hovered upright, her halo of charged hair brushing the ceiling.

"Now," she said, pointing a skeletal finger at the cowering Jayjay, "give me that creature."

Artemis wrapped the lemur in his jacket. "Come and get him," he said.

In the study, Holly was running through Artemis's theory.

"That's it?" said Nº1 when Holly had finished explaining. "You're not forgetting some crucial detail? Like the part that makes sense?"

"The whole thing is ridiculous." interjected Foaly from the monitors. "Come on, fairies. We've done our part. Time to head belowground."

"Soon," said Holly. "Let's just give Artemis five minutes to check it out. All we need to do is be alert."

Foaly's sigh crackled through the speakers. "Well, at least let me raise the shuttle. The troops are holding at Tara, waiting for a callback."

Holly thought about this. "That's good. You do that. Whatever happens, we need to be ready to move out. And when you're finished, do a sweep of the estate, see where that nurse is."

Foaly's focus shifted left, while he put a call in to Tara.

Holly pointed at Nº1. "You just have a little of that signature magic dancing on your fingertips in case we need it. I won't feel completely safe until Angeline is well, and we're drinking sim-coffee in a Haven bar."

Nº1 raised his hands, and soon they were enveloped in ripples of red power. "No problem, Holly. I'm ready for anything."

It was a statement that was missing an *almost*.

In the same split second, the monitors blacked out and the door burst open with a force that actually drove the doorknob into the wall. Butler's huge frame filled the gap.

Holly's smile slipped when she noticed the pistol in the bodyguard's fist and the mirrored sunglasses covering his eyes.

He's armed and doesn't want to be mesmerized.

Holly was quick, but Butler was quicker, and he had the element of surprise; after all, he was supposed to be on his way to China. Holly went for her gun, but Butler was there before her, ripping the Neutrino from her hip.

We have other tricks, thought Holly. We have magic. Nº1 will knock your socks off.

Butler dragged something into the room on a trolley. A

steel barrel with runes etched on the metal.

What's this? What's he doing?

N°1 managed to get off a single bolt; indoor lightning that scorched Butler's shirt, knocking him back a pace. But even as he stumbled backward, the bodyguard swung the trolley past him, slingshotting it into the room. A thick slime slopped from its open mouth, splashing on N°1's legs. The barrel trundled forward, knocking Holly and N°1 aside like skittles.

N°1 stared at his fingers as the magic on each tip winked out like candles in a breeze.

"I don't feel so great," he groaned, then keeled over, eyes flickering, lips muttering ancient spells that did not one iota of good.

What is in that barrel? wondered Holly, releasing her suit's wings from their sheath. Butler grabbed Holly's ankle as she ascended, flipping her ignominiously into the barrel. She felt the thick gunk close over her like a wet fist, blocking her nose and filling her throat.

The smell was repulsive.

Animal fat, she realized with a spasmodic shudder of horror. Pure rendered fat with a few hexes stirred into it.

Animal fat had been used as a magic suppressor for millennia. Even the most powerful warlock was helpless when dipped in rendered fat. You throw a warlock in a barrel of fat, seal it with woven willow bark, and bury it in a consecrated human graveyard, then that warlock is as helpless as a kitten in a sack. The experience would be made even more terrible by the fact that most fairies are devout vegetarians and would be perfectly aware of how many animals had to die to produce an entire barrel of fat.

Who told Butler about this? Holly wondered. Who is controlling him?

Then N°1 was jammed in beside her, and the fat level rose to cover their heads. Holly surged upward, clearing her eyes just in time to see a lid bearing down on the barrel mouth, eclipsing the ceiling light.

No helmet, she lamented. I wish I had my helmet.

Then the lid was on and sealed. The fat found the neck hole in her one-piece and wormed inside, probing her face and invading her ears. Hexes swirled like malevolent snakes, keeping her magic at bay.

Lost, thought Holly. The worst death I can imagine. Sealed in a small space. Like my mother.

N°1 convulsed beside her. The little warlock must feel like his soul was being sucked right out of him.

Holly panicked. She kicked and fought, bruising her elbows and tearing the skin from her knees. Where magic tried to heal her wounds, the hex snakes zoomed in, swallowing the sparks.

She almost opened her mouth to scream. The merest thread of reason stopped her. Then something brushed against her face. A corrugated tube. There were two.

Breathing tubes . . .

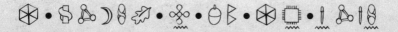

With frantic fingers, Holly felt her way to the end of a tube. She fought her natural instinct to jam it into N°1's mouth.

In the event of an emergency, always take care of yourself first before you attend to civilians.

So Holly used her absolute last puff of air to clear the pipe as a diver would clear his snorkel. She imagined blobs of fat spraying the room outside.

I hope Butler's suit is ruined, she thought.

No choice now but to inhale. Air whistled down to her, mixed with wormy slivers of fat. Holly blew again, clearing the last traces of gunk.

Now for N°1. His wriggling grew weaker as his power waned. For someone with such power, this dunking must be almost intolerable. Holly blocked her own tube with a thumb, then cleared the second one before twisting it into N°1's slack mouth. For a moment there was no reaction, and she thought it was too late; then N°1 jerked, spluttered, and started, like an old engine on a frosty morning.

Alive, thought Holly. We are both alive. If Butler wanted us dead, then we already would be.

She braced her feet on the base of the barrel and hugged N°1 tightly. Calm was needed here.

Calm, she broadcast, though she knew N°1's empathy would be muted. *Calm, little friend. Artemis will save us.*

If he is alive, she thought but did not broadcast.

* * *

Artemis backed away from the nightmare version of his mother that hovered before him. Jayjay screeched and bucked in his arms, but Artemis held him tightly, automatically scratching the tiny brush of hair on his crown.

"Hand over that creature," demanded Opal. "You have no choice."

Artemis circled Jayjay's neck with his thumb and forefinger.

"Oh, I think I have a choice."

Opal was horrified. "You wouldn't kill an innocent creature."

"I did it before."

Opal studied his eyes. "I don't think you would do it again, Artemis Fowl. My fairy intuition tells me that you are not as coldhearted as you pretend to be."

It was true. Artemis knew he couldn't harm Jayjay, even to derail Opal's plans. Still, no reason to tell Opal that.

"My heart is cold, pixie. Believe it. Use some of that magical empathy to search my soul."

His tone gave Opal pause. There was steel there, and he was hard to read. Perhaps she should not gamble so recklessly with him.

"Very well, human. Hand over the creature and I will spare your friends."

"I have no friends," Artemis shot back, though he knew it was a transparent bluff. Opal had been here for a few

days at least. She had doubtless highjacked the manor's surveillance and security.

Opal/Angeline scratched her chin. "Hmm, no friends. Apart from the LEP elf who accompanied you to the past, and of course the demon warlock who sent you back. Not to mention your big burly bodyguard."

Alliteration, thought Artemis. She's toying with me.

"Then again," mused Opal/Angeline, "Butler is not really your friend anymore. He's mine."

This was a worrying statement, and perhaps true. Artemis, usually an expert interpreter of body language and telltale tics, was flummoxed by this crazed version of his mother.

"Butler would never willingly befriend you!"

Opal shrugged. It was a fair point. "Who said anything about willingly?"

Artemis paled. *Uh-oh.*

"Let me explain what happened," said Opal sweetly. "I scrambled the brains of my little helpers somewhat, so they could not report on me, then had them fly the shuttle back to Haven. Then I hitched a ride on your time stream before it closed. Oh so simple for someone with my skill set. You didn't even leave a hex at the hole."

Artemis snapped his fingers. "I knew I had forgotten something."

Opal smiled thinly. "Amusing. Anyway, it became obvious to me that I was, or would be, responsible for this entire affair, so I dropped out of the stream a few days early and took my time getting to know your group. Mother, father, Butler."

"Where is my mother?" shouted Artemis, anger punching through his calm exterior like a hammer through ice.

"Why, I'm right here, darling," said Opal in Angeline's voice. "I am really sick, and I need you to go into the past and fetch a magic monkey for me." She laughed mockingly. "Humans are such fools."

"So this is not some kind of shapeshifting spell?"

"No, idiot. I was perfectly aware that Angeline would be examined. Shapeshifting spells are only skin-deep, and even an adept such as myself can only hold one for short periods."

"This means that my mother is not dying?" Artemis knew the answer, but he had to be certain.

Opal ground her teeth, torn between impatience and the desire to explain the brilliance of her plan.

"Not yet. Though soon the damage to her system will be irreversible. I have possessed her from a distance. An extreme form of the *mesmer*. With power like mine, I can manipulate her very organs. Imitating Spelltropy was child's play. And once I have little Jayjay I can open my own hole in time."

"So you are nearby? Your real self?"

Opal had enough of questions. "Yes, no. What does it matter? I win, you lose. Accept it, or everyone dies."

Artemis edged toward the door. "This game is not over yet."

Footsteps outside and a strange rhythmic squeaking. A wheelbarrow, Artemis guessed, though he did not have much experience with gardening aids.

"Oh, I think this game is over now," said Opal slyly.

The heavy door bounced in fits as it was butted from the outside. Butler pushed the trolley into the room, stumbling after it, hunched and shivering.

"He is strong, this one," said Opal, almost in admiration. "I *mesmerized* him, but still he refused to kill your friends. The stupid man's heart almost burst. It was all I could do to force him to construct the barrel and fill it with fat."

"To smother fairy magic," Artemis guessed.

"Obviously, idiot. Now the game is absolutely over. Finished. Butler is my ace in the hole, as you humans might say. I hold all the aces. You are alone. Give me the lemur and I will go back to my own time. Nobody has to suffer."

If Opal gets the lemur, then the entire planet will suffer, thought Artemis.

Opal snapped her fingers. "Butler, seize the animal."

Butler took a single step toward Artemis, then stopped. Shudders racked his broad back, and his fingers were claws wringing an invisible neck.

"I said get the animal, you stupid human."

The bodyguard dropped to his knees and pounded the

floor, trying to drive the voice from his head.

"Get the lemur now!" shrieked Opal.

Butler had enough strength for three words. "Go . . . to . . . hell."

Then he clutched at his arm and collapsed.

"Oops," said Opal. "Heart attack. I broke him."

Stay focused, Artemis ordered himself. Opal may hold all the aces, but perhaps there is a hole in one of those aces.

Artemis tickled Jayjay under the chin. "Hide, little friend. Hide."

And with that he tossed the lemur toward a chandelier suspended from the ceiling. Jayjay flailed in the air, then latched on to a glass strut. He pulled himself nimbly into the hanging light and hid behind sheets of dangling crystal.

Opal immediately lost interest in Artemis, concentrating on levitating Angeline's body to the level of the chandelier. With a squeal of frustration she realized that such remote elevation was beyond even a being of her power.

"Doctor Schalke!" she called, and somewhere her real mouth was calling it too. "Into the bedroom, Schalke!"

Artemis filed this information, then ducked below Opal to his mother's bedside. A mobile JumpStart defibrillator cart was parked among the row of medical equipment ranged around the four-poster, and Artemis quickly switched it on, dragging the entire contraption to the limit of its cord, to where Butler had collapsed.

The bodyguard lay faceup, hands thrown back as though there were an invisible boulder on his chest. His face was stretched with the effort of moving the great stone. Eyes closed, sweat sheened, teeth clenched.

Artemis unbuttoned Butler's shirt, exposing a barrel chest hard with muscle, scars, and tension. A cursory examination told him that there was no heartbeat. Butler's body was dead; only his brain was left alive.

"Hold on, old friend," murmured Artemis, trying to keep his mind focused.

He pulled the defibrillator paddles from their holsters and peeled back their disposable safety covers, leaving a thin coating of conductive gel on the contact surfaces. The paddles seemed to grow heavier as he waited for the unit to charge, and by the time the GO light flashed green, they felt like rocks in his hands.

"Clear!" he called to no one in particular, then positioned the paddles firmly on Butler's chest and hit the shock button under his thumb, sending three hundred and sixty volts of electricity into his bodyguard's heart. Butler's body arched, and the sharp smell of burning hair and skin assailed Artemis's nostrils. Gel crisped and sparked, burning twin rings where the pads had made contact. Butler's eyes flew open and his massive hands gripped Artemis's shoulders.

Is he still Opal's slave?

"Artemis," breathed Butler, but then frowned in confusion. "Artemis? How?"

"Later, old friend," said the Irish boy brusquely, mentally progressing to the next problem. "Just rest for now."

This was not an order he would have to repeat. Butler sank immediately into exhausted unconsciousness. But his heart beat strongly inside his chest. He had not been dead long enough to have suffered brain damage.

Artemis's next problem was Opal, or more specifically, how to get her out of his mother's body. If she did not vacate soon, Artemis had no doubt that his mother would not recover from the ordeal.

Gathering his nerve with several deep breaths, Artemis switched his full attention to his mother's hovering body. She was twirling below the chandelier as though suspended from it, clawing at Jayjay, who appeared to be taunting her by waving his hindquarters in her direction.

Can this situation get any more surreal?

Just then Dr. Schalke entered the room brandishing a pistol, which seemed too large for his delicate hands.

"I am here, you creature. Though I must say, I don't like your tone. I may be spellbound, but I am not an animal."

"Do shut up, Schalke. I can see I will have to fry a few more of your brain cells. Now, please, fetch that lemur!"

Schalke pointed four fingers of his free hand toward the chandelier. "The lemur is at a considerable height, yes?

How do you suggest I fetch him? Perhaps I could shoot him dead?"

Opal swooshed low, arms and legs twirling like a harpie. "No!" she shrieked, striking him around the head and shoulders. "I would shoot a hundred of you, a thousand, before I let you harm one hair of that creature's fur. He is the future. My future! The world's future!"

"Indeed," said the doctor. "Were I not *mesmerized*, I suspect I should be yawning."

"Shoot the humans," commanded Opal. "The boy first; he is the most dangerous."

"Are you certain? The man mountain looks more dangerous to me."

"Shoot the boy!" howled Opal, frustration sending tears streaming down her cheeks. "Then Butler and then yourself."

Artemis swallowed. This was cutting things a bit fine; his accomplice had better get a move on.

"Very well," said Schalke, fiddling with the safety on Butler's Sig Sauer. "Anything to escape these theatrics."

I have seconds before he figures out that catch, thought Artemis. Seconds to distract Opal. Nothing to do but to reveal the hole in her ace.

"Come now, Opal," Artemis said with a calmness he did not feel. "You wouldn't shoot a ten-year-old boy, would you?"

"I absolutely would," said Opal without a heartbeat's

hesitation. "I am considering cloning you so that I can kill you over and over again. Heaven."

Then *all* of what Artemis had said registered.

"Ten? Did you say you were ten years old?"

Artemis forgot all about the danger surrounding him, lost in the sweet moment of triumph. It was intoxicating.

"Yes, that is what I said. I am ten. My *real* mother would have noticed immediately."

Opal chewed the knuckles of Angeline's left hand, thinking.

"You are the Artemis Fowl from *my* time? They brought you back!"

"Obviously."

Opal reared backward through the air, as though taken by the wind.

"There is another one. Here somewhere, another Artemis Fowl."

"Finally!" said Artemis, smirking. "The great pixie genius sees the truth."

"Find him," shrieked Opal. "Find him immediately. At once."

Schalke straightened his glasses. "At once *and* immediately. This must be important."

Opal watched him go with real hatred in her eyes. "When this is over, I am going to destroy this entire estate just for spite. And then, when I return to the past, I shall—"

"Don't tell me," interrupted ten-year-old Artemis Fowl. "You will destroy it again."

Almost Eight Years Ago

When fourteen-year-old Artemis had a moment to consider things, sometime in between scaling pylons and outwitting murderous Extinctionists, he realized that there were a lot of unanswered questions about his mother's illness. *He* had supposedly given her Spelltropy, but who had passed it to him? Holly's magic had permeated his body in the past, but she herself was hale and hearty. Why wasn't she sick? Or for that matter, how had Butler escaped infection? He had been healed so many times that he must be half-fairy by now.

And of *all* the thousands of humans healed, *mesmerized* or wiped every year, *his* mother was the one to fall ill. The mother of the only human on Earth who could do something about it. Very coincidental. Too coincidental by far.

So, either someone had deliberately infected his mother, or the symptoms were being magically duplicated. Either way, the result was the same: Artemis would travel back in time to find the antidote. The lemur, Jayjay.

And who would want Jayjay found as much as Artemis did? The answer to that question lay in the past. Opal Koboi, of course. The little primate was the last ingredient in her magical cocktail. With his brain fluid in her bloodstream, she would be literally the most powerful person on the planet. And if Opal couldn't nab Jayjay in her own time, she would get him in the future. Whatever it took. She must have followed them back through the time stream, jumped out early, and organized this whole affair. Presumably once she had Jayjay's brain fluid, navigating her way back would not be a problem.

It was confusing even for Artemis. Opal wouldn't even be in his present if he hadn't gone back in time. And *he* had only gone back in time because of a situation she had created. It had been Artemis's own attempts to cure his mother that had led Opal to infect her.

But one thing he now felt sure of was that Opal was behind this. She was behind them and in front of them. Chasing their group into her own clutches. A time paradox.

There are two Opals in this equation, thought Artemis. I think there should continue to be two Artemis Fowls.

And so a plan began to take shape in his mind.

Once the young Artemis had been apprised of all the details and convinced of their accuracy, he had at once agreed to accompany them to the future, in spite of Butler's vocal objection.

"It's my mother, Butler," he said simply. "I must save her. Now I charge you to stay by her side until I return. Anyway, how could they hope to succeed without me?"

"How indeed," Holly Short had wondered, then taken more pleasure than was necessary in watching that arrogance drain from the boy's features when the time stream opened in front of them, like the maw of some great computer-generated serpent.

"Chin up, Mud Boy," she'd said as Artemis the younger watched his arm dissolve. "And watch out for quantum zombies."

The time stream had been difficult for Artemis the elder. Any other human would have been torn apart by such repeated exposure to its particular radiation, but Artemis held himself together by sheer willpower. He focused on the high end of his intellect, solving unprovable theorems with large cardinals and composing an ending for Schubert's unfinished Symphony No 8.

As he worked, Artemis sensed the odd derisive comment from his younger self.

More B minor? Do you really think so?

Had he always been this obnoxious? How tiresome. Little wonder people in general did not like him.

The Present

Back in his own time, in his own house, Artemis the elder paused only to grab some clothes from the wardrobe before quickly exiting his study, warning Foaly and Nº1 to keep silent with a simple *shhh*. He moved quickly along the corridor toward the dumbwaiter shaft adjacent to the second-floor tea room. This was not the most direct route to the security center, in fact the route was circuitous and awkward, but it was the only possible way to pass through the house undetected.

Butler believed he had every square inch of the manor, apart from the Fowl's private chambers, under surveillance, but Artemis had long since worked how to travel through the house without being picked up on camera. This route involved hiding in corners, walking on furniture, traveling in dumbwaiters, and tilting a full-length mirror to just the right angle.

It was possible, of course, that a hostile could figure out the same pathways, coordinates and trajectories, and therefore move about the house undetected. Possible, but highly improbable, and not without an intimate knowledge of nooks and crannies that did not exist on any plans.

Artemis followed a zigzag pattern down the hallway, a second behind a security camera's sweep, then ducked quickly inside the dumbwaiter shaft. Luckily the box was on this floor, or he would have been forced to shinny down the cable, and shinnying was not one of his strong suits. Artemis reached outside and pressed the ground-floor button, whipping his hand back in before the descending box caught his wrist. While it was true that security would register the dumbwaiter descending, it would not set off any red lights.

Once at kitchen level, Artemis rolled onto the floor and opened the fridge door to shield his movement into the pantry. Deep shadows concealed him until the camera swung away from the doorway, allowing him to climb on top of the table and jump outside.

All the time, thinking. Plotting.

Assume the worst. Little Artemis is helpless, and Holly and N°1 are already incapacitated. Quite possible if someone like Butler was mesmerized and doing the incapacitating. Opal is somewhere near the command center, manipulating my mother. It was Opal who could see the magic inside me. Not Mother. She peeled away the spell I had cast over my parents.

And: *Of course B minor. If one starts in B minor, one finishes in B minor. Any fool knows that.*

A suit of medieval armor stood in the main lobby. The same armor that Butler had put on to do battle with a troll during the Fowl Manor siege five years earlier. Artemis approached it slowly, his back flat against an abstract gray/black tapestry, which camouflaged him almost perfectly. Once concealed behind the suit of armor, he nudged the base of an adjacent mirror until it reflected a spotlight's beam directly into the lens of the lobby camera.

Now his path to the security center was clear. Artemis strode purposefully toward the booth. This was where Opal would be, he was certain of it. From there she could monitor the entire house, and it was directly below Angeline's bedroom. If Opal was indeed controlling his mother, closer was better.

It was clear from several yards away that he was right. Artemis could hear Opal ranting from a distance.

"There is another one. Here somewhere, another Artemis Fowl."

Either the penny had dropped, or young Artemis had been forced to reveal their plan. "Find him," shrieked Opal. "Find him immediately. At once."

Artemis stepped quietly into the security control booth. A box room off the main lobby that had served in its time as a cloakroom, weapons lockup, and holding cell for prisoners. Now it housed a computer desk similar to those found in editing suites, and stacks of monitors displaying live feeds of the manor and grounds.

Huddled before the monitor bank was Opal, dressed in Holly's LEP gear. She had wasted no time in stealing the fairy suit. It was mere minutes since Artemis had locked it in the safe.

The little pixie was multitasking furiously, scanning the monitors while maintaining remote control over Artemis's mother. Her dark hair was sweat slicked, and her childlike limbs shook with effort.

Artemis sneaked into the room and quickly punched the code into the weapons locker.

"When this is over, I am going to destroy this entire

346

estate just for spite. And then, when I return to the past, I shall . . ."

Opal froze. Something had made a clicking noise. She turned to find Artemis Fowl pointing a weapon of some kind at her. She immediately abandoned all other spells, throwing her efforts into a desperate *mesmer*.

"Drop that gun," she intoned. "You are my slave."

Artemis felt instantly woozy, but he had already pressed the trigger, and a dart loaded with a Butler special concoction of muscle relaxants and sedatives buried its inch-long needle in Opal's neck, where there was no protection from the suit. This was a shot in a million, since Artemis was not proficient with firearms. As Butler put it: *Artemis, a genius you may be, but leave the shooting to me, because you couldn't hit the backside of a stationary elephant.*

Opal concentrated furiously on the puncture wound, dousing it with magical sparks, but it was too late. The drug was already entering her brain, loosening her control on the magic inside her.

She began to sway and flicker, alternating between her real pixie self and Miss Book.

Miss Book, thought Artemis. My suspicions were correct. The only stranger in the equation.

Intermittently Opal disappeared altogether, shield buzzing in and out. Magical bolts shot from her fingers, frying the monitors before Artemis could get a look at what was going on upstairs.

"*Now* I can do the bolts," she slurred. "I've been trying to focus enough magic all week."

The magic shifted and swirled, finally etching a picture in the air. It was a rough picture of Foaly, and he was laughing.

"I hate you, centaur!" screamed Opal, lunging toward, and then through, the insubstantial image. Her eyes rolled back in her head, and she collapsed, snoring, on the floor.

Artemis straightened his tie.

Freud, he felt certain, would have a field day with that.

Artemis hurried upstairs to his parents' room. The rug was coated in a pool of lumpy fat. Two sets of fairy footprints led from the turgid pearlescent puddle into the en suite bathroom. Artemis heard the power shower drilling against the tiles.

Opal used animal fat to suppress N°1's magic. How despicable. How horrible.

Young Artemis was studying the spreading mass of goo. "Look," he said, noticing his older self. "Opal used animal fat to suppress N°1's magic. How ingenious."

Under the noise of the shower were the sounds of retching and complaining. Butler was hosing down Holly and N°1, and they were not happy or healthy.

But alive. Both alive.

Angeline lay on her bed, wrapped in a goose down duvet. She was pale and dazed, but was it Artemis's imagination or had just a tinge of color crept back into her cheeks? She coughed gently, and immediately both Artemises were at her side.

Artemis the elder raised an eyebrow at his younger self. "You can see how this might be awkward," he said pointedly.

"I can indeed," conceded the ten-year-old. "Why don't I have a poke around in your . . . in my study. See what I come up with."

This is a problem, Artemis realized. My own inquisitiveness. Perhaps I should not have promised not to mind-wipe my younger self. Something will have to be done.

Angeline opened her eyes. They were blue and calm, peering out from tired, dark sockets.

"Artemis," she said, her voice the rasp of fingers on tree bark. "I dreamed I was flying. And there was a monkey . . ."

Artemis shook with relief. She was safe; he had saved her.

"It was a lemur, Mother. Mom."

Angeline smiled wanly, reaching up to stroke his cheek. "*Mom*. I have waited so long to hear you say that. So long."

And with that smile on her face, Angeline lay back and drifted off into deep, natural sleep.

Just as well, Artemis realized. Or she may have noticed the fairies in the bathroom, or the contents of a fat barrel on the rug. Or a second Artemis lurking shiftily by the bookcase.

Butler emerged from the bathroom dripping wet, shirtless, paddle marks scorched into his skin. He was paler than usual, and had to lean against the door frame for support.

"Welcome back," he said to Artemis the elder. "This little one is quite a chip off the old block. Gave me one hell of a jump start."

"He *is* the old block," said Artemis wryly.

Butler jerked a thumb over his shoulder. "Those two didn't enjoy their dip in the barrel."

"Animal fat is poison to fairies," explained Artemis. "Blocks the magical flow. Turns their own power rancid."

A shadow settled on Butler's brow. "Opal made me do it. She . . . Miss Book approached me at the main gates as I was leaving for the airport. I was trapped in my own skull."

Artemis laid a gentle hand on his bodyguard's forearm. "I know. No apologies are necessary."

Butler remembered that he did not have his weapon, and he remembered who did have it. "What did you do with Schalke? Knockout dart?"

"No. Our paths did not cross."

Butler staggered to the bedroom door, Artemis hot on his heels. "Opal is controlling him, though he's making her work for it. We need to secure them both right now."

It took them several minutes to reach the security booth, with Butler pulling himself along the walls, and by

350

that time Opal was already gone. Artemis ran to the
window just in time to see the blocky rear end of a vintage
Mercedes take the bend in the driveway. A small figure
bounced on the backseat. Two bounces, the first time it
was Opal, the second Miss Imogen Book.

Already her power returns, realized Artemis.

Butler loomed above him, panting. "This isn't over yet."

Artemis did not respond to the comment. Butler was
simply stating the patently obvious.

Then the engine noise increased in volume and pitch.

"Gear change," said Butler. "She's coming back."

Artemis felt a chill pass over his heart, though he had
been expecting it.

Of course she's coming back, he thought. She will
never have another chance like this one. Butler can barely
walk. Holly and N°1 will be diminished for hours, and I
am a mere human. If she retreats now, Jayjay will be free
of her forever. Soon Foaly's squad will arrive from Tara and
whisk the little lemur underground. For perhaps five
minutes, Opal has the upper hand.

Artemis planned quickly. "I need to take Jayjay away
from here. So long as he is in the manor, everyone is in
danger. Opal will kill us all to cover her tracks."

Butler nodded, sweat running in rivulets through the
lines on his face. "Yes. We can make it to the Cessna."

"*I* can make it to the Cessna, old friend," corrected
Artemis. "I am charging you with the protection of my

mother and friends, not to mention keeping my younger self off the Internet. He is as dangerous as Opal."

It was a sensible tactic, and Butler knew it was coming before Artemis said it. He was in such bad shape that he would slow Artemis down. Not only that but the manor would be wide open for any of Opal's thralls to stroll in and exact her revenge.

"Very well. Don't take her over seven thousand feet, and watch the flaps: they're a bit sticky."

Artemis nodded as if he didn't know. Giving instructions comforted Butler.

"Seven thousand. Flaps. Got it."

"Would you like a gun? I have a neat Beretta."

Artemis shook his head. "No guns. My aim is so bad that even with Holly's eye to help me, I would probably only succeed in shooting off a toe or two. No, all I need is the bait." He paused. "And my sunglasses."

CHAPTER 15

MURDER MOST FOWL

THE FOWL FAMILY currently had three aircrafts. A Lear jet and Sikorsky helicopter, which were hangared at the nearby airport, and a small Cessna that lived in a small garage workshop beside the high meadow on the northern border of the estate. The Cessna was several years old and would have been recycled some time ago, had Artemis not taken it on as a project. His aim was to make it carbon neutral *and* cost effective, a goal that his father heartily approved of.

"I have forty scientists working on the same problem, but my money is on you," he had confided to his son.

And so Artemis coated the entire body of the craft with lightweight superefficient solar panels, like NASA's prototype flying wing—the Helios. Unlike the Helios, Artemis's Cessna could still fly at its normal speeds *and* take passengers. This was because Artemis had removed the single engine and installed smaller ones to turn the main propeller, the four extra props on the wings, and the landing gear. Most of the metal in the skeleton had been stripped out and replaced with a lightweight polymer. Where the fuel tank had been now sat a small battery.

There were still a few adjustments to make, but Artemis believed his ship was skyworthy. He hoped so. There was a lot riding on the soundness of the little craft. He sprinted from the kitchen door, across the courtyard, and toward the high meadow. With any luck Opal would not realize he was gone until she saw the plane taking off. Of course, *then* he wanted her to see him. Hopefully he could draw her away long enough for LEP reinforcements to arrive.

Artemis felt the tiredness in his legs before he had gone a hundred yards. He had never been the athletic type, and the recent time-stream jaunts had done nothing for his physique, even though he had concentrated hard on his muscles during the trips, willing himself to tone up. A little mind-over-matter experiment that sadly had not yielded any results.

The old farm gate to the meadow was closed, so Artemis scaled it rather than struggle with the heavy bolt. He could feel the heat from the simian's body high inside his jacket, and its little hands were tight on his neck.

Jayjay must be safe, he thought. He must be saved.

The garage doors were sturdier than they looked, and were protected with a keypad entry system. Artemis tapped in the code and threw open the doors wide, flooding the interior with the deep orange rays of the early evening sun. Inside, nestled in a horseshoe of benches and tool trolleys, was the modified Cessna, hooked up to a supplementary power cable. Artemis snapped the cable from its socket on the fuselage and clambered into the cockpit. He strapped himself into the pilot's seat, remembering briefly when he had first flown this plane solo.

Nine years old. I needed a booster seat.

The engines started immediately and virtually silently. The only noise came from the whirring of the propellers and the clicks of switches as Artemis ran through his preflight check.

The news was generally good. Eighty percent power. That gave the small plane a range of several hundred miles. Easy enough to lead Opal on a merry dance along the Irish coast. But the flaps were sticky and the seals were old.

Don't take her over seven thousand feet.

"We're going to be fine," he said to the passenger inside his jacket. "Absolutely fine."

Was this the truth? He could not be certain.

The high meadow was wide and long, and sloped gently upward to the estate wall. Artemis nudged the Cessna from her hangar, swinging the nose in a tight turn to give himself maximum runway. Under ideal circumstances the five-hundred-yard grass runway was more than ample for a takeoff. But there was a tailwind, and the grass was a few inches longer than it should have been.

Despite these considerations we should be okay. I have flown in worse conditions than this.

The takeoff was textbook. Artemis pulled back on the nosewheel at the three-hundred-yard mark and comfortably cleared the north wall. Even at this low altitude he could see the Irish sea to the west, black with scimitars of sunlight slicing across the wave tips.

He was tempted, for the merest fraction of a moment, just to flee, but he didn't.

Have I changed utterly? Artemis asked himself. He realized that he was running out of palatable crimes. Not so long ago, nearly all crime had been acceptable to him.

No, he decided. There were still people who deserved to be stolen from, or exposed, or dropped in the deep jungle with only flip-flops and a spoon. He would just have to put more effort into finding them.

Artemis activated the wing cameras. There was one such person on the avenue below. A megalomaniacal, cold-hearted pixie. Opal Koboi. Artemis could see her striding toward the manor, jamming Holly's helmet down over her ears.

I was afraid of that. She thought to take the helmet. A most valuable tool.

Still, he had no alternative but to attract her attention. The lives of his family and friends were at stake. Artemis took the Cessna down a hundred feet, following Opal's path to the manor. She may not hear the engine, but the sensors in Holly's helmet would throw up a dozen red lights.

On cue, Opal stopped in her tracks, throwing her gaze skyward and capturing the small plane in her sights.

Come on, Opal, thought Artemis. Take the bait. Run a thermal.

Opal strode purposefully toward the manor until she snagged the toe of one LEP boot under the heel of another.

Stupid tall elf, she thought furiously, righting herself. When I am queen . . . No . . . when I am empress, all tall fairies will have their legs modified. Or better still, I will have a human pituitary gland grafted to my brain so that I shall be the tall one. A giant among fairies, physically and mentally.

She had other plans too: An Opalesque cosmetic face mold that could give any of her adoring fans the Koboi look in seconds. A homeopathic hoverchair covered in massage bars and mood sensors that would read her humor and spray whatever scents were needed to cheer her up.

But those plans could wait until she was empress. For

now the lemur was her priority. Without its brain fluid, it could take years to accomplish her plans. Plus, magic was so much easier than science.

Opal slotted Holly's helmet onto her head. Pads inside the helmet automatically inflated to cradle her skull. There was some coded security, which she contemptuously hacked with a series of blinks and hand movements. These LEP helmets were not half as advanced as the models in her R&D department.

Once the helmet's functions were open to her, the visor's display crystals fizzled and turned scarlet. Red alert! Something was closing in. A 3-D radar sweep revealed a small craft overhead, and recognition software quickly pegged it as a human-built Cessna.

She quickly selected the command sequence for a thermal scan, and the helmet infrared detector analyzed the electromagnetic radiation coming from inside the aircraft. There was some waffle from the solar panels, but the scan isolated an orange blob in the pilot's seat. One passenger only. The helmet's biometric reader conveniently identified the pilot as Artemis Fowl, and dropped a 3-D icon over his fuzzy figure.

"One passenger," murmured Opal. "Are you trying to decoy me away from the house, Artemis Fowl? Is that why you fly so low?"

But Artemis Fowl knew technology; he would anticipate thermal imaging.

"What do you have up your sleeve?" wondered the pixie. "Or perhaps up your shirt."

She magnified Artemis's heart and discovered a second heat source superimposed over the first, distinguishable only by a slightly cooler shade of red.

Even at that desperate moment, Opal could not help but admire this young human, who had attempted to mask the lemur's heat signature with his own.

"Clever. But not ingenious."

And he would need to be ingenious to defeat Opal Koboi. Bringing back the second Artemis had been a neat trick, but she should have caught it.

I was defeated by my own arrogance, she realized. That will not happen again.

The helmet automatically tuned into the Cessna's radio frequency, and so Opal sent Artemis a little message.

"I am coming for the lemur, boy," she said, a pulse of magic setting the suit's wings aflutter. "And this time there will be no *you* to save *you*."

Artemis could not feel or see the various waves that probed the Cessna, but he guessed that Opal would use the helmet's thermal imager to see how many hot bodies were on the plane. Perhaps she would try X-ray too. It would seem as though he was trying to hide Jayjay's heat signature with his own, but that was a transparent ploy and should not fool Opal for more than a heartbeat. When the pixie was satisfied that her prize was escaping, then how could she not follow?

Artemis banked starboard to keep Opal in the camera eye, and was satisfied to see a set of wings sliding from the slots in Holly's suit.

The chase is on.

Time for the bait to pretend it is trying to escape.

Artemis peeled away from the estate, heading for the deep purple sea, opening the throttle wide, satisfied by the plane's smooth acceleration. The batteries were channeling a steady supply of power to the engines without releasing one gram of carbon dioxide into the atmosphere.

He checked the tail camera view and was not totally surprised to find the flying pixie in his monitor.

Her control over the magic is addled by the sedative, he guessed. Opal may have had barely enough power to jump-start the suit. But soon the dart's aftereffects will peter out and then there may be lightning bolts flaring across my wing.

Artemis turned south, following the jagged coast. The clamor and bustle of Dublin's high-rise apartment blocks, belching chimneys, and swarm of buzzing helicopters gave way to long stretches of gray rock shadowed by the north-south rail track. The sea pushed against the shore, folding its million fingers over sand, scrub, and shale.

Fishing boats chugged from buoy to buoy, trailing

white sea-serpent wakes, sailors snagging lobster pots with long-handled gaffs. Fat clouds hung ponderously at twelve thousand feet, rain brewing in their bellies.

A peaceful evening, so long as no one looks up.

Though at this altitude, Opal's blurred flying form could be mistaken for an eagle.

Artemis's plan went smoothly for longer than he had hoped. He made sixty miles without interference from Opal. He allowed himself a glimmer of hope.

Soon, he thought. The LEP reinforcements will come soon.

Then his radio crackled into life. "Artemis? Are you there, Artemis?"

Butler. He sounded extremely calm, which he always did before he explained just how serious a situation was.

"Butler, old friend. I'm here. Tell me the good news."

The bodyguard sighed into his microphone, a breaking wave of static.

"They're not coming after the Cessna. You are not the priority."

"N°1 is," said Artemis. "They need to get him below-ground. I understand."

"Yes. Him and . . ."

"Say no more, old friend," said Artemis sharply. "Opal is listening."

"The LEP are here, Artemis. I want you to turn around and fly back."

"No," said Artemis firmly. "I will not put Mother at risk again."

Artemis heard a strange creaking sound and surmised that Butler was strangling the microphone stalk.

"Very well. Another location, then. Someplace where we can dig ourselves in."

"Very well, I am on a southerly heading anyway, so why not—"

Artemis didn't complete his veiled suggestion, as his channel was blocked by a deafening burst of white noise. The squawk left a droning aftershock in his ears, and for a moment he allowed the Cessna to drift.

No sooner had he regained control than a thudding blow to the fuselage caused him to lose it again.

Several red lights flashed on the solar panel display-plane icon. At least ten panels had been shattered by the impact.

Artemis spared half a second to check the rear camera. Opal was no longer trailing behind him. No surprise there.

The pixie's voice burst through the radio speakers, sharp with petulance and evil intent.

"I am strong now, Mud Boy," she said. "Your poison is gone, flushed from my system. My power grows, and I am hungry for more."

Artemis did not engage in conversation. All his skill and quick thinking would be needed to pilot the Cessna.

Opal struck again on the port wing, smashing her forearms into the solar panels and breaking them as a child would break sheets of ice in a pool, windmilling her arms gleefully, wings buzzing to keep pace. The plane bucked and yawed, and Artemis fought the stick to pull the craft level.

She's insane, thought Artemis. Utterly insane.

And then: *Those panels are unique. And she calls herself a scientist.*

Opal scampered along the wing, punching an armored fist into the fuselage itself. More panels were obliterated, and tiny fist-size dents buckled the polymer over Artemis's shoulder. Tiny cracks ran along the dents, slit by the wind.

Opal's voice was loud in the speaker. "Land, Fowl. Land and I may not return to the manor when I have finished with you. Land! Land!"

Each order to *land* was emphasized by another blow on the cockpit. The windshield exploded inward, showering Artemis with jagged chunks of Plexiglas.

"Land! Land!"

You have the product, Artemis reminded himself. So you have the power. Opal cannot afford to kill Jayjay.

The wind screamed in Artemis's face, and the readings from his flight instruments made no sense, unless Opal was scrambling them with the LEP suit's field. But Artemis still had a chance. There was fight left in this Fowl.

He pointed the nose downward, banking sharply

left. Opal kept pace easily, tearing strips from the fuselage. She was a destructive shadow in the dimming dusk light.

Artemis could smell the sea.

I am too low. Too soon.

More red lights on the instrument panel. The power supply had been cut. The batteries were breached. The altimeter whirred and beeped.

Opal was at the side window. Artemis could see her tiny teeth grinning at him. She was saying something. Shouting. But the radio was not operational anymore. Just as well, probably.

She is having the time of her life, he realized. Fun, fun, fun.

Artemis struggled with the controls. The sticky flaps were the least of his worries now. If Opal decided to snip a few cables, then he would lose whatever say he had over the plane. Though it was too early, Artemis lowered the tricycle landing gear. If Opal sabotaged the mechanism now, the wheels should stay down.

They plummeted earthward, locked together. A sparrow on an eagle's back. Opal smashed her armored head through the door window's Plexiglas, still shouting inside the helmet, spittle spraying the visor. Issuing orders that Artemis could not hear and could not spare enough time to lip-read. He could see that her eyes glowed red with magic, and it was clear from her manic expression that any threads connecting her to rationality had been severed.

More shouting, muffled behind the visor. Artemis cast a sardonic gaze at the radio, which sat dead and dark in its cradle.

Opal caught the look and raised her visor, shouting over the wind, too impatient for the helmet PA.

"Give me the lemur and I will save you," she said, her voice *mesmerizing*. "You have my . . ."

Artemis avoided her gaze and pulled the emergency flare gun from under the seat, sticking it in her face.

"You leave me no choice but to shoot you," he said, voice cold and certain. This was not a threat, it was a statement of fact.

Opal knew the truth when she heard it, and for one second her resolve wavered. She pulled back, but not quickly enough to prevent Artemis from firing the flare into her helmet, then reaching up to flick down the visor.

Opal spun away from the Cessna, trailing black smoke, red sparks swarming around her head like angry wasps. Her wing smashed into the Cessna's, and neither survived intact. Solar cell splinters flashed like stardust, and Opal's tail feathers helicoptered slowly earthward. The airplane yawed to starboard, moaning like a wounded animal.

I need to land. Now.

Artemis didn't feel guilty about what he'd done. Flare burns would not hinder a being of Opal's regenerative power for long. Already the magic would be repairing her skin damage. At best he had bought himself a few minutes' reprieve.

When Opal comes back, she will be beyond furious. A true maniac. Perhaps her judgment will be clouded.

Artemis smiled grimly, and for a moment he felt like his old conniving self, before Holly and his mother had introduced him to their pesky moral codes.

Good. Clouded judgment may give me the advantage I need.

Artemis leveled the craft as much as he could, slowing his descent. Wind slapped his face, tugging his skin. Shielding his eyes with a forearm, Artemis peered downward through the blur of propeller spin.

Hook Head peninsula jutted into the blackness of the sea below him like a slate-gray arrowhead. A cluster of lights winked on the eastern curve. This was the village of Duncade, where Butler had awaited his young charge's return from Limbo. A magical inlet that had once sheltered the demon isle of Hybras. The entire area was a magical hotspot and would set LEP spectrometers buzzing.

Dark blue night was falling quickly, and it was difficult to tell hard ground from soft. Artemis knew that a carpet of meadow ran from Duncade to the Hook Head lighthouse, but he could only see the grass strip once every five seconds when it flashed emerald in the tower's beam.

My runway, thought Artemis.

He dragged the Cessna into the best possible approach line, descending in uneven, stomach-lurching swoops. Solar panels frittered away from the nose and wings, streaming behind the craft.

Still no sign of Opal.

She's coming. Make no mistake about it.

With each flash of green, the hard earth rushed up to meet him.

Too fast, thought Artemis. I am coming in too fast. I will never get my legal pilot's license flying like this.

He clenched his jaws and held the stick tightly. Touchdown was going to be rough.

And it was, though not bone-shatteringly so. Not the first time. It was on the second bounce that Artemis was shunted forward into the console and heard the left side of his collarbone snap. A horrible sound that brought bile to his throat.

No pain yet. Just cold. I am going into shock.

The Cessna's wheels skidded on the long grass, which was coated with sea spray and slicker than ice. Artemis scowled, not because of his injuries but because his fate was in the hands of chance now; he had no control. Opal would be coming for Jayjay, and he must do his utmost to distract her.

The outside world continued to intrude most violently on Artemis's thoughts. The front wheel strut glanced off a sharp rock, shearing away completely. For several seconds the wheel continued to roll alongside the plane, until it veered off into the darkness.

Another bump and the Cessna collapsed onto its nose, propeller plowing furrows in the earth. Sheaves of grass fanned the air, and clods of muck rained through the holes in the windshield.

Artemis tasted earth and thought, I don't see what Mulch makes all the fuss about. It's not exactly lobster mousse.

Then he was out of the plane and stumbling toward the rocky shoreline. Artemis did not call for help, and none would have come if he had. The rocks were black, treacherous, and deserted. The sea was loud and the wind blew high. Even if the lighthouse beam had pinned the falling plane's image to the sky, it would be a long while before unarmed, unsuspecting villagers arrived to offer assistance. And by then it would be too late.

Artemis stumbled on, his left arm hanging low, his good hand cupped over the furry head poking from the front of his jacket.

"Almost there," he panted.

A pair of sea stacks jutted from the water like the last teeth from the gums of a tobacco chewer. Hundred-foot-high hard-rock columns that had resisted the erosive power of wind and wave. The locals called them The Nuns because of their sisterly appearance. Head-to-toe habits.

The Nuns were quite the local attraction, and sturdy

rope bridges spanned the chasms from shore to Little Sister and on to Mother Superior. Butler once told Artemis that he had spent many lonely nights on the second sea stack with night-vision binoculars, glassing the ocean for a sign of Hybras.

Artemis stepped onto the first span of the bridge. It rippled and creaked slightly under his feet, but held firm. He saw the sea far below through the slats, flat rocks pushing through the surface like mushrooms through clay. The body of an unlucky dog lay splayed on one of the lower rocks, a stark reminder of what could happen if you lost your footing on The Nuns.

I am hurrying toward a dead end, he told himself. Once I reach the second stack, there is nowhere to go but down.

But there was no choice. A quick glance over his shoulder told him that Opal was coming. He did not even need his shield-filtered sunglasses to see her. The pixie had no magic to spare for invisibility. She lurched zombielike across the meadow, a red haze of magic lighting her face inside the helmet, fists clenched at her side. Her wings were outstretched but tattered and battered. She would not be flying anywhere on those. Only the power of Jayjay could save Opal now. He was her last hope for victory: if she did not inject his brain fluid soon, then surely the LEP would arrive to protect the endangered lemur.

Artemis walked across the bridge, careful not to bash

his dangling arm against the railing. Miraculously he was in little constant pain, but every footstep sent a throb of white-hot agony flashing across his upper chest.

Distract her a while longer. Then the cavalry will surely arrive. The winged, invisible cavalry. They wouldn't abandon me, would they?

"Fowl!" the shriek came from behind him. Closer than he expected. "Give me the monkey!"

The voice was layered with wasted magic. No eye contact. No *mesmer*.

Monkey, thought Artemis, smirking. Ha-ha.

Farther across the chasm. Blackness above and below, starpoints in the sky and sea. Waves growling like tigers. Hungry.

Artemis stumbled toward the first Nun, Little Sister. Stepping out onto a rock plateau worn treacherous. His foot slipped on the surface, and Artemis spun across the diameter of the summit like a ballroom dancer with an unseen partner.

He heard Opal's shriek. For Jayjay to die now would be disaster, as she would be stuck in this time with the entire LEP on her trail and no ultimate powers.

Artemis did not look back, though he ached to. He could hear Opal clanking across the boards, swearing with each breath. The words sounded almost comical in her childlike pixie voice.

Nowhere to go but forward. Artemis almost fell onto

the second span of bridge, pulling himself along the rope rail until he arrived at Mother Superior. Locals said that if you stood at the right point on the coastline at sunrise, and squinted a little, then you could just make out stern features on the Mother Superior's face.

The rock felt stern now. Bleak and unforgiving. Even one false step would not be tolerated.

Artemis dropped to his knees on the mushroom curve of the plateau, cupping his left elbow in his right palm.

Soon, shock and pain will overcome me. Not yet, genius. Focus.

Artemis glanced down to the V of his jacket. The furry head was gone.

Dropped on the Little Sister. Waiting for Opal.

This was confirmed by a sudden shriek of delight from behind. Artemis turned slowly—and with great effort to face his enemy. It seemed as though he had been fighting her forever.

The pixie stood atop the sea stack, almost dancing with delight. Artemis could see a small furry figure splayed on the plateau.

"I have him," Opal cackled. "With all your genius! With your big bursting brain! You dropped him! You simply dropped him!"

Artemis felt a throb build in his shoulder. In a minute, there would be worse coming, he was certain of it.

Opal stretched two hands toward her prize. "He is mine," she said reverentially, and Artemis swore he heard

thunder in the distance. "The ultimate magic is mine. I have the lemur."

Artemis spoke clearly, so his words would carry across the divide. "It's not a lemur," he said. "It's a monkey."

Opal's smile froze, all tiny teeth, and she grabbed what she had thought was Jayjay. The figure was soft in her hands.

"A toy!" she gasped. "This is a toy."

Artemis's triumph was dulled by pain and exhaustion. "Opal, meet Professor Primate. My brother's plaything."

"A toy," repeated Opal dully. "But there were two heat sources. I saw them."

"Microwave gel pack stuffed inside the foam," explained Artemis. "It's over, Opal. Jayjay is in Haven by now. You can't get him. Turn yourself in, and I won't have to hurt you."

Opal's features were twisted with rage. "Hurt me! Hurt *me*!" She dashed the toy monkey against the rock surface over and over again until the dented works fell out.

A metallic voice issued from the speaker: "History will remember this day. . . . History will . . . History will remember this day."

Opal screamed, and red sparks boiled around her fingertips.

"I cannot fly and I cannot shoot lightning, but I have enough magic to boil your brain."

Opal's dreams of supreme power were forgotten. At

that moment all she wanted was to kill Artemis Fowl. She stepped onto the second span with murder in her heart.

Artemis stood wearily and reached into his pocket. "Your armor should save you," he said, his voice calm. "It will be terrifying, but the LEP will dig you out."

Opal scoffed. "More tactics. Bluff and double bluff. Not this time, Artemis."

"Don't make me do this, Opal," Artemis pleaded. "Just sit down and wait for the LEP. No one needs to get hurt."

"Oh, I think someone needs to get hurt," said Opal.

Artemis took his modified laser pointer from his pocket, activating the narrow beam and aiming it at the base of the Little Sister.

"What are you going to do with that thing? It would take a hundred years to saw through this rock."

"I'm not trying to saw through it," said Artemis, keeping the beam steady. "And it's not a rock."

Opal raised her hands, sparks laced like barbed wire around her fingers.

No more talk.

Artemis's laser beam cut deep into the base of the Little Sister, until it pierced the outer shell and reached the vast pocket of methane beneath.

The Little Sister was not a rock. It was the seventh kraken, attracted by the magical resonance of Hybras. Artemis had been studying it for years. Not even Foaly knew it was there.

The explosion was huge, shooting a column of fire fifty feet into the air. The outer shell collapsed under Opal, engulfing her in a blizzard of shrapnel.

Artemis heard the dull twang of her LEP armor flexing to take the shock.

Foaly's armor should save her.

He threw himself flat on the sea stack, suffering the rain of rock, weed, and even fish on his back and legs.

Luck will save me now. Only luck.

And luck did save him. The plateau was hammered with several sizeable missiles, but none struck Artemis. He was hailed with smaller objects and would have a hundred bruises and cuts to add to his list of injuries, but not a single bone was broken.

When the world felt as though it had stopped vibrating, Artemis crawled to the lip of the sea stack and gazed down at the bubbling sea below. A pyramid of rubble steamed gently in the waves where the kraken had been. The great beast would be moving away silently now, to find another magical hotspot. Of Opal there was no sign.

The LEP will find her.

Artemis turned over on his back and watched the stars. He did this often, and the sight usually caused him to wonder how he would reach the planets orbiting those pinpricks of light, and what he would find there. On this evening the stars just made him feel tiny and insignificant. Nature was vast and mighty and would eventually swallow

374

him, even the memory of him. He lay there cold and alone on the plateau, waiting for a feeling of triumph that he realized would never arrive, and listening to the distant shouts of the villagers as they made their way across the long meadow.

Holly arrived before the villagers, gliding in from the north and touching down soundlessly on the sea stack.

"You're flying," said Artemis, as though he had never seen this before.

"I borrowed a suit from N°1's bodyguards. Well, I say borrowed . . ."

"How did you find me?" asked Artemis, though he could guess.

"Oh, I saw a huge explosion and wondered, Now who could that be?"

"Hmm," said Artemis. "A bit of a giveaway."

"Also, I followed my old suit's radiation trail. I'm still following it." Holly touched a finger to her visor, and the filter changed. "That's quite a pile of rocks you dumped on Opal. It's going to take a Retrieval team some time to dig her out. She's cursing like a tunnel dwarf down there. What did you do to her?"

"The seventh kraken," explained Artemis. "The one Foaly missed because it was tubular rather than conical, I would guess. I picked it up on a weather satellite."

Holly placed a finger on Artemis's forehead. "Typical

Artemis Fowl. Beaten to a pulp and still he delivers a lecture."

Magical sparks flowed from Holly's fingertip, engulfing Artemis like a cocoon. He felt comforted and peaceful, like a baby in its blanket. His pains were wiped away, and his shattered collarbone liquefied, then solidified whole.

"Nice trick," he said, smiling. His eyes were glassy.

"I'm here till Tuesday," said Holly, smiling back. "Nº1 filled my tank."

Artemis gazed up at his friend through a red haze. "I'm sorry I lied to you, Holly. Truly. You've done so much."

Holly's eyes were distant. "Maybe you made the wrong decision; maybe I would have made that decision myself. We're from different worlds, Artemis. We will always have doubts about each other. Let's just carry on and leave the past in the past, where it should be."

Artemis nodded. That was as good as he was going to get, and better than he deserved.

Holly pulled a tether from her belt and looped it under Artemis's arms. "Now, let's get you home before the villagers start building a gallows."

"Good idea," mumbled Artemis, drowsy with the aftereffects of his magical makeover.

"Yes, believe it or not, other people do have those occasionally."

"Occasionally," agreed Artemis; then his head lolled back and he was asleep.

Holly reset her wings for the added weight and launched them both off the lip of the sea stack, flying low to avoid the flashlight beams of the locals, which strobed the night sky like searchlights.

Foaly tuned into Holly's helmet frequency while she was airborne.

"The seventh kraken, I'm guessing. Of course, I had my suspicions." He paused. "This would be a good opportunity to mind-wipe Artemis," he said. "Save ourselves a lot of grief in the future."

"Foaly!" said Holly, horrified. "We don't wipe our friends. Artemis brought Jayjay back to us. Who knows how many cures lie in that lemur's brain."

"I'm kidding. I'm kidding. And guess what, we won't even have to ask Jayjay to donate some brain fluid. N°1 synthesized it while he was waiting for the shuttle. That kid is one of a kind."

"I seem to run into a lot of those. By the way, we need to send a team in for Opal."

"They're en route. I think you're in for another rake over the coals from IA when you get back here."

Holly snorted. "What's new?"

Foaly fell silent, waiting for Holly to share the details of her adventures. Eventually he could wait no more.

"Okay, you win. I'll ask. What happened back then—almost eight years ago? My gods, it must have been mayhem."

Holly felt a phantom tingle on her lips where she had kissed Artemis.

"Nothing. Nothing happened. We went, we got the lemur, we came back. A couple of glitches, but obviously nothing we couldn't handle."

Foaly didn't press for details. Holly would tell him when she had processed it herself.

"Do you ever think you might like to go to work and then just come home? No drama?"

Holly watched the ocean flash by below her and felt the weight of Artemis Fowl in her arms.

"No," she said. "I never think that."

CHAPTER 16

A TEAM OF HAIRDRESSERS

LESS THAN AN HOUR later they landed at Fowl Manor. Artemis woke up just as Holly's heels hit the gravel, and was instantly alert.

"Magic is wonderful stuff," he said, pinwheeling his left arm.

"You should have held on to yours," quipped Holly.

"Ironically, if I had not attempted to cure Mother, Opal would have allowed her to recover. It was my journey into the past that gave Opal the basis for her plan, which she instigated by following us to her future."

"I liked you better asleep," said Holly, retrieving her tether. "My head hurt less."

"It's the big time paradox. If I had done nothing, then nothing would have needed to be done."

Holly touched her helmet. "Let me get Foaly on the

⚡🜛◊🜍⚡🜛⊕🜄◊→🜏🜅🜄⊖⌾🜍♆•🜏

com. You two could both talk at the same time."

The exterior lights cast a soft glow on the gravel, setting the stones shimmering like gems. Lofty evergreen trees swayed in the gentle breeze, rustling with life. Like Tolkien's creatures.

Artemis watched Holly stride toward the main doors. If only, he thought. If only.

N°1 sat on the front step, flanked by a squad of LEP officers bristling with the latest weaponry. Artemis knew that his DNA was coded into their guns, and all they had to do was select his icon from a list and there would be no escape. Jayjay had wrapped himself around the demon's crown like a hunting cap and seemed most comfortable there. He roused himself when he saw Artemis and leaped into the boy's arms. A dozen LEP rifles instantly beeped, and Artemis guessed that his icon was being selected.

"Hello there, little fellow. How do you like the present?"

N°1 answered for the lemur. "He likes it fine. Especially now that no one will be sticking any needles in his head."

Artemis nodded. "You duplicated the fluid. I thought that might be an option. Where is Dr. Schalke?"

"He collapsed once Opal departed. Butler put him in a guest room."

"And Artemis Junior?"

"Technically, you are Artemis Junior," replied N°1. "But I know what you are trying to ask me. Your younger self has been transported back to his own time. I sent a Retrieval captain and stayed here as a marker. I thought you would want him out of the way as soon as possible, what with your father and the twins on their way home."

Artemis tickled Jayjay under the chin. "It might have proved awkward."

Holly was troubled. "I know we promised not to wipe him, but I'm not particularly thrilled that there's a little Fowl running around with fairy knowledge in his devious skull."

Artemis raised an eyebrow. "Devious skull? Charming."

"Hey, if the flap fits . . ."

N°1 was a little pale. With a flex of his tail, he lifted his squat rump from the step. "About this no mind-wiping promise. The thing is, nobody told me."

Holly stared at him. "So you wiped him?"

N°1 nodded. "And Schalke. I also left a residual spell in young Artemis's eyeballs so Butler will get it too. Nothing fancy, just a blanket memory loss. Their brains will fill in the gaps, invent believable memories."

Holly shuddered. "You left a spell in his eyeballs? That is revolting."

"Revolting but ingenious," said Artemis.

Holly was surprised. "You don't seem too indignant. I was expecting a speech. Rolling eyes, flapping arms, the whole Fowl thing."

Artemis shrugged. "I knew it would happen. I didn't

remember anything, so I must have been wiped, therefore we must have won."

"You always knew."

"I didn't know what the cost would be."

Nº1 sighed. "So I'm off the hook, as you humans say?"

"Absolutely," said Holly, clapping him on the shoulder. "I feel a lot better now."

"On the positive side, I bolstered your atomic structure. Your atoms were a bit rattled by the time stream. I'm amazed you are still in one piece. I can only imagine how hard you were forced to concentrate."

"Well, you *had* bolstered my atoms, and I have to beg one more favor," said Artemis. "I need you to send a note back in time."

"I've been ordered not to open the time stream again, but maybe we can squeeze back one more thing," said Nº1.

Artemis nodded. "That's what I thought."

"When and where?"

"Holly knows. You can do it from Tara."

"How do you spell *stupendous*?" said Holly, smiling.

Artemis stepped back and craned his neck to peer upward at the front window of his parents' room. Jayjay mimicked the action, climbing onto Artemis's shoulders and tilting his tiny head back.

"I'm afraid to go up, for some reason."

He noticed himself wringing his fingers, and stuffed both hands in his jacket pockets.

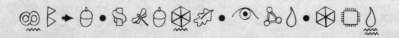

"What she must have been through, all because of my meddling. What she must have . . ."

"Don't forget us," interjected Nº1. "We were submerged in animal fat. You have no idea how gross that is. Eyeball spells are the epitome of good taste compared to animal fat."

"I was turned into an adolescent," said Holly, winking at Artemis. "Now, *that* was gross."

Artemis's smile was forced. "Strangely, all this guilt-tripping is not making me feel any better. The DNA cannons aren't helping either."

Holly gestured at the LEP squad to stand down, then tilted her head slightly as a message came through.

"There's a chopper coming in. Your father. We've got to fly."

Nº1 wagged a finger. "And that's not just a figure of speech. We actually have to fly. I know humans use that expression even when they don't intend to actually fly, so just to avoid confusion . . ."

"I get it, Nº1," said Artemis softly.

Holly raised her forearm, and Jayjay jumped onto it. "He will be safer with us."

"I know."

He turned to Holly, meeting her gaze. Blue and hazel eyes.

She gazed back for a second, then activated her wings, rising a foot from the surface.

"In another time," she said, and kissed him on the cheek.

He was at the front door before Holly called to him.

"You know something, Fowl? You did a good thing here. For its own sake. Not one penny of profit."

Artemis grimaced. "I know. I'm appalled."

He looked down at his feet, composing a pithy remark, but when he looked up again, the avenue was empty.

"Good-bye, my friends," he said. "Take care of Jayjay."

Artemis could hear helicopter rotors in the distance by the time he reached his mother's bedroom. He would have some explaining to do, but he had a feeling that Artemis Senior would not press him for details once he saw Angeline in good health.

Artemis flexed his fingers, summoning his courage, then pushed through into the bedchamber. The bed was empty; his mother was sitting at her dresser, despairing at the state of her hair.

"Oh dear, Arty," she said in mock horror on spotting her son in the mirror. "Look at me. I need a team of hairdressers flown in immediately from London."

"You look fine, Mother . . . Mom. Wonderful."

Angeline ran a pearl-handled brush through her long hair, the luster returning with each stroke. "Considering what I have been through."

"Yes. You were ill. But you are better now."

Angeline turned on her dresser stool, reaching out her

arms. "Come here, my hero. Hug your mother."

Artemis was happy to do as he was told.

A thought struck him. *Hero*. Why had she called him a hero?

Generally victims of the *mesmer* remembered nothing of their ordeal. But Butler had remembered what Opal did to him, he had even described the experience to Artemis. Schalke had been wiped. But what of Mother?

Angeline held him tightly. "You have done so much, Arty. Risked everything."

The rotors were loud now, rattling the windows. His father was home.

"I didn't do so much, Mom. What any son would do."

Angeline's hand cradled his head. He could feel her tears on his cheek. "I know everything, Arty. Everything. That creature left me her memories. I tried to fight her, but she was too strong."

"What creature, Mother? It was the fever. You had a hallucination, that's all."

Angeline held him at arms' length. "I was in the diseased hell of that pixie's brain, Artemis. Don't you dare lie to me and say that I wasn't. I saw your friends almost die to help you. I saw Butler's heart stop. I saw you save us all. Look me in the eye and tell me these things did not happen."

Artemis found it difficult to meet his mother's stare, and when he did it was impossible to lie.

"They happened. All of them. And more."

Angeline frowned. "You have a hazel eye. Why did I not notice that?"

"I put a spell on you," said Artemis miserably.

"And on your father?"

"Him too."

Below, the front door crashed open. His father's footsteps raced across the lobby, then onto the stairway.

"You saved me, Artemis," said his mother hurriedly. "But I have a feeling that all your spell-casting in some way put us in this situation. So I want to know everything. Everything. Do you understand?"

Artemis nodded. He couldn't see how to escape this. He was in a dead end, and the only way out was complete honesty.

"Now we will give your father and the twins time to hug me and kiss me, then you and I are going to have a talk. It will be our secret. Understood?"

"Understood."

Artemis sat on the bed. He felt six years old again, when he had been caught hacking the school computers to make the test questions a little more challenging.

His father was on the landing now. Artemis knew that his secret life ended today. As soon as his mother got him alone, he would be explaining himself. Starting at the beginning. Abductions, uprisings, time jaunts, goblin revolutions. Everything.

Complete honesty, he thought.

Artemis Fowl shuddered.

Some hours later, the master bedroom had been transformed by the whirlwind known as Beckett Fowl. There were pizza boxes on the night table and tomato-sauce finger paintings on the wall. Beckett had stripped off his own clothes and dressed himself in one of his father's T-shirts, which he had belted around his waist. He had applied a mascara mustache and lipstick scars to his face and was currently fencing with an invisible enemy, using one of his father's old prosthetic legs as a sword.

Artemis was finishing his explanation of Angeline's miraculous recovery. "And so I realized that Mother had somehow contracted Glover's Fever, which is usually confined to Madagascar, so I synthesized the natural cure preferred by the locals and administered it. Relief was immediate."

Beckett noticed that Artemis had stopped talking, and heaved a dramatic sigh of relief. He rode an imaginary horse across the room and poked Myles with the prosthetic leg.

"Good story?" he asked his twin.

Myles climbed down from the bed and placed his mouth beside Beckett's ear.

"Artemis simple-toon," he confided.

EPILOGUE

Hook Head

Commander Trouble Kelp himself led the Retrieval team to dig Opal Koboi out of the rubble. They inflated a distortion bubble over the work zone, so they could fire up the shuttle's lasers without fear of discovery.

"Hurry up, Furty," Trouble called over an open channel. "We have one hour until sunrise. Let's get that megalomaniacal pixie out of there and back into her own time."

They were lucky to have a dwarf on the team. Normally dwarfs were extremely reluctant to work with the authorities, but this one had agreed so long as he didn't have to work any of the hundred-and-ninety-odd dwarf holy days, and if the LEP paid his exorbitant consultant fees.

In a situation like this one, dwarfs were invaluable. They could work rubble like no other species. If you needed to dig something out alive, then dwarfs were the ones to do it. All they needed to do was let their beard hairs play over a surface, and they could tell you more about what was going on under that surface than any amount of seismic or geological equipment.

Currently, Trouble was monitoring Furty Pullchain's progress through the kraken debris on the feed from his helmet cam. The dwarf's limbs were a shade paler than usual in the night-vision filter. One hand directed a nozzle of support foam that coated the tunnel wall at stress points, and the other reached in under his beard to rehinge his jaw.

"Okay, *Commander*," he said, managing to make the rank sound like a insult. "I made it to the spot. It's a miracle I'm alive. This thing is as steady as a house of cards in a hurricane."

"Yeah, whatever, Furty. You're a marvel. Now, pull her out and let's get belowground. I have a captain I need to discipline."

"Keep yer acorns on, Commander. I'm readin' the beacon loud and clear."

Trouble fumed silently. Maybe Holly Short was not the only one who would have to be disciplined.

He followed the live feed, watching Furty scoop aside the rock, weed, and shell fragments covering Holly's suit.

Except there was no suit. Just a helmet with its flashing tracer beacon.

"I come all this way for a helmet?" said Furty, aggrieved. "Ain't no pixie here, just the smell of one."

Trouble sat up straight. "Are you sure? Could you be in the wrong spot?"

Furty snorted. "Yep. I'm at the *other* buried LEP helmet. 'Course I'm sure."

She was gone. Opal had disappeared.

"Impossible. How could she escape?"

"Beats me," said Furty. "Maybe she squeezed through a natural tunnel. Them pixies are slippery little creatures. I remember one time when I was a sprog. Me and Kherb, my cousin, broke into a—"

Trouble cut him off. This was serious. Opal Koboi was loose in the world. He put a video call in to Foaly at Police Plaza.

"Don't tell me," said the centaur, running a hand down his long face.

"She's gone. She left the helmet so the beacon would draw us in. Any vitals from her suit?"

Foaly checked his monitor. "Nothing. It was loud and clear until five minutes ago. I thought it was a suit malfunction."

Trouble took a breath. "Put out an alert. Priority one. I want the guards tripled on *our* Koboi in Atlantis. It would be just like Opal to bust herself out."

Foaly got to it. One Opal Koboi had almost managed to take over the world. Two would probably shoot for the entire galaxy.

"And call Holly," continued Commander Kelp. "Inform the captain that her weekend leave is canceled."

Fowl Manor, Almost Eight Years Ago

Artemis Fowl awoke in his own bed, and for a moment red sparks danced before his eyes. They sparkled and twinkled hypnotically before chasing their own tails out of existence.

Red sparks, he thought. Unusual. I have seen stars before, but never sparks.

The ten-year-old boy stretched, grabbing handfuls of his own duvet. For some reason he felt more content than usual.

I feel safe and happy.

Artemis sat bolt upright.

Happy? I feel happy?

He couldn't remember feeling truly happy since his father had disappeared, but on this morning his mood was bordering on cheerful.

Perhaps it was the deal with the Extinctionists. My first major chunk of profit.

No. That wasn't it. That particular transaction had left Artemis feeling sick to the pit of his stomach. So much so that he couldn't think about it and would probably never dwell on the past few days again.

So what could account for this feeling of optimism? Something from the dream he'd been having. A plan. A new scheme that would bring enough profit to fund a hundred Arctic expeditions.

That was it. The dream. What had it been about?

It was just out of reach. The images already fading.

A crafty smile twitched at the corner of his mouth.

Fairies. Something about fairies.

Here's an excerpt from
Eoin Colfer's thrilling novel

available now

CHAPTER 1: THE PRINCESS AND THE PIRATE

Conor Broekhart was a remarkable boy, a fact that became evident very early in his idyllic childhood. Nature is usually grudging with her gifts, dispensing them sparingly, but she favored Conor with all she had to offer. It seemed as though all the talents of his ancestors had been bestowed upon him: intelligence, strong features, and grace.

Conor was fortunate in his situation, too. He was born into an affluent community where the values of equality and justice were actually being applied—on the surface, at least. He grew up with a strong belief in right and wrong that was not muddied by poverty or violence. It was straightforward for the young boy. Right was Great Saltee, wrong was Little Saltee.

It is an easy matter now to pluck some events from Conor's early years and say, *There it is. The boy who became the man. We should have seen it.* But hindsight is an unreliable science, and in truth, there was perhaps a single incident during Conor's early days at the palace that hinted at his potential.

The incident in question occurred when Conor was nine years old and roaming the serving corridors that snaked behind the walls of the castle chapel and main building. His partner on these excursions was the Princess Isabella, one year his senior and always the more adventurous of the two. Isabella and Conor were rarely seen without each other, and often so daubed with mud, blood, and nothing good that the boy was barely distinguishable from the princess.

On this particular summer afternoon, they had exhausted the fun to be had tracking the source of an unused chimney and had decided to launch a surprise pirate attack on the king's apartment.

"You can be Captain Crow," said little Conor, licking some soot from around his mouth. "And I can be the cabin boy that stuck an ax in his head."

Isabella was a pretty thing, with an elfin face and round brown eyes, but at that moment she looked more like a sweep's urchin than a princess.

"No, Conor. You are Captain Crow, and I am the princess hostage."

"There is no princess hostage," declared Conor firmly, worried that Isabella was once again about to mold the legend to suit herself. In previous games, she had included a unicorn and a fairy that were definitely not part of the original story.

"Of course there is," said Isabella belligerently. "There is because I say there is, and I am an actual princess, whereas *you* were born in a balloon." Isabella intended this as an insult, but to Conor being born in a balloon was about the finest place to be born.

"Thank you," he said, grinning.

"That's not a good thing," squealed Isabella. "Dr. John says that your lungs were probably crushed by the alti-tood."

"My lungs're better than yours. See!" And Conor hooted at the sky to show just how healthy his lungs were.

"Very well," said Isabella, impressed. "But I am still the princess hostage. And you should remember that I can have you executed if you displease me."

Conor was not unduly concerned about Isabella having him executed, as she ordered him hung at least a dozen times a day and it hadn't happened yet. He was more worried that Isabella was not turning out to be as good a playmate as he had hoped. Basically, he wanted someone who would play the games he fancied playing, which generally involved flying paper gliders or eating insects. But lately Isabella had been veering toward dress-up and kissing, and she would only explore chimneys if Conor agreed to pretend that the two of them were the legendary lovers Diarmuid and Gráinne, escaping from Fionn's castle.

Needless to say, Conor had no wish to be a legendary lover. Legendary lovers rarely flew anywhere, and hardly ever ate insects. "Very well," he moaned. "You are the hostage princess."

"Excellent, Captain," Isabella said sweetly. "Now, you may drag me to my father's chamber and demand ransom."

"Drag?" said Conor hopefully.

"Play drag, not real drag, or I shall have you hung."

Conor thought, with remarkable wit for a nine-year-old, that if he had actually been hung every time Isabella had ordered it, his neck would be longer than a Serengeti giraffe's. "Play drag, then. Can I kill anyone we meet?"

"Absolutely anyone. Not Papa, though, until after we see how sad he is."

Absolutely anyone. That's something, thought Conor, swishing his wooden sword, thinking how it cut the air like a gull's wing.

Just like a wing.

The pair proceeded across the barbican, she oohing and he *arr*ing, drawing fond but also wary looks from those they passed. The palace's only resident children were well liked, not at all spoiled, and mannerly enough when their parents were nearby; but they were also light fingered and would pilfer whatever they fancied on their daily quests. One afternoon, a particular Italian gold leaf artisan had turned from the cherub he was coating to find his brush and tray of gold wafers missing. The gold turned up later, coating the wings of a week-dead seagull, which *someone* had tried to fly from the Wall battlements.

They crossed the bridge into the main keep, which housed the king's residence, office, and meeting rooms. And this would generally be where the pair would have been met with a good-natured challenge from the sentry. But the king himself had just leaned out the window and sent the fellow running to catch the Wexford boat and put ten shillings on a horse he fancied in the Curracloe beach races. The palace had a telephone system, but there were no wires to the shore as yet, and the booking agents on the mainland refused to take bets over the semaphore.

For two minutes only, much to the princess and pirate's delight, the main keep was unguarded. They strode in as though they owned the castle. "Of course, in real life, I *do* own the castle," confided Isabella, never missing a chance to remind Conor of her exalted position.

"Arrrr," said Conor, and meant it.

The spiral staircase ascended through three floors, all packed with cleaning staff, lawyers, scientists, and civil servants; but through a combination of infant cunning and luck, the pair managed to pass the lower floors to reach the king's own entrance, impressive oak double doors with half of the Saltee flag and motto carved into each one. *Vallo Parietis*, read the legend. *Defend the Wall.* The flag was a crest bisected vertically into crimson and gold sections, with a white blocked tower stamped in the center.

The door was slightly ajar. "It's open," said Conor.

"It's open, *hostage princess*," Isabella reminded him.

"Sorry, hostage princess. Let's see what treasure lies inside."

"I'm not supposed to, Conor."

"Pirate Captain Crow," said Conor, slipping through the gap in the door. As usual, Nicholas's apartment was littered with the remains of a dozen experiments. There was a cannibalized dynamo on the hearth rug, copper wiring strands protruding from its belly.

"That's a sea creature and those are its guts," said Conor with relish.

"Oh, you foul pirate," said Isabella.

"Stop your smiling, then, if I'm a foul pirate. Hostages are supposed to weep and wail."

In the fireplace itself were jars of mercury and experimental fuels. Nicholas refused to allow his staff to move them downstairs. Too volatile, he had explained. Anyway, a fire would only go up the chimney.

Conor pointed to the jars. "Bottles of poison. Squeezed from a dragon's bum. One sniff and you vaporate." This sounded very possible, and Isabella wasn't sure whether to believe it or not.

On the chaise longue were buckets of fertilizer, a couple of them gently steaming. "Also from a dragon's bum," intoned Conor wisely. Isabella tried to keep her scream behind her lips, so it shot out of her nose instead.

"It's fert'lizer," said Conor, taking pity on her. "For making plants grow on the island."

Isabella scowled at him. "You're being hanged at sundown. That's a princess's promise."

The apartment was a land of twinklings and shining for a couple of unsupervised children. A stars-and-stripes banner was draped around the shoulders of a stuffed black bear in the corner. A collection of prisms and lenses glinted from a wooden box closed with a cap at one end; and books old and new were piled high like the columns of a ruined temple.

Conor wandered between these columns of knowledge, almost touching everything but holding back, knowing somehow that man's dreams should not be disturbed.

Suddenly, he froze. There was something he should do. The chance might never come again. "I must capture the flag," he breathed. "That's what a pirate captain is supposed to do. Go to the roof so I can capture the flag and gloat."

"Capture the flag and goat?"

"Gloat."

Isabella stood hands on hips. "It's pronounced goooaaat, idiot."

"You're supposed to be a princess. Insulting your subjects is not very princessy."

Isabella was unrepentant. "Princesses do what they want; anyway, we don't have a goat on the roof."

Conor did not waste his time arguing. There was no winning an argument with someone who could have you executed. He ran to the roof door, swishing his sword at imaginary troops. This door, too, was open. Incredible good fortune. On the hundred previous occasions when Isabella and he had ambushed King Nicholas, every door in the place had been locked, and they had been warned, by stern-faced parents, never to venture onto the roof alone. It was a long way down.

Conor thought about it.

Parents? Flag?

Parents? Flag?

"Some pirate you are," sniffed Isabella. "Standing around there scratching yourself with a toy sword."

Flag, then. "Arrr. I go for the flag, hostage princess." And then in his own voice: "Don't touch any of the experiments, Isabella. 'Specially the bottles. Papa says that one day the king is going to blow the lot of us to hell and back with his concoctions, so they must be dangerous."

Conor went up the stairs fast, before his nerve could fail

him. It wasn't far, perhaps a dozen steps to the open air. He emerged from the confines of the turret stairwell onto the stone rooftop. From dark to light in half a second. The effect was breathtaking: azure sky with clouds close enough to touch. I was born in a place like this, thought Conor.

You are a special child, his mother told him at least once a day. *You were born in the sky, and there will always be a place for you there.* Conor believed that this was true. He had always felt happiest in high places, where others feared to go.

He climbed on top of the parapet, holding tight to the flagpole. The world twirled around him, the orange sun hanging over Kilmore like a beacon. The sea glittered below him, more silver than blue, and the sky called to him as though he actually were a bird. For a moment he was bewitched by the scene, then the corner of the flag crept into his vision. Arrr, he thought. Yon be the flag. Pride of the Saltees.

The flag stood, perfectly rectangular, crimson and gold with its tower so white it glowed, held rigid by a bamboo frame so that the islands' emblem would fly proud no matter what the weather. It struck Conor that he was actually standing on top of the very tower depicted by the flag. This might have caused a tug of patriotic pride in an older islander, but to a nine-year-old, all it meant was that his image should be included on the flag. I will draw myself on after I steal the flag, he decided.

Isabella emerged onto the rooftop, blinking against the sudden light. "Come down from the parapet, Conor. We're playing pirates, not bird boy."

Conor was aghast. "And leave the flag? Don't you understand? I will be a famous pirate, more famous than Barbarossa himself."

"That wall is old, Conor."

"Pirate Captain Crow, remember."

"That wall is old, *Conor*. It could fall down. Remember the slates came off the chapel during the storm last year?"

"What about the flag?"

"Forget the flag and forget the goat. I'm hungry, so come down before I have you hanged."

Conor stamped down off the wall, sulking now. He was about to challenge Isabella, say that she could go ahead and have him hanged for all he cared, *and* she was a rotten hostage. Whoever heard of a hostage *giving* the orders? She should learn to weep and wail properly instead of threatening to execute him a hundred times a day.

He was about to say all of this when there came a dull thump from below that shook the blocks beneath their feet. A cloud of purple smoke oomphed through the doorway, as though someone had cleared a tuba.

Conor had a suspicion bordering on certainty. "Did you touch something?" he asked Isabella.

Isabella was haughty even in the face of disaster. "I am the princess of this palace, so I am quite entitled to touch whatever I wish."

The tower shook again; this time the smoke was green, and it was accompanied by a foul smell.

"What did you touch, Isabella?"

The princess of the palace turned as green as the smoke. "I may have removed the cap from the wooden box. The one with the pretty lenses."

"Oh," said Conor. "That could be trouble."

King Nicholas had explained the lense box to Conor once, delighted to find that the boy's passion for learning equaled his own. *The lenses are arranged in a very specific order,* he had said, squatting low so that his own eye appeared monstrous through the first lense. *So when I remove the cap and light comes in one end, it's concentrated by successive lenses until it can set paper alight at the other. With this little gadget, it might be possible to start a fire from a distance. The ultimate safe fuse.*

Conor remembered thinking at the time that you could leave the box by the window and have it light the fire for you each morning, a chore that he was none too fond of. And now Isabella had removed the cap.

"Did you move the box?"

"Mind your tone, commoner!"

Commoner? Isabella must really be terrified. "Isabella?"

"I possibly placed it on the table, by the window to see the colors passing through."

Obviously, the device had caught the afternoon light, releasing the power of the lenses into the king's laboratory, with the fertilizer, jugs of fuel, and various explosive materials. The concentrated light had landed on something combustible.

"We have to go," said Conor, all thoughts of Captain Crow forgotten. He was no stranger to the power of explosives. His father was in charge of the Wall defense and had brought Conor along on a trip to collapse a smugglers' cave. It was a birthday treat, but also a lesson to stay away from anything that went boom. The cave wall had collapsed like toy bricks swatted by a toddler.

The tower shook again; several floor blocks rattled in their housings, then dropped into the apartment below. Orange and blue flames surged through the holes, and the snap and grind of breaking glass and twisting metal frightened the two children.

"Up on the wall," said Conor urgently. "The floor is falling."

For once, Isabella did not argue. She accepted Conor's hand and followed him to the lip of the parapet.

"The floor is a foot thick," he explained, shouting over the roar of the flames. "The parapet is four feet thick. It won't break."

The explosions went off below like cannon fire, each one issuing a different odor, a different color smoke. The fumes were noxious, and Conor presumed his own face was as green as Isabella's. It doesn't matter if the parapet holds, he realized. The flames will get us long before then.

To Isabella and Conor it felt as though the entire world shook. The stairwell spewed forth flame and smoke as though a dragon lurked below; and from the courtyard came the screams of islanders as chunks of the tower crashed down from above.

I need to get us out of this place, thought Conor. No one else can save us, not even Father.

There was no way to walk down, not through the inferno below. There was only one way down, and that was to fly.

King Nicholas was down the corridor in the privy when his daughter blew up his apartment. He was admiring the new Doulton wash-out toilet he had recently had plumbed into his own bathroom. Nicholas had considered installing them throughout the palace, but there were rumors of a new flush toilet on the horizon, and it would be a pity to be one step behind progress. *We must embrace progress, be at the forefront of it, or the Saltees will be drowned by a tidal wave of innovation.*

When the first explosion rattled the tower, Nicholas briefly thought that his own personal plumbing could be responsible for the din, but realized that not even the bottle of home-brewed ale he had consumed with Declan Broekhart the previous evening could result in such a disturbance.

They were under attack, then? Unlikely, unless a ship had managed to approach undetected on a clear summer's afternoon.

A thought struck him. Could he have left the cap off the lense box? If so much as a spark took flight in that room . . .

King Nicholas finished his royal business and yanked the door open, quickly closing it again as a roiling cloud of smoke and flame invaded the bathroom, searing his lungs. His apartment was destroyed, no doubt about it. Luckily there was no one in his rooms or above them, so the tower's other occupants should easily escape. *Not the king, though. King Nicholas the Stupid is trapped by his own moldering experiments.*

There was a window, of course. Nicholas was a great believer in the benefits of good ventilation. He was a devotee of meditation, too; but this was hardly the time for it.

The king stuffed a towel under the door to stop a draft inviting the fire in, and flung the window wide. Glass and brickwork tumbled past, and the entire structure shuddered as another explosion shook the tower. Nicholas poked his head out for a sideways peek, just in time to see a plume of multicolored smoke expelled from his lounge. *There go the fuel jars.*

Below, the courtyard was in chaos. The fire division, to their credit, had already hauled the pump wagon to the base of the tower and were cranking up some water pressure. If there was one thing they had plenty of on the Saltees, it was water. On any other day, the salt sea spray would have doused the fire; but today, in spite of a stiff breeze, the sea was as flat as a polished mirror.

One man stood near the base of the tower. He cut a jaunty figure in his French aviator's jacket and feathered cap. At his feet lay a large leather valise, and he seemed quite amused by the entire exploding tower situation.

Nicholas recognized him immediately and called down, "Victor Vigny. You came?"

The man beamed a startlingly white smile from the center of his tanned face. "I came," he shouted in the French accent you would expect from one in such attire. "And a good thing I did, Nick. It seems like you still haven't learned to keep a safe laboratory."

Another explosion. Blue smoke and a shudder that rattled the tower to its foundations. The king ducked out of sight, then reappeared in the window.

"Very well, Victor. Banter over and done. Time to get me down from here. Any of that famous Vigny ingenuity make it across the Atlantic?"

Victor Vigny grunted, then cast an eye around the

courtyard. The fire wagon had a ladder hooked on its flank; a rope, too. Neither were long enough to reach the king. "Who designed this thing?" he muttered, hefting the coiled rope onto his shoulder. "Tall towers and short ladders. Just goes to show, there are idiots everywhere."

"What are you doing?" asked a member of the fire brigade. "Who said you could take that?"

Vigny jerked a thumb skyward. "Him."

The fireman frowned. "God?"

The Frenchman winced. Idiots everywhere. "Not quite so lofty, *mon ami.*"

The fireman glanced upward, catching sight of the king in the window.

"Do what he says," roared Nicholas. "That man has saved my life in the past, and I trust him to do it again."

"Yes, Your Majesty. I am at your . . . at his service."

Victor pointed at the ladder. "Lean that against the wall, below the window."

"It won't reach," said the fireman, eager to say something intelligent.

"Just do it, *monsieur.* Your king is getting a little hot under the collar."

The fireman grabbed a comrade, and together they propped the ladder against the tower. Victor Vigny was halfway up before the stiles hit the wall. The tower transmitted its vibrations into the rungs, and Victor knew that it wouldn't be long before it blew its top, like a plugged cannon. The king's apartment and everything above it would soon be no more than dust and memories. He quickly reached the top of the ladder, and threading his legs through the rungs, he slid the rope off his shoulder and down his arm.

"Nimble, ain't he?" commented the fireman to his partner. "But as I intelligently said, that there ladder don't reach."

The debris was showering down now, lumps, shards, and entire granite blocks. There was no avoiding it for the three men working at the ladder. They bore the blows with hunched shoulders and grunts.

"Lean it back," Victor called down, sweat dripping from his face. He tore his feathered cap off as it caught fire, revealing the shock of spiked hair that had earned him the nickname *La Brosse*. "You owe me a hat, Nicholas. I've had that one since New Orleans."

The firemen took the weight of the ladder and the Parisian, pulling him three feet back from the tower wall. Victor Vigny took half a dozen coils in his hand and sent them spinning upward. He had judged the coils accurately, landing the spliced end directly in King Nicholas's hand.

"Tie her off strong now, and be quick about it." Victor cinched the rope to the top rung and then slid down the stiles as fast as he could without stripping the skin from his palms.

"Ladder don't reach," the fireman pointed out, while Victor plunged his hands into the nearest fire bucket.

"I know that, *monsieur*. But the ladder reaches the rope, and the rope reaches the king."

"Ah," said the fireman.

"Now, stand back—if I know your king, that tower has more explosives in it than a similarly sized cannon. I believe we may be about to shoot down the moon."

The fire brigade gave up. They couldn't pump enough pressure to reach the blaze, and even if they could, that fire was all sorts of colors, and pouring water on it might just make it angry.

So they stood back out of the spitting castle's range, waiting to see if the last male Trudeau in the line could save himself from death by fire or fall.

Inside the bathroom, King Nicholas put his Royal Doulton toilet through its most rigorous test. True, the toilet had been constructed to bear the weight of a hefty adult, but possibly not one swinging from a rope tied to its piping. With a dripping towel draped over his forehead, the king put four loops around the evacuation pipe and a few hitches on the end. *I really hope that pipe does not burst. Being burned alive is bad enough, without being found covered in waste.*

The bathroom's stout wooden door was cracking with heat, as though soldiers battered from without. The steel bands buckled, sending rivets pinging around the room like ricocheting bullets.

Nicholas struggled on, wiping his eyes with the towel, inching toward the dim yellow triangle that must be the window. There was no thinning of the smoke, just a faint glow in its center. Just follow the rope, he told himself. It's not difficult. Move forward and don't let go of the rope.

Nicholas tumbled through the window, remembering to hold on to the rope. He juddered to a halt at the end of its slack, like a condemned man on a gibbet.

"Quit your dossing, Nick!" hollered Victor Vigny. "Get yourself down. One hand after the other. Even a simpleton like this fireman here could manage it."

"I could indeed!" shouted the fireman, deciding he would worry about the insult later, if at all.

Below the plume of smoke, King Nicholas could breathe again. Each successive gasp of fresh air drove the toxins from his system and returned strength to his limbs.

"Come down, man! I didn't travel from New York City to watch you swing."

Nicholas grinned, his teeth a flash of white. "I almost died, Victor. Some sympathy would be nice." These simple sentences were a considerable effort, and each phrase was punctuated by a fit of coughing.

"That's it, now," said Vigny. "The old Nick. Down you come."

The king came down slowly, his journey interrupted by several explosions. Once his feet had found purchase on the top rung, Nicholas descended quickly. There were other lives at stake here, after all; and if he got Victor killed because of his own monumental carelessness, the Frenchman would plague him from the afterlife.

Victor had him by the elbows before his boots touched the cobbles, whisking the king away to the relative safety of the keep. They watched from behind an open gorge tower as the king's ladder was seared and blackened.

"What the devil was in there?" asked Victor.

The king's throat whistled with each labored breath. "Some gunpowder. Fireworks. A couple of jars of experimental fuel, Swedish blasting oil. Fuse tape. We have been using the old grain store beneath as a temporary armory. And of course, fertilizer."

"Fertilizer?"

"Fertilizer is important on the Saltees, Victor. It's the future." He remembered something. "Isabella. I must show her that I am unharmed. She must see for herself." He cast his gaze around the courtyard. "I don't see her. I don't . . . Of course.

Someone has taken her to safety. She is safe, isn't she, Victor?"

Victor Vigny did not meet his friend's gaze; his eyes were directed instead over the king's shoulder at the tower's parapet wall. There were two somethings in the midst of the smoke and flame. Two *someones*. A boy and a girl. Perhaps nine or ten years of age.

"*Mon Dieu,*" breathed the Frenchman. "*Mon Dieu.*"

The turret roof was completely gone, apart from ragged blocks around the walls, as though the dragon had grown and now occupied the entire tower. Through swathes of smoke and flame, Conor could see crumbling masonry and falling beams. A thick column of smoke coughed from the tower, which had effectively become a chimney, drawing air from below to feed the fire. The smoke rose like a giant gnarled tree, black against the summer sky.

Isabella was not in the least hysterical; instead an eerie calm had descended over her, and she stood on the parapet, eyes glazed as though she were half asleep and uncertain of the reality of the situation.

The only way down is to fly, thought Conor. It had long been his dream to fly once more, but these were not the perfect conditions.

He had almost flown on his fifth birthday when the Broekharts had gone on a day trip to Hook Head in Ireland to see the famous lighthouse. Conor's present had been a large kite in the Saltee colors. They had set it loose on the windswept seaside pasture, and a sudden gust had lifted Conor to the tips of his toes and would have dragged him out to sea had his father not grabbed his elbow.

Kite. Saltee colors. The flag.

On the parapet, Conor pounced on the flagpole, pulling at the knots holding the bamboo frame. The knots twisted in his hands, pulled by the wind that flapped the flag in its frame.

"Help me, Isabella," he cried. "We must untie the flag."

"Forget the flag, Captain Crow," said Isabella dully. "Leave the goat, too. I don't like goats. Sneaky little beards."

Conor struggled on with the knots. The ropes were thicker than his slim fingers, but they were brittle from the heat and fell apart quickly. With one momentous wrench, he pulled the flapping flag out of the wind, wrestling it to the parapet. It bucked and cracked under him like a magic carpet, but Conor kept it secure with his own body.

He could barely see Isabella now. She was like a ghost in the smoke. He tried to call her, but smoke went down his throat faster than words could come up. He retched and *arrk*ed like a seal, flapping his arms at the princess. She ignored him, deciding instead to lie down on the parapet and wait for her father.

Conor fumbled with his belt buckle, pulling the leather strip out from the loops of his trousers. Then he rolled onto his back and passed the belt behind the flag's bamboo diagonals.

This is an insane plan. You are not a pirate on some fantastic adventure.

This wasn't a plan, there was no time for plans. This was a desperate act. In the melee of smoke, explosions, and jets of flame, Conor struggled to his feet, keeping the flag's tip low, hiding it from the wind.

Not yet. Not yet.

He almost stumbled over Isabella. She seemed to be asleep. There was no reaction when his fingers pulled at her face. *Dead. Is she dead?* The nine-year-old boy felt tears flow over his cheeks, and was ashamed. He needed to be strong for the princess. Be a hero like his papa.

What would Captain Declan Broekhart do? Conor imagined his father's face in front of him.

Try something, Conor. Use that big brain your mother is always talking about. Build your flying machine.

Not a machine, Papa. There is no mechanism. This is a kite.

Flame was climbing the parapet wall, blackening the stone with its fiery licks. Crossbeams, carpets, files, and furniture tumbled into the hungry fire, feeding it. Conor lifted the princess, dragging his friend upright.

"What?" she said grumpily. Then the smoke filled her windpipe, and any words dissolved into a coughing fit.

Conor stood straight, feeling the massive flag flap and crackle in the wind. "It's like a big kite, Isabella," he rasped, words like glass in his throat. "I will hold you around the waist, like this, and then we move to . . ."

Conor never finished his instructions because a further explosion, funneled by the tower, caused a massive updraft, plucking the two children from the parapet and sending the flag spinning into open air like a giant autumn leaf.

The circumstances were unique. Had they jumped, as was Conor's plan, they would have not had enough height for the flag to slow their descent. But the updraft caught their makeshift kite and spun them up another hundred feet, taking them out over the sea. They hung there, in the sky at the plateau of the air tunnel. Weightless. Sky above and sea below.

I am flying, thought Conor Broekhart. I remember this.

Then the flying finished and the falling started, and though it was drastically slowed by the flag, it seemed devilishly swift. Sights dissolved into a kaleidoscope of fractured blues and silvers. The flag caught a low breeze and flipped. Conor watched the clouds swirl above him, stretching to creamy streams. And all the time he held on to Isabella so tightly his fingers ached. He was crying and laughing, and he knew it would be painful when they hit the water.

They crashed into the ocean. It was painful.

When he saw his daughter on the parapet, King Nicholas had tried to scramble up the tower like a dog climbing out of a well. In seconds his nails were torn and bloody.

Victor Vigny had dragged him away from the wall. "Wait, Nick. This is not over yet. Wait. The boy . . . he's . . ."

Nicholas's eyes were wild and anguished. "What? He's what?"

"You have to see it. Come now. We need a boat, in case the wind takes them."

"A boat? A boat? What are you saying?"

"Come, Nick. Come."

Nicholas howled and dropped to his knees as his daughter flew into the air.

Victor watched, amazed. This boy. He was special, whoever he was. Maybe nine, no more than ten. What ingenuity. The explosion took them high; Victor watched their trajectory and then set off for the pier at a run, dragging the king behind him. "The flag could drown them," he puffed. "The frame will collapse, and the flag will wrap around them both."

The king had recovered himself and soon outstripped the others through a trader's gate and down to the jetty. There were already a half dozen boats on their way to the fallen flag. The first to reach them was a small quay punt, sculled across the wave tops by two muscled fishermen. A line of slower vessels trailed behind them to the pier.

"Alive?" Nicholas roared, but the distance was too great. "Are they alive?"

The flag was pulled from the sea, and wet bundles rolled from it. Victor caught the king and gripped his shoulder tight. The little punt spun in a tight circle, and the fishermen pulled for shore, their oars kicking spume from the water. The news traveled faster than they could, passed from one boat to the next. The words, inaudible at first, became clearer with each fresh call. "Alive. Alive. Both of them."

Nicholas sank to his knees and thanked God. Victor smiled first, and then began to clap with delight.

"I came to teach the princess," he shouted to no one in particular. "But I will teach that boy, too—or perhaps he will teach me."

START THINKING LIKE
A CRIMINAL MASTERMIND

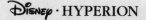

GREETINGS FOWL FANS,

I hope you enjoyed reading about Artemis and Holly. If you did, you will be happy to know that I am busy planning Artemis's next adventure.

But before Artemis returns, I have decided to embark on a very different project. I am writing the official sixth book in the *Hitchhiker's Guide to the Galaxy* series. Most of you have probably already read Douglas Adams's insanely brilliant space series. These are bar none the funniest sci-fi books ever written. The Guides feature Arthur Dent, one of the last humans left alive after the Earth has been destroyed by the remorseless Vogons. Arthur hitches a ride on a spaceship and goes planet-hopping with his friends Ford Prefect, a Betelgeusean journalist; Zaphod Beeblebrox, the two-headed president of the galaxy; and Marvin, the paranoid android.

All this adventuring went on for five books and then Douglas Adams passed away before he could write book six. I am writing the sequel, *And Another Thing...* I hope you will board the spaceship with me so we can travel through Douglas Adams's hilarious galaxy together.